readiscover...

Ritchett

NO PRICE TOO HIGH

Shattered by the bitter end of a passionate affair, Lizzie Wilde leaves her native north east to seek fame and fortune on the London stage. Determined to make her own way in the world, she'll not let her heart be broken again, so when she meets the handsome Captain Ashton, Lizzie resists his advances, for an officer and a gentleman would never marry a lowly actress. With bombs raining down on London, every meeting might be their last, and just as Lizzie dares hope they might have a future, their love is put to the sternest of tests.

NO PRICE TOO HIGH

NO PRICE TOO HIGH

by

Annie Wilkinson

Magna Large Print Books
Long Preston, North Yorkshire,
BD23 4ND, England.

British Library Cataloguing in Publication Data:

Wilkinson, Annie
  No price too high.

A catalogue record of this book is
available from the British Library

ISBN   0-7505-2560-6
ISBN   978-0-7505-2560-2

First published in Great Britain in 2006 by Simon & Schuster
A Viacom company

Cover illustration © Melvyn Warren-Smith by arrangement with
P.W.A. International Ltd.

The right of Annie Wilkinson to be identified as the author of this work
has been asserted by her in accordance with sections 77 and 78 of the
Copyright, Designs and Patents Act, 1988

Published in Large Print 2006 by arrangement with
Simon & Schuster UK Ltd.

Magna Large Print is an imprint of Library Magna Books Ltd.

Printed and bound in Great Britain by
T.J. (International) Ltd., Cornwall, PL28 8RW

Acknowledgements

My thanks to my niece Cathy and her friend Nicki for their kindness in putting me up in London during my travels there, to my friend Heather Ramsay, for all her help with the theatre, to Rilba and William Jones, for help with research and the loan of books, to my family and friends for their encouragement and pleasure in my recent success, to all at 'Hornsea Writers', to Pete Walgate at the Mitchell Centre for taming my computer, to Dr. Robert Colls of Leicester University for recommendations for reading, to my agent Judith Murdoch, my editor, Kate Lyall Grant – and to the late Captain Jack Oughtred whose courage, decency, good humour, determined optimism and zest for life shine through his letters. Many thanks also to his descendants for allowing their publication in 'Destiny – The War Letters of Captain Jack Oughtred M.C. 1915 – 1918' – edited by Alan Wilkinson and published by Peter and Christopher Oughtred. ISBN 1 872167 88 8

I am also indebted to the staff of the Imperial War Museum and to all who have published material on the Great War on the internet, especially www.spartacus.schoolnet.co.uk., www.firstworldwar.com and www.bbc.co.uk /history/war/wwone, to 'The Times' newspapers and 'Punch' magazines of the period, to the BBC and Channel 4 for their programmes and series on the Great War, and to many other writers, some of whose works I have listed below:

Henri Barbusse – *Under Fire* – Everyman's Library

Jaroslav Hasek – *The Good Soldier Svejk* – Everyman's Library

L.J. Collins – *Theatre at War, 1914 – 1918* Macmillan Press Ltd

Hew Strachan – *The First World War* – Simon & Schuster – (also a Channel Four series)

John Keenan – *The First World War* – Hutchinson, Random House

Richard Holmes – *Tommy, The British Soldier on the Western Front 1914 – 1918* – HarperCollins

The Virago Book of Women and the Great War – Edited by Joyce Marlow

Gordon Corrigan – *Mud, Blood, and Poppycock* – Cassell Military Paperbacks.

John Laffin – *The Western Front Illustrated, 1914 – 1918* – Alan Sutton Publishing Ltd.

The Eventful 20th Century – *The War to End Wars, 1914 – 18* – Reader's Digest

Max Arthur – *Forgotten Voices of the Great War* – Random House Audio

And lastly to John Keats and Edgar Allan Poe. I hope they will have no objections to my using their work, but if they have – let them sue.

To my Grandfathers.

Chapter One

'Oh, it's you. I thought you'd be busy.' Lizzie Wilde pushed back a tangled mass of long black hair and, wrapping her old grey dressing gown tight around her, retreated barefoot through the passageway and into her mother's front room. Her eldest sister Ginny, landlady of the Cock Inn, strutted behind her in new high-heeled leather boots, dressed to the nines, irritatingly brisk and depressingly festive. Here it comes, Lizzie thought, the unspoken 'I'll soon set the world to rights for you, so let's get cracking' sort of bustle her sister was noted for.

Ginny stood in the doorway taking off her gloves and inhaling the air. 'I've got a few helpers, so I've maybe half an hour to spare. Oh, that scent, I love it. Pine needles.' She gave a cluck of disapproval. 'You've nearly let the fire out, Lizzie man.'

Lizzie cast an indifferent glance towards the fireplace and lay down on the horsehair stuffed sofa. 'Have I? I hadn't noticed.'

'Not noticed? It's bloody freezing.' She felt Ginny's warm hand against her cheek. 'You're freezing, an' all. You can't sit here on your own on Christmas Eve. Come back with me to the Cock, where there's a bit company, stop you lying about moping and feeling bloody sorry for yoursel'. Take your mind off things.'

13

What difference do you think Christmas Eve makes? Lizzie wondered. I'll never like Christmas again. And as for "a bit company" – that's about the last thing in the world I want. 'There's a bit too much company at the Cock for me, the way I feel,' she said. 'Nothing's going to take my mind off this, Ginny, until I get mesel' put right. So I'd rather be on my own. I'd only put a damper on everybody else's Christmas if I did come.'

Through half-closed eyes, she watched Ginny take off her coat and crouch by the hearth and, with a little tut of impatience, begin carefully arranging small coals on the few remaining embers, easing them up with the poker to let just enough of a reviving draught round them. 'That should get it going again. Now you light the gas mantles, and I'll make us a cup of tea. You haven't let the fire go out in the kitchen, have you?'

'I don't suppose so. Me mam banked it up before she went down to the Cock.'

Ginny bustled off into the kitchen, and Lizzie heaved herself off the sofa to take a coloured spill out of the box on the mantelpiece and hold it to the guttering fire, then carefully turn on the gas and hold the flame just near enough to the mantles to light them without turning their delicate fabric to powder. Now the spill was almost burning her fingers and she threw it hastily onto the feeble little fire. She glanced towards the Christmas tree standing in the corner, dark and sinister. Lizzie ignited another spill and held the flame to some of the tiny spiral candles clamped to its branches. That would please Ginny, at any rate. She threw the second spent sliver of wood into the grate and caught sight of herself in the mirror above the fireplace.

Go to the Cock Inn tonight? She pulled at her hair, a thick, matted mass of black tangles, and lifted her swollen eyelids to reveal a pair of sloe-black stones set in bloodshot whites. She leaned nearer to examine her skin, a pasty grey colour, and as she breathed vapour onto the glass, she noticed that her breath stank. What a bloody mess I am, she thought. I'd be ashamed to be seen tripping down the garden path to use the netty looking like this. I'm going nowhere. She returned to the sofa.

A few minutes later Ginny came in, blew the candles out and turned off the gaslights. 'Come on,' she said, putting a guard up to the fire, 'there's two steaming cups of tea for us on the kitchen table. It's warmer in there and it'll take ages to get the chill off this place.'

Lizzie reluctantly got up and followed her out of the dark front room and into a cheerful kitchen, its fire now burning merrily in the grate. She sat on a hard kitchen chair at a table covered by a cloth of deep red plush, wrapped her cold fingers round one of the cups, and lifted it to her lips. It tasted good. She hadn't noticed how thirsty she was.

'Me mam had left the kettle on the hob, and full to the top,' Ginny said. 'It was just about boiling. So what are we going to do with you, like?'

'What I've asked you to do, I hope. Help me to make myself right again, one way or another.'

'I wish you wouldn't do it, Lizzie. It's not right.'

'No, but you did it.'

'I had no choice.'

'Neither have I.'

'You have. I'll look after the bairn, if you can't.'

'And wouldn't they all have a field day with that, round here? I should think our family's given 'em enough to keep 'em all yattering for the rest of the century, without me giving 'em any more. And think what it would do to my mother. Hasn't she had enough grief through the years? And she really hoped I was going to be settled with Tom. She moved heaven and earth to help that bonny little courtship along, and look where it's got us. No, Ginny. Nobody knows except you and our John, and nobody's going to know, especially not *him*, or his bitch of a sister. But I wouldn't be surprised if she's got a bloody good idea.'

She paused, and took a few grateful gulps of one of the best cups of tea she'd ever tasted in her life. 'Do you know what she said when we were in "The Cock" one night?' Lizzie did a perfect imitation: '"Inferior minds and inferior morals *do* have a tendency to go together, don't they?" with that maddening upper class attitude she's got, and I thought then Tom must have said something to her, told her something about us. It was just the way she looked; I knew that comment was meant for me to chew on, and I have an' all – ever since. And now she's poisoned him against me, and I'm left holding the baby.'

'It might not be her doing though, Lizzie. There's more men than him have ditched a girl after they've got what they wanted, and if they fancy themselves gentry and they see you as belonging to the lower orders, you can nearly

16

guarantee it'll happen. And if he'd been anything like a man, he wouldn't have told her anything about your private business in the first place.'

'He tells her everything. And it's her doing all right, because there was no sign of any end coming the last time I saw him, we were as right as rain. And that's the trouble, do you see? She was jealous to death whenever he took too much notice of me because she thinks he's her property.'

'He's not much of a man then, is he, if he lets her think that? Not much of a man if he sends you a letter, either, instead of having the guts to face you.'

Lizzie sat for a moment or two looking into her cup, feeling the tears pricking her eyes and a lump fit to choke her filling her throat. She breathed in the steam from the tea, and swallowed hard, determined to force the feeling down, but she couldn't help it, it would come out. 'Oh, Ginny, you make me feel like screaming! Can't I make you understand? He's the man I love, he's the man I'd set my heart on. I wanted him more than anything else in the world, and she turned him against me! She's ruined everything – everything! I could kill her! But I've still got some pride. She's never going to have the satisfaction of seeing me dragging mesel' about with a swollen belly. If I haven't got Tom, I won't be having any baby. I'll have to get rid of it and that's all there is to it. And then I'm getting right away from here. I'm going to London to work on the halls like you did.'

She watched her sister closely but there was no reaction from Ginny, who sat in stern silence, jaw set, grinding her teeth. Lizzie felt a wave of panic

17

wash over her.

Cheeks flushed, and eyes suddenly imploring, she begged, 'You will help me, won't you?'

With her heart in her mouth Lizzie went down to the Cock Inn the day after Boxing Day, to see Ginny alone, well out of the way of her mother, and the rest of the family.

'I'll not be getting in touch with anybody in London about this job, and that's flat,' Ginny told her. 'It can be done just as easy in Newcastle. There's plenty of scope for that trade there, same as any other port. And it'll be a lot safer nearer home, an' all. You're only seventeen, Lizzie man, and if anything goes wrong, you'll need your own family to look after you. We'll take the train tomorrow, to see a landlady I know through the Licensed Victuallers. She knows just about all there is to know about what goes on in Newcastle, and she knows a woman who's supposed to be very good. She ought to be an' all, she wants two guineas.'

'I don't care where it happens, just when. I can't leave it much longer, can I?'

'No. Not if that's the course you're set on.'

What had she hoped for? That Tom Peters, the man she adored, the man she'd have laid her life down for, would discover he had a heart and come galloping back on his white charger to rescue her? Or even just a conscience; that would have done.

Well he hadn't either, and now she sat beside Ginny in the back kitchen of a grey-haired stranger with a strange profession, sipping tea

18

laced with brandy and making small talk as if there were nothing amiss. But there was, or they wouldn't be here.

The pleasantries were soon done with, and it was down to business. Ginny handed over the money and the woman counted it, then gave a satisfied nod and put it behind the clock on her mantelpiece. 'All right. Now, how old are you?' she asked.

'Seventeen.'

'Have you ever been to anybody like me before?'

'No.'

'Good. I don't like dealing with people other folk have meddled with. They make some right messes, some of them.'

'Has anybody ever died?' Lizzie asked, not that she was in a frame of mind to back out. Rather die than carry on with this.

'Not from anything I've ever done they haven't,' said the woman, and Lizzie's sharp eyes took everything in as she tossed a jug and a bowl and a strange assortment of tubes and pipes into a jam pan full of boiling water and put the lid on. 'We'll leave that lot to bubble for ten minutes, while we have this cup of tea, then your sister can sit in the front room for a bit while we set you right again.'

'What happens?'

'You squat over the bowl and give yourself a thorough good wash with plenty of soap and water, then you go and lie down. I pour the boiling water off the things and leave them to cool a bit while I wash me hands. Then I put something very safe in a bowl and pump it through the syringe

19

with the tube on the end. That primes it so there's no air in it to do you any damage. When that's done, I take the tube between my fingers like this,' she held up two long, midwife's fingers to demonstrate, 'and I feed the tube up to where the baby's lodged, and pump a bit of the solution in to kill it, and then it's all over. You can get dressed and go home.'

'Will it hurt?'

'Not a bit, and it'll not take long either, if you keep still and do as you're told.'

'Don't I have to wait for it to come away?'

'No. It might take a couple of days to do that. You'll be all right at home. Did you bring plenty of clean rags – thoroughly clean, mind?'

Lizzie nodded. 'What's in the solution?'

The woman tapped the side of her nose with her long, skinny forefinger. 'That's for me to know. Don't fret, I'll still be here, if you're ever in trouble again.'

Don't you fret, either, thought Lizzie, because if I'm all right after this lot, no man's ever going to get near me again.

Clean, quiet, and discreet. The woman was everything the landlady had said she was, and more. She was dispassionate. The thing was done as if it were a dreary but necessary routine, and really not very interesting. There was very little shame, it was not a massive ordeal, and Lizzie came away from her house feeling nothing but relief, as if an enormous weight had been lifted off her. She sat beside Ginny on the way back to Old Annsdale, bundled up in wads of old linen, hoping she wouldn't start bleeding on the train. What an embarrassment that would be, if she leaked through her clothes and onto the seat. There would be more shame in that than all the rest of the business put together. Thank God it would be dark when they got off.

Ginny's stepson Philip was playing with three-month-old Pip when they got back to the Cock Inn. 'Ithn't he a grand little lad, Lizzie?' he beamed.

'Aye, he is that,' she agreed, not sparing the child a glance. She went up the stairs and into Ginny's bedroom to examine herself in the long mirror. She looked no different, and if everything had gone according to plan, she wasn't going to look any different now, and thank God for that. She sucked in her stomach and tightened her belt a notch, then turned this way and that, gazing critically at her reflection. Her figure looked good; fit to be seen anywhere, and she was going to be seen on the stage in London, and she was going to earn some money, just like Ginny had. No bulging belly, no brat hanging off the end of her breast was going to get in her way now.

The Westminster chimes of Ginny's clock began, and they all stood in a circle with hands crossed in the Cock's concert room, the very place where Lizzie set eyes on Tom for the first time at a fancy dress party thrown in aid of the miners' strike fund. The memory of that night returned with such force that she could almost see him, could almost hear the banjo. A good-looking young fellow dressed in knee breeches, which showed a

21

pair of well turned calves, he was definitely a cut above the rest. He'd been rattling out ragtime tunes, and when he'd looked up at her with that roguish twinkle in his blue eyes, my God, it turned her knees to water, and she'd decided in that instant, he was going to be hers. She'd just looked at him, and he'd put his banjo aside and the next thing she'd known, she'd been in his arms and dancing on air.

The phantom was gone, and now Lizzie stood surrounded by friends and family with tears filling her eyes, achingly alone. She determinedly swallowed them down. She would get over all this, and she'd go on to be a success in the London Music Hall, just like Ginny had. She'd make her New Year's resolution now. She'd start as she meant to go on in 1913, and she didn't mean to let any man get in her way, or get the best of her ever again. Once bloody bitten, twice shy. Before the twelfth stroke, she felt something slip inside her, but she couldn't very well break the circle so she stood there, holding hands with her mother on one side and Ginny on the other, smiling and singing 'Auld Lang Syne' with the rest of them. Then the singing stopped, and they all listened for the tall dark 'stranger' – her brother Arthur – who did the honours every year as the Cock's first foot.

Lizzie slipped away, up to Ginny's bathroom, to see what the matter was. She was covered in blood, and on removing the pad she saw it – tinier than Tom Thumb, a defenceless little thing curled up on its gory cushion, with its knees flexed under its chin, and its arms crossed over its head, as if to protect itself.

'Oh, dear. Oh, dear.' What a mess she was in. She filled the bath with hot water and stripped herself, and looked at the poor little creature again before climbing in to wash off the blood and the stench of it. 'Pity for you,' she whispered. 'Pity you didn't have a better father. You wouldn't have been as quick into the world then, and you wouldn't have been as quick out of it, either.' She sank down into the hot bath until the water covered her ears and drowned out the sounds of the revels downstairs. Her black hair floated in tendrils on the surface of the water, and although she couldn't wish the little thing alive again, she put her hands to her face and began to weep.

Tom Peters had done one thing for her, if nothing else. He'd given her the kick up the arse she needed to get out of Annsdale. Both Annsdales come to that – the newer, grimy mining village of Annsdale Colliery, and the ancient rural village, where her mother's cottage stood. The sooner she saw the back of them both the better as far as she was concerned. All she had to do now was to persuade Ginny to use her influence with her friends in London, to help her get a start. It wasn't proving easy, but Lizzie intended to stick at it until she'd worn her sister down. She continued her battle of attrition the next time they were alone in the bar of the Cock Inn.

'You're mad, Lizzie,' Ginny told her. 'You'll never be able to finish your apprenticeship if you leave now. You'll never get another job as good as that round here, and what will Mr Surtees think, after all he's done for you?'

Lizzie tilted her chin and looked at Ginny with a determined gleam in her black eyes. 'Aye, it's a bad job about Mr Surtees, and I'm sorry. And it is a good apprenticeship, but I don't want to waste my life sitting in the back of a tailor's shop making bonny clothes for other people, seeing nobody and being seen by nobody. Let our Sally leave that Doctor's family she works for, and maybe Mr Surtees'll give her my job. I think I can do better. I've got a bit of talent that might get me somewhere. I don't want to stay here and end up like our Emma, slaving after a man and a houseful of kids and living from hand to mouth.'

'You want to try your luck on the music halls. All right, but there's plenty of chances to work in the Tyneside music hall, Lizzie, there's no need to go to London.'

'There is. I want a fresh start, where nobody knows me, where nobody's going to be sticking their noses into my business all the time. I bumped into our Emma's next-door neighbour when I went to the Co-op in Annsdale Colliery to get me mam's messages, and do you know what she said? "Oh, I heard you and your Ginny were up in Newcastle the other day. What for did you gan to Newcastle, like?" As if it's any of her bloody business why I go to Newcastle. But it's all round the village, and it'll not be long before me mam finds out we were up in Newcastle. Like after Tom jilted me, and some of them were asking: "Why, are you not walking out with Tom Peters now, Lizzie?" There's probably a gaggle of them some-where, all putting two and two together this min-

24

ute. There's too many nosey buggers like them round here, minding everybody else's business. And I liked London, Ginny man. I'll never forget that time we went to see you on the Halls. It was magic.'

Ginny looked unhappy and unconvinced. 'All you saw was the surface gloss. You didn't see much of the hard work, and you didn't see any of the squalor, or the corruption. London's not a safe place for a lass on her own, Lizzie. Especially a good-looking lass who's got no money and no family to help her.'

Lizzie had the answer to that one. 'There's nothing can happen to good-looking lasses in London that doesn't happen everywhere else an' all. I'm living proof of that. But that'll never happen to me again, Ginny, either in London or anywhere else. Anyway, you managed, and you did all right.'

'Did I? I had some hard times before I started doing all right that you know nothing about.'

'Well, I'm not frightened of hard times, Ginny, and I'm not frightened of hard work, either. I've had some hard times here, and they couldn't be any worse in London. And you had some good friends, an' all, friends that might be able to help me get a start, if only you'll ask 'em.'

'What will me mam say?'

'When I'm a success, and she sees I'm happy, she'll say "Good!"'

Lizzie won the day, and Ginny wrote to her old friends Mr and Mrs Burns, her songwriter and his wife, who agreed to help Lizzie find a job, and to put her up until she found somewhere to stay.

25

It couldn't be for long, though. Now that the Underground was stretching out in all directions, they were soon to be retiring to the suburbs.

She would be much better in the theatre rather than in music hall, Ginny had told her, because if you do a revue or a play you're with the same set of people and you have the chance to make friends, but moving from engagement to engagement in music hall, you spend your life in isolation. So here Lizzie stood, beside Mr Burns in front of one of his old friends, Frank Osborne, the manager of de Lacey's theatre.

'Well what can she do?'

Mr Burns looked uncertain, and the manager turned to Lizzie.

'Can you dance?'

'Yes, I can dance.'

'Can you sing?'

'Yes, I can sing.'

'What else can you do? I'm not a charitable institution, you know. If I'm paying anybody, I want my money's worth.'

Lizzie put her hands to her ears and smoothed back her hair with a gesture and facial expression of mild irritation which were a perfect imitation of the manager. In the manager's accents she asked, 'Well, what can she do?' and then snapped 'Can you dance? Can you sing? What else can you do? If I'm paying anybody, I want my money's worth.'

'I see. You're a passable mimic. Anything else? Any other reason why I should throw good money at you, rather than at any one of a hundred other job hunters?'

'I'm good with a needle. I could make costumes, but I don't want to do that, I'd rather be on the stage. But I'm willing to do anything. I can do anything you want doing, as long as it doesn't need a man's strength.'

'All right. Irma's told me to get rid of her dresser so there's room for you there. Irma's the star. Do you know what a star is?'

'I think so.'

'Well, I'll tell you what a star is. A star is the sole reason the people pay their ticket money. If there's no star, there's no money handed over at the box office, and if there's no box office takings, there's no show, and if there's no show, we're all in the workhouse before we're much older. There's only one star here, and she's got to be kept happy. If she likes you, I'll take you on for a month's trial. If you don't shape up, you're out. And by the way, I'm known to everybody round here as "the governor".'

Lizzie nodded. 'Yes, governor.'

Chapter Two

Lizzie tactfully kept trying to steer the conversation away from it, but Irmgard Meyers would keep on returning to the topic of the war.

'French and Russians they matter not,
A blow for a blow and a shot for a shot;
We love them not, we hate them not,
We hold the Vistula and the Vosges-gate,

27

We have but one and only hate,
We love as one, we hate as one,
We have one foe and one alone–
ENGLAND!

'Have you ever heard anything like it? They call it the "Hymn of Hate", and they're singing it in every café and music-hall in Germany.'

Lizzie's face was a picture of scorn. 'Silly buggers. It's a pity they've got nothing better to occupy their time.'

'But can't you see, Lizzie, hatred of England is being deliberately whipped up in Germany. It's official policy. Uncle Herman says the man who composed that pleasant little ditty got the Iron Cross. *"Gott strafe* England" is what people say to each other instead of "Good morning" or "Good afternoon" now. It's actually rubber stamped on letters and printed on postcards. It's engraved on jewellery – all sorts of things, brooches and cufflinks – even on wedding rings!' She handed Lizzie her blue stage costume. 'Just put a stitch in it, will you? You're quicker than anyone else.'

'Being neither one thing nor the other can't be easy, at times like these,' Lizzie said.

'I was born and brought up here, but now I'm accused of being German. If I went to live in Germany, they'd call me English, and I'd have an even worse time of it than here, and things are bad enough here. Have you heard about that sketch at the Coliseum, the one with the performing dogs they called "Everyday Life in a German Town?" They're calling it "A Day in Dogville" now, and they've changed the bloody backdrop to a huge Union Jack!' Irma laughed but the sound was mirthless, and Lizzie saw anxiety in her blue eyes.

'It's getting bad, isn't it?' Lizzie conceded. 'I went to a dance after the show the other evening, and there was one of that family of German equestrians there, the ones who're playing at the Hippodrome. She told me they've just gone and changed their names from Gaertner to Griffiths.'

Not only that, but as she'd walked from her lodgings to de Lacey's theatre, Lizzie had passed a German pork butcher's shop with its windows smashed and had seen the fat proprietor trying to shield his quivering wife from the abuse of the mob. It certainly wouldn't help to tell Irma that.

'I'd change my name, if I thought it would do me any good. But I'm too well known,' Irma shuddered. 'I've played here under my own name for so long that people aren't going to forget. And this is the muck we have to use now.' Irma smeared her face with Clarko's greasepaint. 'People can say what they like about the Germans; they make the best stage make-up. This stuff can't touch Leichner's. But we've got Marie Lloyd and Gladys Cooper endorsing the patriotic brand, so it's tantamount to treason to use Leichner's now.'

'It's asking for your skin stripping off, more like,' said Lizzie. 'Like young Leni, what was her name? The one who got a good helping of acid mixed into her jar of cold cream?'

Irma shuddered. Leni was a particular friend of hers. 'Leni Reichensthall. Don't remind me.'

Feeling against the Germans was so strong in

England you could almost reach out and touch it. Exotic stage names chosen for their aura of glamour now had an aura of treachery and the slightest association with the land of the hated Hun could make anybody an object of fear and suspicion. A Polish juggler they knew who had been brought up in Germany couldn't get work anywhere and Carl Hertz, the famous magician, made a public announcement claiming that he was an American.

Irma had been the idol of her adoring public until the outbreak of the war that was to have been over by Christmas, but Christmas had come and gone, the war went on, and in spite of her talent, her astonishing good looks and her generosity, the public's love affair with Irma was nearing its end. *Life's Enchanted Cup* had been wildly successful at the start of its West End run, but now audience numbers were beginning to flag. And Lizzie had been there when one of the stage hands had asked Irma outright, 'Meyers is a German name, isn't it?' Caught off guard, Irma had blushed and said that Meyers was just a stage name; her real name was Mildred Jones, and she'd been brought up in India.

Lizzie knew it was a lie. Irma's father was a German who had gone back to Munich after the death of his English wife, and she had told Lizzie that as a child she had spent most of her summer holidays with Uncle Herman and Aunt Hildegarde. Lizzie kept her secret. Since her arrival at de Lacey's, first as Irma's dresser, then as dresser and understudy, Irma had proved a friend and ally. They had a strong rapport, shared the same slightly cruel sense of humour and made each other laugh, but now things were changing. Lizzie had tried to put a bit of heart into her friend, reminding her that some of the soldiers who'd been fraternizing with the enemy after the Christmas Truce were supposed to have said that they'd rather shoot their own generals than them lads they'd shared cigarettes and goodwill with, but that consolation hadn't lasted long. Poor Irma. It was doubtful that anything Lizzie could say would make her laugh now, or give her any reassurance.

German spies and informers were suspected everywhere, even in the ranks of the aristocracy. Lord Haldane, a lifelong bachelor, was accused of having a German wife, and had been threatened with violence in the street. 'Blood is said to be thicker than water, and we doubt whether all the water in the North Sea could obliterate the blood ties between the Battenbergs and Hohenzollerns when it comes to a life and death struggle between Germany and ourselves,' the magazine *John Bull* thundered, and England's First Sea Lord, Prince Louis of Battenberg, had to resign. If people like that could be threatened, what hope was there for a poor little half-German actress? Even Royalty were feeling the effects of British distrust of the foreigner, and it was rumoured that the exalted Saxe-Coburg-Gotha family were toying with the idea of adopting a less Hunnish name.

Lizzie unwound a length of blue silk thread and bit it off, moistening the end between her lips before threading the needle. Without raising her eyes to the young man at the dressing room door she said, 'I'm sorry, but Miss Meyers isn't here.'

'I see. In that case, I'll wait.' His cut glass accent was deeply, pleasingly masculine.

Lizzie shrugged. Plenty of men were still susceptible to Irma's Teutonic charms, in spite of the war. Irma was one of the 'women who will' – but only on her terms. She once described her strategy to Lizzie: 'I allow myself to be taken to lunch at a nice little place in the West End, and on the way we might pass a certain shop window, and I might say, "Oh, isn't that a dear little necklace," or bracelet, or pair of earrings, or beautiful fur, or whatever it might be, before walking on. Then, when he comes to see me again, he might just have something for me, beautifully wrapped, and how surprised and pleased I am when it turns out to be the dear little whatever it was. And if there is no gift, or not enough of one, then I'm so sorry, but I have an engagement. He soon understands. Men value what they pay for, and the more a thing costs them the more highly they esteem it.'

So if this idiot wanted to stand there and wait, Lizzie wouldn't stop him. She lifted the stage costume and inserted the needle. Just a few stitches, and that little tear in the blue silk would be invisible to the audience.

Irma's admirer pulled up a stool, hitched his trousers a little at the knees and sat solemnly at Lizzie's elbow. He was not in khaki. Her glance took in a well-cut suit of grey flannel, a face that was clean-shaven except for the thin moustache adorning his upper lip, and a thick thatch of wavy brown hair parted at the side and swept back.

'I say, you're awfully clever with your needle.'

'Yes, I know. It's one of the things they pay me for.'

'And terribly badly, I should think.'

'"With fingers weary and worn, with eyelids heavy and red, a woman sat in unwomanly rags, plying her needle and thread..."' Lizzie recited. 'But no, it's not quite the "Song of the Shirt".'

'No, of course not.' He paused, and observed, 'Your voice has a lovely lilt to it. You're not from London.'

This stage-door-johnny had an irritatingly acute ear. Until that moment Lizzie had felt confident that she'd obliterated every trace of her native North East of England from her speech. A little piqued, she raised her head to stare into a pair of lustrous grey eyes whose depths held a speculative gleam. 'Where am I from then?' she demanded.

'Somewhere near Newcastle, at a guess. You sound a bit like Lieutenant Yates, one of my fellow officers.'

Ah, so he was in khaki, but not today. Probably on leave as she hadn't noticed any sign of a wound. His lips suddenly parted in a smile, and his eyes lit up with genuine amusement. 'He'd been working as an administrator of the railway in East Africa and came back to join up, and when he went to the recruiting office the sergeant asked him what school he went to, and he said Heaton – meaning Heaton Arts and Crafts. The sergeant thought he'd said Eton, so he sent him for training as an officer instead of a private soldier. I think I'm the only one he's let on to, so far.'

How funny that anyone with an accent like hers

should be taken on as an officer! 'Yes, that's really funny, isn't it?' Lizzie gave a faint smile. 'I'm not sure how long Miss Meyers will be. I seem to remember she's with the governor, and time's getting on, so I doubt very much she'll have time to see you before the play starts.'

'I don't mind waiting. That dress you're wearing, I suppose you made it yourself.'

'Why do you suppose that?'

'Because I shouldn't think you could afford it otherwise.'

Lizzie raised an eyebrow, but otherwise her face was expressionless. She made no reply.

'And I wouldn't call it "unwomanly rags", either. It becomes you, and not slightly! The blue sets off your black hair and eyes wonderfully, and the shorter length, for a girl with pretty ankles, well! You're quite a sight for sore eyes, Miss...?'

A sardonic smile crept over Lizzie's features. He'd dredged for a compliment, and he'd managed to find one. Perhaps he thought he'd get the understudy on easier terms than the leading lady. What a bonny game of fox and goose this specimen of the masculine race must think he was playing. If she'd been young and green, she might almost have thought him sincere, but she was nineteen years old and nobody's fool.

She ignored the unspoken question, and didn't give her name. 'I think you'd better save your compliments for Miss Meyers. She's the one you've come to see, after all.'

He'll get no honeyed words from me, if that's what he's hoping for, Lizzie thought. She raised her work to her teeth and broke the thread with a vicious yank. Weak, deceitful wretches, that's what men were, a set of Judases who'd betray you with a kiss. She abhorred them to her soul.

Irma sat with her back to her mirror, brushing her blonde hair and surveying them both, her face alive with malicious laughter. She was obviously intent on having some fun at their expense.

'The boy stood on the burning deck,
His back was to the mast.
He swore he would not budge an inch,
'Til Oscar Wilde had passed.
But Oscar was a cunning chap,
He threw the lad a plum,
And as he bent to pick it up,
He stuck it...

'Well, you'll know where he stuck it, Georgie boy! No relation of *yours*, was he, Lizzie? Oscar Wilde? *Wilde*, I mean?'

Georgie rapidly closed the dressing room door. 'Shush, shush, bitch! I don't mind how much you insult me but don't do it so loudly, or you'll get *me* two years on the bloody treadmill!' His matinée idol features had turned pale and his big, slightly short-sighted brown eyes were wide with a look of alarm that drew a deep-throated chuckle from his tormentor.

'Shush, shush, bitch! Don't get Georgie into trouble!' Lizzie mimicked, exaggerating his voice and expression. 'And don't cast any aspersions on me either. My name might be Wilde, but none of my family were ever wild in quite the way that

Oscar was.'

Georgie pursed his cupid's bow lips. 'That's right, Eliza. You tell her.'

'I will, Georgie, and I have a plan to outwit her. You can take me dancing at Fred Karno's, so that we'll be seen by everybody who is anybody in London in each other's arms, doing a scandalous tango. Then no one will ever suspect you.'

'And how do you propose that we get there and back, my dear, when we've got shows to do here?'

'Just as his hotel guests do, take a ferry up the Thames. Or go by train, if we must.'

'I love you dearly, Eliza, but I'm not made of money. So if you want to tango with me, you'll have to be content with the disreputable den we always go to. It's open when we can go, and it doesn't cost a bloody fortune. And you can say one thing for the clientele there, at least they can dance, most of them.'

'Come on, then.' She took him by the hands, and dragged him out of his seat, then remembered. 'Oh, by the way, Irma, one of your admirers called to see you.'

'Who was it?' Irma brightened.

'Somebody I've never seen before, and I don't know his name. I forgot to ask.'

'Oh, never mind. I'm engaged tonight, and for the next few weeks probably, so I shouldn't have had time to see him anyway.'

'Tonight, Irma? Do you mean all night?'

'Yes, darling. He's passed the test.'

'Ooh, naughty! Well, if you can't be good, be careful,' said Georgie.

'And if you can't be careful, remember the date,'

36

Lizzie warned. 'Come on, Georgie. The stage is empty. You can help me practise until I'm perfect. "Masks and faces, both gay and laughing..." she sang, leading Georgie through the wings, stopping only to wind up the gramophone and place the needle at the start of a recording of the song. Humming along, they strode onto the stage.

Georgie loved to tango. His right hand soon pressed Lizzie's left shoulder blade and his right elbow comfortably supported her left one. 'She likes you *awfully much*, Lizzie,' he said. 'I think Irma's one of those ladies who're strangely susceptible to the charms of their own sex.'

'You should talk. Aren't you "strangely susceptible" to the charms of yours, Georgie?'

'Quite, but I admit it, and Irma never has and never will. That's the reason she so enjoys baiting *me*. I suspect she nurses a secret passion for you.'

'Rubbish, Georgie. You know Irma! How many lovers has she had since I came to de Lacey's? A dozen or more?'

'Exactly my point! Never the same man for very long; and there are those who "bat for both sides", so to speak. Tantalizing thought, isn't it?'

'Well, she's never said anything to me. You shouldn't fall into the trap of thinking everybody's tarred with the same brush as you, you know, Georgie!'

'My dear, I don't. I've never had the slightest suspicion of you, for example. Oh, but I do so love to dance with you, Lizzie. You're as light as a feather. All my other partners have two left feet compared to you,' he told her, lifting her right hand until he was supporting both her arms in a horizontal line, in regal ballroom fashion.

'Then sack all your other partners, Georgie.' Lizzie put her right hand behind his left arm and a sigh of pure pleasure escaped her as he propelled her smoothly, sensuously across the stage. Gliding along in Georgie Bartlett's arms, following his lead to the throb of the music, Lizzie felt perfectly calm, perfectly safe, and as happy as she ever expected to be.

Too soon, the record stopped. 'Play it again, there's a love,' she called to someone in the wings she had mistaken for one of the stage hands; but the stocky frame of the governor walked out of the shadows, slowly clapping his hands.

'You're good. Very good.' His hooded, dark eyes fixed them with a thoughtful stare. 'A bit more practice, and you could be exhibition dancers, but the party's over, and it's time to go home now, children. You should get your beauty sleep, Lizzie. Miss Meyers is a bundle of nerves these days. We never know when we're going to need you.'

He put both hands to his head, to smooth back his slightly receding black hair, a gesture that told them he was annoyed, and worried. Irma had become very difficult and unreliable, always pleading illness or fatigue. She'd failed to appear at more than one matinée, and was now demanding a week off.

The following evening Lizzie stood behind Irma, massaging the knotted muscles in her shoulders, but to little avail. She was jittery when Lizzie helped her into the stage costume, and by the time she got to the wings to wait for her cue she was gasping with nerves. Lizzie turned to the props table and handed her a porcelain cup and saucer and a pair of crocheted gloves before she went on. 'Good luck,' she whispered.

With a brittle smile Irma stepped onto the stage and started speaking her lines, and Lizzie knew she would be all right. She would just nip back to the dressing room for that jacket she'd just finished knitting in royal blue – an almost perfect copy of the nicest one in Gorringe's. Long, and with two pockets and a sash.

The man with the grey eyes was waiting by Irma's dressing room door.

'How did you get in?' Lizzie demanded.

'Through the door, as you did, I assume.'

Lizzie took the huge bunch of vivid red tulips interlaced with myrtle that he proffered, and leaned her nose towards them before laying them on Irma's chair. 'They're lovely, but you shouldn't have been able to get in that door. It should have been locked, or the doorman should have been on it.'

'Should it? Perhaps he was called away, or something.' He shrugged.

His expression was too innocent to be altogether convincing. Lizzie picked up her jacket and frowned. 'He'd better be a lot more careful in future, or the governor will give him the sack. I'm afraid Miss Meyers won't be able to see you. She has engagements until well into next month.'

The grey eyes appraised her. 'It isn't Miss Meyers I came to see. The flowers are for you. I hope you'll do me the honour of having supper with me.'

Lizzie ushered him out of the dressing room and locked the door. 'I'm sorry. I'm here until late every evening, and when I'm free my partner takes me to the Hole in the Wall.'

'The Hole in the Wall? Where's that?'

She didn't reply, though she heard him call after her as she went in search of the doorman. Leaving a stage door unguarded like that was asking for trouble, from all sorts of pests, thieves, and idiots.

The voluptuous, insistent beat of the tango pulsed through Lizzie's mind and limbs and the world disappeared. Except for the music, and a consciousness of Georgie's body against hers she was hardly aware of her surroundings. One by one, other couples left the floor or stood on its periphery to watch not so much a dance, but sensuality to music. The music stopped and Lizzie, dressed in dramatic beaded black with her lips painted a daring red, was roused from her trance when a rather familiar figure tapped Georgie smartly on the shoulder.

'I say, excuse me, old man, you've hogged this girl to yourself for long enough, and now it's somebody else's turn, if you please.' He was halfway across the dance floor with her before Georgie had collected himself enough to say:

'This isn't an excuse me, but be my guest. You will anyway.'

There was a rap on the dressing room door, and an instant later the callboy's head appeared. 'Oh, there you are. Somebody to see you.'

In stepped a young man Lizzie had never seen before, and the door closed after him. He gave a slight bow, then one shoulder twitched upwards, then the other, and then his chin jutted forward. 'Captain Ashton sends his compliments, and asks for the pleasure of your company at supper on Saturday night.' His accent was almost imperceptible, but she recognized it immediately. It could be none other than Lieutenant Arts and Crafts from Heaton.

'Captain Ashton?'

'Yes. It was he who danced with you at the Hole in the Wall.'

'Then he should come and ask me himself.'

The emissary cleared his throat and resumed his squirming. 'Well, he has an engagement, and – it's rather delicate. He wishes to avoid any misunderstanding when you meet.'

She couldn't take her eyes off him. 'What about?'

'About the real purpose of the meeting.'

'And what might that be?' Little freak. With an innocent smile on her face Lizzie looked steadily into his eyes and waited.

Eventually, wriggling like a worm on a pin, he said, 'Captain Ashton wishes you to spend the night with him.'

'I see,' she said. 'If Captain Ashton likes me enough for that, he should come with a proposal of marriage. That would stop any misunderstanding.'

There was a silence, as if the remark were too silly to merit a rational answer, then he said: 'He's serious. It's you he wants, and before we go back to France. He'll reward you, and very handsomely.'

Enraged, Lizzie leapt to the door and held it open. 'Why, there'll be two chances of that! None, and bugger all!'

Now his whole torso was agitated, but Arts-and-Crafts stood his ground. 'He says you can name your price.'

'A lot more than he can afford, or anybody else.'

'Name it.'

'All right, then,' she said, with a tilt of her chin. 'A hundred pounds.'

He was suddenly still. 'A hundred pounds for the night?'

'No. A hundred pounds for a whole hour of my very valuable time.'

'That's rather steep.'

'Yes, so is the Ritz. What do they say about the Ritz? If you have to ask the price, you can't afford it. And tell him he'll have to arrange the hotel. Tell him I've no objection to the Ritz, or Claridges, would you, Lieutenant Yates?'

Cheek! She slammed the door hard behind him. That would be the last she'd ever hear from either of that pair. After she'd calmed down, Lizzie began to wonder what Irma would make of that little scene. Irma would never have lost her temper, and she wouldn't have sworn. Only stupid people swear, and Lizzie could have kicked herself for it. What superlatively caustic or utterly crushing remark would Irma have made? Lizzie stared into the mirror, mimicking her: 'Oh, I may be easy, but never make the mistake of thinking I'm cheap! I'm never that. Motto: always look ravishing, sweetheart! Never let your appearance slip, and put a high value on yourself. If you look a wreck stay at home, because if men see you like that you've lost the illusion, and you can never get it back. They never put as much value on you again.

'The big difference is that I'm not easy,' Lizzie muttered, and then she laughed aloud, because if she had been, even Irma couldn't say that demanding a hundred pounds wasn't putting enough value on yourself. Not that she'd ever get the hundred pounds. Not that she wanted it. Not like that, anyway.

So, he was Captain Ashton was he, the man with grey eyes? And Captain Ashton had wanted her, and because she worked in the theatre, he had assumed she was for sale. 'Men,' she breathed. 'I hate them. I hate them all.'

'What do you think? I've had someone biting on my line!' Lizzie saw a spark of interest in Irma's blue eyes and she became immobile waiting for more, but Georgie knocked on the door and, as usual, entered without waiting for an invitation.

'But I had to throw him back in.' Lizzie wasn't sure she wanted Georgie to hear what she had to say. He always had the latest scandal, and how he enjoyed passing it on. Lizzie delighted in her impression of Georgie-with-a-secret. When he was going to say something utterly treacherous or exquisitely malicious, his eyes would shine, and he would blurt a little of it out and then hesitate, not from any compassion for his victim, but because he was so thrilled with the power his news gave him that he wanted to prolong the moment. He liked to savour his juicy morsel and have his audience on the edge of their seats and almost salivating in anticipation. Then he would deliver it. He was so easy to mimic, and Lizzie found him hilarious – when he was discussing other people.

Irma shrugged herself into her dress, in disgust. 'It sounded for a moment as if you were going to say something interesting,' she protested. 'I don't know why you bothered to open your mouth.'

'Throw him back in?' said Georgie, his eyes lighting up. 'Are you talking about that fellow who crushed all your toes the other night?'

'Yes,' said Lizzie, a little reluctant. 'That one with the thin mouth and the shifty, deep-set eyes. I hope he's a better soldier than he is a dancer, or we might as well demand a truce.'

'Oh, *that* one! His eyes didn't look shifty to me, sweetheart, they looked gorgeous! So *penetrating*, dear!'

'Gorgeous, my foot. They're too deep-set, and the colour – it's not a colour at all – it's like a slate roof after a downpour.'

'It is! They have exactly that lustre, but it's beautiful! And his mouth! I could have kissed it myself!'

'No, his lips are much too thin. And the way he stands, as if he were waiting for somebody to take his photograph! What a poseur.'

'He just wanted you to notice him, Lizzie.'

She contemplated Georgie for a moment or two, and then decided. It couldn't hurt to tell them, because nothing was going to come of it. 'Do you know what he's had the impudence to do? He's only sent his friend to offer me money for my services, as if I were a cheap tart.'

Georgie seemed less than shocked. 'Cheap? How cheap?'

'He asked me how much I wanted, and I said a hundred pounds.'

Georgie pulled a face. 'I don't call that cheap. You should have sent him to me, darling. I'd have looked after him for nothing.'

'Shut up, Georgie,' Lizzie laughed. 'I doubt you're his type.'

'I doubt you are either, now. I should think you've priced yourself out of something *sublime!*'

After the start of the third act the callboy came and nudged Lizzie's elbow as she stood by the props table.

'He's here again,' he murmured. 'He wants to see you.'

'I'm busy,' she hissed. 'Tell him I can't see him.'

'Go on, Lizzie, see him for me. He's given me a good tip.'

'I can't see him. Irma might forget something she needs if I do. Anyway, I don't want to see him. Tell him he's wasting his time.'

The callboy sighed and went off on his errand, but was back a few minutes later with an envelope. Lizzie gave a little cluck of exasperation and pushed it into her jacket pocket.

She remembered the letter just as they were ready to leave.

'What does he say?' asked Irma, turning to the

mirror and stretching her lips over her teeth for a careful application of lipstick. Lizzie hesitated and when she spoke her voice sounded strange, even to her.

Holding a bundle of five pound notes, she said, 'He says I'm to meet him at the Ritz for supper on Saturday, as near to half-past-ten as I can manage, but if I do go he'll expect me to stay the night!'

Irma turned to face her with her top lip only half painted. 'My God! let me see.' She took the letter from Lizzie's hand and quickly scanned it. 'Yes, and that's all he says, no reference to the money.' She cast the letter aside and transferred her gaze to the bank notes with the air of a cashier. 'I can tell you there isn't a hundred there. Count it sweetheart, count it.'

There were ten.

'Will you go?'

'I don't know.'

'He might have the other fifty for you if you do. That's probably his idea, half in advance, and half after you-know-what,' said Irma, her face perfectly serious.

'Do you think so?' Lizzie sat down, suddenly weak at the knees.

'A hundred pounds! My God! You'd better pull all the stops out and give a fine performance for that money. Make sure he enjoys himself.'

'I'm not concerned with him. I'm concerned with myself, keeping myself safe and making sure I don't *get into trouble.*'

'I could give you a few hints there, and a hundred pounds would be more than enough to make you right again even if you did, with plenty left over. Women don't get offers like that every day, not even actresses, and he's not bad looking, if Georgie's to be believed. How long do you think it would take you to earn that much?' Irma gave her a quizzical look, then shrugged and returned to the mirror. 'But you're not the type. You'll be true to your provincial roots, and miss a golden opportunity.'

Lizzie watched her for a moment or two. 'It is a lot, isn't it? More money than I've ever seen in my life before. I could do a lot with a hundred pounds. Get some decent lodgings, for a start.'

Irma raised her eyebrows and grunted her agreement through stretched lips.

'And I must say,' Lizzie continued, 'I'm curious. I'm curious to know whether he would hand over another fifty pounds. And if he did, I'm curious to know how I'd feel, after doing it for *money*. It's horribly low, isn't it?'

Irma snapped the lid back on her lipstick and laughed. 'I wonder what Georgie will say?'

'On second thoughts,' said Lizzie, rising from her chair and handing Irma her coat, 'I think I'll just hang on to the fifty in case he comes back for it, and not go. You're right. I'm not really the type.'

They were quiet for a moment or two, buttoning coats and adjusting hats, then Lizzie added, 'I'll tell you what, though, Irma. I wouldn't mind hearing your hints, anyhow.'

Chapter Three

The cold winds of March had persisted until the last week in April but now they were gone, and it was fair and warm. With her fifty pounds clutched in a hand thrust deep into her coat pocket Lizzie sped along Oxford Street towards her favourite haunts, the large department stores. The window displays looked marvellous, full of colourful fashions, but not half as brilliant as they looked before the war, when they were lit up after nightfall. Half the lights in London were dimmed after dark, these days.

She slipped into Selfridges and walked past banks of early spring flowers and foliage, all still at their best although it was nearly a month after the usual time. The flowers at Selfridges always impressed her with a sense that some effort had been made to please her, with a sense that she, as a customer, counted for something.

She hurried along to look at the evening dresses, some sheath-like to the knee, with floating gauze underskirts edged with bands of silk, others high-waisted Empire lines, their straight sides softened with draped crossover bodices. How many yards of crepe de Chine and voile and satin might that one take, how many beads, how many yards of thread? She stood for a while pondering on the construction of a beaded ivory evening gown, fit for a queen.

No. There wouldn't be time to make a passable copy of that before her appointment at the Ritz, and she certainly had no intention of parting with the five guineas demanded for it. Her black dress would have to do. A delicious frisson of fear shot through her at the thought that she might go to the Ritz, that she might meet him there after all. Despite the warmth of the day she shivered, and the shiver gave her pleasure.

The orchestra began to play. How wonderfully civilized Selfridges was, she thought, making her way to ladies' underwear to sigh over petticoats of crepe de Chine and chiffon as delicate as cobwebs. Titillated by the thought that she might actually wear them for Ashton she asked for other, unmentionable garments to be taken from drawers for her and carelessly inspected them. Then, quite undaunted by the supercilious gaze of the middle-aged lady assistant she ordered that the flimsiest be wrapped for her.

The cosmetics counter. Perfumes, rouge, powder, and lipstick, all blatantly displayed to the customer at Selfridges, not hidden, as if they were something to be ashamed of. She liked that. Of course, she wouldn't go to the Ritz, but how it thrilled her to think that she might, and to imagine what would happen after supper if she did. She should be safe there after all, and Captain Ashton didn't strike her as a Jack the Ripper. All that would happen would be the something that's supposed to be 'a fate worse than death', which was a long way off a fate worse than death now, for her, at any rate. And with somebody as high up as a Captain – that would be something, wouldn't it?

She glanced at the clock and dashed down to the bargain basement for a pair of stockings, in agonies of impatience at the slowness of the assistant who took her money. Better get a move on, or she'd be late at de Lacey's, and she wasn't going to risk that, and maybe getting on the wrong side of the governor. Clutching her tiny parcel in one hand and her money in the other she made a swift exit and shot along Oxford Street, her thoughts at the Ritz with the man with grey eyes, doing the something that Irma always referred to as 'you-know-what'. And, of course, there was the other fifty pounds to think about. Really, that would be the best of all, if only she could get a hold of it.

'Another bloody white feather,' said Georgie, twirling a bit of down between his thumb and forefinger. 'I'll have enough to stuff a mattress soon.'

He was making light of it, but Lizzie could see he was rattled, and with reason. There were posters everywhere, directed at the young women of London, asking: 'Is your "Best Boy" wearing Khaki? If not, don't YOU THINK he should be?'

'Point them out to me, Georgie. I'll tell them you're more of a woman than they are,' Lizzie quipped, but jokes and levity were no match for rousing sketches like 'The Slacker' or 'The Enemy' run by some of the music halls, or patriotic plays like *Tommy Atkins* and *England Expects*. One of the newest songs was a gung ho call to action called 'We don't want to Lose You But...'

sung by Vesta Tilley, who had taken to herding men onto the stage during her performances to get them enlisted on the spot. There was no comfort from the trade magazine either; *The Era* was publishing the names of artistes who had signed up and those who had fallen on the field of battle in a column entitled 'The Profession with the Colours'.

Georgie sighed. 'Things are getting hot, Lizzie. The governor's talking about putting a note on the theatre bills to say that the men in the cast are either too old to enlist, or unfit to serve.'

Lizzie pulled a face. 'Not much of a choice, is it, Georgie, enlist and go and live in a horrible army camp with no proper bathrooms and lots of nasty men shouting at you and making you get up at the crack of dawn, or admit you're a dud,' she sympathized.

'No. Throw myself on the mercy of the Hun, or on the mercy of the British public. I think I shall throw my lot in with the Hun. He can't be any more vicious than some of our young ladies. I can't hold out much longer, Lizzie, old friend. You've no idea how it feels to see a pretty young thing trip towards you, beaming all over her face as if she'd been waiting all her life to see you, and then to have one of these pushed at you and think for one awful moment that she's actually going to spit on you. It quite shatters one's nerves.'

He reminded her of some defenceless animal at bay. 'But you'd be no use to the army, Georgie!' she exclaimed. 'What's the point in them giving you a gun? With your eyesight, you couldn't hit a barn door. What use would you be to them?

There'll be plenty of time to join up if you can't get out of it. Both my brothers are in France, and they reckon the war's going to go on for years. Once you're in it, there'll be no getting out. Hold out as long as you can, that's my advice.' She saw him waver and slipped her arm through his, her tones cajoling. 'Hang on a bit longer, Georgie. You can't go now, not when we've just perfected our tango. How can I be expected to manage without you?'

And seriously, how would she? She and Georgie had been friends since she first came to London, only seventeen years old, to work at de Laceys, and he'd been her dancing master, her mentor, her jester, her favourite butt, and a protector of sorts. He was her lifeline, the only man she ever went out with. If Georgie went, she'd have no life worthy of the name at all. She felt a flash of anger. Bloody bitches with their feathers. They were going to ruin everything.

Such plush and gilded opulence as she saw in the dining room at the Ritz Hotel would have left Lizzie utterly overawed, had it not been for her absolute determination not to be so. She crossed one leg over the other and leaned back in her chair, looking idly about her. A society woman sat at the next table, smoking a cigarette and occasionally feeding titbits to a pampered little dachshund which sat on a chair beside her with a ridiculous ribbon of red, white and blue tied round its neck.

Ashton nodded towards the dog. 'He's making sure we know whose side he's on.'

'It doesn't pay to take chances, these days.' She smiled vaguely back at him, thinking how elegant the woman looked, holding her cigarette. Streams of waiters were passing with plates which left the most mouth-watering aromas in their wake. One of them stopped at her elbow to place a trout in front of her, which lay on a bed of some unfamiliar pale green herb. He set another before Ashton, poured two glasses from a cut glass decanter whose contents gleamed the palest yellow, and was gone. Lizzie uncrossed her legs and watched intently as Ashton lifted his fish slightly and separated the flesh from the bones with one deft and delicate sweep of his knife.

After a moment or two she copied him with an off-hand air, her knife only a degree less skilful than his. 'How can you afford all this?' she asked, not raising her eyes from the fish. 'Is Daddy very rich?'

There. She'd mentioned the unmentionable, and asked the question nice people never ask. She had underlined the fact that she was a girl no officer or gentleman would ever be able to present to his family, even if he might be more than happy to show her off to his more disreputable friends. To hell with it. She took a small mouthful of her fish and chewed it in silence, awaiting his reply, sensing his eyes on her over the decanters and the pyramid of imported fruit.

'He's rich enough, I suppose. And I'm a bit of a gambler. I've had the most unbelievable run of good luck lately.'

'You must have, to pay for all this, and on top of a hundred pounds.' She looked up and met his eyes, and in an instant decided to tell him, as cool as may be. 'And you won't even be getting my virginity.'

He was silent for a moment, then: 'That's all right,' he said. 'You'll be getting mine.'

She felt her eyebrows rise a little, and glanced up, suspecting him of making game of her. But the eyes that met and held hers were clear and innocent, and the expression on his face was guileless, almost solemn. She looked intently at her plate during the long pause that followed. Better make some conversation, she thought. Say anything to break the silence. 'What's it like in France?' she asked.

'Bloody,' he said. 'That's why we're both here. I want to drink deeply from "Life's Enchanted Cup", while I still have the chance.'

When he closed the bedroom door behind them and glanced towards the ornate bed with its thick covering of rose-patterned silk Lizzie's knees almost gave way and her hand flew to her chest, she had such palpitations. Calm down, calm down. She must be calm, cool, icy, even. Play it like Irma would play it. She cast an eye round the room, noting a screen covered in light green watered silk, but no washstand.

Her eyes darted to his face. He was contemplating her, already tugging at his bow tie. 'You're nervous,' he said.

'There's nothing the matter with me.' She dropped Irma's silk wrap on the back of a chair, all gilded wood and petit point embroidery, and raised her foot nonchalantly to the seat, but her

54

fingers trembled a little as she pulled at the ankle ribbons on her up-to-the-minute shoes. He watched her hold them by the heels and put them carefully under the chair.

She straightened up, and managed to keep the tremor out of her voice when she said, 'My dress fastens down the back. Will you help me?'

The just passé straight v-necked dress, which had looked like a mermaid sheath on Irma skimmed Lizzie's hips. She felt his fingers fumbling with the fastenings, and then his warm hands on her skin as he pushed it away from her shoulders. She shivered.

'A good thing there's a fire,' he murmured.

'Yes.' She looked towards it, burning brightly in the centre of a beautifully carved fireplace of tortoiseshell coloured marble, and then turned her face up to the ceiling light, glaring mercilessly down from its white glass bowl. Looking at him again, she saw that his eyes were quite blue in the light of it, and there were golden lights in his brown hair. Without a word he crossed to the doorway and switched it off while she picked up her dress and placed it carefully over the chair and then waited for him, more comfortable in the gentler light of fire and table lamps. Still fully dressed himself, he put his hands under her slip, to lift it gently over her head.

'Isn't it funny,' she gasped, 'it should be Irma here with you, not me.'

'No. It's not funny at all. You're the one I want.'

'Then why did you ask for Irma, in the first place?'

'She was highly recommended as a woman of

55

pleasure. A couple of fellow officers have enjoyed her charms. These are funny little garments, aren't they?' he commented, trying to unfasten her bust bodice.

She took it off. 'You should have had Irma. You could have compared notes with them.'

'I could, but I want you. Like a spoiled child who looks into a toyshop window and says, "That's the one I want", and you're the goods. No other will do.' He briefly touched her breasts, then grasped her flimsy silk knickers with both hands and pushed them down to her knees.

Lizzie stepped out of them and turning her back on him hurried to take cover under the bed-clothes. He unfastened his trousers and dropped them to the floor, his shirt with double cuffs, socks and underclothes – all silk, she noticed – were soon scattered after them. She saw a firm, well-muscled body as naked as her own, and a swell of flesh arising from curls of brown hair above a pair of strong thighs. He threw back the covers and got into bed. Without invitation, he covered one breast with his hand, his grey eyes gazing down into hers. 'Are you sure you're not nervous?'

'I've said so, haven't I?'

'Well, I am. I'm like that man who sings "I'm shy, Mary Ellen". So you teach me what to do, Lizzie, and – be gentle with me.'

She searched his face, and her eyes narrowed into slits as she looked suspiciously into his, but she could find no hint of mockery in them. They were as calm as millponds, two tranquil pools of innocence, and around his mouth there was not so much as the ghost of a smile. He seemed

56

perfectly sincere.

Still, there was a limit to what he ought to expect. 'Giving lessons wasn't part of the bargain,' she told him.

'No?' He paused, and began to pull the pins out of her hair, whilst digesting this piece of information. He put them carefully on the bedside table, and ran his fingers through her hair, frowning and chewing his lip, as if deciding on a strategy. 'Then as I won't be charged with cowardice, I must assume command, and start with a reconnaissance,' he said at last, and lowered his mouth to lock hers in a brief kiss. 'I'll discover the lie of the land, and decide upon my line of attack, and then let instinct be my guide. If I stick doggedly to my objective, I shall be the victor.' His lips travelled further, gently nuzzling ear, neck, and shoulder. 'And I'll do better without these.' Impatient of constraint, he pushed the bedcovers to the floor and then paused, to take a good look at her. She caught her breath in sudden fear at this brutal exposure of her nakedness, blushing and trembling as she saw his reaction to the sight of her lithe body written in his face.

'Oh, you are a beauty.' He was still for a moment, then his lips travelled to her right breast. 'Here's Hill 60, and we must take the high ground.' He cupped her breast in his hand, and she felt a heat inside her, knowing that he would take her nipple into his mouth even before he did so. His hand travelled further down her body, over her belly and the mound above her thighs, finally coming to rest between them.

'And here I find the enemy's trench. I consider

it my duty to take this trench, and quell the enemy with enfilading fire.' He grasped her knee and, pushing it firmly aside, knelt between her legs to spread her thighs. 'And here, I suspect, I'll find a dark little dugout, underneath all this camouflage. Ah, there it is.'

'Oh! Oh!' she gasped with shock as she felt him press his fingers gently into her.

He seemed satisfied with what he had found, and gave her a reassuring smile. 'Oh? Oh, yes. A sturdy trench mortar will be enough to despatch the owner of this, I think.' He lowered his gaze again to his mark, and she watched him grasp himself with the other hand. Her heartbeat quickened at the sight of the reddened, glistening point, soon directed downwards and pushing its gristle hardness against her. He threw all his force against the breach, and with a few hard thrusts he gained his entrance – to begin the rout in earnest.

He seemed transported onto another plane. His face showed such ecstatic absorption in his own sensations that it began to pique little tremors of delight in her, and gazing into his grey eyes she encircled him in legs and arms. At length a burst of molten pleasure started at the point of his thrusting, and each beat of her heart washed its ripples from belly to breast, to neck, to brow, to thighs to toes, to fingertips, until a tingling warmth suffused her and left her limp. Her grip on him relaxed, but he was not finished with her yet. He quickened his pace, and though already up to the hilt in her lunged ever harder inwards. He groaned, and groaned again, and sank to rest on his elbows with his flushed cheek warm against hers. 'At last,' he gasped, still breathing hard, 'the trench raider has made his conquest. And I claim you for my prisoner. Say, "I surrender".'

She wanted to, to lie there and surrender to that voluptuous torpor paralyzing her limbs, but instead she tried to push him away and force herself up to carry out Irma's instructions.

He held her fast. 'Say it, prisoner. Say, "I surrender", or don't expect honourable treatment.'

'All right, I surrender. Did you see a washstand?'

He let her go. 'No, but the bathroom's over there.'

She'd wondered where that door led. She slipped out of bed and snatched up her borrowed overnight bag as she made her way over thick wool carpet and through the door to lock it after her. A bathroom in a bedroom, had anybody ever seen the like of it! Fumbling in her bag she soon found the bowl, which she quickly filled with warm water and a large pinch of the crystals Irma had given her. She put the bowl in the enormous porcelain-white bath and retrieved the Higginson's syringe, an implement she had met with once before. She clambered into the bath and made her relaxed limbs support her to squat. Holding one end of the syringe in the mild antiseptic she gave the bulb several hard squeezes. The pink liquid spurting out of the other end told her she'd primed it properly, just as Irma had shown her. She inserted it into the place just vacated by Captain Ashton, and keeping the distal end well below the liquid in the bowl she pumped the bulb to give herself a thorough douching. A few minutes later, wrapped in one of the hotel's thick white towels, she emerged bag in hand to find him sitting up in bed, torso still bare but the sheet providing decent covering for the rest.

'What on earth were you doing in there?'

'Washing your muck out,' she said, looking for the best place to put her bag.

She heard a gasp, and then the sound of a cigarette case snapping shut. 'What a charmer you are, Elizabeth. You have a glorious turn of phrase. You're not much better than our colonel, who tolerates the men's visits to the brothels because he feels "they must get rid of their dirty water". Really, it's well worth a hundred pounds to hear such a compliment.'

'My mother's the only person who ever calls me Elizabeth,' she said, discarding her towel to get into bed beside him, hoping she would be able to sink deep again into that divine lethargy that had not quite left her.

'No she isn't. I just called you Elizabeth.' He tapped the end of his cigarette against the bed-side table and put it to his lips. She sank back against the pillows to luxuriate in the warmth and comfort of the most comfortable bed she had ever lain upon in her life, idly watching him fumble for a match, her nostrils catching the acrid whiff of brimstone as he lit up.

He inhaled deeply and lay quietly for a while, blowing smoke rings into the air. Her eyes began to close, and she made neither protest nor move-ment when he pulled the cover aside to inspect her nakedness. 'Very pretty. A pretty little figure, and a generous black muff, to match your hair. Beautiful firm breasts, and pink nipples. Sugar and spice, and all things nice, that's what little girls are made of. But you haven't learned your trade very well, Elizabeth. It's the business of a prostitute to be pleasing – or so the other fellows tell me.'

She was warm and half asleep, too drowsy to reply or to feel any hurt or voice any objection to the name he called her. He put his cigarette in the ashtray and pulled her to him, nuzzling her neck and stroking her hair.

'You're adorable, Lizzie.'

She stiffened, and her eyes opened wide. Now where had she heard that before?

'You're adorable, Lizzie,' he repeated.

'Of course I am.' Her tone was sardonic.

'You're adorable, Lizzie.'

She said nothing, but arched her eyebrows and turned her head away.

He kissed her. 'You don't like compliments. Fair enough, let's talk about something else.'

'What?'

'You. Your family, and where you were brought up, and why you came to London.'

That lovely feeling of relaxation and drowsiness was spoiled now. She turned to face him.

'Light me a cigarette, will you?'

He did as she asked, and placed it between her lips. She inhaled, and was convulsed by a paroxysm of coughing. Through eyes blurred with tears she saw an expression of amusement on his face as he took the cigarette from her. 'I see that's the first one you've had. I don't approve of women smoking. I don't want to get you into any bad habits.'

'That's rich,' she croaked, as soon as she had breath to speak.

61

The grey eyes gave her a penetrating stare for a moment or two. 'Well?'

'Well what?'

'You haven't answered my question. About your family, and where you come from, and why you came to London.'

'I was brought up near Durham, my father's dead, and the rest of my family still live there. I came to London because I wanted to.'

'Did your father die in France?'

'No. He died when I was about eleven. Long before the war started.'

'How did your mother manage?'

'Our Ginny helped her, and our John. They're both a lot older than me,' she said, her accent becoming more Geordie the more she thought of home. 'Give us it back, then.'

'Are they your brother and sister?'

'Yes. Come on, then. Give us it back,' she insisted.

He turned and stubbed out the cigarette. 'Are they the only ones?'

'What for did you do that?'

'I told you. And I asked you if Ginny and John were your only brother and sister.'

She was obviously not going to get the cigarette and frowned, annoyed but resigned. 'No. There's our Emma and our Sally, and our Arthur. Our Sally's the only one that's not married, apart from me. And before you ask, me brothers are both in France, because they'd joined the Territorials for the sport and the bit of holiday it gave them every year. Only they got more sport than they bargained for soon after the war started. Our

Arthur's a gun layer, and our John's a sergeant.'

'Do you write to them?'

'No. They've got their wives to write to them, and me mother.'

'Why don't you write? Can't you? Can't you read and write?'

'Of course I can bloody read and write. What do you think I am?'

'I know what you are. And here's your other fifty, by the way.' He reached for an envelope and dangled it before her, then had second thoughts and pushed it under his pillow.

She flushed. And I know what you are, an' all, she thought, you're a bloody arsehole. And if it hadn't been for her other fifty quid, she would have told him so.

'I'll give it to you later. You're annoyed with me for asking all these questions, aren't you?'

'A bit. But I'll put up with it, because it's the business of a prostitute to be pleasing, or that's what the fellows say.'

He placed a finger firmly on her lips. 'Don't say that.'

'You said it.'

'I know. But I don't like you saying it. Young ladies shouldn't swear or use bad words, not even young lady prostitutes. And anyway, I don't want to be reminded of it. Let's change the subject. There's something else I want to talk about. You like poetry, and I want you to read some of mine out loud to me. We have lots of poets at the Front, but their stuff's not half as robust as mine. Here.' He handed her a dirt-begrimed exercise book, open at the page, and she scanned the verse:

63

Shells

A roaring from the guns and from the shells!
What a tale of terror, now, their turbulency
  tells!
In the startled ear of night
How they scream out their affright!
Too much horrified to speak,
They can only roar and shriek
Out of tune,
In a clamorous appealing to the fury of the fire,
In a mad expostulation with the deaf and
  frantic fire,
Leaping higher, higher, higher,
With a desperate desire,
And a resolute endeavour,
What a tale their terror tells
Of despair!

How they clang and crash and roar
What a horror they outpour
On the bosom of the palpitating air!
And the ear it fully knows,
By the twanging,
And the clanging,
How the danger ebbs and flows:
And the ear distinctly tells,
In the screeching
And the squealing
How the danger sinks and swells,
By the sinking or the swelling in the anger of
  the shells,
Of the shells, shells, shells, shells,

Shells, shells, shells
In the clamour and the clangour of the shells!

'Those are our shells of course, dealing despair to the enemy. I wouldn't give any credit to theirs, never mind the fact that half of ours are duds, and they've got ten times as many as we have. Go on then, read it out.'

She did as he asked, and gained his approval. 'Hmm,' he nodded, 'you can read after all, and with feeling. That was good, Elizabeth.'

'I'd rather you didn't call me Elizabeth.'

'Got you, Elizabeth. So what do you think of my poetry? Rather good, isn't it?'

'Yes, it's pretty robust, as you say,' she said, through clenched teeth, and thought: on the bosom of the palpitating air? What sort of bloody rubbish is that?

He seemed pleased. 'Yes, it is. And you do read well Lizzie, very well indeed.' He leaned towards her, took hold of her waist, and pulled her down into the bed. 'Let's make love.'

'"Routing the enemy's dugout" doesn't sound much like making love, Captain Ashton.'

'It doesn't, does it? But that's how you got my virginity, and now in return you ought to make love to me properly. Unless you're one of those despicable types who have their evil way with a chap and then leave him high and dry, it's the least you can do.'

Lizzie lay perfectly still and silent, watching him.

He sighed. 'Oh, dear, I see all the responsibility falls on me in this business, so I'll do the love-making. If I say I'm going to cover every inch of

65

you with kisses because your skin tastes like honey, would you believe me? Would that sound like making love?'

'I would pretend to believe you for the sake of being plea...'

He pressed a finger to her lips to silence her. 'And so do you want me to make love to you?'

'I'll have to get out of bed again if you do.'

'No, you won't,' he whispered, nibbling at her ear.

Oh, yes, I bloody will, she thought. But, mindful of her fifty quid and considering this was the business of one of her profession, she capitulated, and allowed him to indulge himself in a lot more you-know-what with her, and this time accompanied by kisses, squeezes and tender murmurs rather than talk of routs and conquest. All of a piece with his wilful self-delusion that what they were doing was 'making love', she supposed.

He might as well have saved his breath. For all his sugary compliments, Lizzie Wilde wasn't such an idiot that she nursed any illusions about the officer class and its intentions towards penniless, unprotected girls like her.

Chapter Four

He ran his hands over her limbs, abdomen and breasts after completing his final conquest of her the following morning. 'Your skin is so soft, Lizzie,' he whispered.

Your skin is so soft, Lizzie. The memory of her first surrender to Tom Peters caught her on those words, sharp and unexpected as a bayonet thrust, and Ashton saw the perfidious tears that welled up to betray her. She turned her head away in a gesture at once proud and careless. 'When you get back, you'll be able to recommend me to your fellow officers. But don't forget to tell them how expensive I am.'

'Is that what you want?'

'No.'

He put his arms around her, squeezing her to him and preventing her from getting out of bed. 'Neither do I. But what I should like is to go to Kew, to see the gardens. Have you ever been to Kew?'

She shook her head. Why, no. She'd never been to Kew, or anywhere else much.

'Then don't let's part just yet. The gardens are bound to be looking at their loveliest just now, and the glasshouses are quite spectacular. You're free on Sundays, so come.'

Irma had impressed on her the need to beware of devaluing her favours by giving them too freely, and she wavered, wondering whether it would be judicious to favour him with her company any longer. She shook her head again. 'No, Captain Ashton. What I should like is the money you owe me.'

He released her and held out the envelope. She took it from him, but put it in her bag without counting it.

'Ah, that shows you have faith in me. You take me for an honest fellow. So come with me to Kew.'

Hardly knowing how it had happened, she found herself depositing her bag alongside his in the Left Luggage at the station. 'It's unbelievable,' he told her as they made their way to the train to Richmond, 'one comes to London, and one is stunned to see everything going on as if there were no war at all. "Business as usual" hardly expresses it. The papers are full of sports and games, and football matches, and people are enjoying themselves at theatres and fashion shows, no end of amusements. I was at Waterloo with Lt Yates a couple of days ago – he had orders to report to Southampton for embarkation back to the Front. We'd given ourselves plenty of time, but what we hadn't made allowances for were the enormous queues of racing men struggling for the trains for the Hurst Park Races, and none of them prepared to let the fighting men – the mere defenders of their country – get in their way. I think they'd rather have trampled us to death. And I thought, they're not going to *watch* the geldings' race; they're running it. Able-bodied men, hordes of them in the prime of life, swarms and swarms of them, and I don't exaggerate. The upshot was that Yates and a lot of other officers missed their train. Everybody was muttering about it, all except the racing men, of course. Even the porters were saying what a disgrace it was, and I thought, roll on conscription, and give all these blighters a taste of what we've had to put up with during the past few months. I heard of a young girl who was killed while she was washing a step in Scarborough – killed by a shell from a German battleship...'

'That was months ago – wasn't it before Christmas? They bombarded Hartlepool, didn't they? I remember my mother writing about all the damage, and there were hundreds of people killed.'

His eyes darkened. 'Yes. Teesside is a prime target, because it makes munitions and other things necessary for the war effort. One can understand why they would bombard Hartlepool, it's a port and a military target. But I suppose being Huns they couldn't resist having a pop at a lot of women and babies and innocent civilians in Whitby and Scarborough as well. How any man can stay at home and go about amusing himself at races while that sort of thing's happening I don't know. And if the people here had any idea of some of the things they've done in Belgium and France, well...'

It was a shame for them all, Lizzie thought, for everybody who'd been killed, but it was Georgie and the tango that most concerned her when she asked, 'Do you think conscription will come?'

She felt strong hands encircle her waist, to lift her onto the train. 'It should, and as soon as possible, but it depends what the politicians are planning. If they merely want to drive the Germans out of France and Belgium, possibly it won't, but that will leave Germany free to build up her armies and navy again, and then what a fine revenge she'll wreak on us. The people who talk about peace can have no idea what a disservice they're doing to their country. The German government will stop at nothing to defeat us, there's absolutely nothing they won't stoop to if they think it will help them gain their ends; and how anybody can fail to see that after attacks on civil-

69

ians *and* the poison gas attacks, I simply do not know.'

He stopped to open the door of an empty compartment, and stood aside to let her enter, closing the door carefully after them. He took a seat opposite and flashed her a rare smile. 'I say, this is s'nice. Just the two of us.'

'S'nice?'

He laughed. 'Surely you've heard it, that ridiculous song, "I Do Like a s'Nice s'Mince s'Pie." They sing it in the ranks all the time. They've got us all at it – "s'nice s'mince pie, s'nice s'mince pie, I don't like ham, lamb or jam and I don't like roly poly; but when I sees a s'nice s'mince pie, I arsks for a 'elpin' twice...".'

'Oh, yes, that.'

The smile faded. His eyes darkened and his brows came together in a sudden frown. 'To go back to what you were saying before, no, we haven't enough men to carry us through another year, and we haven't enough shells either. We'd have made a better fist of it at Neuve Chapelle if we'd had enough artillery to suppress the enemy trenches, and enough reserves to follow up our success...'

He must have caught the look of blank incomprehension on her face, for he gave a short laugh and stopped. 'I'm sorry. None of this means anything to you, and I really must stop thinking about it. We're sent on leave for a rest from all that, and I ought to make the most of it.'

'Well, you've already gone a long way towards doing that, haven't you?'

'Yes, I have. I've drunk deeply from life's en-

70

chanted cup, and there's nothing more enchanting in it than you, Lizzie.'

'You're mad,' she told him, adjusting her hat, white silk in the latest cloche style with lilac ribbon round the crown that she'd given thirty-five shillings for. 'Fancy paying a hundred pounds for a girl, and after only seeing her twice!'

'If you'd been with us these past few months, you wouldn't call me mad. Money's only money, after all, and I can't spend it when I'm dead. So if I want the best doll in the toyshop I shall have her, and I shall come back and play with her again next time I get leave.'

'You'll find it very expensive to play with me, unless you marry me.'

He gave a mock sigh. 'It's an awful pity, but in my case rather the high-priced dollymop than the wife. The wife would prove ruinously expensive. My father's a diamond merchant, and I want to keep my fingers in the till. He'd slam it shut so hard he'd cut them off if I married without his approval.'

'And what would your mother have to say to that?'

'My mother is no longer with us.'

'Why not? Did he cut her off?'

He didn't answer, and she saw that she'd touched a raw nerve. His mother was probably dead, perhaps quite recently. Best to change tack, then, and get back to the original question.

'Can't you make your own living? Would it matter that much, if your father cuts you off?'

'Yes, I could make my own living but it would be slow. I shouldn't get as far as I want as fast as

I'd like without him. Anyway, how can *you* ask *me* that, Miss Hundred Pounds a Night? I daresay we've both seen enough of life to know that poverty is not a pleasant thing, and the sad fact is that he's got all the money.'

Wrong. That was the wrong answer. The right answer would have been 'I'd make any sacrifice on earth to call you my own,' or anything along those lines. He gave a little shrug and the thin lips parted in a grin which seemed to express regret at his vulnerability. She answered by drawing back her own lips in a smile that she knew would look pleasing.

'Come on. I want to show you the Palm House. This is my favourite part of Kew, I think,' he said, steering her towards a huge glasshouse. Once inside she stared about, enthralled by so much light and greenery and by the ornate framework of wrought iron painted a brilliant white, which vaulted high above her like thick white lace, dwarfing her, dwarfing even the trees it contained.

He watched her for a moment or two, then said: 'And how do you like your architecture made of glass and iron, Lizzie?'

'It's magical, like something out of fairyland.'

'It is rather, isn't it? And all owing to the miracle of modern engineering. Do you know, it's almost 400 feet long, and a hundred feet wide, and sixty-odd feet high. I should love to be able to construct something like this one day.'

'Then I'm sure you will.'

'Perhaps. Come and see it from the mezzanine floor.'

She followed him up a white spiral staircase, and along a gallery supported by cast iron pillars, to look down at the trees, and up at the arched glass roof above them. 'Architecture, Lizzie, and engineering. If I survive the war there'll be no more soldiering for me. I shall start to rebuild everything that's been destroyed.'

'All on your own?'

He laughed. 'Perhaps not. I might need one or two people to help me, and you for an appreciative audience, to keep me going with encouraging comments like, "Oh, that's rather impressive trusswork, Freddie," or,' he leaned to whisper in her ear, "I do so admire your front elevation, my love!"'

'It's amazing,' he said, as they strolled around 300 acres of garden, 'How three months of spring seem to have been concentrated into a single week. See how well the daffodils and narcissi are looking, and nearly a month after the usual time. And here the earlier tulips are coming into flower. And the celandine are still out. They're usually gone by the middle of April, and they're still here, with the bluebells, and even a few anemones. It's extraordinary. Do you like gardening, Lizzie?'

'I don't know. I never had much time for it. My mother and Sally did most of it after my father died, and John did all the digging.'

Hearing the chirruping and twittering of birds surrounding them Lizzie looked up to try and spot them. Instead she saw leaves of vivid and tender green, half transparent, so that the sun shone through them as through stained glass. 'Look up there, Freddie,' she said, and squeezed his elbow.

He looked up, laughing, then the smile faded and the jocular mood was gone in an instant. 'Maple leaves, the emblem of Canada. Oh, Lizzie,' he said, his pace slowing, 'those valiant Canadians. One can only imagine what their mothers will suffer.'

'What about the Canadians?'

He came to a halt. 'You must have heard about the gas attack at Ypres a couple of weeks ago, when the Germans pushed the Allies back. The French colonials got a bad dose of it and they fled – one could hardly blame them, but they left a huge gap in our lines for the Germans to exploit. The Canadians were all the rawest of recruits who'd only just come up the line, but they stepped into the breach and held it against four German divisions with heavy artillery. Once more unto the breach, dear friends, once more, or close the wall up with Canadian dead! Saint Crispin's day couldn't touch it. They fought through two days and nights, under their officers until their officers were killed, and then they fought on their own courage and initiative. Luckily the German infantry attacks were confounded by their own gas, and the Canadians were able to fire at them at close range. They fought like Trojans, but their losses were enormous.'

'Whose, the Canadians' or the Germans'?'

'Both, I suppose.'

Lizzie was used to seeing words like 'losses' and 'casualties' on newspaper hoardings, but had previously been too wrapped up in her own survival to ponder very deeply on what those words meant,

74

or take the slightest notice of what was happening at the Front. Now Ashton's agitated manner struck their meaning home. 'Their losses were enormous,' she repeated. 'I suppose that means there were heaps of dead soldiers. How awful!'

'And how courageous,' he said. 'It makes my blood boil, to think of an enemy that will sink to using something as filthy as poison gas, but that's the latest weapon of the Kultur they're so fond of boasting about. I ask you, Lizzie, what perverted imagination incubates such weapons? What depraved brain orders them to be unleashed on fellow men? There's nothing chivalrous about their conduct of this war, and the worst of it is that we shall have to become as foul as they are, or we shall lose, and then God help us all.'

'Do you believe in God?' she asked.

'I don't believe in anything much, except man's infinite capacity for cruelty and destruction.'

She hesitated, then asked, 'What about the Angel of Mons, then?'

'I know people who saw slagheaps and colliery works at Mons, making things difficult for the artillery, but I've never met anybody who saw any angels. It's like stories of bullets and shrapnel never hitting the wayside crucifixes that you see all over France and Belgium. They're lies that sell a lot of newspapers, principally because people want to believe such things.'

'But you still believe in the war.'

'We guaranteed Belgian neutrality, and the Germans violated it. They've overrun Belgium and France and they've committed the most horrible atrocities. It's an obligation of honour to turn them back, and it's in our own self-interest to do it, and decisively.'

They resumed their walk in silence, past rhododendrons just coming into flower, on and on towards birches and larches still in their tenderest foliage. 'That's the willow wren,' he told her, stopping to listen to chiming birdsong. 'Isn't it enchanting?' He cast his eyes skyward. 'You know, Lizzie, not so long ago I looked up like this after some pretty heavy shelling, and I saw a man's legs dangling from a tree. Just the legs. Nothing else left of him.'

At a loss for what to say to this, and not knowing how to respond to the distress she saw on his face, she averted her eyes and said nothing. The silence was broken only by the rustling of leaves in the balmy breeze, and far in the distance she fancied she heard the mellow harmony of church bells.

She walked down a dingy, narrow Soho street, back to her rented room in a three-storey house of multiple occupation with neither garden nor bathroom, and sanitation that turned her stomach. Let him see her home, she thought, not a chance! Never in this wide world would she let anybody whose opinion she cared about see her in these surroundings. But she'd be out of here tomorrow as soon as it was light, bag and baggage, and they wouldn't see her backside for dust.

The stench of unwashed bodies and rotting vegetation overpowered her when she let herself in the front door and groped her way up two filthy, debris-strewn flights of stairs. On reaching her landing she stepped gingerly over rotting floorboards and unlocked the door to her room, pushing it open to reveal a stark interior – bare boards, a bed, a table upon which stood a mirror flanked by two candlesticks, and a chair. Once inside, she deposited her bags on the chair and with a sigh of relief carefully locked the door behind her. She struck a match and lit the candles and then drew the curtains, mulling over the events of the past twenty or so hours.

Like a good courtesan she had allowed Ashton to indulge his little fantasy, and now the fantasy was over. It's a strange game, love, she thought, and nine times out of ten it's nothing to do with love at all. It's to do with satisfying men's lust, and lust for conquest, and from now on she would play the game to her advantage, not theirs. Ashton liked her, she was certain of it, and had she been the daughter of a family that lived in Belgravia and sent its sons to public school, that liking might well have ended in marriage. As it was, she would serve his purpose until Daddy chose him a suitable wife, or he chose her himself. That was the sort of love he was holding out to her. Spoiled child was right. The man really was an arsehole.

She undressed and hung her clothes carefully on the back of the chair, slipped into her nightdress, then took the ninety odd pounds she had remaining out of her bag and looked at it. This was more use to her than any amount of love. She'd spend it judiciously, first and foremost to get some lodgings she wouldn't be ashamed to be seen in, not like this stinking hovel. Captain Ashton had got what he'd paid for, and she owed him nothing. He'd left her swearing that he loved her to distraction, but in the end he reminded her of a drowning man, clutching at a straw called Lizzie, and she determined to throw him off, before he dragged her down with him. His kisses and caresses didn't mean he loved, they meant that he wanted to *be loved*.

She would never fall into that trap again. Never. Her brother John had tried to warn her against Tom Peters, had told her 'don't get too fond', but that didn't go far enough. She stooped to look in the mirror and pull the pins out of her hair, and gave her reflection a wry smile. I have some better advice for you, my pet, she thought. *Don't get fond at all.*

She quickly blew out the candles and got into bed. She wouldn't have given Ashton this address for all the tea in China. She must have been mad to let him have her mother's, and to half-promise that she would write to him. And why on earth had she given him that good-luck charm, that little gold horseshoe that John's wife had pressed into her hand before she left Annsdale? It must have been worth a couple of guineas, at least. Stupid girl, to let stupid sympathy gallop away with her like that.

After a few minutes she ran her hands caressingly over her body, wondering at the erotic excitement she'd felt with Ashton. It had probably been the fear that had caused it, the terror and the thrill of stepping so far out of all bounds of decency and morality. Or perhaps it was the novelty of it all. Could he really have been a virgin? She recalled his face when he told her so, its candid, frank sincerity; his eyes so innocent, and found she still could not disbelieve him.

He must be a damned quick learner, then. Perhaps it was sheer instinct with some men. Whichever way it was, there was no denying that his lovemaking, as he chose to call it, had been very good. Or 'awfully s'nice,' as he'd kept telling her before they parted. 'Awfully, awfully s'nice.'

It was becoming harder and harder to divert Irma from her almost constant state of moody apprehension but Lizzie's tale of her encounter with Captain Ashton, with every shred of tenderness and human sympathy expunged was just the tonic Irma needed.

'Oh, my poor, dear, provincial darling, it's quite the sad and shocking story of the innocent country girl who comes to London, isn't it? And now you're one of the fallen! Do you feel terribly degraded?'

The sparkle in Irma's eyes and the eager smile on her lips assured Lizzie that what she had left in her tale was salacious enough. Only the most sordid gossip got such a gratifying reaction from Irma.

Degraded. Lizzie pondered on the word for a moment. 'I felt a lot more degraded living in those horrible lodgings in that foul back alley,' she declared. 'I shan't have to do that any more.'

'You've no regrets, then, sweetheart?'

Lizzie, with her head tilted to one side, cast her eyes heavenward. 'Why yes, Irma, as a matter of fact I have,' she said, after a couple of seconds' reflection. 'I wish I'd asked for guineas now.'

Irma wriggled in ecstasy. 'Oh, my darling Lizzie, I'm so proud of you! Three times in one night! And he should have been mine, you slut! I ought to scratch your eyes out.'

'Not a word of it to Georgie, or I'll be scratching yours out,' said Lizzie, though not much caring now if he did find out. She could control him in the same way that Irma did if she wanted to, by hinting that details of his furtive little forays down certain back streets might reach the wrong ears, that his little peccadillos might become public knowledge if he dared to let hers out.

When she thought about it, Lizzie realized that she had another regret about her night with Ashton. If she had realized at the outset that he would meet all her demands and that she would actually spend the night with him she would have made him take her to The Karsino on Tagg's Island in the Thames. Fred Karno was the most brilliant impresario in London, and his slapstick comedy was a hit in America, as well as in England. Charlie Chaplin had been spotted there with Karno's Troupe, and was now the highest paid actor in the world. It would do her no harm at all to be seen by Karno, Lizzie thought. And she'd wanted to dance a tango at the Karsino's Palm Court Concert Pavilion ever since Irma had told her about it.

But it would have been useless. Ashton had two left feet, and he certainly wouldn't have wanted to give a hundred pounds to watch his 'young lady' dance with other men all night.

She followed Georgie's lead, blissfully and without a thought in her head, until he nodded towards a couple who were gazing entranced into each other's eyes, billing and cooing like a pair of turtledoves. 'Don't they make an enchanting picture? Is that love, do you think?' he laughed, turning her so that she got a good view of them.

'Perhaps. And it might last until the end of the month, and then he'll send her a letter to say he's engaged to be married to somebody else.'

'On the other hand,' said Georgie, 'it might last 'til death do them part.'

'Hmm.'

'Such cynicism, in one so young. Methinks my Eliza has been crossed in love.'

'Love, Georgie, is a blood sport, like the fox-hunting up where my family live.'

All the same, she kept a wistful eye on the lovebirds, who were still engrossed in each other when Georgie swept her past them for the fiftieth time. 'Oh, Georgie,' she sighed, 'I'd love a tall, dark, handsome man to put his arms round me and protect me from the world, and make love to me, and tell me he loves me, and really, really mean it.'

He pulled her in closer. 'Oh, so would I, Lizzie. So would I!'

He was playing the fool. 'Silly bugger!' she threw her head back and laughed, until glancing at his face she saw that his eyes were unusually moist.

Lizzie set out for work a little late, feeling well satisfied with herself after tidying her new room in her vastly superior lodgings. She was installed in a Georgian house in Bloomsbury, a place

Georgie had told her about, and from where she could see the windows of his little flat on the opposite side of the square. It was amazing how living in a place that was not a slum and having a few decent possessions made you feel more human. As if you counted for more in the world, which you did, no doubt about it. But now she'd cut it a bit too fine and she'd better shift, if she was going to get to de Lacey's on time.

The place was deathly still when she dived through the stage door. Cast and stagehands were standing together talking in hushed tones, and nobody was making any effort to get anything done. Irma was looking more tense than ever.

'What's up? Why are you all sitting looking at each other? Has somebody died?' Lizzie demanded

'Haven't you heard?' the callboy piped up. 'The *Lusitania*'s gone down, off Queenstown.'

'The governor's going off his head,' said one of the chorus girls. 'His wife and kids were on that ship, coming back from a visit to her cousin in Canada. He's gone for the first train up to Liverpool, to get across if he can.'

Lizzie had heard the paperboys crying something about the *Lusitania* and Queenstown as she'd raced through the streets to the Theatre, but neither name meant much to her and she'd taken very little notice.

Where was Queenstown? It was on the tip of her tongue to ask, when one of the stagehands gave her the paper. No need to show her ignorance, then. She took it, and read for herself:

82

Saturday 8th May 1915. The Cunard liner *Lusitania* was torpedoed by a German submarine off the South coast of Ireland yesterday afternoon and sunk, with over two thousand people on board. Telegram from Queenstown: Torpedo boats, tugs and armed trawlers all in except *Heron*... Total number of survivors 658 and 45 dead... Kinsale fishing boats might have a few more.

Irma shuddered, her face white. Lizzie caught her eye. 'Well, we can't help it, can we?' she shrugged, laying the paper aside.

'Oh, the callousness of youth!' Georgie exclaimed.

'They're saying a lot of people were killed by the torpedoes. I reckon they can give up on anybody they haven't found already.'

'They're sending people to the naval and military hospitals, but they haven't given any names out yet.' The doorman's face was a picture of gloom.

'I'm not callous at all, but there really isn't much we can do about it, is there?' said Lizzie, 'except make things worse by letting the show go to pot. And then the governor'll be in the bankruptcy courts. That'll give him something to thank us for, I'm sure.'

In sombre mood, everybody drifted back to work, and the curtain went up on their jolly little play only ten minutes late. They played to a theatre that was barely a quarter full, and as was usual for a matinée, most of the audience were women. Irma gave an uninspired performance.

That evening the theatre was half full and with a larger proportion of men, some of them in uniform. Ten minutes to curtain up and still no Irma. Lizzie put on the costume. She was pitched into the part before she had much time to consider her nerves, and played it exactly as she'd seen Irma play it so many, many times before. She got as much applause as Irma usually did, and came off stage flushed and energized.

'That was a great performance, Miss Wilde.' Bert was a man in his fifties, whose short, muscular frame and belligerent expression always put her in mind of a bulldog. A leftover from the last of the sailing ships, Bert had taken the job of flyman, to climb up to the gantry backstage and change backdrops whenever necessary, or scatter 'snow' at the right moment, or drop a dead pheasant onto the stage when the leading man 'shot' it. 'Give our own English girls a chance, that's what I say,' he continued. 'Knock the German variety into a cocked 'at.'

Lizzie smiled. Her acting had been adequate, but a long way off great. She hadn't rehearsed enough for that, but she was pleased by the compliment. 'It's all the help I've had from everybody else, Bert,' she said. 'And if we all carry on the same way, I think we should manage to keep things ticking over until the governor comes back, don't you?'

'Yes I do. I 'ope she never comes back. It's time we sent the 'ole bloody lot of 'em packing, going for merchant ships with their bloody submarines, drowning innocent women and kids. This country's crawling with bloody Germans, spying on us and plotting to do us all in.'

'Irma's English,' Lizzie said, 'and she's been a good friend to me.'

'Hmm,' he snorted. 'Irmgard Meyers. She sounds English, I don't think.'

'But Bert, your name's German, come to that,' said Lizzie. 'Your first one, at any rate.'

'Bert? That's a good English name, that is. There's nothing German abaht me, Miss. If I thought my name was German, I'd go and cut my throat.'

Nothing was seen or heard from Irma the following day, or the day after that. Her trunks and her props lay where she had left them in her dressing room, but when Lizzie went to see her she discovered she'd given notice to quit and was gone, leaving no forwarding address.

Life would lose some of its spice without Irma and her wicked wit, Lizzie thought, retracing her steps to the Theatre, and there was something horribly unpleasant about the manner of her going. But the more people who left, the more openings there were for other people, and if she worked like a slave, the governor might make her promotion permanent. There'd be no slum lodgings ever again if she could work a flanker like that. Her step became livelier, and a smile accompanied her little sigh, and her shrug. She would miss Irma, certainly, but it's an ill wind that blows nobody any good, and as Irma herself used to say: 'Your best friend is the pound in your pocket.'

Chapter Five

Lizzie's conviction that none of them would ever see Irma again grew with every day that passed. By the time Thursday came her acting was surer and her confidence in her performance was increasing. She was beginning to make changes in the way she played the part, trusting her own interpretation and beginning to live it. The audiences seemed to like it. Everybody was pulling together to keep the show going until the governor got back, and everything was going better than they could have expected. A few of the cast had arranged to go out to supper after the show on Friday night to celebrate their success.

Costume off and hanging out of harm's way, all greasepaint removed and her own lipstick carefully applied, Lizzie stepped out of her dressing room wearing Irma's wrap, right into an argument between the doorman and the flyman.

'We didn't ought to be starting a quarrel with ordinary German people, even if the German subs are torpedoing passenger ships. There's no bloody excuse for these hooligans who go about smashing their shops up,' the doorman was protesting. 'And they're not even getting Germans half the time. Two out of the three poor sods done over by the Kentish Town mob were Englishmen, and I know that for a fact because my sister's eldest had to go to Marylebone police station as a witness. Half of these so-called anti-German demonstrations are just an excuse for a lot of thieving. We can't blame everything that happens in the war on a poor barber or a little German shop assistant who's had no contact with Germany for years, except for a letter she might send once in a blue moon.'

'Ah, but what's she telling 'em in 'er letters, eh? All about what's going on in this country, where the army camps and shipyards and munitions factories are, that's what, or 'ow many troops are setting out on which trains – she might be telling 'em anything, for all we know. You don't know what they might be doing. I 'ope the people in Parliament aren't as soft as you, or we'll lose the bloody war.'

'There can't have been many soft people in Canning Town,' said Lizzie. 'I heard there were fifteen German shops attacked there.'

'I'm not soft. I fought in the Boer war, before some of you lot were out of your nappies. I'd willingly suffocate the Kaiser, or any of his family, or any of the German generals with their own poison gas. I'd hold their heads in it with my own hands if I could. But I'm dead against picking on innocent bystanders, people who've got nothing to do with it.'

'Like Irma, you mean,' said Lizzie.

'Yes, like Irma, Miss; people making her life a misery until she can't see anything for it but to up and off. And German shops weren't the only ones who copped it in Canning Town – a lot of English ones were damaged alongside 'em. And the cowards that did it weren't content with taking money from the tills, they were in people's houses pinching their furniture, and bedding, and even their clothes. No, I don't go along with that. If they want to fight Germans, let them get out to France and fight them. A bit of army discipline'd do that lot good.' He gave Bert a withering glance, and with his words loaded with meaning he repeated, 'People like that.'

Bert's ruddy face reddened further, his chin jutted forward and his dark eyes flashed fire. 'There's forty thahsand bloody GermHuns roaming wherever they like round England, plotting and spying, and it says in the paper that the GermHuns in that prison ship in the Solent stand hooting and yelling insults at our troop transports going past. If our boys did the same in Germany, they'd get strung up for it! We feed their lot, but our lot are used for slave labour and kept half-starved in prison camps in Germany – they're forever writing home begging for bread. I've seen that with my own eyes, because I've seen letters from my sister's bloke. We're too bloody soft for our own good here. What do you think the Germans did at the start of the war? Turned all the English out of their houses and jobs, and left them to get home the best way they could. I wonder what the people who were turfed out of Germany have got to say about what's going on here? I wonder what the governor thinks about it all, with one of his kids dead, and the other one missing?'

The doorman lost heart in the argument at that, and shuffled back to his post, his lined face downcast. What would the governor think to it all, and what sort of state would he be in when he got back to London? Lizzie wondered. They'd had only one telegram from him, to say his son was dead, his daughter missing, and his wife still in hospital and he'd be back as soon as he could. But he'd be pleased at the way they'd managed, if he was capable of being pleased at anything. There was nothing much they could do anyhow, except soldier on and wait.

Georgie and the rest of the party came laughing and jostling each other down the corridor, and swept her along with them. They were soon crammed together in a cab, Lizzie sitting on Georgie's knee. 'Do you think I dare take Irma's stage costumes in, Georgie?' she asked, wrapping her arms round his neck. 'You don't think she'll be back, do you?'

Georgie didn't think Irma would be back, so Lizzie decided she'd get the alterations done on Sunday. If she made them a dead fit, they'd set her figure off, and that might encourage the governor to give her the part permanently. It would also make sure they wouldn't fit anybody else, which would be an added incentive for him to decide in her favour. And she ought to get Irma's name scratched off the programme and her own written in instead. But maybe that was going a bit too far. Maybe she'd better wait until the governor got back before she started asking for stuff to be sent to the printers.

She hoped to God she'd get the curse on time. It would be a bloody nuisance if she didn't, especially with no Irma to go to for aid and comfort.

British Expeditionary Force
Monday 10th May

Dear Lizzie,
  It's a lovely evening. A little distance from me, there's a field of yellow turnip flowers rippling in a breeze which wafts their scent, something like meadowsweet, towards me, to mingle with the heavy scent of the lilacs in the cottage gardens. A single spider's thread is glinting in the sun, spun out between two stems of euonymus, and every time the wind blows them apart I think the thread will break, but it only stretches, and relaxes again. It seems a miracle that something so fragile can be so strong, and I think of the thin little thread between us and hope it's an omen. The sky's a brilliant blue, with swallows wheeling about under wispy white clouds. High above me a lark is singing its heart out. I swear they sing louder here, as if they're trying to drown out the noise of the bombardment. Far in the distance I can see a scout plane, which looks no bigger than a fly and there are shells bursting silently around it, like white puffs of smoke. A few seconds later one hears explosions, very faint. At this distance I feel very detached from any sense of the danger the airman is in, but if he gets hit, he's had it. They have no parachutes.
  We're a long way behind the lines and I would say I wish you were here with me, except that one is never quite out of reach of the shells. Most of the cottages here have been destroyed by the shelling and the people have all gone away,

leaving the place to the brutal and licentious soldiery.

Apart from the noise of the guns, very faint and far away just now, and the blighted houses, this profusion of nature's loveliness reminds me of you and the day we had at Kew. I enjoyed our day together immensely. You did too, didn't you, just a little bit? It was very sweet of you to give me the lucky horseshoe. It's in my breast pocket, and I know it's going to keep me safe when we go up the line.

I wish I could have had another half an hour with you. I know I should have been able to make you promise to write to me if I had. I hope you will write. I'm longing to get leave so that I can see you again, but that won't be for ages yet. I think of you all the time.

Yours ever, and xxxxxxx ad infinitum,
Freddie.

Lizzie's heart missed a beat when the letter arrived on Saturday. He'd written it on Monday evening, and her mother had sent it on to her. Supposing he'd posted it on Tuesday, that meant it had taken five days to get to her. She put her letter under her pillow and set off to work light of heart. She would read it when she got back, over and over again. And she would write to him, after all.

Georgie was waiting in her dressing room, looking very subdued. 'The governor's back. He's been telling me what happened to his wife. It was terrible, Lizzie. She was with a lot of other people who couldn't get into a lifeboat because of the list of the ship, and when it went down it sucked them all down with it. She'd been holding onto the children but the boy got tangled up in the wreckage, and she lost her grip on him. When she surfaced she still had the little girl, but the boy was nowhere to be seen.'

Lizzie shuddered. 'She must be out of her mind.'

Georgie nodded. 'It wasn't until they were rescued that she realized the kid was dead. You'd better go and see him. He's got something to say to you.'

The governor was slumped in his captain's chair dressed in sombre black, his bloodshot dark eyes looking out of a face that was thinner and older. 'You were the closest to Irma, Lizzie. Do you know why she left?'

Lizzie's eyebrows twitched upwards for a fraction of a second. She stared at him, but said nothing.

'She didn't think I was going to blame her, did she? I don't hold Irma responsible for this. Irma's half English, and even if she weren't, I don't hold her responsible for murders committed by the German High Command.'

'I know, but a lot of people seem to, and she couldn't stand any more of it. The *Lusitania* going down was the last straw.'

'Do you know where she's gone?'

'No. But wherever it is, it won't be Germany.'

The governor slumped further down in his seat and heaved a great sigh. 'I abandoned this ship for a while, Lizzie, and you've helped to steer a steady course. I've got to thank you for that. You've done well with Irma's part from what I've heard, so it's yours until she comes back. If we don't hear from her within another month, it's yours as long as the play runs. Ethel can be your understudy.'

Lizzie's face brightened. She smiled and opened her mouth to thank him, but he held up his hand, and shook his head.

'I won't be here much for the next two or three weeks. I've a lot of business to attend to, so I'll have to trust you all to manage without me. If you go on as well as you've begun, we'll be all right.

'We're burying our daughter on Monday, did you know, Lizzie? Poor little Annabel, she was only five years old, and my son...'

The query about her pay that had been on the tip of her tongue died with her smile, and Lizzie stared in horror at the tears that began coursing out of the governor's reddened eyes and down his sagging cheeks. She had never seen her father or either of her brothers cry; it was the first time in her life she had seen any man cry. Embarrassed, helpless and silent, she stood and watched him, wishing herself almost anywhere else in the world, and was so very, very thankful when without another word he got up, wiped his eyes, squeezed her hand, and left.

She had her part, but not the pleasure she'd expected to feel at knowing it was hers. She felt only her own deficiency in the face of a good man's grief, and went back to her dressing room full of joyless resolution to do the only thing she could do for the governor, and play the part well. She just hoped he'd remember about her money.

She'd felt little misgivings about his letter all day, and when she got back to her lodgings she saw why: 'I *know* I should have been able to *make* you promise...' The words jumped out at her, and she knew it was too true. He sensed her weakening will, and that just a little more persuasion, just a little more pressure would make her give in to him, would make her love him. He wanted to confuse an honest commercial exchange with real affection, and now she realized what the game was she could put a stop to it. Thank God she'd seen it in time, otherwise she might have done it again. She might have fallen into the trap of believing a lot of easy flattery and been gulled into allowing a man to control her with lies and take advantage of her by deceit – again.

No. With a sinking heart she knew she couldn't allow it. No man would ever betray her again, because she would never betray herself.

Most of the cast and the theatre staff wanted to attend the funeral, to show their respect and sympathy for the governor and his wife. There were no advance bookings for the Monday matinée, so the performance was easily cancelled. The loss of income wouldn't be enormous, and they'd work all the harder for the rest of the week. Mourning clothes presented no difficulty for Lizzie. Everything she had was black or dark blue.

She and Georgie arrived at the church early and sat at the back, in a pew near the aisle. Before the service started the church was packed save for those pews closest to the altar reserved for the family. When the cortege arrived people had to squeeze aside to allow passage for the bearers. Their burden was pitiful, a little white coffin unembellished except for a silver cross and five white lilies. The mother and father followed it up the aisle. For all her ordeal, the dead child's mother appeared to be holding up better than her husband – he looked near to collapse and was leaning heavily on his brother. The rest of their families followed close behind.

Lizzie stole a glance at Georgie, who stared straight ahead with a face as pale as marble. She knew exactly what he was thinking, but how much use did he think he would be to the British Expeditionary Force? He didn't know one end of a rifle from the other. And he'd be even less use in the navy. What could he do other than entertain people, for pity's sake? She'd have to talk him out of any nonsense about enlisting, because, quite apart from their dancing, the whole show would go to pot if he left, and then where would they all be, the governor and his wife above all?

She turned again to the little coffin, now standing alone in the aisle. How terrible, how unspeakably awful it all was, and all the more so because there were two drowned children and only one to lay to rest.

Ashton was right. If the Germans could stoop to drowning babies, they had to be defeated. They had to be. She suddenly thought of her brothers, defending them all at the Front. Perhaps she should write to them. Perhaps she'd send them one of those new Gillette safety razors apiece she'd seen advertised – no stropping, no honing, a guinea a set. They would be handy things to have in the trenches. She wavered, not certain that Arthur really deserved one – after all, he was a gun layer and, as Ashton had told her, behind the lines and not in the worst danger. Still, he was doing his bit, she supposed. A mixture of rage and pity combined with a rare burst of generosity, and she decided she *would* send them both one. And she'd send them some of those Horlicks tablets, too, so they could suck them when they couldn't get a cup of tea.

She rose to her feet with the rest of the congregation, and took up a hymn book, as the organ began to play the twenty-third psalm. They were halfway through it before she found the place and joined the singing:

'Yea, though I walk through death's dark vale
Yet will I fear no ill...'

The governor was on his feet, but looked utterly crushed, too broken to sing. It was all too ghastly for words.

Everything in Lizzie's garden was as rosy as it could be when she stepped out of the theatre with Georgie and others of the cast on the last night in May. The danger of his enlisting seemed to be gone, and to her intense relief all peril of any little inconvenience that might have arisen from her dalliance with Ashton was passed. One or two theatre critics had noticed her and were writing favourable reviews, and the governor had rewarded her with an increase in pay. She had just given a first rate performance. She was walking on air.

'Girls and boys come out to play,' she laughed, glancing upwards, but instead of the moon and the stars she saw the strangest thing suspended in the sky – silvery bright and silent, and shaped like an enormous cigar. 'Good Heavens! What's that?' she exclaimed, gazing at it in fascination.

'That, my dear, is a Zeppelin,' said Georgie. 'And it'll soon start dropping bombs, if I'm not very much mistaken.'

No sooner were the words out of his mouth than there was a terrific blast, and then another. The ground quivered when a third shook a building further down the street to its foundations, sending its windows splintering in all directions, and blowing out the ironwork along the outer wall. Then came another explosion, and a red blaze in the distance. The faces of a couple of the chorus girls were contorted in fright and their screams and shrieks added to the din. Lizzie thought of Ashton's words: 'The civilians will not escape. Every man, woman and baby, every cat and dog will be in this war. They'll see to that.'

Georgie spread his arms out and began urging and shepherding them all along. 'Come on. Let's get to the Underground. It must be safer than it is here.'

They began to run, and ran on and on until, gasping for breath, they reached the Underground and clattered down the steps as fast as they could go, down, down, down, speechless, saving their breath for gasping and hurrying, and rushing headlong towards safety, deep in mother

97

earth. Lizzie got halfway down and then stopped, and crept back up to the mouth of the Underground, unable to tear herself away from the sight of the silent silver balloon, now ascending in a night sky reddened by fire. Streaks of light were lancing the skies, searchlights, she supposed, and sirens were shrieking. She could smell smoke. 'My God,' she said. 'My God, my God,' then turned and raced down the steps to join the rest of them.

Walking back to her lodgings after all the noise of the raid had ceased she passed a group of men digging through the wreckage of somebody's home, trying, they said, to find survivors. She shuddered and hurried on, praying to God that her own little room and its meagre contents would be safe.

'Where's Ethel?' asked Lizzie the following day.

'Oh, Lizzie, she can't come in today, it's terrible,' a skinny girl with die-straight brown hair volunteered. 'A bomb fell through the roof of her cousin's house and into the bedroom where their five kids were sleeping, and the house was in flames straight away. Her husband thought he'd got them all out, but in the commotion he missed little Ethel, named after our Ethel. The poor little mite's dead! She died from suffocation and burns. The father and the kids, they've all been burned, and Ethel's had to go over and help her cousin to look after them all, because there's nobody else, and she'll be doing everything, I shouldn't wonder, because what will her cousin be fit for after something like that? If it were me,

I'd never stop weeping!' As if to prove the point, she burst into floods of tears.

'Oh, Mae!' Lizzie jumped to her feet and put an arm around the girl. 'Has anybody got a clean handkerchief?'

A handkerchief was produced, and Mae dabbed at her reddened eyes and nose. 'And she was such a happy little girl,' she sniffed. 'But the doctor thinks the others are going to be all right. The bomb said Krupps, Essen.'

'Sent a nice little present to that family, didn't they, Krupps, Essen? And don't think little Ethel's the only one, neither. There's a woman dead after she had to jump out of a window to get away from the flames, and a couple who were burned alive while they were saying their prayers, and there's other kids dead. And they won't be the last.' Bert's face was puce with rage, and he pulled at his shirt collar. 'I blame the Government. Bloody useless! I don't know what we bloody pay 'em for! "Many Fires Reported, but Those not Absolutely Connected with Airships" – I suppose everybody in London decided to set their own houses on fire, eh, is that it? Well, they have to make out it's not as bad as it is, with the Germans raining bloody bombs on us, and no bloody guns, no nothing to fight 'em off wiv!' Bert held up a copy of the *Daily News* and smacked it with the back of his hand. 'They're trying to make out there was only one fire worth getting excited about. Do me a favour.' He tossed the paper onto a table in disgust.

'Well, we must have heard about a hundred explosions before we got to the Underground,' one of the chorus girls chimed in. 'And there was plenty after, I daresay.'

'They're not going to tell us anything, if they can help it. It's censorship. It's always the same when there's a war. You never get told the truth,' said the doorman, his expression gloomier than ever. 'They always try to make out everything's all right, when nine times out of ten everything's all wrong.'

'That bloody Irmgarde. I bet she was a spy. What wiv people like her, and bloody useless people in Parliament, we'll all be bombed and burned in our beds before long. I bet the bloody Germans are cruising across the Channel this minute. They'll probably be stomping all over England this time next week, spraying us all with their GermHun bullets and kicking the shit out of us wiv their GermHun boots. Don't worry, I know all abaht it. I know one or two people who've been in Belgium, and they tell the bloody truth abaht it, mate. We'll get a dose of what the Belgians got. There'll be blood and guts all over the place.'

'Oh, they wouldn't do that, would they?' one of the girls squealed. 'We're not soldiers. We've got nothing to do with fighting.'

Bert gave her a look of contempt. 'Why do you think they bayoneted them Belgian babies? 'Cos they'd caught 'em throwing grenades, or something? But don't you worry. They'll have *something else* in store for you.'

'If they do manage to get cross the Channel, they'll probably gas us all,' said the callboy in a very matter of fact manner, with a wink in

Lizzie's direction.

'Nonsense!' Lizzie exclaimed, seeing by the alarm of some of the girls' faces that the callboy's joke had gone far enough. 'A piece of nonsense! We've still got the best navy in the world, and the Germans won't get past it, submarines or no submarines. Take no notice of them. Napoleon couldn't invade us, and neither will the Germans.'

'That's right, Lizzie. A bit of sense, at last,' said Georgie. 'Come on now, noses back to the grindstone, everybody. We're all on our honour to make this a play worth seeing and push the ticket sales up, so let's get on with it. We've wasted enough time already.'

Chapter Six

A few days later, Lizzie awoke to find two letters for her, one from neutral Holland. A broad smile covered her face as she opened it, murmuring 'Irma.'

Dear Lizzie,

Here I am, safe in Amsterdam. I've found somewhere to live, and now I'm writing to all my friends, both in Germany and in England, to let them know my address.

Tell the governor I'm very, very sorry about his wife and children and about leaving, but I couldn't have stuck it in England any longer, Lizzie. My nerves were in shreds.

Uncle Herman sent me the latest hit –
Zeppelin, flieg,
Hilf uns im krieg,
Flieg nach England,
England wird abgebrannt,
Zeppelin, flieg.
Which means: Zeppelin fly,
Help us win the war,
Fly against England,
England will be burned,
Zeppelin, fly.

What do you think to that? I'm so glad I left before the Zep Raid. I shouldn't have liked to feel responsible for that as well as the *Lusitania*.

Amsterdam is very pretty and I should love to get work in the theatre here, but alas! I speak no Dutch. Still, I have a nice, dull Dutchman who seems to have made himself responsible for my welfare. He speaks neither German nor English, but we manage to communicate – *somehow!* I must close, as the worthy burgher's knocking on the door as I write, and it's vital to keep him amused, perhaps for the duration. Oh, mercy!

Give my love to Georgie. How I miss you both.
Yours in exile,
Irma.

How typical of Irma! She's already got a man eating out of her hand! Lizzie felt glad and relieved, and put the letter aside with a laugh. When she turned to the other one, her smile was a little less certain.

British Expeditionary Force
8th June 1915

Dear Lizzie,
  We march to the front line and how we sweat with the heat of the sun and our uniforms. The men carry roughly sixty pounds of pack and equipment on their backs, so they boil. While we're here, the men sweat with the exertion of digging and repairing trenches and latrines, and I often work beside them, although strictly speaking officers aren't supposed to. But it's better than the boredom of mere supervision. The real work begins after dark. Parties of us are out in no man's land on patrol, or trench raids, or repairing or laying barbed wire – a job everybody hates because it's impossible to be quiet. Every now and then the enemy sends a flare up and we all freeze for ten to fifteen seconds until it dies, like children playing statues; except that if we move, an enemy sniper will put us 'out' for good with a bullet through the head. Some of us break into a *cold* sweat at that thought, me included. You've no idea how long fifteen seconds can seem. If we keep very still, and happen to be very lucky, they don't spot us and we all get back into our trench alive. I was out with a raiding party yesterday from about midnight until three o'clock. We captured half a dozen Germans and brought them back for interrogation without losing a single man, which is rather wonderful, *n'est ce pas?* I swear it has something to do with my lucky horseshoe.
  There's no hope of any washing or changing clothes until we return to billets, so for days at a

stretch I live between two clay walls with a lot of brutes who stink like otters, and who are infested with lice, and I, regrettably, am in the same condition. Otherwise, the outdoor life is very healthy, and we're all as fit as fleas, but most of us are very keen to get behind the lines and back to civilization.

How different it all is from the scents of the gardens at Kew. How different too from the scent of a certain dark lady, the memory of whom is the last thing in my mind before I go to sleep – a very pleasant change from the unrelieved sight, sound and over-ripe stench of men.

You'll be pleased to know that a Zep was shot down over Flanders yesterday. One of our chaps saw the Zep raid in London and gave us a vivid account of it, which has made me even more anxious to hear from you, especially as you now lack the horseshoe. I enclose a little enamelled silver badge for you, a black cat with sapphire eyes to keep you lucky.

I look for a letter from you every time the post comes. I'm simply bursting to know how you are. Write and tell me you're safe, at least.

With love, Freddie

She slowly folded the letter and put it under her pillow. She'd only just managed to put him out of her mind, and now here he was again, disturbing her peace. She stared into the stony eyes of her little black cat, and wondered if the captain would have written to a lady of his own class to tell her about sweat and latrines and lice. She doubted it, somehow.

Thank God she had work to do; she'd be too busy to think about him. She poured water from the ewer into the basin and, in descending order, gave the three fs a thorough good wash – face, you-know-what, and feet – with the armpits thrown in for good measure. She finished by dabbing a little eau de Cologne behind her ears, or eau de Provence, as some were calling it now, and wondered what it must be like to live among a herd of stinky soldiers, in a smelly trench, with the scent of latrines wafting over on the breeze.

'When are *you* going to get your khaki on, Mr Bartlett?' They were waiting at the stage door when she and Georgie arrived together; a pair of hussies with malicious little eyes and chins jutting self-righteously upward. One of them loomed towards him until she had him almost pinned against the wall. Georgie did nothing to defend himself, whereupon the girl produced a white feather and stuck it up his nose.

Lizzie leaped at her like a wildcat, teeth and claws bared, to snatch the feather from Georgie and shove it right up his assailant's nose. 'You mind your own business!' she hissed, 'And don't you come round here again pestering people, or I'll give you a lot more than a bloody feather. Your boys in khaki will never want to look at your faces again when I've finished with you.'

They gave Lizzie a look, and having got the measure of her scuttled off pretty quickly. Elated at her triumph, she turned to Georgie. 'Did you see the looks on their faces? That'll set me up for the day.'

'You shouldn't have done that, Eliza,' Georgie protested. 'It might affect the box-office takings if word gets round. Anyway, it wasn't necessary. I've made my mind up. I'm going to join up.'

Shocked and dismayed, she followed him through the stage door. 'You're what?'

'"Joining the colours," to use the theatrical phrase.'

'But why, Georgie, what for? Not just because of the harpies, surely.'

He sighed. 'No, not just because of them. Because I can't skulk here any longer while better men are out in France and Turkey defending us all. I can't hold off any longer, Lizzie. The war's not going to be over, and the army needs soldiers.'

'But you're *not* a bloody soldier, Georgie! And no, the war's not going to be over, it won't be over before every man in England is either dead or maimed for life. Have you seen the casualty lists in the papers?'

'I can't help it, Lizzie. I'll have to take my chance. Besides,' he gave her a wry smile, 'England's so tedious these days. Blue paint muffling all the street lamps for fear of Zep raids, hardly anybody daring to go out except in daylight, and then only to some ghastly committee for endless fundraising for Belgians and sending things out to Serbia and whatnot. And all this *earnestness* about sock knitting and other dreary things! It's all splendidly patriotic, of course, but I ask you, how can we survive the boredom? I mean to say, if we're all so set on pulling together that we can never criticize other people, or laugh at their little foibles, or take unholy pleasure in their downfall, life loses all its snap! Such excess of virtue makes one question the point of existence. All things considered, Lizzie, I've decided that as that's how things are going, I shall outdo everybody in cliché and "do or die for King and Country". In short, rather a clean and sudden end from rifle fire than a long drawn out one from ennui.'

'Oh, Georgie, you *fool!*' Lizzie exclaimed.

'Yes, aren't I?'

'You don't know what you're letting yourself in for.'

Georgie's lips twitched. 'Some rather delightful officers, I hope. I shouldn't at all mind starting with your Captain Ashton. Love in a trench, Lizzie. It would make a wonderful title for a play.'

'And what about the rest of us? What about the governor?'

'What about the governor?' The governor himself, who had followed them in just in time to hear the tail end of their discussion, demanded to know.

Thoroughly vexed, Lizzie sat at her mirror removing greasepaint after the most trying performance of her short career. 'It's for him to decide. If he thinks he ought to go, then he must. I won't interfere,' the governor had told her when she asked him to talk Georgie out of enlisting, and so Georgie had disappeared to some God-forsaken training camp somewhere. The governor had found a stand-in, an old ham of about sixty with badly dyed black hair and a memory like a sieve, who went by the name of Dorrien. Lizzie was constantly on edge, anticipating his next missed cue, until she became so concerned with reminding him of his lines that her own performance was suffering. The old imbecile was beginning to make her look as bad as he was himself, and ultimately it was bound to affect her reputation as well as ticket sales. She hurled the greasepaint-smeared cotton wool into the bin, and screwed the lid back on the cold cream as if she were wringing his stringy old neck. On a balmy Sunday night like this, in the middle of July, Georgie would have whisked her off to a dance after the performance, and she'd have gone home feeling tired and happy. As it was, she would go home and mull over every mistake and hitch in the performance until it made her feel ill. It really was the bloody limit. She thrust her stool back so savagely when she stood up that it crashed over. The callboy entered as she bent to pick it up.

'Don't you ever knock?' she snapped.

'I did knock. You can't have heard me. There's a porter waiting to see you from Charing Cross Hospital. Says he's got an important message.'

The look on his face spoke volumes about how a little success goes straight to some people's heads, and Lizzie knew she'd better smooth it over with him somehow before he decided to punish her by being a trifle too late with her call.

She carefully pinned her lucky black cat on the lapel of her new lilac linen jacket, put on her white silk hat and set out for the hospital.

His eyes lit up as soon as he spotted her walking

down the ward. 'I'm awfully glad you could come,' he said, as soon as she was within earshot. Indeed, he did look so awfully glad that Lizzie thought that if he were a dog, he'd be wagging his tail. He also looked pale, and the pallor of his face contrasted strikingly with the brilliance of his eyes.

She sat down beside his bed. 'What happened to you?'

'I stopped a little shrapnel ball. Got it in the shoulder, a clean wound, but I lost rather a lot of blood. They gave me morphia in the field ambulance, and after that I don't remember much, except I found myself in Valhalla, with the most beautiful women you could ever imagine. They were all blue-eyed blondes and all falling over themselves to wait on me hand and foot, and they must have thought me very ungrateful, because all I kept saying to them was, "Yes, you're all very nice, but only a black-haired girl with black eyes will do for me." So they had to throw me out of Valhalla, you see, and here I am, back in merry England with my black-eyed girl beside me.'

'What's Valhalla?'

'Valhalla...' he mused for a moment, 'it's a sort of exclusive afterlife club that only admits the very best warriors, and it's run by a Norse god called Odin. He sends the Valkyries – their name means the choosers – to pick the bravest fighters and bring them back. As soon as they arrive all the arms, legs and heads are sorted out and put with their rightful owners, and they're magically reassembled, to spend their time drinking and carousing with old Odin and being waited on by his stunning young spear maidens.'

'An officers' club with women. I should have thought you'd be glad to stay there.'

A faint blush rose to her cheeks when he beckoned her nearer and whispered, 'Oh, no, it wouldn't be at all interesting. They're all virgins, you see. Things are much better arranged here on earth.' The grey eyes searched her face, and her blush deepened a shade before he went on: 'And another thing is, as soon as they've feasted, they have another battle and tear each other limb from limb, then get patched up, and then have another feast. It's all very monotonous, and I was nearly trapped there. A fellow who came across with me told me he thought I was never going to wake up again. I'd been out for over twenty-four hours. So when they came with another dose of morphia I said I didn't want any more of it.'

Her gold horseshoe was tied on a bit of dirty string round his neck. 'The lucky charm wasn't so lucky after all,' she said.

'Perhaps it was,' he grinned. 'I'm lucky I didn't get it in my lung, or anything vital. I'm lucky still to be alive and safe in Blighty, with a bit of unscheduled leave whilst I convalesce. It's a very pleasant prospect, if I can persuade you to come and see me. Some men pray for a Blighty wound.'

'Blighty. That's a funny word.'

'Isn't it? I'm told it's the Hindustani word for home. Whether it is or not, it seems to have caught on.'

'How long do you think you'll be in hospital?'

'A week or two. And then if I'm lucky they'll

allow me a month or so to get fighting fit again, and they'll have me back in France. You never answered my letters, Lizzie.'

'I know. I wasn't sure I ought to come to see you here either. The circumstances of our last meeting were so very ... so very ... *peculiar*.'

The corners of his mouth turned down a little, and he bit his lip. 'Peculiar isn't the word I'd have chosen. Wonderful, perhaps. Delightful. Awfully, awfully...' he hesitated, searching for the word.

'S'nice?' Lizzie laughed, in spite of herself.

'Exactly! And why did you come, if you weren't sure you should?'

She cast up her eyes and grimaced. 'Because you're doing your patriotic duty, I suppose, and it seemed to be the least I could do, now you're wounded.'

'Quite right. After all, you've taken my virginity, and now I think you've got some responsibility for me. I'm glad we agree about that. You must come and see me every day, and help me get better.'

One of the nurses was passing by, and turned to stare.

Lizzie went hot all over. 'Keep your voice down, Freddie.'

He lowered it to a stage whisper. 'But I'm not complaining. I didn't mind a bit. Come and see me every day, won't you?'

'No,' she said, and the look on his face made her relent. 'I might come and see you a couple of times.'

He took her hand and squeezed it. 'Promise you'll come as often as you can. If you don't, I'll come down to de Lacey's and tell them all what

111

you did to me at the Ritz.'

Well, what else was there to do in the dreary empty hours now both Irma and Georgie were gone? She might as well go to see Ashton. It seemed to please him, and she could take no hurt from a man lying wounded in a hospital bed. She would keep a tight control on her dealings with him and everything would be perfectly all right.

She went to see the ward sister and got permission to visit outside the regular hours. A couple of days later she sat by his bed for an hour or so, telling him about her trials at the theatre.

'I say,' he said, 'I didn't realize I was in company with an actress. I bargained for a seamstress. I have a strong partiality for seamstresses.'

'How's that?' Lizzie's brows twitched into a suspicious frown.

'Because that's what I thought you were when I first saw you; you were so deft with your needle.' The wan lips parted in a smile as he added, 'But now I find I'm particularly drawn to actresses, and seamstresses are a thing of the past.'

'And how long will you be drawn to actresses?' she demanded.

Without the slightest hesitation he replied, 'As long as you're one.'

She smiled. 'Well, that's all about me. Now tell me all about you.'

'Oh, there's not much to tell. I'm an infantry officer who got a bit of unscheduled leave after getting a cushy one in a battle.'

'Has the battle got a name, like Mons, or anything?'

'You could call it the battle of Boesinghe if you wanted to glorify it with a title. We took the enemy trench and the sliver of ground they gained when they gassed us in April, and I've heard since that Daddy Plumer came to congratulate us and tell us what a jolly good show it was, only I was out of it before then.'

'Daddy Plumer?'

'The General. He promised us the action will go down in history.'

'The Germans must have been asleep, if it was so easy.'

'No ... there was a bit of opposition.'

'And I suppose plenty of the men got killed.'

He nodded. 'About 600, I think. And thousands wounded.'

She raised her eyebrows. 'It must have been a jolly good show, at that rate,' she said.

She went to see Ashton every other day for a week, and looked upon it as doing her bit for King and country – even if it was only raising the morale of one captain. After a week, she started going every day, until the end of his fortnight's stay in hospital. On the day before his discharge she saw an older man coming out of the ward, who stopped and stared so intently at her as she passed by that she couldn't forbear turning her head, to find herself face to face with an older version of Ashton. The light of recognition died in his eyes when he saw her full face, and without a word he turned away from her and proceeded down the corridor. She shivered slightly at a sensation her mother would have described as 'someone walking over my grave' and went on, pausing at the entrance of the ward to watch Ashton sitting in a chair by his bed. His gloomy expression brightened the moment he saw her. Lizzie sat at the other side of the bed and gave him a smile.

He said nothing about his father. 'I'd like to go shopping tomorrow morning, to replace some lost kit,' he told her. 'Will you come with me?'

'What do you need?'

'Some new uniform, unless you know a young needle-woman who could patch up a service jacket torn by shrapnel.'

'I shouldn't think you'd be able to get the blood stains out even if I did,' she said; not at all keen to stretch patriotism so far as to take on the task of repairing ruined khaki. 'Unless you do it straight away, you never can.'

'So the tunic's had it,' Ashton conceded. 'I'll have to get another. And I need a haversack, field glasses, belt and revolver and a whistle on a cord.'

'What happened to the ones you had? Did you lose them on the battlefield?'

He frowned. 'That's the infuriating part about it. It's a remarkable thing, but stretcher-bearers at the Front can go out onto the battlefield and heave their insides out to bring a man back over mud and shell craters, and go toiling and sweating with the weight of him along duckboards through miles of communication trench, and still keep his kit strapped to him. Yet as soon as he gets to the field ambulance it's against orders for his equipment to be carried the few feet needed to put it into the ambulance with him.'

Puzzled, Lizzie asked, 'If he's already in an

ambulance, why does he have to be carried to another one?'

'Oh, a field ambulance isn't a vehicle. It's a house, or a barn, or some other such place kitted out to receive wounded. Well, as I say, I got to the field ambulance with all my belongings strapped on me, but the orderlies took them off with my clothes and laid them at my side on the straw. Before they gave me the morphia I asked them to strap my kit on the stretcher, so that it would go with me when I was moved, but they wouldn't, and I hadn't the strength to argue the point.' He nodded to a man across the ward. 'Fellowes over there said he refused to move until the medical officer let him take his belongings, and they got to the clearing hospital with him. He lay on the floor that night with them beside him, but the following morning when they were putting him on the stretcher to the hospital train the orderlies told him again that he couldn't take his kit. He was a bit wiser than me and in a better condition to argue, so after a fearful row with the RAMC Captain about it, they let him take his things.'

'It's a pity you didn't do the same.'

'They tell you it's the order that they can't take your kit on the stretcher, and you take them at their word when they say they'll send it on. But lots of wounded are complaining that they've lost everything. Lieutenant Broom here was wounded at Ypres in November and lost literally everything he had, didn't you, Broom? He was wounded again last month after only a week at the Front, and now he's lost all his kit for the second time.'

Lieutenant Broom lowered his newspaper, and

115

nodded confirmation.

'It's an outrage, Lizzie,' said Ashton, his grey eyes smouldering with resentment. 'It's a scandal that we should be put to the expense of buying everything again.'

'Rob all my comrades,' said Broom. 'That's what some chaps say RAMC stands for.'

'I don't say it's that, but once the stuff's parted from its owner, I don't wonder he never sees it again,' Ashton said. 'You should see those places, Lizzie, when the wounded are being brought in by the hundreds. One can only wonder at the medical staff, with such a tremendous amount of work in such utter chaos. I should think things just get pushed to one side until nobody can remember whose is which, or where the owners have gone. I don't blame the medical staff, I blame the order.'

Broom looked sceptical. 'You're too charitable. I've heard that in the town near the clearing hospital I was taken to, there's a shop selling second-hand field glasses, supposed to be the property of wounded officers. I suppose if I went there, I should be able to buy mine back.'

Lizzie found it easy to believe. 'That's probably what's happened to yours, Freddie.'

He shrugged. 'Perhaps. The worst of it is I had quite a bit of cash in the case with my field glasses. If I'd had any sense I'd have put it in my breast pocket, but I only thought of that afterwards.'

Oh dear, Lizzie could almost hear Irma whispering – on your guard, sweetheart. This is just a roundabout way of telling you he's hard up.

Chapter Seven

He rested his hands on her waist as, dressed in her newest white V neck linen blouse with the wide collar and lace inset panels that she'd got for three guineas at Gorringe's, she stood with her back to him facing the camera. She'd let him persuade her to have her photograph taken with him, and immediately after his discharge from hospital here they stood, in the studio of a grey-haired lady photographer.

'That's about right.' She had posed them sideways against a backdrop of Italian scenery and now hovered about them, lifting their chins a fraction, or turning their faces a hair's breadth this way or that. At last she was satisfied and, encouraging them to 'Hold it there', she hastened behind her tripod and took hold of the bulb. 'That's right, now watch the birdie!' They both stared solemnly into the middle distance, somewhere beyond the concertina front of the camera. The light flashed and the photographer squeezed the bulb.

'And now a little snap of Lizzie,' Ashton said. 'Just head and shoulders, I think.'

'Oh, no,' said Lizzie, 'The governor's had some taken for the bills and theatre posters. You can have one of those.'

She caught his eye and he grinned, then turned to the photographer. 'Just the one together, then.'

'It will be a good one, I think,' said the lady,

carefully removing her plates, 'but I'm very busy at the moment, so it might be a couple of days. Come back on Wednesday or Thursday.'

'It's amazing how many women are doing jobs like that these days, isn't it?' Lizzie commented when they stepped out into a street busy with people streaming to and from shops, offices and courts.

'It is, and look up there. There's a woman conductor on top of that motor-bus, collecting the fares from a couple of Tommies!'

'Here's a shock for you, Freddie,' Lizzie teased. 'The driver's a woman, as well.'

'Good Lord, I hope not! I hope this war isn't going to go on much longer, or we won't have any women left. They'll all have turned into men.'

'I'm getting on the bus, Freddie. I might as well ride back to de Lacey's, and it goes past the military tailor's in the Strand. That's where you're going, isn't it?'

He seemed reluctant. She watched him look minutely at the driver as they boarded the bus, and smiled at his too evident relief when he'd convinced himself it was a man.

'I don't see how we can keep ticket prices down, if the Government slaps this entertainments tax on us,' the governor told them. 'And we'll be in for more Zep raids, now the nights are getting longer. People will be too scared to come into London, especially if there's a full moon. I've sent a lot of free tickets for the slowest houses to the hospitals for the nurses and the poorer servicemen, just to try and keep the theatre filled. The fact has to be faced; we have to stay in the black if we want to stay afloat, and so I've no alternative but to cut your money for the time being, and we'll only do a couple of matinées during the week. You'll get your old rates back if and when things get better.'

And when might that be? Lizzie wondered. After Irma's last letter, she was sure he was right about the Zep raids, but even without them she suspected things were never going to get better at de Lacey's. The governor seemed to be losing his grip on the place since the tragedy with his kids. He'd lost all his old fire and enthusiasm, as if the theatre no longer mattered. He was talking like a beaten man; and although Lizzie was playing the leading lady, things weren't half as much fun at de Lacey's since Georgie and Irma's departure. In fact, they weren't any fun at all. The salary had compensated, in a way, but now even that was threatened. Maybe it was time to be on the lookout for alternatives. Fred Karno was reputed to be stingy, but a good boss otherwise, and although his custard-pies-in-the-face style of humour didn't especially appeal to Lizzie, she was sure her talent for mimicry could be adapted somehow to suit Karno's muddle and mayhem sketches. And she might have the chance of a tour in America if only she could get in with him.

They had no sooner stepped into the palm court pavilion than Ashton was hailed, 'I say, if it isn't our old school chum Ashton! How long must it be since we've seen you? What have you been doing with yourself? You have enlisted, I suppose?'

Freddie gave a curt nod, the expression on his face as far away from pleasure as possible at this unexpected meeting with a trio of 'old school chums'.

'And is this your ladyfriend?' another asked, openly ogling Lizzie. 'Mind if I take her for a spin on the floor?'

Lizzie was in sparkling form, quick to grasp every opportunity to parade herself and her talents to whoever might care to see them – Fred Karno, with a bit of luck. 'I shouldn't mind,' she said, not waiting for Ashton's reply. 'As long as you can dance.'

'Oh, I can dance. Second Lieutenant Carruthers, at your service.' He offered her his arm and led her towards the floor, but lowered the arm as they walked and then, altogether too familiar, placed it round her waist. 'What's a pretty girl like you doing with that bounder? One might almost take you for a stage beauty. I say, haven't I seen you in something?'

'You might have, if you've seen a piece called *Life's Enchanted Cup*. It's running in the West End.'

'And I suppose you're the leading lady.'

She nodded as he turned to take her in a dance hold. 'And how long have you known Ashton?' he demanded, steering her clumsily round the floor.

'Not long.'

'An actress,' he grinned. 'The dirty dog! But he was always a bit of a dark horse. We knew him for years at school, without really knowing him at all. A bit of an enigma, our Freddie. Quite a hit with

120

some of the masters because he did rather well in exams, but tended to keep most people at arms' length, unless you count hobnobbing with the menials!'

He threw back his head and laughed, putting his dancing out of step so that they had to stop to pick up the rhythm again. 'Never thought he'd take up with an actress, though! But he was always one of those people you never can tell about.'

'Oh, really?' she looked pointedly beyond him to the ornamental latticing painted on the walls, and then up to a domed roof to study painted scenes of Hampton Court, and other places of interest.

'Yes. I always think there's something a bit suspicious about people who are too reserved, don't you? One can never get to the bottom of who they are, or what they think, or what they might be capable of. One wonders what it is they have to hide.'

'There's a lot of suspicion about these days, I've noticed. And have you been unreserved enough to tell Captain Ashton about your suspicions?' she asked, suddenly finding herself a partisan in Ashton's cause.

'Captain Ashton! He's a Captain is he, by God! But I'm not really surprised. No, I haven't told him. That would be rather awkward, wouldn't it?'

'Not for an unreserved person, surely. Tell me,' she hesitated, 'I'm not very well up on army matters – tell me, does a captain outrank a lieutenant?'

The lieutenant stiffened slightly. 'Of course he does.'

Lizzie gave him a beaming smile. 'Oh, excuse me,' she said. 'It's nothing to do with your only

121

being a second lieutenant, it's just that you're a very poor dancer.'

'I'm afraid you must excuse this young lady, Carruthers. She's engaged.' It was Ashton, looking into her eyes and holding out his arm for her. She took it, and allowed him to lead her through the large French windows and into the gardens.

They walked on in silence for a while, then Lizzie said: 'So, aren't you pleased to see your old school chums, Freddie?'

'No, I'm not. They might call themselves chums, I wouldn't. They were far too conscious of their class, and their pedigree to be chums of mine. I hated school, Lizzie, simply hated it. My schooldays were the most miserable years of my life, and the happiest day of my life was the day I left.'

'And you're not conscious of your class, and your pedigree?'

'Oh, yes, I am, very much so. And I hate being in the company of people I went to school with. I wish you hadn't danced with Carruthers.'

'I wouldn't have, if I'd known it would upset you.'

'Of course it upsets me. I love you.'

'You never told me that.'

'I told you that night at the Ritz. And now I'm fearfully jealous if you talk to anybody else. I want you all to myself.'

Other strollers passed by with smiles and nods, and a little distance away a young couple were clambering out of one of the many small boats provided for the amusement of the guests. She watched them in silence for a while.

122

'It's an odd sort of love, though, isn't it, Freddie?' she said at last, as though musing to herself. 'It isn't love with marriage in view because of your father, and since you've told me all your cash was lost with your kit, it's not likely to be love for money, either. The sort of "love" I think you have in mind deserves one or the other, but you seem to think I should be happy to do without either.'

'No, I don't. I told my father I had a passion for an actress who I couldn't afford, and since I got the Military Medal he evidently thinks I deserve to be indulged, because he laughed and gave me a very generous allowance. So I've booked us a room here. They give preferential rates to officers.'

A flush of anger rose to her cheeks at that. 'Ah. I see. You know, Freddie, I'm evidently the contrary one this time, because that doesn't please me either. For one thing, I'm not a whore. For another, you seem to take me for granted.'

'Take you for granted? Good God, I should think so too! I haven't brought heaps of cash so I can stand on ceremony with you, Elizabeth! If a man can't take a girl for granted at a hu...'

She pressed a finger against his lips. 'When I stayed at the Ritz with you I was very hard up, Freddie. I didn't know you from Adam, and I thought I should never see you again, and the whole thing seemed quite impersonal. So even though it was frightening, it was a pretty straightforward choice to make. Now, I'm earning much better money, and I'm beginning to know you, and somehow that makes it much, much harder.

Much more ... embarrassing. I shall get my own room.'

Anger began to colour his cheeks. 'How on earth can it be harder? What is there to be embarrassed about? We wouldn't be doing anything we haven't done before and now you know me, you must realize what a thoroughly decent sort I am. And you liked it as much as I did, you were revelling in it – no woman can sham that flush of pleasure that spreads over her cheeks and chest, no, not even an actress; so don't attempt to deny it. I can't understand you, Lizzie!'

She stood stock-still and stared at him. 'What? What was that you said? How could you know such a thing?' she demanded sharply, jabbing an accusing finger in his face. 'Freddie, you were lying when you told me you were a virgin. Weren't you?'

A party of passers by stopped and stared goggle-eyed at the sight of the outraged girl and her blushing escort. Freddie gave them a look of fury, took her by the elbow, and steered her out of their hearing.

'And you haven't been listening,' she continued, as he propelled her along. 'When I was poor I took a big chance with myself because I was driven to it. Now I'm better off, I don't want to run any risks. I've got a good part now, and I should have a lot more to lose if...'

Through clenched teeth he hissed: 'If I made you pregnant, I'd see you were looked after.'

'But the only way you could do that would be to marry me, Freddie.'

'No, it isn't. I can provide for you without that.'

124

'And you imagine I'm going to risk my career, my whole life, on a promise like that?'

'All right, then. I would marry you. I suppose.'

'And what about your father, then? If you won't marry me before, why on earth should you marry me afterwards? As far as you're concerned I'm just a naughty little actress you'll amuse yourself with until Daddy decides it's time for you to get married. Isn't that it, Freddie? And then you'll marry to suit him, and yourself too, probably, and it won't be to me, or anybody like me.'

He stopped and put his good arm around her to pull her fiercely to him. 'No. That isn't it at all. I admit I haven't thought as far ahead as you have. The sort of things that happen in France prove that many of us have a very short lease on life, and so I don't look very far into the future. But I've never had any dishonest intentions towards you, Lizzie.'

'You were looking far enough into the future to start rebuilding Ypres and the rest of devastated Europe,' Lizzie said. 'And if I'm going to stay the night, I shall have my own room. I'll get it myself, and I'll pay for it.'

'No, you won't. If that's what you want, I'll get it for you. I must say though, Lizzie, I'm pretty fed up about it.'

By the time he went to get a room for her, there were none to be had, and still hoping to see the elusive Mr Karno, Lizzie had reconsidered her idea of returning to London on the ferry. In an effort to please her, Ashton made a few brave

125

attempts at dancing, and she kept a sharp eye out for the famous impresario well into the small hours.

He did not show himself. Disappointed, she let Ashton lead her upstairs to a very pretty room. She undressed behind a screen, down to a crepe de Chine bias cut sheath of pale lilac, a triumph of French seaming and shell edging with little violet and white roses she had worked in bullion stitch around the cleavage and hem during unoccupied moments at the theatre.

He was sitting in an armchair when she emerged, and looked so done in that for a moment Lizzie actually thought of sleeping on the floor and letting him take the bed. Then he looked up at her with eyes that reminded her of a puppy begging to be petted. It hardened her and without a word to him she climbed into the bed alone.

'Will you put the light out, Freddie?' she murmured, sinking down between the sheets and pulling the covers up to her neck.

She heard a heavy sigh. 'Just give me a few minutes.' He went to a writing table and switched on the lamp, then turned off the centre light and sat down to begin writing.

'Surely you're not writing letters at this time of night. Why not leave it until morning?'

He continued to scribble. 'I won't be long.'

Exasperated, Lizzie turned over and closed her eyes, but the light disturbed her, and prevented sleep. At length, he tossed a sheet of paper onto the bed and went behind the screen to undress.

She took up the paper and read:

La Belle Dame Sans Merci

Oh, what can ail thee, knight at arms,
Alone and palely loitering,
The sedge is withered on the lake,
And no birds sing.

I see a lily on thy brow,
With anguish moist and fever dew,
And on thy cheek a fading rose
Fast withereth too.

I met a lady in the meads,
Full beautiful, a faery's child,
Her hair was long, her foot was light
And her eyes were wild.

I made a garland for her head
And bracelets too and fragrant zone.
She looked at me as she did love,
And made sweet moan.

She took me to her elfin grot
And there she gazed and sighed full sore,
And there I shut her wild sad eyes
With kisses four.

And there we slumbered on the moss
And there I dreamed, ah, woe betide,
The latest dream I ever dream'd
On the cold hillside.

'You're not going to pass that off as one of your
own, are you, Freddie? I might only be a little

127

dresser turned actress, but I seem to remember that poem,' she said, as he reappeared buttoning his silk pyjamas. 'It's Keats, isn't it?'

He nodded, his grey eyes looking hopefully into hers for a moment. Getting no reaction, he switched off the lamp and she heard his footsteps padding towards the armchair. 'Well, I'm over here on the cold hillside, Lizzie, and my bloody shoulder hurts.' He sounded very petulant.

'Does it, Freddie?' she commiserated.

'Yes. It's hurting like hell. It must be all that dancing. You're an awful, heartless, calculating whore, Lizzie. You're enough to drive a man mad.'

'Why are you calling me a whore, all of a sudden?' Lizzie smiled into the all-concealing darkness. 'Is it because I won't take your money and sleep with you?'

She fancied she heard laughter in his voice when he answered: 'Yes.'

'And what would you call me if I did sleep with you?'

'I should call you a very sweet young lady, and the darling of my heart.'

She gave an exaggerated yawn. 'Good night, Freddie.'

'Good night, Lizzie. Sleep tight.'

Sleep tight. Implying, of course, that *he* would not. The reproach reverberated in her mind for a few minutes, and conscience smote her. After all, he had borne up bravely with the dancing, and to leave him suffering in that chair really would be heartless. And what if it did him some real harm?

'Come and get into bed, Freddie, if you're sure you can behave yourself.'

He was beside her in an instant, and sounding much enlivened. 'I am. I wouldn't have the strength tonight, anyhow, so you're quite safe.' He snuggled down beside her, very close. 'I say, I'm frightfully bucked about this, Lizzie. I was feeling rotten, you know.'

Yes, you're frightfully bucked with yourself for having worn me down, thought Lizzie. 'This far and no further, Freddie,' she warned, 'or I'll send you back to the armchair.'

'It's true, though.'

'What is?'

'There is something wild in your eyes some-times, and other times there's something very sad.' He turned towards her and ran his hands over her silk slip, over the mounds of her breasts and her belly, 'And the last time we were in bed together, you "looked at me as you did love, and made sweet moan..."'

She removed his hand. 'Nothing of the sort, Freddie. Go to sleep.'

'Well, you made sweet moan, anyway. And it was awfully...'

'S'nice, I suppose,' she said, and it was with an effort that she prevented herself from shaking with laughter.

The waiter left the tea tray on her bedside table, opened the curtains, and was gone. She glanced towards Ashton. He did look pale in the sunlight; his lips were almost bloodless. Yesterday's dancing must have been quite a trial for him. She would leave him to sleep whilst she ran down the corridor to the bathroom. She got out of bed and slipped on his dressing gown.

On her return she tossed it over the armchair and examined herself in the gilt mirror over the fireplace, quickly running her fingers through her sleep flattened hair to fluff it up. That looked better, thick and glossy – shortish at the front to make a becoming frame for her face, and just to the points of her shoulder blades at the back. She wondered for a moment whether she should have it all chopped. The bob was all the rage among the more daring young flappers. She bit her lips to put a little more colour into them, then wetting her fingers with spit she carefully smoothed her eyebrows. That looked much better. She turned sideways and pushed her shoulders back a little, noting the curves of breasts and hips under the silk of her petticoat with dispassionate approval. If that sight couldn't madden any red-blooded man with desire, nothing could.

The man in question was still asleep, and Lizzie wondered how the night might have gone if a fair measure of his blood hadn't been poured out on the fields of France. She poured herself a cup of tea and slid back down the bed, then felt him stroking her hair.

'It's like silk.'

'I thought you were asleep.'

'I know you did, but I had one eye open. I was watching you, especially when you were preening yourself in the mirror.'

'Sly old Freddie. I shall have to watch out for you, if you're as cunning as that.'

'Give me a kiss.'

'No.'

'Why not? A kiss can't hurt.'

'A kiss, Freddie, is as a prologue to a play. Men never want kisses but they want more besides, I've heard, and as one thing leads to another, I won't give you a kiss.'

'You seem to know a lot about men.'

'Yes. Some's what I've been taught, and the rest I discovered for myself. But all in all, I've got a pretty good idea of them.'

He sat up, looking disgruntled. 'Well, give me a cup of tea, then.'

She poured it, and handed him a cup. 'You'd approve of my understudy, Freddie. Since the Zep raid, she'll kiss anybody in khaki, and if they've got a wound stripe, she'll do the rest as well. She reckons it's only fair to do everything we can for the soldiers. Because they're trying to protect us.' Ethel had also said: 'And the poor things might get killed,' but Lizzie thought it better not to mention that.

'She sounds a very warm-hearted girl.'

'She is. And you'd like me to be so warm-hearted.'

'Yes, but not so indiscriminate. I should like you warm-hearted exclusively towards me.'

'Ethel probably wouldn't appeal to you, anyway. She's a pasty blonde with an underdeveloped figure.'

'Well then, I've nothing to hope for from Ethel.' He put his left arm round her and hugged her to him. 'Did you sleep well, my faery's child?'

'Yes, thank you, Freddie.'

'And will you take me to your elfin grot?'

His voice was so coaxing and his expression

131

such a mixture of appeal and devilry that for two pins she could have lain beside him and done anything he wanted, for no reward other than to please him. She checked herself. That feeling had been her downfall once before.

'No, I will not. Come on,' she urged, and jumped out of bed to disappear behind the screen with her clothes. 'Let's go down to breakfast. I've got to be back at de Lacey's in time for the matinée, and I want to have a quick look round to see if we can see anything of Fred Karno.'

He threw back the covers and put on his dressing gown, collected his toilet things and went in search of a bathroom. She dressed quickly and took extra care with the application of her lipstick. She was determined to make the right impression if they did chance on Mr Karno. She was still in front of the mirror carefully putting the last pin in her hair when Ashton returned. He stood behind her, wrapped his arms around her and began nuzzling her neck. Pleasant little shivers ran down her spine.

'Stop it, Freddie.'

'Why? You like it.'

'No, I don't.'

'Yes, you do. I can tell by the sound of your voice.'

'Well, stop it anyway.'

There was something unfathomable in the grey-blue eyes that met hers in the sun bright surface of the mirror, but he desisted in his nuzzling, and moved away from the window to pull his trousers on.

'You should get dressed behind the screen.'

'That would be a little ridiculous, Lizzie. There isn't a bit of me you haven't already seen.'

She gave him a look, but said nothing. He finished dressing and threw his things into his overnight bag.

'Well, that's the Karsino,' he said. 'I had a present for you, but I don't think I dare give it to you now, we're such strangers.'

'What is it?'

'Well,' he hesitated, 'It's regimental crested undies. Every subaltern in the army seems to have a copy of madam Venn's catalogue. Have you seen her advert in *The Tatler?* I got you some of the new camiknickers, in cream silk. They look delightfully sporty. Chemise and knickers united into one flimsy garment. I was sure you'd like them.'

She laughed. 'Sporty? Is that what you call it? You are a naughty one, Freddie.'

'Do you want them?'

'No,' she lied, 'you should save them for your wife. Aren't you bringing your bag?'

'I'll let the porter fetch it. They can send it on for me. Officers are forbidden to be seen carrying things.'

'But you're not in uniform.'

'Well, I don't want to carry it anyway.'

'No wonder you lose things,' she said, fearful for the regimental crested undies.

As they left the room, Lizzie spied Lieutenant Carruthers advancing along the corridor and threw her arms round Ashton to give him a scorching kiss.

'I say, Lizzie, why couldn't you have done that in there?'

'Safer for me out here,' she whispered, demurely fingering his lapel. 'Thank you for bringing me, Freddie.'

'It was – almost – my pleasure.'

She glanced surreptitiously at Carruthers' carefully averted eyes. That would give him something to chew over in the officers' mess.

Chapter Eight

Army Training Camp
July 1915

My dear Eliza,

How right you were. It's absolutely frightful. My dear, the very worst thing is, there's no privacy, and I really mean *no* privacy. All one owns is a numbered bed place along a grey painted wall, where one throws down one's bed board and palliasse, in a line of other bed boards and palliasses that stretches into infinity, with a view of still more bed boards and palliasses along the grey painted wall on the other side of the room. There are fifty men sleeping in this one room! Think of it! One cannot escape without a pass, and one has to be back in this hell-hole by half past nine, for roll call. And the sergeant, my dear, is so *rude!* Lights go out at ten o'clock, and then people start to cough and splutter, and argue, and spit on the floor, and a creature who has soused himself in beer in the canteen might deposit his stomach contents somewhere, and then several brutes start snoring. One tries to sleep, but the palliasse on the board is too hard, and the blanket rubs the skin off one's neck, and the lorries and motor-buses and cars going along the road outside all night long sound as if they're driving down the middle of the barrack room. Sleep is impossible, and then that filthy sergeant comes in at reveille to execrate anyone who isn't out of bed before the bugler has put his instrument to his lips. The food is unspeakable, bread and margarine, and fat bacon, and stews made of gristle and congealed grease.

Did I say that lack of privacy was the worst thing? I exaggerated. I had hoped, Eliza, that my short sight would get me a reprieve or some civilized employment manning the telephones somewhere. Instead, I am disfigured by the ugliest pair of spectacles you ever saw in your life, which I have to wear at all times and which have succeeded in ruining my appearance by making hideous little indentations on either side of my nose. I should very much like to lose them, but the penalty for that, I assume, would be death, and I'm much too cowardly to put it to the test.

At least we're dressed in khaki, and not the horrible post-office blue that some of Kitchener's army are wearing. It took me a week to master the art of rolling on puttees and even now they're usually too thick at the ankles and too tight round the calf. I'm used to having a dresser, Lizzie! But I shall probably get a rifle soon, and I promise you, the first person I shall shoot is that damnable sergeant.

I'm hoping for some leave at the end of August, and I shall fly back to London and civilization for tea dances, and tango parties, and other *pleasant pursuits*. I hope to see you.

By the left, left, left turn, right turn, about turn, on the right heel and the left toe, on the left heel and the right toe, left, left, left... Just thank your lucky stars you were born a woman, Lizzie.

Love from your friend in Hades (which I now know is situated somewhere on the South Downs),

Georgie

'Oh, poor Georgie,' Lizzie murmured, thoroughly conscience-stricken. If only she'd remembered to tell him to say he went to Eton.

'How's the portrait going?' she asked, as Ashton held out a chair for her.

She lowered herself gracefully onto it. 'All right.' He pulled out another for himself and sat down. 'He's making me look impressively clean cut and warrior-like. I think my father will be pleased with it.' He took out his silver case, and put a cigarette to his lips.

She took the case from him and helped herself to one, before snapping it shut and handing it back, looking him defiantly in the eye and smiling slightly as she leaned forward for a light. He gave her a mildly disapproving frown, but lit her cigarette. 'How much is it costing him?' She was intrigued. She'd never known anyone who'd had a portrait painted before.

'I haven't a clue. I never thought to ask.'

She took a draught of smoke and leaned back in her chair, holding her cigarette in practised fashion between her fingers; fully conscious of her attractions and of the elegant pose she'd rehearsed before the mirror. 'What happens when you go there?'

'I go in my uniform, and the parlour maid shows me into the studio, and then I pose for hours, and if I'm to stay and pose in the afternoon they very kindly give me lunch, and I make small talk with his wife and daughters. It's frightfully boring. If I'm meeting you I tell them I have an engagement, and I don't stay to lunch. I go back to the flat in Knightsbridge and as our cook and maid have deserted us to do their bit in the munitions factory, I make a spot of lunch and then I get changed and come out again.'

'I should have thought the portrait painter's parlour maid would be working in a munitions factory by now.'

'She's rather advanced in years.'

'Even so. How old are his daughters?' She asked, affecting not to care.

'About the same age as you, and they're both awfully pretty.'

She saw his sly smile as he waited for her reaction. He was trying to make her jealous. She gave a careless toss of her head. 'I suppose they're just the sort of girls your father would approve of.'

There. That wiped the smile off his face. 'Oh, Lizzie, don't let's get on to that. You're always off with me for hours when we do. Listen, they're playing a tango. Come on, we can't miss it, not just as I'm getting the hang of it. And I shan't be here much longer. I've got my embarkation orders.' He stood up and offered her his hand.

Oh, damn the bloody war. She had begun to look forward to their *thé dansants* between shows. Even if his dancing couldn't touch Georgie's, he was improving, and it was better than no dancing at all, or going without a partner like those pitiful wallflowers sitting round the edge of the room. She stood up and let him lead her onto the floor. He took her in a firm dance hold.

'When do you go?'

'In a week. The first of September, to be exact. Will you miss me, Lizzie?'

'Of course I'll miss you. I'll have nobody to take me dancing.'

'You'll have lots of stage door Johnnies crowding round, and wanting to take you out.'

'Yes, but they're usually an odd lot. There isn't one of the usual crowd I'd be seen dead with. And life will be nothing but work, work, work, and for less money than I got before, especially with the governor's new scheme of doing charity matinées twice a week. I shall probably be too tired to be bothered.' She sounded crabby, even to herself.

'I'm glad, I don't want you going out with other men. But cheer up, Lizzie. It must be better than working in a munitions factory.'

'You don't say, "Cheer up, the war will soon be over." People have stopped saying that altogether now.'

'I know. I say, Lizzie, my father's going to join his wife at their house in Norfolk next weekend. Come and stay at the flat. I'll take you dancing after the show on Saturday night, and then we'll have a lovely Sunday together – my last one before I go back to France. I've kept that little garment for you. You could try it on.'

'No, Freddie. I don't think that would be a good idea at all.'

'Oh, go on, Lizzie, be a sport. It might be ages before I see you again.'

'No.'

Stay overnight in his father's flat being a sport and trying on sporty little garments with nobody else there, after everything she'd said? Either he was mad, or he thought she was.

She heard one rap on her dressing room door the following evening, and before she could draw breath to say 'Come in,' it was flung wide open.

'What a journey I've had! Trains crammed full of troops and munitionettes, and all sorts of people. Oh, but what a relief to be here, Eliza old thing.' He kicked the door shut behind him, flung his hat on the peg, and spread his arms wide for her.

'Georgie,' she squealed, jumping up to hurl herself at him and hug him, before standing back to take a good look. He appeared remarkably clear-eyed and healthy. 'Oh, Georgie, to see you in khaki! But I must say, you do look rather well in it. Honestly Georgie, I've never seen you look so well. You're as brown as a berry. And you've put on weight.'

'Pure muscle, Eliza. All those route marches, all that drill. "Hon parade – come halong there, at the double – para-ade 'shun! Form fours! By the left, left, left! Move to the right in fours!" That bloody drill sergeant's certainly turned me into a killing machine. Pity my sole ambition is to kill him.'

'You idiot,' Lizzie laughed. 'But I thought you said the food was muck.'

'It is, but when you've marched for about twenty miles carrying a full pack plus rifle and bayonet, and entrenching tool and handle, and 150 rounds of ammunition in web pouches, oh, and I nearly forgot the water bottle, well, you're so hungry you'd eat just about anything. And you could sleep on just about anything as well, and we do. Oh, but Lizzie, I can hardly wait to get into my own little flat, and my own bed.'

'I'll bet!'

'Come over when you get home, and we'll have a cup of tea together. I've decided I'm giving the flat up after this leave, Lizzie. The war's not going to be over for ages, and it's ridiculous to keep paying the rent on it. I can't afford it anyway, on a shilling a day army pay. You can have my nice lace net curtains if you like – they'll look rather well up at your windows. And if you fancy anything else, you can keep it for me – three years or the duration. I'll leave the rest of my stuff with my mother.'

'You've no idea how much I've missed you, Georgie,' she said, and meant it. It was marvellous to have him back, to share a laugh with him, and know he expected nothing else. No pretence on either side, no complications, everything equal, and straightforward, and easy. Friendship, pure and *safe*.

'Tomorrow? Saturday night!' Ashton protested. 'What do you mean, you can't come out with me tomorrow? I've been looking forward to it.'

Lizzie had saved the news until they got back to the theatre for the evening performance, and now she sat, just changed into her costume, applying greasepaint at the mirror. 'Yes, but Georgie's only got a few days leave, and I promised him we'd go dancing.' It was only a tiny lie. She hadn't promised; she'd let Georgie assume she would go dancing.

'What! You do realize I've only got a few days left, Lizzie? And then I'm back to France. Probably to the front line. I might never see you again.'

'Come with us then. Georgie won't mind. In fact, I know he'd like you to.'

She saw a glint in the grey eyes, and a flush spreading over his still pale cheeks. The dark brows came together in an angry frown. 'But I wouldn't like it. I don't want to come and watch you dancing with another man. I don't want that bloody gigolo there at all. I want you all to myself.'

'Georgie's not a gigolo,' she said, although she was not entirely sure what the word meant.

'All right, then,' he challenged. 'I'll come on condition that you come back to the flat with me afterwards, and spend the night.'

'No.'

The flush deepened. 'Why not? Are you going to spend the night with him?'

Insulting question. Her eyes flashed his fire back at him, and her cheeks reddened. 'I'm not even going to answer that,' she said.

'Do you love me, Lizzie,' he demanded, 'or not?'

Do you love me, Lizzie? Someone had asked her that question once before and it had been a prelude to treachery, and she had been a fool. Men! Treacherous, scheming swine, always trying to manoeuvre a woman into sacrificing her interests to theirs, forever trying to encroach on her liberty, to confine her, to hem her in and nail her down. Nothing mattered to them but what *they* wanted, there and then, and never the slightest concern for what might happen to *her*, afterwards. She'd thought she had Ashton under control, but now she saw she'd been deluding herself. Well, then, if she couldn't control him, she wanted no more to do with him. She'd send him packing.

'No, and you don't love me either, because if you did, you wouldn't treat me as some sort of camp follower. If you loved me,' she turned towards him and stared him straight in the eye, 'you wouldn't want to put me at risk of landing at the workhouse door with my bloody shameful bundle while you're gone to France and either dead or amusing yourself with some other woman.'

He stared as determinedly back. 'You didn't mind my amusing myself with *you* for the price of a hundred pounds.'

'No, and I've already told you why, because the temptation was too much to resist, and I was lucky not to get caught out. But now things are going all right for once. I've got a good part, and the money's all right, and I'm not going to bugger it up for myself. So go to hell, Freddie.'

She felt his fingers digging into her shoulders as he pulled her round to face him, his eyes blazing. 'And what if I were to give you two hundred? You'd soon abandon your scruples then.'

'You'd soon abandon yours too, if you had nothing, Mr High and Mighty. People like you can never understand what it is to be without money, to watch other people eat and pretend you're not hungry because you've got no money to get anything with, or to wonder whether you can keep a roof over your head for the next seven days, or be perpetually on the look-out for people you owe money to, so that you can jump into some dark corner before they spot you. The hundred pounds you keep throwing in my face got me out of all that, and now I'm earning decent money of my own I won't take any more risks. I struck a bargain with you, and I kept my part of it. We're quits, and you can take your hundreds and shove them ... in a very dark and private place. So go to hell, Freddie.'

'And have you ever gone without anything to eat, Lizzie, or been without a roof?'

'I've never been without a roof, but I've seen people who have, and it'll just as easily happen to me as to them if I don't watch out.'

There was a rap on the dressing room door, and the callboy shouted, 'Everything all right, Lizzie? You're on in five minutes.'

'Yes, everything's all right, thank you. Mr Ashton's just leaving.'

'Lizzie, if...'

'Goodbye, Freddie.'

His foot made sharp contact with her waste bin

and sent it crashing to the other end of the dressing room. He left without another word, slamming the door behind him hard enough to shake the foundations.

To hell with that. His tantrums would get him nowhere with her. Clever women are women who play men at their own game, she thought, leaning forward to concentrate on the task of covering her eyelids with blue powder. They're women like Irma, who keeps her own end in view and treats men as a means to it. Once the end is achieved, the means can be dispensed with. Irma's end now was to survive the war in peace and comfort, and she had a man to help her do it. She would be careful to give him the impression that he was no end of a fellow, that she had the highest regard for him, that she adored him, in fact. But she did not adore him, and if she were to meet another man who could do more for her she would very civilly and very elegantly dispense with her worthy burgher, with no more qualm of conscience than she would suffer at discarding an outworn shoe. Lizzie looked intently into her mirror to gauge the effect of the blue. Too much, even for the stage – especially near the brow. She reached for a lump of cotton wool to wipe some of it off. Clever women don't *give* the sort of trust and devotion that can devastate them and ruin years of their lives when it's betrayed, she told her reflection, they *take* it. With them, the boot is entirely on the other foot. That's the difference. They keep the boots of treachery firmly on their own feet. They keep control. And she would follow their example.

Now the colour looked well, emphasizing the

black of those eyes wherein Ashton had seen 'something soft and sad'. With her nose almost touching the glass she subjected her eyes to a minute examination. Her lover was deluding himself. He'd seen 'something soft' because he wanted her soft. But she was not soft, and never would be again, and her eyes were as dead and hard as two flints, to match the flint Tom Peters had left her for a heart.

'All right, Lizzie?' In full evening dress, with silk muffler hanging round his neck, Georgie held his arm out for her as she stepped out of the stage door. 'Let's go and make a grand entrance, let them all see we're back, show them how a tango should be danced. You'd better enjoy yourself while you can. I bet the Zeppelin raids start again soon, now the dark nights are coming. Then you won't see half so many people about at this time, especially when it's a full moon.'

Lizzie glanced upwards. The moon was in its last quarter, and covered by drifting, grey clouds. A few short months ago London had been wonderful after dark, with its street lighting and its brilliantly lit window displays, and always alive with people. There were still people, but not as many as before. Now London was a place of darkened shops and theatres, and electric globes muffled in blue paint, and dark streets, and *menace*. She shivered, and suddenly wished Ashton were with them. Stupid girl. Even he couldn't protect her from a bomb.

Taking Georgie's arm, she hurried along beside him. 'I got a form to fill in today. It seems everybody gets one that's not in the armed forces. A lot of questions about how old I am and what my occupation is, and who I work for, and whether I can do any other sort of work, and all sorts of nosey questions. It's to do with the National Registration Act.'

'Oh, dear. I suppose that means that Lloyd George might send you to replace one of the men who've gone off to war – in a munitions factory, or as a farmer's girl – or perhaps he'll send you to one of those sweatshops to make uniforms for us. That would be more in your line.'

'He wouldn't do that, would he?'

'Perhaps not, if you can convince him that your little play's essential to the maintenance of public morale.'

'It's getting really serious, isn't it, the war?' she said, glancing up at him.

His expression was very solemn. 'Now it's begun to affect you personally, Lizzie, indeed it is. Extremely serious.'

'Are you being sarcastic, Georgie?'

She'd spoken sharply, and he raised his eyebrows. 'Just teasing,' he said, 'you can still stand a bit of teasing, surely?'

She gave a little toss of her head. 'Well I'm certainly not going to tell them I can do tailoring.'

'I'd be very careful to read the small print before making any false declarations if I were you, old thing. There will be penalties.'

That sounded ominous. 'Hmm,' she said, 'I hadn't thought of that. Still, I suppose that sewing uniforms would be better than working in a munitions factory and turning as yellow as a canary, or getting myself blown up, and for nothing more than twenty-five bob a week.'

'Twenty-five bob sounds pretty good going to me,' said Georgie, 'considering it's about five times as much as they pay us poor Tommies for getting blown up at the Front.'

'You've never been near the Front, Georgie.'

'And you've never been near a munitions factory, but these are mere quibbles. This is Georgie Bartlett, idol of the West End stage risking his tender skin. The mere thought that I *might* get blown up should entitle me to as much as a munitions worker gets. And if you were to throw all the impertinence I have to put up with from that bloody sergeant into the equation, you'd realize I'm entitled to ten times as much.'

'You idiot, Georgie. Those girls probably have to put up with far worse from their foremen, and you get bed and board and clothing along with your shilling a day. They have all that to buy for themselves.'

'I know. How I envy you, though, being a woman. You're excused it all.'

'How so? I could still be pushed into a munitions factory.'

'Ah, but if you're clever you'll pre-empt them by becoming someone's wife. Then the Government will recognize your duty to stay comfortably at home.'

Georgie's dancing was as skilful as ever, but it couldn't dispel the vague feeling of discontent that had settled on her since her quarrel with Ashton. She glided round the floor in his arms wrapped in her own thoughts, and only gradually became aware of a thickset man of around thirty with a thatch of blond hair and a matching moustache, who had passed them several times, with a mousy little partner in a dowdy blue dress. She saw him look pointedly towards Georgie, and raise his eyebrows for a fleeting second.

Georgie's eyes never left the man's face. 'There's someone who understands me, I fancy,' he murmured. 'Rather a stunner, isn't he?'

'Not exactly tall, dark and handsome,' Lizzie said, feeling very ungenerous.

'No, a gorgeous blond, and so *masculine*, my dear!'

When they left, the fellow was leaning on the railings on the opposite side of the street, his partner gone, and there was that come-hither look again, as soon as he caught sight of Georgie.

'See that? The way he's looking at me? It's making me feel quite weak at the knees. I say, Lizzie, do you mind if we part company? I think I've found a soul mate, and I'd better make the most of it. It'll be ages before I get another chance.'

'You filthy little beast, Georgie.'

'But you love me all the same. I'll see you tomorrow.'

The man tilted his chin slightly, and Georgie hastened at the command, just, Lizzie thought, as an adoring little lapdog might trot to her master.

So be it. She'd heard enough about regimental sergeant majors and drill sergeants and about life in the tents and huts of training camps for one evening, and although Georgie's dancing had been as smooth and sensuous as ever, she hadn't enjoyed her evening. She watched him for a while, running eagerly along beside his soul mate in the direction of Soho, very glad to know no more than she did about Georgie's darker side.

Where was Ashton, she wondered? Was he in the flat in Knightsbridge, or was he out as well, trying to make the most of his last few days of freedom? Perhaps he was looking for a 'soul mate'. Or perhaps he'd found her, and was back at the flat with her this minute, dressing her in cream silk undies decorated with his regimental crest.

The following day she sped along the landing towards the bathroom before anyone else was up and returned to her room shivering in her dressing gown with her wet hair wrapped in a towel. She pushed up the window sash a couple of inches and looked out onto the square, rubbing her hair dry and contemplating the dreary hours waiting to be filled before the evening performance. She combed her hair and spread it over her shoulders to dry, then crossed the room to a chest of drawers to retrieve a bundle of letters tied with red ribbon. She might as well pass the time reading the ones from her brothers again. She must have had them three months and it was about time she wrote back. The late August sun felt hot through the glass and she turned her chair to let it fall on her back. Lovely. She was beginning to feel warm again, and if she sat here for a while her hair would soon be dry. Arthur's few lines were the first that came to hand.

Dear Lizzie,
Well, here I am in France, bonny lass, keeping you all safe from the bloodthirsty Hun with my eighteen pounder. We keep popping a few over with your name on them. I got the razor all right. It was all right until I ran out of blades, so I hope you'll take the hint and send some more. I'll keep the cutthroat just in case you forget. I've told all the lads you're in the theatre, and they're all looking forward to you coming out here with a nice long chorus line to do the cancan for us, see if you can get your toes up higher than the lasses in Paris.

I'll maybe see you Christmas 1965, Lizzie man. That's how long we reckon it'll take to win the war.
All the best,
Arthur

Just like our Arthur, Lizzie thought. Give him an inch, and he wanted a mile. She wished she hadn't bothered to send the bloody razor now. She tossed the letter on the bed and had just unfolded one from John when the sound of footsteps prompted her to leap up and look out of the window. Ashton! No, it wasn't Ashton. Just a dreary old woman on her way to church, making her habitual stop for another dreary old woman who had a couple of rooms downstairs. Lizzie sat down again and took up John's letter.

Dear Lizzie

It's funny, but before I came here I thought all Germans were the same, but when you think about it, how can they be? In England, Geordies and Londoners are as different as chalk and cheese, and the lads from Birmingham are different again. It's just the same with the Germans, we're finding out.

I've been in a lovely quiet sector for the last month. The lads opposite are from Saxony, and their attitude is 'we're Saxons and you're Anglo-Saxons, so why should we fight each other?' They like to live and let live, so we all have a quiet life here. If any of our lads start shooting, they'll shout across, 'You want a fight, Tommy? Wait 'til the Prussians come. They'll give you a fight.' So they don't fire at us, and we don't fire at them. It suits us all right. The lads lie about in the sun for hours, and read books, and write letters home, and I've got plenty of time to make myself look bonny with my nice new razor. But if you get opposite the Prussians, they give you hell, and the Bavarians aren't far behind them. I hope the censor doesn't bother to read this or it'll not last long, this peace and quiet. The senior officers will be round to instil a bit of offensive spirit into us all.

The razor's lovely, bonny lass, and it makes shaving a lot easier, but you shouldn't have spent your money. You've got enough to do looking after yourself in London. I hope you're going on all right. Go on back home if you're not.

Write as often as you can. We all like to get letters.

Love,
John.

PS We heard something about our Arthur that gave us all a laugh a week or two ago. A little French lad stopped him with, 'Hey, Tommee! You want to buy feelthy postcard?' Well, that bairn was a good judge of character, because our Arthur gave half a week's pay for a brown envelope, hoping for an eyeful of the French at their filthiest. When he tore it open all he'd got was a picture of a pigsty, but by that time the lad was half a mile down the road, running like the clappers.

PPS I'm hoping to get a bit of leave soon, but nothing's ever certain in the army, so it might not come off. If it does, could you get back home for a few days? It would be nice for my Mam.

Fond of John though she was, Lizzie must have jumped up half a dozen times during her reading of that letter, to look out of the window and see who was knocking, or whose the footsteps were. If she was going to do that, she might as well face the window, and keep a lookout while she wrote. She turned her chair, combed her hair again and settled down with pen and paper. No, she wrote. She wouldn't be able to get home. She was doing all right in the theatre just now, and she daren't risk missing an opportunity.

An hour or so later she startled to a knock on the door of her room. The letter writing must have absorbed her more than she'd realized, because she hadn't heard anyone at the front door. Casting pen and paper aside she jumped up to answer it. The disappointment must have shown on her face when she saw it was only Georgie.

'What's up, old girl? You look as if you've lost a pound and found a shilling.'

'Nothing. I was just writing letters.'

'Don't do it too often. It obviously doesn't agree with you.'

'You look chirpy enough for both of us. Did you have a nice evening with your soul mate, or was it the whole night?'

Georgie pulled a 'keep that out' sort of face and tapped the side of his nose with his forefinger. Lizzie shrugged in convincingly affected indifference and returned to her chair, whereupon Georgie sat on the bed facing her, eager to reveal all.

'Oh, all right then, I might as well tell you. You'll get it out of me anyway. I had a marvellous evening, and the most wonderful thing; we're in the same regiment, but different divisions of course, as he's in the regulars. I'm in love, Lizzie. It's the real thing this time. I was with him for hours, and then I tore myself away to snatch a few hours' sleep in my nice, soft bed. But the bloody bed was too soft, and what with that, and thinking about *him*, I tossed and turned for ages, and finally had to rip the blankets off and lie on the floor, and then I slept like a baby. The army's a very uncivilizing influence.'

'I think that's the point of it, Georgie. They train you to kill people, don't they?'

'You know, Lizzie, you were like a bear with a sore head all yesterday evening, and I can see you're going to be no better today. You're not a bit interested in my news, or that divine fellow I'm dying to tell you about. I've a good mind not to ask you over for lunch.'

'Oh, go on, Georgie, ask me. I don't want to bother cooking; some of the other tenants always leave the kitchen in such a filthy state. And we can decide which bits of your furniture you want me to look after. And I'll even let you tell me about your new friend.'

'And you won't have to spend any of your own money on feeding yourself either, you crafty little cat.'

Lizzie kept up her vigil at Georgie's window, until it was time to leave for the evening performance, when he decided he'd walk down to the West End with her.

'I don't suppose you'd fancy giving the old ham a night off and playing leading man?' she asked him, as they approached the theatre.

'That would be too insulting to him, wouldn't it? Besides, I never, ever work for nothing, and I'm sure the governor wouldn't pay two of us.'

'Well, I'm going to speak to the governor about him. He's hopeless.'

'Give him a chance. He might improve.'

'He's had six weeks of chances, and he's no better. A leading man ought to be able to act, or at least be fit to look at.'

Work, work, work; that was what she needed, then she wouldn't have to think. She threw herself into the performance, and the leading man never made a slip. To show her thanks for this small but significant mercy, and mindful of Georgie's accusation that by taking her bad temper out on him she was making the 'poor fellow' worse, she flashed him an approving smile before tripping back to the dressing room to remove costume and make up. She told the stage doorman to let Captain Ashton in if he arrived, but that tap on the dressing room door that she was constantly on the alert for never came.

There was no sign of Ashton on Monday either, and he was due for embarkation first thing Wednesday morning. He wasn't going to come. When she got home on Monday evening she took the photograph off her mantelpiece and looked at the two of them, her face impassive, his full of – what? Something like hope, possibly. They might have made a handsome pair. She shoved it face down into a drawer before undressing and getting into bed.

It was just as well for her it had all ended. Or perhaps it wasn't, it was hard to decide. He had been generous, there was no denying it, and that was a very endearing trait in a man. And had he really offered her *two* hundred to spend the weekend with him or was her memory playing tricks on her? Was it two hundred pounds? 'Good God!' she exclaimed, and turned over to bite into the pillow. If she'd had any sense she'd have been careful to preserve that association, as a hedge against hard times, that's what Irma would have done. Irma would have played him like an angler plays a trout, and feelings wouldn't have entered into it, not on her side, at least. That's where I went wrong, Lizzie thought. I let feelings get in

155

the way of brain – again! Not very clever, my lass. Go and sit in the corner with the dunce's cap on.

And the mantelpiece had looked horribly bare and dreary without the two of them, side by side, gazing out at her.

Chapter Nine

The racket from the chorus girls' dressing room filled the corridor so that it was a few moments before she noticed him, filling her doorway as she stood by the wall mirror ready to pin on her hat.

'I leave for France tomorrow morning, Lizzie. I came to say goodbye.'

'Good heavens – Freddie.' She hesitated, tweaking the strands of hair that lay on her forehead until they were arranged to her satisfaction. 'Well,' she concentrated on her reflection, 'I hope they send you to a nice quiet sector where nothing horrible happens. Opposite some peaceful Saxons, maybe.'

'So do I. You never gave me your photo.'

'Do you still want one?'

'Of course. It's nice to have a pretty woman to look at now and then.'

She reached into a cardboard box on the shelf above her mirror and found a photograph. As she gave it to him their hands touched briefly, turning her skin to gooseflesh. 'Are you going to keep it next to your heart?'

'Not so near, I think. Perhaps I'll pin it up in

156

my billet.'

'Or your dugout.'

He looked briefly into her eyes, then transferred his gaze to the picture. 'It says "love, Lizzie" on it. If that were true, I would keep it next to my heart. I wish you were an advocate of free love, Lizzie. It's a wonderful philosophy. All the best philosophers are saying so. I'm sure people can be happy living together without marriage.'

He was trying to turn her into his kept tart now, as if she had no prospects of her own, and nothing better to do than what he wanted. She wondered what Irma would do, and began to realize that she wasn't like Irma, and never would be. She really had too much pride for that game, and she'd no intention of playing it. 'Are all the best philosophers men, by any chance?' she asked.

'Of course not. There are a lot of independent-minded women among them, just like you, Lizzie.'

'Not like me, Freddie. I'm not an advocate of free love and I'm not an advocate of living together without marriage either. I'm an advocate of dancing. Would you like to take me?'

'What's wrong with the gigolo?'

'Nothing's wrong with the gigolo, as you call him, except he's not here.'

'Hmm. Well, we both know I'm not very good at dancing. Not as good as him, anyway.'

There was an uncomfortable pause. Lizzie crossed the room to retrieve her jacket, carefully left hanging well out of reach of clouds of powder. He took it from her and held it out for her to slip her arms into the sleeves. 'I'd much rather be helping you off with it,' he said, as he

157

drew it up to her shoulders.

She ignored the comment. 'Did you have a nice weekend?'

'Yes. I had a wonderful weekend. I went out and found some very good bad company, and enjoyed myself no end.'

'You'd have had even more fun with me, taking me dancing, or to the races, or something.'

'I wanted to take you dancing, if you remember, before that frightful actor chap stuck his nose in and you wouldn't ditch him. But "or something" in the flat would have been fun. I'd have had the most fun getting my big doll to dress herself in tiny little undergarments so that I could have the pleasure of taking them off again, but you wouldn't let me. You are a spoilsport, Lizzie. You spoiled all my sport, anyway. You told me to go to hell.'

'But you didn't go to hell, Freddie. You went out and found some bad company, and had a wonderful weekend.'

He began playing with a strand of her hair. 'That *was* hell, Lizzie. And I didn't really enjoy myself very much – because you're the only bad company I really want.'

So, he'd had a rotten weekend. Good. He deserved a bit of punishment. She gave a little smile of satisfaction and wondered whether, if she held out long enough, she could make him crack and offer her marriage. And if he wouldn't – well then, he could go to hell. 'It is a dilemma, isn't it, Freddie?' she said, giving herself a cool and approving once over in the mirror before putting on her hat. 'Your father won't approve of me, so that cuts one avenue off, and as long as I can earn enough money of my own I shall stay on the straight and narrow, so that blocks the other. There's really no way forward.' She jabbed the hatpin into place.

'I see. In that case, I hope the play folds and you have to come to me in rags and throw yourself on my mercy. Then I shall pay you back for torturing me, you witch. I shall install you in a little garret somewhere and violate you three times a day, and every time I'll think to myself "That's right. This is the only language this heartless trollop really understands, and that's another hu..." but I won't say it, as it's bound to get me into trouble.'

'And you'll think to yourself, "That's another hundred pounds I've saved." That's what you were going to say.'

He assumed an innocent expression. 'Not necessarily.'

'If you're making wishes, Freddie, wouldn't it be kinder to me if you wished for your father to have a change of heart?' She searched the grey eyes. 'Or perhaps your father is just a convenient excuse? Could that be it, Captain Ashton?'

'I usually keep my wishes within the bounds of possibility, Lizzie, but I don't mind wishing him a change of heart, if it'll please you. And I'm not lying to you.'

'Ah, but men like you don't consider that lying to women like me counts as lying at all.' She ran her toes along the floor under her dressing table, and, finding her shoes, slipped them on.

He watched her tie the ribbons. 'They're the

159

ones you wore that night at the Ritz. I wish I had you there this minute.'

She nodded, quickly completing the task and ignoring the last comment. 'Yes. They're perfect for dancing, but if you don't want to take me, I might as well go home.'

'No. I won't take you dancing. But I will take you to supper – if you'll come.'

The train was waiting in the station, a long segmented snake that seemed to stretch for miles. The nearest carriages were first class, and she could see officers smartly dressed in uniforms trimmed with red tabs and gold braid being served by waiters. They certainly did themselves proud, sitting there in the lap of luxury. Further along she saw that the carriages were rather more Spartan.

She had planned to take Ashton by surprise whilst with his father, to walk up to him unannounced, to acknowledge him and stand there brazenly waiting to be introduced, and then watch their reaction. One look at the press of people convinced her she should have stayed in bed. There would be no hope of finding them among this heaving throng of soldiers, officers, servants, factory workers, wives, mothers, children, porters and railway staff. She cheekily stood on some unattended luggage to scan the mass of people again and again, but neither of the two men was anywhere to be seen.

'Lizzie! Lizzie!'

She spotted him, alone, and without much luggage – the porters would be dealing with that.

Looking as pleased as punch he sped with long easy strides towards her.

'I say, this is a s'nice surprise. And have you come all this way, just to see me off?' He put his hands on her waist to lift her down.

'Freddie, you're breathless. Are you sure you're fit to go back?'

'What else am I to do, if I can't get you into bed? I might as well go off and get shot. But you have given me a surprise, Lizzie. Perhaps you like me, after all. Just a little bit.'

No need to disillusion him by telling him she'd come to catch him with his father and put him on the spot. She tilted her head and laughed teasingly up at him. 'Perhaps. Just a little bit.'

'You know, I hardly slept last night. I'm in an awful fix about you.'

'Why?'

'That fellow Georgie, for a start. I want to know how things stand there. I've the most frightful feeling there's something between you two.'

'There is. We both like dancing.'

'More than that.' His expression was so intense it was comical, reminding her of a jealous child who wanted to wrench a favourite toy from the clutches of a hated rival.

'With Georgie?' her eyebrows shot up in disbelief. She began to laugh, and then said: 'He was our leading man and he can dance. Actors spend a lot of time together, and we became friends. He's good company. And that's all there is to that.'

'Are you sure? Has there *ever* been anything else? Has he ever been your lover?'

She felt bubbles of laughter rising to her throat again and it must have been infectious.

'Why are you laughing?' he demanded, laughing too, in spite of himself.

'You're jealous of Georgie, that's why. You've no idea how funny that is, Freddie. It's ridiculous.' She might have said more, might have told him about Georgie's predilections, but held her tongue. It would have been difficult to find the right words, and she wouldn't have shamed Georgie for the world, or been the means of bringing any trouble on him.

But Freddie seemed to catch her drift, for his mouth turned down in an expression of disgust. 'Oh, I see. I suspected it at once, and then when I saw you dancing together I thought I must be imagining things, but I was right after all. The blighter's a bloody shirt-lifter.'

'What a rotten thing to say, Freddie.'

'It's true though, isn't it? I detest the blighters. So do most men who've had to survive public school ... well, better not say any more about that.'

'I wouldn't say anything wrong about Georgie for the world. He's been the best friend anybody could have. He took me under his wing when I first came to London, and he's looked after me ever since, in his way.'

'I don't want him looking after you any longer. Let him find somebody else to look after. I don't want the blighter putting his filthy hands on you. And I can't stand the thought of my next leave being spent like the past few days, Lizzie.'

'Then what's the answer, Freddie?'

'I don't know. I wish you'd relent and let me set you up in a nice little flat. My father's exceptionally generous at the moment – he gets his money's worth in being able to bore his friends at the Athenaeum with boasting about the son who's commanding a company at the Front. A dispute with him would be a severe blow to the treasury; it would hurt us both in the long run, and other people besides. And I should have to work my way up from the bottom, whatever I did. You know how long that takes. And there are other things about me you might not particularly like, things I don't speak about.'

'What are they?'

There was frantic activity as the guard blew the whistle and the wheels of the train began to turn. 'There isn't time now. This is my train to hell, Lizzie, and I mustn't miss it.' They raced towards the train. He jumped aboard and slammed the door behind him, then hung breathless out of the open window.

'I'll tell you next time I see you. Write to me, Lizzie, won't you?'

'Yes.' She touched his cheek. 'And I never meant it you know, Freddie, about going to hell. Come back safe!'

He clasped her hand and held it, until the train picked up speed and forced him to let go.

She waved until she lost sight of him, then hopped on a bus outside the station and went up to the top deck. She took a seat near the front, and sat looking down on the busy streets, exulting in the knowledge that Ashton wanted her as much as she'd wanted Tom Peters, that he was suffering the same tortures and agonies that she'd endured three years ago. She recognized the signs. Yes, it looked as though she'd captured her officer, but not the money that should have gone with him. That was just her luck, though – never any ointment without its fly.

As they passed over Waterloo Bridge she looked down at the Thames with some satisfaction. She'd withstood Ashton's pleas and persuasions, and his tantrums. She had held out, and used her brains, and the result would be an offer of marriage, she was sure of it. The words of one of Marie Lloyd's latest numbers popped into her head:

Dear, dear! Hm, hm – don't fret.
If a fellow says, 'Wilt?' will she wilt? You bet!

Yes, being Mrs Captain would be a step up in the world, and it would also save her from any danger of munitions factories or farms, or any other slave labour scheme Lloyd George might have in mind for surplus women. It was an awful pity that he'd taken against Georgie though.

A hilarious thought flitted into her head, and suddenly her face was wreathed in smiles. Perhaps it might even be possible to remove that ugly fly. If father was going to cut up rough about having an actress for a daughter-in-law, well, why tell him about the wedding at all? They could save that news until Freddie had his partnership, and everything else he wanted.

Her smile stretched from ear to ear, and a glow of triumph burned in her breast. She hadn't been Irma's understudy for nothing, after all.

'It's sick-making. This is what I call courage above and beyond the call of duty or whatever the phrase is. I fully deserve the military medal for this sacrifice, if not the VC. But what's the alternative? Keep paying rent on a flat I'm never going to be in, for God knows how long, on army pay? It can't be done, Eliza old thing. Oh, but my lovely lace curtains, how well you've hidden me from my nosey neighbours, and what wonderful times I've had standing behind you, spying on them. Parting is such sweet sorrow! My only consolation is that you're going to a good home.' Georgie stood at the window overlooking Bloomsbury Square, taking down his cream lace curtains, almost the only things remaining in his flat.

Lizzie laughed. 'You are an idiot, Georgie.'

'Maybe, but when it's taken one years to get a home together, it really is a horrible feeling to be breaking it apart.'

'Take me dancing. It'll take your mind off it.'

'I can't. I already have an engagement.'

'With your soul mate in Soho, I suppose. Well that should cheer you up.'

'It will, undoubtedly. But that reminds me. I saw your Captain Ashton wandering around one of the seedier streets in that part of town on Monday night, and he saw me. He was in no mood for conversation, though – barely acknowledged me.'

Having no wish to hurt his feelings, Lizzie had confided nothing about her last meeting with Ashton to Georgie. 'What do you suppose he was doing there?' she asked, feeling an unexpected chill at the thought that his comments about finding bad company had been more than vain words.

Georgie's eyebrows lifted, and he looked askance at her through half-closed eyes. 'What are men usually doing when they wander round places like that in the evenings, Lizzie? Your guess is as good as mine.'

He helped her put his beloved lace net curtains up at her windows before she went down to de Lacey's for the evening performance. On her return, she lit the paraffin lamp of etched cranberry glass that she was keeping for him and sat in its rosy, cosy glow embroidering a new camisole, chewing her lip and wondering what in God's name Ashton *had* been doing in those dubious parts of Soho that Georgie knocked about in. And something else niggled her, something she'd hardly noticed at the time; that Ashton had said about losing his father's money... 'It could hurt us both, and other people besides.'

'What other people?' she asked the empty air.

British Expeditionary Force
2nd September 1915

Dearest Lizzie,
Men have been pouring onto the ship in endless streams of khaki along with supplies of every sort, boxes of ammunition, food for men and horses, and just about everything else you can think of. The decks are swarming with men, smoking and laughing, or huddling in corners to play cards, or standing at the rails looking

166

towards England, most probably wondering if they'll ever see home again. Except for the rawest recruits they all know what's facing them, but they sing and joke and make the best of things.

A couple of minutes ago we had the command: 'Put your cork jackets on, gentlemen!' I was already wearing mine. War is such a game of chance the only thing to do is stay lucky, and it's as well to give luck a helping hand, *n'est ce pas?*

I'm very glad we got a few things straightened out and now I'm more fed up than ever about being shipped back, especially as I won't get any leave for ages. The powers that be will think I've had my fair share, and that it's some other poor devil's turn. In ordinary circumstances I'd be the first to agree; but wanting you is making me very selfish. I seem to have no room in my mind for anybody else, especially when I think about the coming winter and the probability of more Zep raids.

Look after yourself, won't you, and write to me as soon as you can.

XXXX by the shipload,
Freddie

Plenty about love, but nothing about marriage, Lizzie noted. Nothing about his wanderings in Soho, or any mysterious other people either, and she'd very much have liked to know more about that.

A week after Ashton's return to France, Lizzie took a cab home. No sooner had she let herself into her room than the most terrific explosion

167

made her almost jump out of her skin. She flew to the window and threw up the sash to lean out, but could see nothing, so ran back down the stairs to see the darkened streets thronged with women and children screaming and running about in their night-gowns, and other people with necks craning upwards. The night was clear, and Lizzie was sure she could make out the tiny figures of the crew aboard a massive yellow Zeppelin which was drifting eastwards, illuminated by searchlights and the fires below. Anti-aircraft guns began to send shrapnel into the sky, their shot sounding meagre compared with one fearsome explosion after another raining down from the dealer of death beyond their reach. After an age the noise stopped, and the night sky was red with fire. More excited than terrified, Lizzie went with some of the crowd to see the damage. The bomb had exploded in the centre of Queen Square, shattering windows but mercifully injuring no one. Lizzie looked towards the Alexandra Hospital for Children and shuddered to think of the murder and maiming and mutilation that might have been done there, and was being done in other parts of London.

'What was it Irma had said: *'Zeppelin flieg, England wird abgebrannt'*? Perhaps it would – all of England – be burned. 'Every man, woman and baby, every cat and dog will be in this war. They'll see to that.' Lizzie shuddered at the thought.

A letter from Ashton arrived a few days later.

B.E.F.
17th September 1915

Darling Girl,
I got your letter about the Zep raid the other night, and we've seen the papers. I can tell you it's made us more resolved against the enemy than ever. One sees and hears enough in Belgium and France to set one against them, but to hear of helpless civilians being burned alive in their peaceable houses *at home* simply makes one's blood boil. The stark conclusion is that to win this war we will have to become more Prussian than the Prussians and crush German militarism out of existence. They leave us no alternative. I can't say very much, but something might occur soon to lead us along that path and give us a fitting revenge, but not, I'm glad to say, on women and children.
Yours 'til death,
Freddie

After that came nothing but field postcards, which never said any more than: 'I am quite well. Letter follows at first opportunity.'

Georgie took her dancing a couple of times, before returning to his training camp. With all her favourite companions gone, Lizzie's life settled into a routine of four matinées a week, two of them for charity, and six evening performances, sending and receiving letters and scouring the newspapers. She could learn little about what was happening in France and Flanders; there was more about the Dardanelles and Gallipoli and Sulva Bay, places which held no interest for her at all.

At last, at the end of September she saw some good news about the Western Front. 'A Real British Victory at Last' the *Daily Mail* proclaimed, above an account of the Battle of Loos. This was a breakthrough and the Huns were on the run, at last. Thank the good Lord for that, thought Lizzie. The war would soon be won.

Chapter Ten

A couple of weeks later they were playing to a full house and had just started the third act when the electric lights suddenly dipped. A second later an almighty blast shook de Lacey's to its foundations.

A man in the stalls leaped to his feet. 'Those bloody Germans with their Zeps again!'

Interrupted mid-sentence, Lizzie turned towards the audience, anger overriding the fear in her. She could do nothing to stop murder and mayhem dropping from the skies, but she would do her damndest to forestall a stampede in the theatre. She fixed the man with a determined stare, increased the pitch and volume of her voice a fraction, turned to Mr Dorrien, and gave him her hand.

'...just like you to know how very much I enjoyed it,' she smiled, willing him to carry on.

'Oh, Miss Carmichael, the pleasure was entirely mine, I do assure you...' he responded. The man sat down again and the rest of the audience kept their seats, despite the blasts outside.

When the play was over and they were taking their bows he whispered to her: 'Coolness under fire, Miss Wilde, coolness under fire. Well done.'

'Well done yourself,' she grinned. 'Shall we round the evening off with a few patriotic songs, do you think?'

He nodded and she stepped forward to gales of applause, striking a John Bullish attitude and holding her arms out for silence.

'Was that the Kaiser, sending us more love gifts from the Fatherland, do you think? Don't they realize that it'll take more than a few German bombs to spoil the show when British audiences are out to enjoy themselves?' she demanded, as soon as she could be heard.

The audience rose to its feet, and she couldn't go on, for torrents of cheers, whistles, and applause. When the noise abated she continued, 'And now, as we're all in this together, let's round off the evening with a sing-song.'

The musicians struck up with a series of songs calculated to hurl defiance at the enemy and put some starch into British backbones. Audience and cast sang with gusto, and when the orchestra ended the medley with 'Rule Britannia', the people in the audience rose to their feet and the noise of their cheering would have drowned out a 600 pounder.

Later, Lizzie and others in the cast joined crowds

of men in khaki, men in naval uniforms, men in suits and bowler hats, a couple of kilted soldiers from some highland regiment and a handful of women, all wandering around the Strand and Aldwych, surveying the damage. Bombs had crashed into the pavement outside the Strand Theatre and the Waldorf Hotel next to it, but apart from minor damage the buildings had escaped, or hundreds of people might have been killed. There were bodies lying about as it was, and Lizzie fancied that she saw one of them move. She ran over to a woman to do what she could to help her, and Mr Dorrien followed. He turned the woman over and Lizzie shuddered at the sight of her eyes, wide open and cast upwards so that only the whites showed. She was dead, and so, presumably, were all the others. There was nothing to do but wait for the authorities to remove them.

They followed the trail of destruction to Exeter Street, where the rear of the Lyceum had been hit. Flames were leaping into the night sky from a hole in nearby Wellington Street. Somebody said a bomb had set the gas main alight.

They'd all had a closer shave than she'd realized. Lizzie wondered what *The Times* would have to say about London being a sitting duck for enemy raiders and still lacking any real defence against them. Not enough to fill two column inches in the middle of the paper, if the last raid was anything to judge by. It was probably just as well to play the raids down. The attitude of 'business as usual' had been disparaged by Ashton, and perhaps rightly so – then. But

172

instinct told her that 'business as usual' was the only possible response to this sort of outrage. That, and fierce and swift retaliation.

She took the letter out of her pigeonhole and pinched it between finger and thumb. This was a real letter at last, and not just a sheet. She went back upstairs to her own room and settled herself by the window to read in comfort.

B.E.F.
15th October 1915

Dearest Lizzie,
  We've had a very trying time of it lately. I'm surprised still to be in the land of the living and able to write to you. I see no harm in telling you this now that the show's over. There was a big push on the 25th to take back some of the ground we lost, and a certain little mining town. We thought we'd won the battle, then on the 26th the deluge started, both of rain and of enemy fire. We were all desperately tired and wet, and some of the men were famished, not having eaten for forty-eight hours. I ended up commanding men from three different divisions, the telephone wires were smashed so that orders from higher command were an impossibility, and I saw men mown down all around me; we were picking our way over their bodies. The din was frightful, what with the rattle of machine guns and rifles – a lot of the firing coming from a tall slag heap, and the screeching of shells from their fifteen pounders, and the noise of shrapnel hitting the pylons. The

173

field was simply covered by the bodies of men, just like a flock of sheep lying down, and only a few of us left standing. The Germans let the survivors stagger from the field without a shot, so that tells you what sort of a show it was, to wring pity from an enemy like the Hun. It's the worst thing I've ever been in, and it dragged on for days.

You can't imagine how horrible it is to stand helplessly by watching men gasping and heaving against the slow drowning caused by *our own* poison gas, seeing their eyes popping out and listening to the poor devils struggling for breath, knowing that there's absolutely nothing you can do for them. It's the most horrible thing one could ever see. The sight of men hanging helplessly on barbed wire that was supposed to have been cut and wasn't, and being riddled with bullets runs a close second. And then hearing the wounded groaning and shrieking in no man's land after the attack, and having to wait until dark to bring them in makes you feel like screaming yourself. The poor bloody stretcher-bearers hardly knew where to start. We were bringing them in all night, night after night, and the Germans let us. Then they'd give us a few warning shots at dawn to get us out of the way before they began the strafe in earnest. But what a filthy job it is to bring the dead in, especially when they've lain out for days. During roll call after the show was over I kept looking at my once shiny buttons, blackened by the gas, as the missing men's chums kept answering, 'Over the hill. Over the hill'.

The gaps in our ranks are awful. There are

corpses piled up at the clearing station awaiting burial, and lots of relatives to be written to. What a ghastly task that is, but not a hundredth part as bad as it is to get such a letter, I suppose. That seems to be the most solid achievement of this wonderfully well planned battle – the annihilation of our own army. We threw five divisions into it, and whole battalions of men have gone west. There's some truly impressive intelligence behind it all.

I hope you don't mind me writing about these things, but I can't get them out of my brain for long. You'll probably get this letter with half of it blacked out anyway and I shall be facing a court martial for spreading alarm and despondency, or something of the sort. And none of it would matter so much if we hadn't lost everything in the counter attack. Sir Douglas Haig thought that machine guns were 'much overrated' and that two per Battalion would suffice. I wonder if this massacre will have changed his mind?

Do you remember Yates? He's survived, and we're both away from the trenches and back in billets. We're going to a village a couple of miles from here to have dinner soon, to get out of it for a bit and have a change of scene. We're also hoping for a good feed, of course, and we may drink rather a lot of champagne to celebrate the fact that we're both unscathed. It's nothing short of miraculous. My little horseshoe does seem to be doing its work, doesn't it?

Poor Yates was in a bit of a state the other day, he was sitting there and his legs seemed to take on a life of their own. You should have seen them

– they were dancing a jig almost – it was remarkable. Quite funny in a macabre sort of a way. He thought of going to see the M.O., but he's all right now. It's amazing how one or two good long sleeps restores people.

I think I must have had a tiny dose of gas, I felt it in my nose and throat, a sort of tickling sensation, and then as though someone has my chest in a vice. But you can't always smell it because of the fumes of the explosives. Never mind, like Yates, I'm getting rapidly better. A couple more days rest and we'll both be as right as rain. I'm holding up quite well. In fact, I'm holding up as well as anybody. It's queer, but you can see the most hideous things, and think you'll never be able to put them out of your mind, then a couple of hours later you're laughing with your comrades and forgetting everything, especially after a good meal. I think most of it's relief at not having gone west yourself, and I suppose if it weren't so, you'd very quickly go mad. War seems to make us callous. I suppose if it didn't, we couldn't carry on. No good getting depressed, is it?

The post's just come, and I see I have three letters from you. Yates has seen them. I laughed at him and said, 'So there! She does love me.' It's bucked me up no end, I can tell you, very much so. I'm going to make him sit and wait until I've read them all before we go out. I'm simply longing to see you again, but God knows when. Nothing's been said about leave, and I don't expect it will be, for me. I'll be at the very bottom of the list. I hope you're looking after yourself. Be very careful not to get in the way of any German bombs.

Love and kisses ad infinitum.

Freddie

PS Did you read in the papers about their shooting Nurse Cavell? Perfectly frightful, isn't it? I would say more, but words fail me.

PPS Thinking about you stops me getting too depressed, especially thinking about something very s'nice. I think you know what I mean. I could do with some of that sort of s'niceness just now. *Ma cherie, la vie est breve,* and I hope you'll remember that when I see you, and be *very s'nice* to me.

It almost made her wish she'd let him have his own way at the Karsino – but no, she thought, keep your head, Lizzie. Men are such fickle, contrary creatures that if you had, he'd be cooling by now. She read the letter through again and put it behind their photograph on her mantelpiece, wondering if that had been the 'Real British Victory at Loos' that the *Daily Mail* had been crowing about.

The Zeppelin raids seemed to have a startling effect on the governor, rousing him from his somnambulist state and galvanizing him into action. The following Monday morning he pounced on them all after the matinée. 'We start rehearsals for pantomime next week. I've got a good script for *Cinderella,*' he announced.

With all the crocks and old fogies you've taken on for men's roles? Lizzie wanted to say, but prudently kept her mouth shut. Mr Dorrien had proved himself after all, but it was going to be uphill work doing anything with the rest of them. Still, if the pantomime was a flop nobody was going to lay the blame at her door.

She piped up. 'I want to be principal boy. I can slap my thigh as well as Vesta Tilley, and I can do a pretty good imitation of her, too: "I joined the army yesterday, so the army of today's all right!" she struck a Tilley pose with an imaginary swagger stick, becoming a larger than life version of the artiste. '"I say, you fellows, I'm awfully bucked to be in the army – having a simply ripping time! And don't the girls all favour a chap wearing khaki, with his shiny buttons and Sam Browne belt!"' To ram the point home she burst into the chorus of 'Jolly Good Luck to the Girl Who Loves a Soldier'.

'Yes, all right,' said the governor. 'We'll have to change the words, alter the tune a bit, stick a few jokes in it for the kids, and a bit of innuendo for their parents, but we'll keep it in.'

'We should do Jack the Giant Killer, and call the Giant Fritz, and I could kill him with a mock Lee Enfield, or some contraption that shoots eggs – or custard pies would be better still. Something along the lines of Karno's Circus. That sort of thing's very popular these days. A muddle somewhere. Give him a drunken Dame for a wife, if Mr Dorrien can do a drunk, that is. And I can "do" Marie Lloyd and Florrie Ford, if you want a burst of either of them to liven things up.'

'Of course I can do a drunk,' Mr Dorrien protested, pushing back his black hair with grey roots.

'We're doing Cinderella. Ethel can play Cinders

178

and one of the chorus can understudy her. We'll give the ugly sisters those German helmets with a spike coming out of the top they call *pickelhaubs*, and they can have German style moustaches as well, just to please you. Your ideas aren't bad, but you'd better make sure you're not ill. It'll be hard to get an understudy for that lot. I'm impressed.'

Not half as impressed as you're going to be by the time I've finished with the part. I'll see to it we get some good reviews, Lizzie thought. 'I'm never ill,' she assured him.

She was determined she'd be a hit with Vesta Tilley's 'Tommy', although judging by the letters she'd had from Ashton recently the army of today was far from all right for the average private or junior officer. Karno's 'muddle somewhere' seemed to be a lot nearer the mark, and a bloody murderous muddle at that. But that was no concern of hers, a struggling little actress on the London stage. Better to concentrate on matters she could influence, important things like how much she was going to be paid, and her costumes. They must be authentic. 'Thing is, governor, I can do a good take-off of Vesta, but if I'm to get the audience with me, I'll have to have a proper uniform, and one that fits, not something that fits where it touches, like the regular Tommies.'

'All right, Lizzie,' he agreed. 'You can go to Ellis's military tailor's, and get measured.'

Well, that was settled, then. The next thing was her place on the bill. She was going to be top, or there'd be hell to pay. It might be worth getting the governor to invite the press to a preview, too.

It could certainly do no harm to talk nicely to some of those gentlemen.

26th December 1915

Dear Freddie,

The governor let *Life's Enchanted Cup* run right until Christmas Eve, it's been doing so well lately, and he worked us all to death with rehearsals for pantomime at the same time without giving us a penny more in pay, which was very nice of him, I don't think. He's getting meaner and meaner, and more of a demon for work than ever these days, so we're all suffering from brain fag, puffy eyes, aching feet and broken backs, but apart from that we're in perfect health. Time's flown, because we've hardly had time to... I could use a very vulgar word here that's quite common in the theatre where very few people stand on ceremony – but I'm too much of a lady, you'll be glad to know. On Christmas Day I slept all day, and today we opened with *Cinderella*, with plenty of ragtime tunes and custard pies and naughty jokes about the Kaiser and his *pickelhaub*, which won't be understood by the children – unless they're very advanced, Mr Dorrien says – which we hope they're not. I shouldn't wonder if we'll be in trouble with the censor, especially as today's a Sunday. Some people are sticklers, and it would be just our luck to have had them in the audience tonight. I'm playing Tommy Buttons, you remember, so I get most of the best jokes, and sing 'Keep the Home Fires Burning', with the audience joining in.

180

They all enjoyed it, and even the purity brigade can't object to that.

I'm writing this at twelve o'clock at night, because I'm too wide awake and wound up after all that to think about going to bed. I'm just glad to be doing something different to *Life's Enchanted Cup*. I was getting really bored with playing Violet. I shall enjoy pantomime – it was a scream tonight. We had a little party in the crush room after everyone had gone, and plied the pressmen with drink – we desperately want some good reviews. They all loved the show, and I think we'll get some, except from a rather straight-laced bluestocking lady journalist, who wouldn't have anything alcoholic. She's the first lady reporter I've ever seen, but they say there are a few now. The war's turning everything topsy-turvy isn't it?

This is the longest letter I've ever written to you, isn't it? I think about you all the time, but I had hardly a minute to myself to write before. I hope you had as good a Christmas as possible, Freddie, drinking plenty of champagne in the estaminets with Lieutenant Yates. I should like to be there to keep an eye on you and keep you away from all those naughty French girls. I've heard all about them – don't think I haven't. You'll be all right talking French to them, but it's no good talking it to me, Freddie – I don't understand a word, except maybe '*Au revoir*'.

Lots of Love, from Lizzie.

PS Of course I'll be nice to you when you get back – just as nice as you are to me.

PPS I hope you're completely better from the

gas now, but I expect you must be, if you were out having meals and chasing French girls with Lieutenant Yates.

She read the letter over and smiled. Better not tell Ashton she'd charmed, flattered, wheedled and joked a couple of half drunken reporters into letting her write her own generous review to 'save them the trouble'. Somebody as jealous as him, it might give him the wrong idea about her altogether. Or rather, it might give him the right idea about how her calculating little business brain was beginning to work, and that would be even worse. She sealed the envelope and put it in her bag, to post the following morning.

British Expeditionary Force
31st December 1915

Dear Lizzie,
    Thank you for your good wishes for me during the festive season. I spent it back in the suicide ditch, but farther north this time. Alas for me, there was no champagne, and no French girls, but I had a family of very impudent French rats for near neighbours – they had the flat above mine in the dugout. Mother rat seemed to be teaching her children a few circus tricks, because they kept leaping out of their parlour and doing back somersaults onto me – I suppose I provided a nice soft landing. It was all right until they landed on my face – that really is the limit. So I put my pillow on the other end of the bed and let them land on my boots. We never kill them, or at least I

don't. Their corpses stink too much. I'm also dispensing a lot of Christmas cheer, if not goodwill, to other, smaller and more irritating creatures. But apart from the livestock, we had very little to disturb us, except the cold. We sleep in our boots and greatcoats there, with the blankets, but we're never warm enough.

The opposition were very quiet, apart from the sound of their carols and Merry Christmases shouted across to Tommy, and all that. We haven't had the sort of fraternizing that went on last year though. It's queer, sometimes one absolutely hates their guts, and at other times they seem like decent fellows, no different from ourselves. I suppose we can't blame them for the actions of their staff and politicians. It's all an awful tangle. All I can say is that the morals of war are horrible, and make beasts of us all at times. Better not to think about it too deeply.

I shall have a few serious words with that manager of yours when I get back for working you too hard, but that should all be over now if you've finished with *Life's Enchanted Cup*, and you're doing the pantomime rather than rehearsing it. During the past week, your eyes will have stopped being puffy, and your feet will have stopped aching, and your back must have mended itself by now. I hope so.

It seems that her sufferings haven't stopped my fiancée from having a high old time over the festive season, at any rate. I'm delighted you're a great hit as principal boy, but how I hate to be left out of your triumphs. I do love you, Lizzie, completely and absolutely.

I may be getting some leave in February, fingers crossed, so I'll see you then. I hope you can manage at least a few days off. I must finish now, or I'll miss the post. You will write back by return, won't you?

Oceans of Love and Mountains of Kisses from your

Freddie

'My fiancée.' A hint of marriage there, but a hint wasn't enough; it might be just a ploy to keep her sweet. Was he really hooked, or just stringing her along? If she held out long enough, a real proposal would come, with a nice, expensive engagement ring at the very least. And if it didn't, he could bugger off; she couldn't really care less about him.

She cut out the pantomime reviews from various papers to send to him. He would bring them back when he came on leave, and then they could go into her scrapbook. The ones she'd suggested herself were brilliant, of course '...Miss Wilde's is a new and exciting talent, not to say comic genius, and some of our established artistes will have to look to their laurels...', and the like. The surprise came at the piece written by the lady journalist, who thought the show '...a thoughtful and patriotic piece, a tribute to the extraordinary courage of soldier and civilian alike, and an inspiration to all who see it...' Lizzie laughed aloud. What pish! The piece was nothing but a string of unlikely incidents concocted to provide a reasonable excuse for a lot of ridiculous antics and filthy jokes, and thoughtful patriotic inspiration had had very little to do with it. Still, if that was what some people wanted to believe, it couldn't do her any harm. She tucked the cuttings in an envelope and then sat down to write.

'As soon as I read about the panto in the paper, I said to Ollie, "This is too much. I bet she got those reporters drunk and made them let her write her own review," and I'm right, aren't I?'

'You know me too well, Georgie,' Lizzie laughed.

He almost danced with glee. 'I knew it! I just knew you'd had a hand in those write-ups, they sounded so exactly like you when you're being at your most ironic! How could they take you seriously? You'll do well in show business, my darling, you're so deliciously devious. But honestly, it's not bad. The governor sent me a couple of tickets for old times sake, and I was laughing my head off and clapping like mad in the stalls – didn't you see me?'

'No. But the censor's made us take the Kaiser jokes out. They won't have Royalty mocked, not even him. So have you got Ollie with you?'

Georgie pulled a face. 'Sadly no, he's back in France. I was reduced to bringing Mama, and I've sent her home in a cab.'

'All the way to Pimlico? It'll cost a fortune.'

'She can afford it.'

Lizzie laughed, and threw her hairbrush at him. 'Georgie, you cad. Your own mother!'

He picked up the brush and returned it to her, with a rueful grin. 'I know. I fear I've proved rather a disappointment to her in many ways, but

185

she puts a brave face on it. Seriously though, she is rolling in it – not like me. I'm nothing but a shilling a day soldier now. Oh, Lizzie, I do miss all this. Ollie says that the army in France spends half its time just waiting about for something to happen, waiting for the ration cart, waiting for the post, waiting for orders, waiting to go up the line, waiting to be relieved. If it really is like that, I shall start a concert party. But for now, I've got four days embarkation leave, so get that slap off your face and get your glad rags on. It's Tango Time!'

Chapter Eleven

The more successful the pantomime became, the more morose the governor looked. Nothing they did seemed to please him or lighten his mood, and Lizzie was in two minds about asking him for any time off. But it was already nearing the end of January, and Freddie would be in England by the end of next month, and after all his ordeals in France, it would be a pity to disappoint him. He only had ten days and he was talking about their going up to Annsdale to see her family. She was getting excited at the prospect. If she was going to ask, better do it as soon as possible, and play on the governor's sense of patriotism.

'I'd like a couple of weeks off, at the end of February, if possible governor,' she told him one night, after they'd had a full house, and five curtain calls. 'My young man's had a rather hard time of it in France, and he's due some leave then.'

'The end of February, you say? Well, Lizzie, I'll tell you something. You can have a couple of years off. In fact, if you rely on me for employment, you'll be having the rest of your life off. I thought I was going to be able to stave it off, but I'll be lucky to see February out before I'm in the bankruptcy courts, and everything I own will be in the hands of the receivers.'

'What, this theatre?' Lizzie looked at him aghast.

'No, not this theatre, Lizzie, it doesn't belong to me. But all my property will be seized to pay the creditors.'

Lizzie wasn't entirely sure what bankruptcy meant, but she knew what it wasn't going to mean. It most certainly was not going to mean any bailiff charging into de Lacey's and carrying off anything that could be of any use to Lizzie. During the course of the following week, Irma's copper trunk and all her stage costumes – those beautiful dresses and costumes and hats and gloves that had adorned 'Violet' – quietly made their way, with sundry other items, out of the star's dressing room at de Lacey's and into Lizzie's room in Bloomsbury Square – and as soon as they'd rung the curtain down for the last time, her pantomime costumes would follow in their wake.

She crept into the court at the start of the bankruptcy hearing while the statement of affairs was being read out. The governor was sitting staring straight ahead, like a man in a trance. It seemed he owed a phenomenal sum, nearly ten thousand pounds. Lizzie thought of the man she'd known when she started at de Lacey's and could have wept. And this, after the tragedy of his children.

The official receiver stood up, turned towards the governor and frowning over a pair of gold-rimmed spectacles perched on the end of his thin nose, he began his meticulous examination, and the governor's public ordeal.

It became apparent that the catalogue of his disasters had begun years ago, after his partner died and the executors demanded an account. He either couldn't or wouldn't pay what they demanded, and so they began proceedings. After five years they got a judgement against him for almost two thousand pounds, with half as much again added on for legal costs. The governor had borrowed money and managed to pay a thousand and fifty. But since 1911 he'd produced a series of plays at a loss of nearly six thousand pounds, and, try as he might, he'd never been in a position to pay any more. He lost over a thousand on *Vice Versa* at the Globe Theatre and then took it on tour at a loss of another two hundred and fifty. In 1912 he produced *The Chalk Line*, but it was killed on the first night by the coal strike, and that, and the tour lost him about four and a half thousand. Since then he'd made a modest profit on *Life's Enchanted Cup*, but couldn't tour with it because the trains were always packed full of soldiers. The pantomime had also been a hit, but made nowhere near enough to compensate.

The governor stood up to emphasize the fact that his last two shows had made a gain in spite

188

of the war, and that given time there was every chance he would recoup his losses. Both registrar and official receiver looked unimpressed.

'Give him a chance, can't you?' Lizzie felt like shouting. 'He'll do all right now, if you leave him alone.'

But the petitioning creditor was howling for his pound of flesh, and after all their hard work the whole enterprise at de Lacey's was to be thrown down the drain, and all the cast, crew, back stage, and front of house thrown out of work, not to mention the governor himself. Sickened, she left before the examination was concluded.

She pondered on the fiasco during her long walk back to Bloomsbury Square. If only he'd settled at the outset, he could have avoided all those costs. Sorry though she was for him, there was no avoiding the fact that the governor had been a very silly man, and the upshot of his silliness was that she would soon have no job, and no money, and perhaps no nice room in Bloomsbury Square if she couldn't find something well paid enough to cover the rent. A loser in love, and now in her career, she'd be homeless before long if she didn't watch out.

How wonderful it must be to be safely married, and leave some man to worry about all that sort of thing. Perhaps if she played her cards right she could get Freddie to propose; he had called her his fiancée in his last letter. She must look her best, and smell wonderful, and be very, very pleasing. Do everything to please him, stopping just short of you-know-what. Unless he was just playing her along that should spur him on to marriage. He could have any amount of s'nice-ness afterwards.

A man who would pay a hundred pounds for one night might not think marriage too high a price, and the best of it was that if she could capture Freddie she would have the security of a respectable marriage without the inconvenience of a husband except for his occasional few days leave, because there was no sign yet of any end to the war. Lord Kitchener had said at the start that it would take at least three years, and men were enlisting for 'three years or the duration'. Freddie would be kept busy in France for a long time yet, and she would be free to make a name for herself.

'I half expected to have my leave cancelled. I've absolutely been on tenterhooks about it, so it was some relief when we got past the embarkation officer at Boulogne, I can tell you.' He picked up his valise and, still talking, followed her upstairs to her flat. 'All the chaps were cheery when we set out, but we cheered up even more then, and not slightly! As soon as I'd been to my father's for my things, I went to find you at de Lacey's, but the place was dark, absolutely no sign of life there at all.'

'No, and there won't be, until someone else takes it over. The governor's a bankrupt. It looks as if you got your wish, Freddie. The whole show's folded, and here I am in rags, throwing myself on your mercy.'

'Oh, Lizzie, I'm most frightfully sorry. I wouldn't have had it happen for the world!'

She stopped outside her door and looked up at

him. His face was a study: a mask of commiseration which entirely failed to prevent his underlying glee shining through.

'Hypocrite! You wished for your chance to pay me back, and now you have it.'

'Then I shall pay you back with love,' he laughed.

'And violate me three times a day?'

'Yes. You'd like that, wouldn't you? But you'll have to let me in first.'

She led him into her room and lit the cranberry glass lamp. That, and the small fire burning in the grate gave the room a rosy glow and made the dismal February afternoon cheerful. Freddie stooped to pick up a camisole half trimmed with lace, with the needle and thread stuck through, that she'd left on the chair. When he put it beside the lamp his smile had faded.

'What's the matter, Freddie?'

'Oh, nothing. Your sewing, it suddenly reminded me of somebody.'

'Who?'

'Somebody I loved and lost a long time ago,' he shrugged, unbuttoning his greatcoat, and then his face brightened. 'You've got our picture on your mantelpiece, I see.'

'Yes, I like to have one or two things like that. They take the bareness off, don't they?'

He took off his coat and held it up for her inspection, poking his finger through a hole in the back, about eighteen inches from the hem. 'If that bullet had been a little higher! Think of it, Lizzie,' he laughed. 'The sort of injury every soldier dreads! The one they make filthy songs

191

about to march to! How terrible that would have been, for me and all my young ladies, French as well as English!' He hurled the coat on the bed, then caught her by the wrist and took her in his arms to hold her tight and give her a long, lingering kiss. 'Of course, there's only one I really care about, and I'd have hated the Hun to deprive her of the benefit of my...'

'Of your what, Freddie?'

'S'niceness, of course. Or me of the benefit of hers,' he said, his eyes drawn to the bed as if to a magnet. 'I'm badly in need of some love, Lizzie. It's only the thought of coming back to you that's kept me going these past few months.' His mouth descended on hers again, in a kiss that made her feel weak at the knees.

Dangerously weak. She pulled away from him, before she lost the will. 'Are you sleeping at your club, or at your father's tonight?' she asked. Wherever it was, he sure as hell wasn't sleeping with her. There were a few things she wanted to know about Captain Frederick Ashton before she started any more of those antics.

His grip on her tightened until she cried: 'Freddie, you're hurting me!'

'Not half as much as you're hurting me, though! Honestly, Lizzie, I've been through hell and high water for you. Who else do you imagine I'm thinking of when bullets and shrapnel are whistling past my ears and all my other parts? Who do you think I'm defending when I face all that? Or even when we're simply living in all that filth and foulness we put up with in France, counting off the hours to the relief, or the next meal, or the next post, or counting the weeks and days until our next leave?'

'All your young ladies, I suppose. French as well as English.'

'No. You, Lizzie. You and you alone. And if I were a woman, and a fellow had gone through all that for me, I'd do anything for him. Absolutely anything.'

'Then if you were a woman, you'd certainly wake up alone one of these days, with a little bun in your oven, while the fly-by-night who used to tell you that everything he did was for you goes off with a better catch. So lucky for you you're a man, Freddie.'

'Not when I'm your fiancé, you tormenting trollop. You must have a heart like a stone. What will it take to melt it?'

She held up her left hand and placed the naked third finger against her chin, and with her head tilted to one side cast her eyes heavenward in reflection. 'I can't think, Freddie. Can you?'

'Yes, I can. If I can't get you into bed now, let's get out of here as quickly as possible, and go for something to eat. I'll take you to a wonderful little restaurant I know in Soho, and wine you and dine you and wine you again, until you're drunk enough, but not too drunk, and then I'll bring you back here and give you something to bring a sparkle to those wicked black eyes.'

'Hmm, Soho,' she said. Unless Georgie had been mistaken, restaurants weren't the only things he knew about in Soho.

He ushered her into a very ordinary looking little

193

place that looked like a galley, buzzing with the noise of a crowd of chattering customers, many of whom hailed him by name. An old French waiter came over, and with profuse apologies for the crowding squashed them into a table near the window and gave Freddie the menu.

He handed it to her. 'What would you like?'

'Oh, I don't know. I can't tell what most of the dishes are. Anything will do, as long as it's not fish. Whatever you're having.' She appraised various gaudy posters of women wearing dresses of deep décolleté advertising various wines and spirits which brightened up the walls, while Freddie gave their order in fluent French. The man eventually scurried away, almost falling over himself to be of service to *'le capitaine'*.

Now was the time to ask *le capitaine* what it was that he'd been doing in Soho, and what that mysterious thing was that he never spoke about. Illuminated in the flame of a candle held in a wine bottle, his eyes had a warm lustre. She caught his glance and smiled, then looked away and began playing with the rivulets of wax encrusting the bottle, peeling pieces off, and working them in her fingers like putty whilst she pondered on the most delicate way to broach the subject. She could think of nothing other than to come straight out with it. 'Georgie told me he'd seen you in Soho,' she said, after a moment or two. 'But not this part. One of the more notorious parts, as a matter of fact.'

He burst into laughter and leaned back in his chair the better to see her face. 'Did he, by God! I wondered exactly what it was that was on your mind, Lizzie. And what was *he* doing in notorious parts of Soho, might I ask? And what business has he got to be telling tales about me?'

'Oh, Georgie tells tales about everybody, or he wouldn't be Georgie. And he's my friend, Freddie. He tries to look out for me. He says you saw him.'

'He's right, I did. And did he tell you what I was doing in Soho?'

'No. But only because he didn't know.'

'Couldn't he guess?'

'Whether he could or not, he didn't.'

'Would you like to know what I was doing in Soho, Lizzie?'

'Yes, I would.'

'Then I shall tell you. Much later.'

'Why not here and now?'

'Much too long and complicated a story, and this is neither the time nor the place. But I will tell you, Lizzie, since you ask. Is there anything else you want to know about me?'

'Yes, there is. I want to know everything. Especially what it is you've never told anybody.'

The waiter was back with the first course, and after that, they had very little opportunity for conversation, because he was constantly at Freddie's elbow, wanting to know if this or that was all right, or if he needed another thing. After the meal Freddie lit a cigarette at the candle, but stubbed it out before he'd half smoked it and called for the bill, eager to be off.

They were just approaching Bloomsbury Square when he suddenly said: 'You want to know everything. Well, my father was already married when he met my mother, and she became his mistress. You know what that means for me.' His tone was light, and his profile in the light of the streetlamp was impassive.

She felt herself blush to her provincial, chapel roots, and they walked on in silence until she asked: 'I suppose that's the thing you've never told anybody.'

The hand he had supported in the crook of his elbow was suddenly left to support itself as he lowered his arm. 'Yes. The legal maxim is: "Those born of sinful intercourse are not counted as children." In law, that is.'

'I didn't know that, Freddie. What are they counted as, then?'

Without breaking step he took hold of her hand and held it. 'For the purposes of inheritance, they're not counted at all. They have no right to anything. Of course, they can be provided for in a will, but as far as I know, my father hasn't made one. Perhaps he thinks he's likely to outlive me and he may be right, the way things are going in France; but if he were knocked down by a motorbus tomorrow I should have no claim on anything.'

'In that case, I wish him a long life,' she said.

He squeezed her hand. 'So do I. He's got more money than he can count, and the more I distinguish myself in France, the more generous he becomes.'

'Then he might be generous enough to let you choose your own wife.'

'Perhaps he will, given time, but I can't wait for

196

that. I want to set you up in a nice little flat, where we can...'

'Wait a minute, Freddie.' She let go of his hand to find her key and let them both into the house. He followed her up the dark stairway and into her own room, where she threw off her coat and hat, and turned to face him.

'You've just told me that children born of sinful intercourse aren't counted as children, and have no rights of inheritance, and in the next breath you want to set me up in a nice little flat where we can have no end of sinful intercourse, and I can have the name of a whore and produce a lot of children who don't count as children. Are you quite barmy, Freddie, or do you think I am?'

Unbuttoning his greatcoat he said: 'No ... yes ... no... I mean, I want to set you up in a flat where we can live together and love each other and I'll work like a slave and my father will buy me into a partnership and then I'll be able to provide for us, and then we will marry, whether he relents or not.'

'No.'

'But Lizzie, use your head. If I survive this war I shall be able to offer you far more money and security that way than if I marry you now.'

'No, no, and a thousand times no.'

'You're wrong to mistrust me, Lizzie. The fact that the law wouldn't recognize any children would mean nothing in practical terms, because I *have* made a will. Before Loos when lots of us were writing our last wills and testaments I made mine leaving everything I have to you. Absolutely everything.'

She looked at him open-mouthed. 'Did you, Freddie?'

'Yes. Now will you agree? I couldn't do better than that if we were married, could I?'

Except I'd get a pension for the rest of my life, she thought, and I suppose officers' widows don't do too badly. And anyhow, wills are easily changed, and men are fickle. 'I've got a better idea,' she said. 'We'll get married and say nothing about it until you've got your partnership and everything else you want.'

'Deceive the old man, you mean?'

Far rather that, than deceive the young trollop. 'Yes,' she said. 'It's no more than he deserves.'

He tossed his coat onto the bed and sent the hat spinning after it, and with his hands up sank into her armchair. 'All right, you win. I don't really like deception, but I see my offensive's failed. I'm beaten. You win.'

She fell onto his knees and clasped her arms round his neck, looking intently into his eyes. 'And I claim you for my prisoner. Say: "I surrender".'

'Yes, trollop,' he laughed, 'you've carried all before you in the counter-attack, and I'm shot, shelled, gassed, and machine gunned into defeat.'

'Say it, then.'

He groaned. 'I surrender. I knew I should have to, in the end. That's why I went to the Inns of Court and got a special licence. We can be married anywhere you like, as long as we can find a parson willing to perform the ceremony.'

'Freddie, you monster. Were you just teasing me about living together, then?'

'No. Marriage has other serious disadvantages for me.'

'What?'

'Well, when we're respectably married I shan't be able to call you things like heartless whore, or tormenting trollop, which is such a relief to my feelings when you're being at your most damnable, Lizzie. You will promise to be a sweet, loving little wife, won't you? A faithful, kind little wife, and always be s'nice to me?'

She looked into a pair of hopeful grey eyes, and wondered what was supposed to be the difference between a child born in wedlock, and one not. There were no marks of the devil on him. His face was as handsome as the general run of faces beneath the traces of anxiety and battle fatigue still lingering there. She felt a stab of sympathy for him. 'I shan't be damnable, as you call it, when we're married, because I'll feel safe whatever happens, and I'll be more able to trust you. And just to prove it I won't ask you to explain what you were doing in the worst streets in Soho.'

'That's nice of you, Lizzie,' he said, beginning to pull the pins out of her hair. 'But I'm going to tell you, anyway. Do you remember my doing this once before?'

'I'm not likely to forget, am I?'

'You've got beautiful hair. The way it's cut at the front reminds me of raven's wings. I'm glad you haven't had it all cut off. I thought you might have.'

'I almost did, to play Tommy Buttons.'

He leaned towards her to kiss her. 'Is it bedtime yet?'

'Time you went to your father's, or to sleep at your club, do you mean?'

'Yes, of course. That's why I brought my valise, so I could leave it here and sleep somewhere else.'

She gave him a sidelong look and raised her eyebrows.

'I keep trying my luck, don't I?' he smiled, making no move to go.

She made no move to make him, and in the end she got up and made cocoa for them both on Georgie's gas ring.

'Isn't this wonderfully peaceful and domestic?' he said when she handed him a cup. 'So peaceful it seems totally unreal, after everything that's happening in France. I'll do everything I can to make you happy, you know. You can be absolutely sure of that.'

He really meant it. She sat on the footstool beside him and on an impulse took his hand, to kiss it and hold it against her cheek.

After a long pause, he said: 'Ashton's not the name on my birth certificate, or my certificate of baptism, and I had to show the certificate of baptism to get the marriage licence.'

'What is your real name, then? Your mother's name, I mean?'

'Bowman.'

'Hmm,' she mused, 'Lizzie Bowman. I like the sound of it. Much better than Lizzie Wilde.'

'Why not Lizzie Ashton?'

'Yes, that's all right as well. But I like Bowman better. It sounds so English. So ... "once more unto the breach..." sort of thing. It suits you, Freddie.'

'Does it? I envy the bowmen of Agincourt, Lizzie. They had one leader who was a leader, and no allies or politicians to confuse the issue, and their battle was over and done with in the space of a day, with only a hundred or two dead – nothing but a minor skirmish compared to our shows. But are you sure it doesn't bother you?'

'What?'

He felt for his cigarettes and matches, then slowly lit a cigarette and inhaled deeply. 'The fact that I'm illegitimate. Not exactly what you took me for, am I? Of course, there's a cruder word than illegitimate, but I won't offend you by using it.'

She pulled herself up to sit beside him on the chair arm. 'Why not? You offend me by saying bad words about me. Give me a drag on your cigarette, Freddie.'

He held the cigarette to her lips for a moment. 'I don't offend you at all, because we both know I only use them when you've exasperated me to the limit, and I only mean them in that instant, and they're not really true anyway. But "bastard" is absolutely true, at least when it's applied to me. Does it bother you, Lizzie? I want to know – not that I can do anything about it. But I think we must be straight with each other now we're to be man and wife, don't you?'

Straight with each other? She turned her face to blow the smoke away, pondering on that for all of two seconds before deciding against it. Still, she could give an honest answer to his first question. 'Well, it doesn't seem to be bothering me at the moment, does it, Freddie?'

'Shall I tell you what I was doing in Soho?'

'Yes, if you like.'

'I used to promise myself I'd find my mother one of these days, only I never got round to it because time seemed endless, and there was always something more pressing to do until the war. Then it seemed as if I were looking down a telescope and things that used to be a long way off – like death – were suddenly very near, right at the end of my nose in fact. So I began my search, starting with the streets whose names I remembered. I wanted to use my father's money to help her if I could. I wanted to lavish it on her. I thought she had a perfect right to it. Does that shock you?'

'No. Not at all.'

'She had such a pinching, scraping sort of a life, you see. My mother really did know something about dodging into doorways to avoid people she owed money to. I remember her bundling us up in clothes in the middle of the night and the next thing we knew we'd be on a cart pulled by a horse with its hooves muffled by rags, moving on under the stars to a new address – an exercise generally known as a moonlight flit. It was quite exciting. We thought it was a game.'

'Why did she have to run away from the rent man, if your father's so well off? Is he so bloody mean he let you live from hand to mouth?'

'The short answer to that is yes. He had a spite against her, you see. My brother was born when I was about three, and my father knew he couldn't be his. I think he had some doubts about me after that. Of course, he stopped paying the rent on the flat we were in, and that was when we began our gipsy lives. Soho was the last place we lived. I say, Lizzie, I've brought a drop of whisky. Have you got a glass?'

She had a couple of very nice cut glass tumblers, another loan from Georgie, and brought him one. He got up and took a silver hip flask from the pocket of his greatcoat and poured himself a generous measure of golden liquid. In the mellow light of the lamp it gleamed beguilingly through the facets of the glass. She picked it up and inhaled the aroma, sipped a little, coughed and pulled a face, and handed him the glass as he sat down again. 'I don't know how you can stand the stuff. It's horrible,' she said, resuming her seat on the footstool.

'I'm glad you think so. But it gets us through some trying times.'

'Well, how did you all survive, if she got nothing from your father?'

'She eked a living for us making embellished blouses – you know, the really fancy ones in beautiful colours, with beading and lace and whatnot that were in fashion years ago, that the big department stores used to sell for pounds and pounds. She used to manage about seven a week, at tenpence or a shilling each. Later on she started making copies of Paris fashions for ladies who were better off than us, but not well off enough to buy from the shops – a sort of corner dressmaker. And she did get something from him. He used to arrive now and then to slap a few pounds down on the sewing machine where she was working. Even at that age I sensed it gave him some satisfaction to see her slaving like that.'

'So that's who I reminded you of when you first saw me. Your mother.'

He nodded.

'And is that why you've always had a partiality for dressmakers? And why you were so interested in what they paid me at de Laceys?'

'No. It was just that you filled me with lust.'

She gave a little tut of disapproval. 'Go on then, with what you were telling me.'

'Where was I?'

'He slapped money down on the sewing machine.'

'Oh, yes. Well, he never spared my brother a glance, but he used to have a very good look at me. I certainly used to feel myself under inspection, I can tell you, and then he'd be off, and we wouldn't see him again for weeks. But the day I was seven he came and carried me out of the house and bundled me into a motor car, and my mother ran down the street after it, screaming, with tears streaming down her face. My brother was bawling his head off too.'

'I shouldn't think you were very happy, either.' She waited for him to go on, but he was silent so long that she had to prompt him. 'Well? What happened next?'

He looked at his cigarette, burned to ash. He lit another and inhaled as if his life depended on it. 'I found myself in a house like a mausoleum and I was put to bed in a room on my own, instead of the bed I was used to sharing with my mother and my brother. I was angry and terrified. They very soon discovered I could barely read, and I proclaimed my lowly origins every time I opened my mouth. So they had an illiterate who spoke and behaved like a member of the criminal classes on their hands, and I was determined to make myself so objectionable that they'd take me back where I belonged.

'My father's wife had three little girls. I think she thought I might contaminate them in some way. They all disliked me intensely, which is hardly surprising. A week later I was a boarder at a crammer, worrying about my mother and aching for home, and wishing I were my brother instead of myself. I ran away a few times and once I got all the way back home. My mother wept to see me, but my father had put a watch on the house, and after he'd been to see her she told me I'd have to go back to school. I was absolutely devastated and I hated her for it – for years afterwards. And when I got back to school the headmaster made me stand outside his office for the rest of the day, waiting for a caning.'

She was surprised to see a broad smile on his face as he went on: 'I think he intended it as a sort of refinement of cruelty, but by the time he came out for me I was shaking with laughter. Nerves, I think, but in the end I'd laughed myself into such a state I didn't give a hang about the beating. But it was pointless to run off home again and I had nowhere else to run to, so I had to stick it.'

She sat on his knee and traced the contours of his face with her fingers, from broad, masculine brow to firm chin, and then kissed a cheek already growing rough with bristle, murmuring, 'Oh, dear. Poor little Freddie.'

He took another puff of his cigarette. 'Well, because of his accent, poor little Freddie was soon dubbed "the Beast of Bethnal Green" by the other boys, and he quickly learned that boys are pack animals who get their thrill from the quarry's fright, and if they can make him cry or run, well – that's the high point of their pleasure. That cadre we met at the Karsino used to amuse themselves like that with boys who didn't quite "fit in". They made my life a burden for a time, but I would rather have died than knuckle under. They were so determined to make me crack that they nearly drowned me in a bath one night. Lucky for me one of the masters heard the commotion and spoiled the fun, and I was left pretty much alone after that. So, poor little Freddie soon toughened up, you see.' He stubbed out his cigarette and took a mouthful of whisky, looking at her through speculative, narrowed eyes. 'And then he grew into lecherous big Freddie, Freddie the libertine, terror of the fair sex, particularly actresses who go by the name of Lizzie Wilde.' He put down his glass, leaned towards her and kissed her again and again, slowly and sensuously. With mounting excitement she responded kiss for kiss until she felt his hand on her breast.

She removed the hand and in very decided tones said: 'Sorry, Freddie, but that's as far as the s'nice games go with Lizzie Wilde; she's a reformed character. You'll have to wait for Lizzie Bowman.'

He frowned, his grey eyes darkened, and a flush spread across his cheeks as he pushed her away and stood up. 'I've asked you to be my wife, and you've accepted. I've got the licence in my pocket – we can be married within the week. I've told you everything there is to tell about myself, things I've never told another living soul, and still, *still* you won't trust me, you heartless, heartless ... tormenting ... exasperating...' He snatched up his hat and his greatcoat with the bullet hole eighteen inches from the hem, and with a final 'bloody actress!' hurled himself downstairs and out into the freezing February night.

Chapter Twelve

'You won't understand a word any of them say, you know, Freddie,' she told him as they boarded the train the following morning. 'I shall have to translate everything. Except for my mother of course. She was very well brought up. Her father was a schoolmaster – a headmaster as a matter of fact. And you'll probably understand our Ginny, come to think of it, she was a singer on the halls and lived in London for three or four years...'

'I shall probably understand them all,' he said, squeezing on behind her.

'Ugh!' She wrinkled her nose in distaste at the sight and smell of a carriage full of trench foul veterans, all of them privates or non-commissioned officers. 'Phew, it's a bit whiffy,' she said, flapping her hand in front of her face.

'Shush,' he murmured, taking hold of her hand to still it. 'Do you think they don't know it? Don't you think they hate it more than anybody? They'll have been travelling all night, most of them, straight from the Front, with no time to clean up, and I doubt if many of them have more than four days leave. Sit down and make the best of it.'

'But they're probably crawling with lice,' she hissed.

'No doubt they are, and so was I, a couple of days ago. Don't worry, Lizzie. Just sit down and cross your fingers and hope you don't get typhus,' he said, ushering her up the aisle.

She sat down next to a haggard looking private of about forty whose head was swathed in bandages and closed her eyes, listening to Freddie discussing the Government's recently introduced Conscription Act with the sergeant behind her. All the blighters who wouldn't volunteer to help their country were going to be *made* to do their bit now, and not before time. She listened to him growing warm on the subject of shirkers and profiteers, and passionate about *'bloody reporters and their newspaper patriotism,'* and the corners of her mouth twitched upwards.

What a nasty turn he'd given her, though, when he'd rushed out into the night, and in that moment she knew how different from Irma she really was. She was sick of uncertainty, of wondering whether she would find another decent job, tired of wondering how long she would be able to pay the rent, fed up of doing battle for herself. She wanted a man to do battle for her. She wanted to be respectable. She wanted to be Mrs Captain, and how very glad she'd been when

Freddie returned half an hour later, throwing gravel at her window, begging to be let in. She'd tried to feign displeasure when she went down to open the door for him, but he saw through it and told her so, and her relief was so immense that she threw herself into his arms and shed tears. They had such a wonderfully softening effect on him that he carried her back upstairs and with kisses and fondlings began another campaign of gentle s'niceness. But marriage lines in the hand are worth any amount of promises in the bush, and her brain wasn't so addled with emotion that she was in any danger of losing sight of her own interests. So, wary of offending him again she struck on the happy thought of pleading the curse as the reason for refusing him in the first place, then feeling his gaze concentrated on her she blushed at the lie, and was glad to see he took her blushes for evidence of modesty.

What an outpouring of concern and chivalry that had brought forth, so much that Lizzie thought if she were capable of loving any man, it would be him. He was her slave. He'd hardly known what to do to make amends, and they'd lain in each other's arms for most of the night, as chaste as two angels. She closed her eyes to savour the memory, wishing she could close her nose as easily.

She had only herself to blame. The first class carriages had been full, and Freddie had wanted to wait and travel first class on a later train. She was the one who had been too impatient, who had wanted to be off. What a journey this was going to be. She may as well make herself as comfortable as possible and catch up on her lost sleep, if that were possible on this overcrowded, stinking cattle truck.

I want to go home, I want to go home,
I don't want to stay in the trenches no more,
Where whizzbangs and shrapnel they whistle
  and roar.
I want to go over the sea, where the Kaiser can't
  fire shells at me,
Oh my, I don't want to die; I want to go home.

I want to go home, I want to go home,
I don't want to visit la belle France no more,
For oh, the Jack Johnson's they make such a
  roar,
Take me over the sea, where the snipers, they
  can't get at me,
Oh my, I don't want to die; I want to go home.

Amid the soporific clatter of the wheels and the mix of murmured conversation and muted singing which drifted into her drowsy slumbers there came a familiar baritone. It couldn't be. The singing stopped and she opened her eyes just as the train screeched into York Station. When the crush and jostle of many people getting off with their belongings and a few others getting on was over Lizzie got up and wandered down the aisle looking to right and left, and then on into the next carriage. And there he was, in front of her – her brother John with his eyes closed, just falling into a doze with his head lolling against the back of the seat. She stood rooted to the spot for a moment, surprised to see him, and imagining his surprise on seeing her. She stole forward and put a hand on his shoulder. An instant later she felt her wrist roughly grasped and gave a yelp of pain as she stared into a pair of eyes whose depths held all the wariness and mistrust of a wild animal.

It was a second or two before he recognized her, and became himself again. 'Why, it's our Lizzie! Why did you not let me know you were coming home, bonny lass!'

'I could say the same thing,' she said, ruefully rubbing her wrist.

'Sorry. I'm a bit too quick for civilization. It comes of spending too much time where you can hardly be quick enough. I didn't know I was coming home mesel', until a couple of days ago. This is the leave I should have had four months since.'

'Come on, John. There's somebody I want you to meet.' She took her brother by the hand and dragged him forward until they reached a couple of seats next to Ashton, vacated when passengers got off at York. 'Freddie, this is my brother John. John, this is Captain Frederick Ashton. We're getting married. In fact, you can give me away, John.'

'Can I?' She was surprised to see John give Freddie as smart a salute as was possible on a train. Freddie returned it, then offered his hand.

'This puts me in a bit of a quandary, sir. Do I treat you as a brother-in-law, or as a superior officer?'

'A brother-in-law, of course!' Lizzie exclaimed.

'A brother-in-law, of course,' Freddie repeated, 'in private. But when we're in public and in uniform we'd better observe the necessary form, for both our sakes.'

The awkwardness between them that the difference in rank made was marked, and after John had gone back to 'join the lads' she commented on it to Freddie.

'I can't help it, Lizzie. I meant no slight on your brother, but it would be no good to either of us if we were reported for fraternizing. We'd lose both rank and pay. That's what happens to officers and NCOs. Privates are sentenced to field punishment.'

'What's that?'

'Being made to do drill for hours with a full pack, and then being roped hand and foot to something like a gun wheel for hours at a stretch, day after day. The modern substitute for a flogging, and not at all pleasant. But once we're out of uniform rank won't count for anything, and we'll get on splendidly together.'

Walking between the two men along familiar streets, Lizzie saw a profound change in John. His eyes were everywhere. 'Plenty of good sniping positions round here,' he remarked to Freddie. 'Over there, just behind that hedge.'

He nodded towards the spot where laughing Tom Peters had taken her hand and pulled her out of sight of prying eyes to give her his first sweet kiss, and she winced at the memory of his treachery.

'All right, hinny? I didn't want to frighten you.' It was John who spoke, John who saw the expression of pain that flitted across her face.

'Yes, I'm all right. Just a bit cold, that's all.' She took hold of both their hands. 'Can't we forget about the war for a bit? You've come home to get away from all that.'

Freddie looked over her head towards John, and with a voice full of irony said: 'Forget about the war, sergeant. That's an order.'

A few yards further down the road, John clasped her briefly in his arms. 'Aye, well, this is where we part company, bonny lass. I'm going home to Elsie, although I'm ashamed to, in this state. Tell me Mam I'll be along later. Goodbye, Captain Ashton.' With a smart salute to Freddie, he turned and marched away in the direction of Annsdale Colliery. Lizzie watched him go, a stark outline against the white background of a snow filled sky.

'How do men live in trenches, on days like these?' she shivered.

Lizzie gave a short rap on her mother's door, and led Freddie inside. A couple of her sister Emma's boys were playing on the clippy mat and her mother was busy at the frame, stitching a quilt. She glanced up and started at the sight of them, then pushed the frame aside and came forward, smiling a welcome through sudden tears.

'Our John's at home, an' all,' Lizzie told her when they were clasped in each other's arms, 'but he's gone straight home. I suppose he'll be round to see you after he's said hello to Elsie. I don't know how long that's going to take.'

'Oh.' Her mother produced a handkerchief from her apron pocket, dabbed her eyes and blew her nose. 'Why, it'll take a while, I suppose. He's been away eighteen months, so they'll have plenty to talk about.'

Freddie raised his eyebrows for a fraction of a second, and gave an innocent smile. Lizzie introduced him to her mother and then nodded in the direction of the two boys. 'Where's our Emma?'

'In Newcastle, in Elswick's munitions factory. Our Ginny's looking after three of the lads, and I've got these two. She says she might as well make hay while the sun shines, and get a bit of money put by while she's got the chance. Oh, but it's tiring work, Lizzie, and it's dangerous. She walks from the station nearly too tired to put one foot in front of the other. And fancy, John's home as well, is he? And why did neither of you write, for pity's sake?' She rested a hand on Lizzie's arm, a gesture part welcome, part reproach. 'The first time you've been home since you went to London, Lizzie! I wish you'd let me know you were coming. I've nothing in the house to feed you on.' Her manner a little guarded, she turned to Freddie and said: 'Give me your hat and coat, Captain Ashton. I'll hang them in the hall, and Lizzie'll take you into the front room while I make us a cup of tea.'

Freddie took off his greatcoat and handed it to her, with Emma's boys gazing at him in fascination. No wonder, Lizzie thought. Tall, broad shouldered and trim in his service jacket and Sam Browne belt, he was the very model of a hero.

The old Norman church loomed ahead, an eerie sight in the fast fading light, seeming to Lizzie like a ghost from a bygone age. The stillness of the air was suddenly broken by the flight of an owl, in search of unwary prey. Freddie nodded towards the bell tower, illuminated by the quarter moon.

'Now there's a good sniping position. I should certainly put a man up there to pick off a few of the enemy.'

'I went to a service in St Aidan's when the *Titanic* went down,' Lizzie said, and remembered the feel of Tom's arm round her waist as they walked through the archway afterwards and her dreams of walking through it again as his bride. 'That's where I wanted to get married.'

'Then I'll go and see about it.'

That wasn't what she'd meant. The words expressed a long dead hope and had come out before she thought to check them, but she could hardly tell him that. She glanced up at the bell tower and had a sudden vision of laughing Tom Peters hiding there, taking careful aim with his Enfield rifle. With a shudder she said: 'I doubt the Rector would agree to it.'

'Why not?' he challenged.

'Why, you know what it's like in villages. We're pretty far down the pecking order here, and to make matters worse, the Rector's son wanted to marry the girl that ended up marrying our John. It caused a bit of a stir at the time, and more than a bit of ill feeling.'

'I see. And there's been ill feeling ever since, I suppose? Well, never mind. I'll go and talk to him. Is his son at the Front?'

'How do I know?'

Freddie frowned. 'Well, whether he is or not, I'll

make it very clear that only an absolute bounder and a traitor to his country would refuse a service-man in wartime. He won't say no. He won't dare.'

'Aye, Martin's away in France,' Ginny told her, 'although I don't know where. I don't think he does either, most of the time. So I'm having to manage on me own, and I've got our Emma's bairns to look after while she's at work. But I can't say business here's booming. What with Lloyd George's new licensing laws, and a lot of the men working away, I'm hardly rushed off my feet. And now our Phil's enlisted an' all. He's barely sixteen and they've taken him, even though a blind man can see he's nowhere near old enough. Martin'll go mad when he finds out. I daren't write and tell him. But what about you, what's happening?'

'We've been to me Mam's, unpacked our cases, had a cup of tea and Freddie's gone down to see the Rector about us getting married. The sooner the better, he says. I thought our John might be here,' said Lizzie, looking round the empty pub. 'He's had plenty of time.'

'Aye, well, it'll take him at least three hours to say hello to Elsie. He'll be along when that's done. Ee, but you're coming up in the world, our Lizzie. Fancy you marrying an army captain! When's it to be?'

'As soon as the Rector will marry us. A day or two at most. Freddie's got a special licence.'

'Is he Church of England, like? I suppose he is, being a captain.'

'I suppose so. I never asked. He's gone because

216

he thought I wanted to get married there.'

'It would be the last place I'd pick, and that stuck-up old hypocrite would be the last parson I'd ever want to do my wedding. And only a couple of days? You're not giving us much time, Lizzie man!' Ginny said, and then with a sly smile and her eyebrows raised, asked: 'And where's me Mam putting you two to sleep, then?'

Lizzie frowned. 'Why, where do you think? She wanted me to sleep with her, but I wouldn't. So I'm in the room I used to share with our Sal, and Freddie's in the one our John and Arthur slept in. And I don't want you making any of your bawdy comments when he gets here, either. I want you on your best behaviour.'

'Is there not a law against standing drinks for people now?' John asked.

'Aye, there is,' said Ginny. 'There's a law against just about everything. But we don't take much notice. We're far enough away to do just about anything we like here.'

Freddie laughed. 'What will you have, John?'

'A pint of beer, thanks Ca... Freddie.'

Ginny pulled the pint. 'And I suppose you'll want a whisky, Freddie?'

'Yes, a good Scotch malt will do for me.' He took out a ten shilling note.

'You can put that away. These are on the house,' Ginny told him.

Smiling her approval, Lizzie asked: 'Well, what did the Rector say?'

'He wasn't there. They said he'd been out with the Hunt and they'd expected him back half an

217

hour ago, so I waited for a while, and then I got tired of it. I'll go on the way back.'

It was only a week to Ash Wednesday, and if the Rector couldn't or wouldn't marry them before then it would be too late, because he wouldn't marry them during Lent. She recalled the Rector's cold hostility towards them after the breach between Elsie and his son, and imagined him performing their wedding ceremony with that familiar expression of icy disdain on his face. Him and Tom, they would be like two bad fairies at a christening, with the memory of Tom's sister Alice to make a third. Seized by misgivings she said: 'I've changed my mind about a church wedding, Freddie. Let's just go into Durham and get married in the registry office.'

'Suits me, as long as you're sure. I'd much rather have a civil ceremony. I've never been enamoured of parsons, and some of those in France have put me off religion for life.'

John was grinning from ear to ear.

'What?' Freddie asked. 'What have I said?'

'Nothing that I haven't thought,' John told him.

Lizzie was surprised to see the Rector on the doorstep the following day. Her mother ushered him into the front room, and disappeared into the kitchen to make tea, leaving her and Freddie to deal with him. He'd heard that a Captain Ashton had been looking for him, and full of patriotic duty and Christian charity, he was willing to do what the Captain wanted – provided he could give satisfactory answers to a few pertinent questions, of course. Freddie caught her eye and raised a quizzical eyebrow The corners of her mouth twitched downwards and she gave a barely perceptible shake of her head.

'It's awfully decent of you to have come, sir, and I'm most frightfully sorry to have troubled you,' Freddie told him, 'but you see, we want to tie the knot with the least delay, and so we've decided on the registry office in Durham.'

The Rector's smile became a grimace. 'I advise you most sincerely to reconsider. Matrimony is a very serious thing, a thing to be undertaken only once and until death do you part. It should be solemnized in the presence of God.'

'I suppose,' said Freddie, 'that *that* is simply a matter of opinion.'

The Rector pulled himself up to his full height and faced Freddie squarely. 'You're mistaken in your supposition, young man, it's "simply" a matter of fact.'

Freddie fleetingly raised his eyebrows and inclined his head slightly, but returned the Rector's gaze with a mouth set in a resolute line and eyes that did not waver.

'Then as you seem to be quite decided, I won't stay to tea,' the Rector said, 'and I sincerely hope that your marrying in such haste will not lead to a leisured repentance.'

Freddie gave a slight shrug. Lizzie stood up and prepared to show the Rector out.

He hesitated in the doorway. 'Please give my apologies to your excellent mother, Miss Wilde. I hear you're living in London now?'

She nodded confirmation.

'Perhaps you sometimes see something of those

old friends of yours there – Miss Peters and her brother? I hear she's working as a VAD in one of the London hospitals. He's in the North-umberland Fusiliers, unless I'm much mistaken. I was at his wedding, but not officiating. I'm well acquainted with his uncle. A very good family, as I daresay you know, and he chose his wife well.'

Tom was married, then. How she did it she would never know, but Lizzie kept her face a blank, and staring straight through him, mur-mured an indifferent 'Indeed.'

The Rector gave her a venomous smile, and turned again to Freddie. 'Good day to you, sir.'

Poisonous, poisonous, poisonous old viper! He knew! With her feelings a tumult of pain, shame and fury she led him to the door.

She'd managed to avoid Annsdale and all the humiliation associated with it for the past three years. What on earth had possessed her to let Ashton bring her back to the place?

Chapter Thirteen

'We've been to the registry office, and they can marry us on the sixth,' Lizzie announced after Freddie had gone upstairs to inspect the uniform he'd had cleaned to wear for the wedding. 'As long as you sign permission.'

John was sharing a cup of tea with their mother, his legs stretched out before the fire. Their mother sighed and replaced her cup in the saucer, her mouth drooping at the corners, her face full of misgiving. 'I don't know, Lizzie,' she murmured, rolling her eyes towards the ceiling. 'Who is he? He might be another brides in the bath man for all we know. We know nothing about him.'

'What? Marry me and do me in, for what I've got? And him a Captain in the British Army? It's not very likely is it, Mother?'

'What about his family then? Why haven't we heard anything from them?'

'His father's away on business, and anyway, they don't get on all that well.'

Her mother's eyes were full of alarm. 'Does that mean he doesn't agree? Or hasn't he had the chance? Have you asked him?'

'Look, Mother,' said Lizzie, her jaw set in an obdurate line, her mind intent on having it her own way, 'if you don't sign, we'll go to Scotland and get married, so you won't stop us, you'll just make it a sight harder than it needs to be.'

The heat rose to her mother's cheeks. 'Well then, Miss Impudence, you'll only have yourself to blame if it all goes wrong, won't you?' The flush was followed by a sudden pallor. 'You're not pregnant, are you?'

Stung to anger, Lizzie retorted, 'No I'm not bloody pregnant! What do you think I am? Do people *have* to get pregnant in this family before they can get married?'

John straightened and gave her a warning look. 'That's enough, Lizzie. You've gone far enough, now.'

Cheeks burning, she cast him a smouldering glance and fell silent. After a moment or two her mother looked into her face and asked, in gentler tones, 'Are you sure you love him, Lizzie? Are you sure he's the right man for you? You haven't known him long, and we don't know him at all. That's all I mean.'

Still sullen, Lizzie said, 'I've known him a year, and I know him well enough to know he'll be all right.'

'I think she's right, Mam, if that's any comfort to you. I haven't known him two minutes, but I get a good feeling off him,' said John. 'I reckon he'll be as good a husband as most, as long as she treats him all right.'

'I'm doubtful,' her mother said. 'But if *you* think he's all right, I'll sign.'

How typical of her mother, she seemed to think that nobody but her favourite boy had any sense at all, Lizzie thought, but she could hear Freddie coming down the stairs again and put on a cheerful smile, determined to lighten the atmosphere with pleasant chatter.

'If you can play whist, you can learn to play bridge,' Freddie assured them, offering John a cigarette. 'The first thing you've got to do is value your hand. It'll improve your mental arithmetic, if nothing else.'

'What a cheek!' Elsie laughed. 'There's nothing wrong with my mental arithmetic.'

'Nor mine, either,' said Lizzie. 'Men seem to think women aren't capable of anything. And what about offering me a cigarette?'

'Not good for you,' said Freddie, 'and you mustn't set a bad example to your sister-in-law.'

'I never thought women aren't capable,' John protested, 'and anybody that did doesn't think so any more. As long as they get the separation allowance, most women seem to manage without men altogether.'

He looked so despondent that Lizzie wished she hadn't spoken, and Elsie protested: 'You know I hate you being away, John. I want you at home.'

'I know you do, bonny lass, but I've been away that long my own bairns don't know me, and I'm one of the lucky ones. Some lads find out they've got no wife or sweetheart to go back to, if she's got somebody nearer at hand – some conchie, or some bugger who's been crafty enough to get himself into a reserved occupation so he's got a clear field with other men's women.'

'That won't happen here,' Elsie said. She reached into the dresser and tossed a pack of cards onto the plush-covered mahogany table. 'Deal the cards out, then, and tell us how we value the hand.'

Freddie drew out a chair for Lizzie, and one for Elsie.

John dealt the cards. 'Away, then Lizzie. Set your cards out into suits.'

Freddie showed her how to set out her hand and add up the points. 'The suits have a ranking – clubs are lowest, then diamonds, then hearts, and spades are the highest. Aces count four points, kings three, queens two and knaves – or jacks – they count one point.' Then he leaned over Elsie's shoulder to help her. She looked well tonight, with her cheeks pink from the warmth of the fire, her dark hair pinned up; lamplight gave it a deep red lustre. She was wearing a beautiful pair of pearl drop earrings that John had brought back from France, and it wasn't as if Lizzie was besotted with him or anything, but the sight of Freddie's lips near those pretty little ears gave her an unexpected pang of jealousy. It was ridiculous, but she certainly did *not* want Freddie finding any other woman more attractive than her.

'Did you know, Freddie, that it was Elsie gave me that little horseshoe you're wearing?' she said. 'Sorry, Elsie, but I thought Freddie had more need of it than me.'

'Then I'm glad you gave it, Lizzie, and I hope it keeps him safe.'

'Superstition,' said John. 'If it's got your name on it, you'll get it, never mind lucky charms.'

'That's your superstition,' laughed Freddie. 'My charm's mine, and I'll tell you why. Fritz gave us a pretty lively time of it early last month. I was in support quietly drinking my afternoon tea when they started a massive artillery bombardment. Of course, I had to get to my post pretty quickly, so,' he felt for the string round his neck and retrieved the trinket, 'I touched my little horseshoe for luck and ran for it. I managed to get there without being hit and got the platoon sergeants to put the men under cover, all except the sentries – although I could hardly make myself heard. The ground was simply shaking with the impact of the shells. Even the rats were panicking. Just imagine it, hundreds of guns going at it like the clappers, and rapid *and* machine gun fire as well, and our gunners weren't long in replying, so the noise was simply deafening. We'd stood a fair bit of it when the Bosche let off mines under our trenches, and the earth heaved up into the sky like a mushroom, clods of earth as big as a horse flying through the air.'

His grey eyes sombre, Freddie raised his eyebrows and gave the two women a grim nod. 'I'd never really had the wind up before, except at Loos, but I did then. We heard later that men further down the line were buried alive in their dugouts. Then our bombers came to reinforce us and things quietened down a bit. I turned in at about eleven, but their guns started again at one o'clock and we all had to stand to arms again. The first strafe had been bad enough but it was nothing compared to the second. The whole place was simply jumping with reports, absolutely alive with them. We stuck it pretty well, and attacked the Bosche on our left, and he returned our fire, and not slightly either! Things eventually quietened down again, but we stayed ready for another attack, but do you know, in the end, our company had only half a dozen wounded and *not a single man killed*, and whether John believes it or not, I give all the credit to a certain lucky charm that came to me through the two charmers sitting beside us just now.'

'Aye, and they're not the only charmers, by the sound of it,' John laughed. 'Well, you got off light there, Freddie but I think its probably got more to do with the luck of the draw, and maybe a good leader. Away then, Elsie, let's see how lucky you are. If you've got ten points or more, you might have a bid.'

They'd played a few slow and laborious hands when Elsie put her cards down and listened. 'That's Ellie, crying.'

'Leave her. She'll soon turn over and go to sleep,' John said, but by the time they'd finished the hand, Ellie was in full flood, and Elsie went through the adjoining door into the kitchen and up the wooden stairs to her.

John stood up. 'Why, she might be a few minutes, so come and have a seat by the fire, Freddie. Away and put the kettle on for a cup of tea, Lizzie man. Put the pies in the oven, an' put the peas on an' all, while you're at it.'

Lizzie went into the kitchen and put the kettle on the range, trying to catch the snatches of conversation wafting through the open door. The men had begun talking in curiously quiet tones, and she strained to listen. Well, if they thought they were going to leave her out of the most interesting bits of the conversation, they'd find they were mistaken. Four mutton pies were standing on a baking sheet and there was a pan of soaked peas on the hearth. She slammed the pies into the oven and put the peas on the range and was back in the living room before they'd had time to utter another sentence.

She joined them by the fire. There was a silence, then John said, 'We can talk in front of our Lizzie, she's not easily upset. Freddie was just telling me the first dead man he saw in France had killed himself, Lizzie. Feller took his boot and sock off, put the rifle barrel in his mouth and squeezed the trigger with his toe. Blew the top of his head off

226

after hearing his wife had gone off with another chap.'

'Well, I'm not quite as heartless as John makes me out to be,' she assured Freddie. 'I think it's a shame.'

'You were saying that the worst of it was, you had to write to his wife, and tell her,' John prompted.

'Well, it's so awfully difficult, isn't it? Although I thought it would have served her right to know it, in the end I couldn't bring myself to say anything about the suicide. I just said he'd been killed in action and left it at that.'

'Things have turned out all right for that one, then,' John said, 'she's got a new man and she'll be able to claim a widow's pension she doesn't deserve. There's a lot of women have got a lot to answer for. I'm just very thankful my wife's not among them.'

'There's a lot of men have got a lot to answer for, an' all,' Lizzie protested.

'I agree, but there's no man been the cause of any woman having to face a firing squad, as far as I know, and that's happened a time or two in France.'

'When?' she demanded.

'To a sixteen-year-old I won't name, because as far as his family know he died a hero. He absconded, and got picked up by the redcaps trying to board a train, but when it came out that he'd tried to get home because of a letter from his lass saying she'd got somebody else, his commanding officer gave him seven days' field punishment, and told him if he tried that one on again he'd be in front of a court martial on a charge of desertion. Well, as soon as he got loose he absconded again, only this time he intended making sure he got past the redcaps so he burned his uniform and set off in civilian clothes – God knows where he got them from. Next thing is he's up in front of a general court martial for desertion. Well, there's no defence so the court's got no option but to give him the death penalty, with a recommendation for mercy. Unlucky for him there'd been a few breaches of discipline in the battalion and it didn't help him at all. Somebody decided an example had to be made, so the only mercy he got was a firing squad. The night before he got shot they gave the poor little bugger that much rum he passed out. He had to be carried to the place of execution – an abattoir wall, as it happens. We had to tie him to a pole, blindfolded like they are and with an envelope pinned to his jacket to show where his heart was. But nobody wanted to kill him, and so he was still alive after they'd fired. It was a right bloody balls up, man. In the end the commanding officer shot him through the head with his revolver. I was sick to my stomach – and when we went through his pockets there was a letter to his poor mother and one for the lass who'd let him down. I wouldn't like to have been her, getting that, but I doubt she did. I doubt they were ever sent. He haunted me for months. I went back to where we'd buried him a week or two after, and somebody'd nailed a board to the cross with: "Enlisted at sixteen. My King and Country's Gratitude" scrawled on it, and I thought whoever'd written that had done right. I changed my mind about pacifists there and then. I wished I'd been one myself.'

There was absolute silence for several moments, then Freddie asked, 'But how can men be pacifists when other nations threaten theirs?'

'I'll just go and see how the supper's getting on,' said Lizzie, and escaped, to sit by the kitchen range. They weren't bothering to keep their voices down now John was off on one of his socialist political speeches – he was beginning to sound like Ginny's husband. Freddie was countering with his 'once the sword is drawn against you, you've no choice but to fight' argument. She took the lid off the pan to stir the peas, and staring into the pan saw not them, but a sixteen-year-old tied to a post, blindfolded and with an envelope pinned to his chest.

'But what are we to do?' Freddie was saying. 'We've simply got to win, and to win we must have discipline. Didn't you see those pitiful streams of fugitives tramping the roads in Belgium and France, poor women with their children, fleeing their homes to save their lives, with whatever they could carry? You must have heard the stories of lads and girls being taken from their homes to God knows where, for Heaven knows what. And these are our allies, John, and if we let the Germans dominate Europe they'll soon start to dominate us. It might happen here – it *is* happening here. Think of what they've done to Scarborough, and Whitby, and Hartlepool. And the Zeppelins – killing our own women and children in their beds. Can we let that go unpunished? If we're not men enough to defend what's ours – well, all I can say is, we deserve to lose it.'

There was a creaking sound from the stairs as Elsie stole softly down them. 'Are they on about the war again?' she murmured.

'Yes, they are, and not very cheerful, either,' said Lizzie, flooded with grief for that young soldier, for the anguish that had brought him to an abattoir wall, and a firing squad, and a poor, shameful little grave. John saw how wicked it had been, so why couldn't Freddie?

Elsie put a hand on her shoulder, her eyes full of concern. 'Why, what's the matter, Lizzie?'

'Nothing,' she said, and releasing her breath in a long sobbing sigh she delved into her pocket for her handkerchief and blew her nose. 'I've just got a bit of a cold. Did you make the pies yourself, Elsie?'

'Why, yes. There's nobody else to do it.'

'You've learned to cook since you lived at my mother's.'

'Don't speak too soon. You haven't tasted them yet,' said Elsie.

'I should think this is the first time you've ever eaten pie and peas out of a bowl, with a spoon, Captain Ashton,' Elsie said.

'Freddie, please,' he reminded her. 'Yes, it is, and jolly good they taste too.'

'It'll make a nice change from champagne and caviar,' said John, with a sly smile.

'Yes, this is much more luxurious,' Freddie grinned, happily tucking in, and Elsie smiled too, at the compliment. Whatever his shortcomings, he seemed happy not only to tolerate her family, but to make himself one of them.

'Well, you've had the pie and peas,' said John, when the meal was over. 'Now try a glass of Newcastle brown ale.' He pulled the caps off a couple of bottles whilst Elsie stacked the bowls to take them through to the kitchen. Freddie accepted, and offered John a cigarette, but he had both hands occupied with bottle and glass, and Lizzie took it. Freddie frowned and shook his head disapprovingly, but gave John another, and lit his own and theirs. Lizzie inhaled the smoke, and conscious of Freddie's eyes on her, blew it nonchalantly down her nose. Elsie came in with tea and Freddie, with his cigarette dangling on his lip, dealt another round of cards.

'This is how we waste our time in France,' he told them.

'That's not what you were saying earlier,' Elsie said.

'Oh, but that sort of thing's a rarity. Most of the time we're just hanging around in support lines or in billets, waiting for something to happen. I bet John hadn't a clue how to play auction bridge before he went to France, had you?'

'No, I hadn't.'

'Nor had I. We've had plenty of time to learn, you see. But do you sometimes think, John, that it's England that seems like a dream, and France that seems like your real life?'

'Why, France has been real enough for the past year or more, I'll agree with you there, and I spent a lot of the time dreaming about being back in England. This is the first time I've been home on leave, and half of it's gone already. You look forward to coming home for months, and as soon as you do the days run away from you faster and faster and before you've had time to turn round it's time to go back. Still, I can see my little sister married, and who would ever have thought that?'

'A happy coincidence,' said Freddie, 'and a good opportunity for us to meet.'

'How many times have you been on leave, Freddie?' asked Elsie.

'Three. But once was after I'd been wounded. They gave me a few days before I went back.'

'Next time I'm on this earth I'm coming back as a captain. They seem to be on leave the best part of the time,' John teased. 'And I'll get better rations, an' all – roast sirloin instead of bully beef, and bread and potatoes instead of bloody dog biscuits. And even a servant to wait on me, polish my buttons and clean my webbing, make sure I get my hot water for shaving every morning, and a nice breakfast.'

'Come back as a brigadier,' said Freddie, 'they do even better. You can spend your war in a French chateau sleeping on feather beds, with the chatelaine attending to your every desire.'

'No, I'm happy enough among the men when I'm in France, and my wife's the only chatelaine I want.'

'Same here,' Freddie smiled at Lizzie. 'But you might well be a Captain before much longer, John, the way things are going. Fritz creates regular vacancies for new officers.'

'He creates regular vacancies in the ranks an' all,' said John.

'Shush,' said Elsie. 'Don't talk about it; it upsets Lizzie. Let's think about cheerful things while you're at home. What do they say at the Front? Keep merry and bright! I've got twelve points and no long suit. Can I bid?'

Chapter Fourteen

The strains of 'Celeste Aida' drifted from some far distant place as she felt his lips brush gently against hers. With her heart swelling with love for him she gazed into his adoring eyes and returned his tender smile. She was the one he wanted, the one he worshipped, his one and only love, and he had come back to her. He was her heart's desire and she was his, and life without him had been worse than death.

Now he was here beside her, and to feel his warmth against her was pure joy. She twined her cold limbs round him and kissed his cheek, imploring, 'Never leave me again, Tom. Promise me you'll never, never leave me again. Promise me, promise me.'

With all the blankets thrown off, chilled to the marrow and hugging a lifeless bolster she opened her eyes to shattering reality. He was gone, and gone for good, and on this bitter cold March day she was to be married to somebody else. Shivering, she let go of the bolster and climbed out of bed.

Her mother had put the tin bath before the kitchen fire, and was carefully filling it.

'The water's just hot enough. I lit the fire two hours ago. Get in now, while I make you some breakfast.'

'I couldn't eat any breakfast. I'll just have a cup of tea.'

Her mother pressed her, but Lizzie was adamant, and was eventually left in peace to bathe and drink her tea. Feeling a little warmer, she dried herself before the fire while her mother emptied the bath and tidied the kitchen. Getting into character for the part she was about to play, she dressed carefully in the elegant, light blue costume salvaged from the wardrobe of *Life's Enchanted Cup* and pinned up her hair. Then, with the fire thawing her she leaned towards the mirror above the mantelpiece, and began applying her red lipstick.

'Oh, Lizzie! That stuff on your mouth, and today of all days,' her mother protested, 'And I don't see why you couldn't have had a Christian wedding in the chapel either, instead of going to the registry office like a heathen.'

'It's all the same wherever you go. As long as you get the marriage lines, you're married just the same.' She rubbed her lips firmly together for a moment, then stretched them wide. Perfect. Not a hair out of place. Cool, calm, resplendent.

'You're not. You're half married in the registry office, and not the half that matters most, either,' her mother insisted. 'You're not married in the sight of God.'

'I'll be married enough for what I want,' Lizzie

said, putting on a white felt hat and fur-trimmed wrap, more salvage from the liquidators. She turned to her mother with a smile as bright and brittle as ice. 'There. How do I look?'

There wasn't a car or a carriage to be had, so Lizzie and her handful of relatives had no option but to take the train to Durham and walk to the registry office in Claypath, then cram into the anteroom and wait to be called in. She sat down on a hard chair and took stock of all her relations. They'd done their best, but they really were a set of old-fashioned, shabby country bumpkins, apart from Ginny, perhaps, and Elsie, maybe. Emma and Elsie kept complimenting her on her dress, her fetching little boots and her hair, and telling her how lovely she looked. She smiled her thanks, wishing she could say the same for them, but Emma looked ill, with dark rings under her eyes and her skin tinged yellow from working at the munitions factory and her husband Jimmy, a winder at the local pit, looked no better either. And although she'd once been reckoned the belle of Annsdale, even Elsie's gloss and glamour couldn't stand the cold light of day, and she was still wearing the same brick-red costume Lizzie had given her three years ago. Emma's boys looked clean and well brushed, but their clothes were either too big or too small – obviously cast-offs. Elsie's children, a boy of about four and a girl of two, were better dressed. All the children were staring at her, entranced. She gave them a brief smile now and then, wondering what Freddie really made of them all. The son of a diamond importer – he must wonder what on earth he was marrying into. She remembered his mother and brother, and consoled herself with the thought that they were probably still living from hand to mouth in the East End, and looked no better.

Tom's wedding must have been a far better show than this. They'd probably been driven to church in garlanded carriages, or Daimlers or Rolls Royces, with the ceremony conducted in a flower filled cathedral with a couple of hundred distinguished guests and a choir and peals of wedding bells, then on to a reception like the scene Lizzie had played so many times in *Life's Enchanted Cup* – with champagne and caviar, expensive gifts, and flattering speeches and the bride looking like a queen in lace and pearls.

Not like this cold and charmless place. She glanced towards Freddie, self-assured in faultless khaki with gleaming buttons and polished belt. He caught her eye and gave her a glad smile, and she pitied him for his blind trust in her. He was here for her sake, and without a soul of his own to cheer his wedding day and she thought how terrible it would have looked if they *had* gone to church, with hardly anybody on her side and nobody on his.

The Registrar called them, and because she wasn't twenty-one, he asked Lizzie's mother to sign permission for the marriage. After a fraction of a second's hesitation she did, and the ceremony began.

'I solemnly declare that I know not of any lawful impediment why I may not be joined in matrimony to Elizabeth Wilde,' Freddie repeated after the registrar.

Was there any impediment, she wondered? He wasn't the one she loved, but was that a lawful impediment? Well, if it was, she wasn't going to admit to it. She could never have Tom, and so it hardly mattered who she married. Captain Freddie, the dashing army officer and budding architect, would do very well, and so when her turn came she repeated the formula. John came forward with the ring, and Freddie slipped it onto the third finger of her left hand and, prompted by the registrar, called on 'the persons here present' to witness his taking of Elizabeth Wilde to be his lawful wedded wife. His voice was strong and clear, and he looked full of optimism. She glanced at his handsome, happy face and thought: Can't you sense I don't love you? That thought was quickly followed by another: Perhaps you'll be killed on the battlefield, or die of wounds somewhere, and then it won't matter that I never loved you.

It all seemed unreal, less real than a dream. Lizzie could see her mother holding her best lace handkerchief before her streaming eyes, but for herself, she'd felt more emotion playing Violet on the stage. Her turn again. She parroted the words perfectly, and it was all over, except for the signing of the book.

She watched Freddie's profile as he took up the pen, and thought he looked the perfect bridegroom. He *was* the perfect bridegroom, and she was struck by the pity of not loving him. He inscribed his name and as he handed her the pen he gave her a smile that lit up his whole face. By sheer reflex she returned the smile, took the pen from him and carefully wrote her name under his. After John and Ginny had witnessed their signatures the registrar handed Lizzie her marriage lines. Smiling her happy bride's smile she took them, wondering where Tom was at that instant, and whether he ever thought of her.

Mondays were slack days in the Cock. They rarely had any custom in the best room, so all the bar staff had been roped in to wait on the guests. Any stray customers would be served in the taproom. The best room looked wonderful, polished to brilliance with its roaring fire and glowing lamps reflected in the brass and copper ornaments. Ginny had seated them in the middle of a long trestle table covered with snow-white damask, decorated with swags of ivy and a few spring flowers and positively groaning with food of the wholesome, unadorned, rustic variety: thick slices of roast ham, roast pork, roast sirloin, a large ham and egg pie, bowls of winter salad and every variety of pickles, including Lizzie's favourite pickled damsons – her mother's speciality; fresh baked bread and pastries and fruitcake left over from Christmas. Freddie sat on Lizzie's left, her mother on her right. John was seated next to Freddie, and Ginny sat next to her mother, who leaned over her to speak to her new son-in-law.

'If there's one thing Ginny excels at–' their mother hesitated slightly before using his name, *'Freddie* – it's putting a decent spread on. I don't know how she's done it, in so little time, and with all the shortages...'

Lizzie choked the boasting off. 'Mother! It's not the Ritz, you know.'

'It looks better than the Ritz to me,' said Freddie. 'Better than anything I ever had there, anyway.'

Lizzie smiled then, and set herself out to be pleasing. 'It's a pity we couldn't have a dinner, Freddie, but at least we've got hot soup to warm us up for a start, and then baked potatoes with butter to go with the rest.'

'Aye, this is where we all congregate whenever we've got something to celebrate,' John concurred. 'The U boats will have to sink *all* our shipping to stop our Ginny making a splash for something like her sister's wedding. I don't know how you do it, bonny lass.'

'I'll tell you what the secret is,' Ginny laughed, 'I help other people, whenever I can, that is; and now I need a bit help, they're doing me a good turn.'

Lizzie's younger sister Sally hurried in, breathlessly removing her coat and scarf as she walked and flinging them on the coat stand. 'I'm sorry I couldn't get here in time to see you married, Lizzie man. The Doctor was going to drive me to the station for the early train, but there was an accident, and he couldn't. So I helped him with the patient, but I'm that vexed about it, I am really.' Flushed with her exercise she stopped, and looking at Freddie offered her hand. 'Oh, and you must be my new brother-in–law!'

Looking as pleased as punch, Freddie rose to his feet and shook her hand.

Lizzie demanded, 'You? Helped him with the patient?'

'Aye, I often do, when he needs a bit help. This morning it was a young lad that had taken a fall and broken his arm. I had to help him set it, soaking the plaster of Paris bandages for the pot and that. Fetching and carrying for him, you know,' she added, taking her seat at one of the small tables set below the wedding party where Elsie, and Emma and Jimmy sat keeping their children in order, among a handful of friends and neighbours. Sally pulled in her chair and looking at Lizzie with a self-deprecating little smile added, 'I help him in the dispensary an' all, measuring medicines out and putting them into bottles, counting pills out and things, and I explain how to make poultices and that – to the patients, you know. He's so busy now a lot of the doctors have gone to France or to the military hospitals. He says I'd make a good hospital nurse, and although he'd be sorry to lose me I ought to go because there's plenty wants doing, with all the wounded men coming back.'

A hospital nurse? Sally? Lizzie could hardly believe it, and would have gone on with her interrogation, but her mother gave her a nudge. John was on his feet to say a few brief words of congratulation, welcome and gratitude and to give the usual compliments and good wishes, including those of absent friends. 'I know they'll all send you their best wishes for a long and happy married life, as we all do. And now I hope you'll all join me in raising your glasses to the happy couple.'

After the toast Freddie stood up to thank them all, and ended by telling them: 'You won't be surprised to know that I fell for Lizzie hook, line and sinker the very first time I saw her in de Lacey's theatre, and I promise you all I'll love her and cherish her for the rest of my days.'

Jimmy clambered up onto the dais at the end of Ginny's concert-cum-function room. He opened the piano lid and played the first few bars of the Destiny Waltz, then paused. 'Away then, let's see you dance your first waltz as man and wife,' he urged.

All eyes were on the newlyweds. Freddie caught Lizzie's hand and swung her round to face him, then propelled her into the middle of the floor. 'I might not be much good at the tango,' he murmured, 'but I can dance anyone else off the floor doing a waltz.'

'All right, Freddie,' she humoured him, thinking he was no better at the waltz than he was at the tango, but no matter, there was a round of applause from the spectators. The rest followed, including Lizzie's old employer Mr Surtees and his wife. With both their men in France, Ginny began to dance with Kath, Arthur's wife. Sally and Emma soon followed suit, and the children began to hop around the floor too. The few lads had come out of the taproom and were standing in the doorway to see what was going on. They soon regretted it.

'Away, why should women have to dance with

each other when there's all these bonny lads standing about?' Ginny demanded, physically dragging them into the room and allotting them partners.

As soon as they had cleared away the tables in the best room and done the washing up, Ginny's barmaid, Maudie, came to join the party with her husband Ned and the other helpers. The strains of the Northumberland pipes were added to those of the piano. The floor was full, and the newlyweds stood out to watch the other dancers.

'Oh, Lizzie, I rue the day you left me,' Mr Surtees was at her elbow. Grey hair thinning on top, but still luxurious round the sides, moustache flourishing on upper lip, he put her in mind of Lloyd George. 'I can get as many orders for uniforms as I can fill,' he told Freddie, 'but I haven't enough workers.'

'Enough, Mr Surtees? When I was here, you only had me.'

'Why, I've got four lasses now, all working hell for leather, but they're not a patch on you, Lizzie. What'll you take to come back?'

'I can't come back, Mr Surtees. I'm a married woman now.'

'And maybe your husband's needing a new uniform?' The tailor appraised Freddie with a professional eye, touching him on the shoulder and turning him, the better to see the way the sleeve was set. 'Why who's made this? They heven't got it sitting right at the shoulders. When you want a one that fits you right, Captain, you come to me. I'll mek you a better one than you'll get anywhere in London.'

242

'Get away with you, Mr Surtees – it fits perfectly. It came from Ellis's military tailor's in the Strand,' Lizzie laughed.

'And how much did you give for it?' Mr Surtees' large, bright hazel eyes looked over his spectacles, expectantly into Freddie's.

'Goodness, I'm not sure. I mean, I can't quite remember,' said Freddie. 'About four guineas, I think.'

Surtees turned to his wife, 'Hear that, Mary? About four guineas – *he thinks!* Ee, these Southerners, they must hev money to burn. Away, lass, Ginny's waving at us. They want another pair for the dancing. Excuse us, Captain.'

And what was going into the Surtees' bank account every week, Lizzie wondered? They were certainly doing all right out of the war. When she'd gone to Ellis's to be measured for her pantomime outfit she'd looked round that snooty, polished place and thought the same, that she wouldn't complain if she had a pound or two less than Ellis in the kitty. Winners and losers, that's what war creates, and John was right. The losers are the patriotic cattle who volunteer to defend their country by throwing their lives away at the Front, and the winners are the people who stay quietly at home feathering their own nests and keeping themselves and their own well out of harm's way. She knew which side she'd rather be on.

Now some more traditional tunes set a livelier pace. Lizzie stood out with Freddie and watched the others: Ginny and one of the lads from the taproom, John and Elsie, Mr and Mrs Surtees

243

and Ned and Maudie, all dancing a reel.

'I say, Surtees can go rather, can't he? For a fellow his age.'

'I don't know why they had to start that,' Lizzie murmured. 'It's not the sort of music you're used to at all.'

'Perhaps not,' he smiled, clapping to the beat of the music and nodding encouragingly at the dancers, 'but it's traditional, and now I'm married to a Northern girl, I shall get used to it. I shall grow to like it.'

'You don't have to bother for me. I haven't been a Northern girl for the past three years.'

'Don't frown, Lizzie. You're a Northern girl born and bred.'

'Hmm!' She gave a little snort of dissent, 'I don't have to stay the way I was born and bred. I can change things, and I have. I'm a London girl now, and a bit more refined in my tastes.'

'Don't become too refined to know the value of what you have here,' he said.

'What have I got here that's so marvellous?'

'A family that loves you, Lizzie! Your own mother, and brothers and sisters. People you can count on. People who put themselves to a lot of trouble to make you happy.'

Emma was the first to leave. 'These bairns are falling to sleep. I'll have to get them home to bed, Lizzie man, and I've got to be up at the crack of dawn tomorrow, to get to work,' she said. The dark rings under her eyes were darker still, her skin seemed yellower. Lizzie had seen many a girl like that on the buses in London, and heard some of their conversations about friends injured in the machinery, and about a doctor telling them: 'Half of you girls will never have babies.' And no one was supposed to know that some girls had died of TNT poisoning.

'No wonder they call you canaries,' she said. 'You ought to pack it up, Emma. It's making you look hideous, and it'll make you ill, as well.'

'Thank you very much.' Emma bridled. 'But I'll stick it until I'm a lot more hideous, 'til my eyes start to turn yellow. They say it's all right before then.'

'Who's they?'

'The doctors.'

'The majority of them'll say anything the Government tells 'em to say, man,' John chipped in. 'I know that with some of the lads they send back to the trenches.'

'They can't *make* you work there. You're a married woman with five children,' Lizzie persisted.

'Aye, I am, and that's why I want the money. And as long as me mam and our Ginny and Elsie will help look after the lads, I'm going to earn as much as I can, while I've got the chance.'

'Just make sure it doesn't end up with five bairns needing another mother, will you?' said John.

'I'd better come with you, Emma. Our two are falling asleep as well,' said Elsie.

'I'll walk on home with the lasses, and then I'll come back for a bit of crack,' John said.

The lads from the taproom had never been more than reluctant dancers and, all except Sally's partner, excused themselves. Having lost her partner, Ginny took up her usual station behind the bar.

Freddie nodded towards Sally and her partner. 'They seem to be getting on well.' Jimmy must have thought so too. He began to play a waltz. Lizzie felt herself swept off her feet and onto the dance floor to join the few remaining couples.

'Happy?' Freddie asked.

She nodded.

'How long do you think the party will go on?'

'Until two or three o'clock in the morning, maybe later, if I know our Ginny.'

He groaned and leaned towards her, nuzzling her ear. That familiar, pleasant little tingle ran down her spine, and made her smile. 'We needn't stay that long,' she said.

'I wish we'd booked a hotel. The thought of your mother being near...'

'She's got more tact than that. She's staying at the Cock, and so is our Sally. We'll have the house to ourselves.'

He pulled her close into him and she caught her breath at the shock of a large erection pressed hard against her. Both amused and scandalized she laughed, and looked into a pair of smouldering grey eyes, but didn't move away. He gave a long sigh, warm on her neck and redolent of erotic pleasure, tantalizingly delayed.

The few people left had made themselves comfortable in the best room before John and their mother came back and Ginny shut the door on the last of the customers.

'Where've you been Mam?' asked Sally. 'I

246

haven't seen you for ages.'

'No,' Ginny teased, 'And you were too busy with that canny little lad from the taproom to miss her until now.'

'You brought him to partner me, Ginny. It wasn't my idea. Anyway, I haven't got time for lads. I'm going to be a hospital nurse.'

'A hospital nurse? You?' Lizzie challenged. 'You haven't got the education. And you're not strong enough.'

'The Doctor seems to think I'm strong enough,' Sally protested, 'I've learned a lot since I went to work for him. He says I'm a good help.'

'And what's his wife doing, while you're "helping"?'

'Whatever she likes. I only do it because she won't. She's squeamish. She doesn't like sickness, and she can't stand the sight of blood, or people in pain, so she's not much use to him in that way.'

'But you can't stand the sight of blood, and you went as a housemaid, not an apprentice.'

'I went to work for the Doctor, and I do the sort of work he wants me to do. And I've got used to the sight of blood and all sorts of things, and he says I'm good with the patients.'

'Bravo, Sally,' said Freddie. 'We can't have too many good nurses.'

'Maybe Lizzie thinks there's nobody can do anything but her,' Arthur's wife smirked.

Lizzie gave Kath a resentful glance. 'Nothing of the sort. I just don't think nursing's the sort of work our Sally wants. She's never been strong for one thing, and they see some horrible sights for another, or so I've heard.'

247

'Aye, and those horrible sights are men, Lizzie,' said John. 'Somebody's got to help them.'

'Why, let's change the subject,' her mother protested. 'This is supposed to be a celebration.'

'You can change the subject as often as you like, Mother,' Ginny said. 'But it'll come back to the war. It always does.'

Chapter Fifteen

The church clock struck midnight as they passed, and a new moon hung above the tower like a silver blade in a sky studded with stars. A ghostly apparition loomed out of the blackness towards them and passed with a whoosh of its wings. She shivered.

Freddie held up the hurricane lamp, and with his free arm round her waist pulled her closer into him and moved her along, almost at a trot. 'Don't be frightened. It's only a barn owl.'

'I know that. I'm just cold. My teeth will be chattering before long.'

'I've got the cure for that,' he laughed. 'Just let me get you inside, and I'll soon warm you up. You'll find I'm on fire. Better get all those lovely clothes off as fast as you can, or I won't answer for what will happen to them. They'll be rent from top to bottom.'

'Freddie, you beast!' she exclaimed.

'I know, but I can't help it. I don't know how I've contained myself this past week. I'm ... I'm starving for love ... dying for it ... simply exploding for want of you.'

'Heavens, Freddie, what will you say next?'

'Something absolutely frightful, I fear. Better get you inside and into bed before we find out.'

They'd arrived at the cottage and he flung open the door, which her mother rarely locked. 'Wait there,' he said, and set the lamp down in the hallway. She caught her breath and laughed as he swept her up into his arms and carried her over the threshold, kicking the door shut behind him and striding on and up the stairs.

'Which room are we in?' he demanded, when they were halfway up.

'Mine, I suppose. You'd better put me down, Freddie, or you won't have breath left for anything.'

'Don't bet on it.'

She saw a faint light from under the bedroom door as he gained the landing, and when he pushed open the door there was a fire in the grate and the room smelt of polish. He set her down on the clippy mat beside the bed. The bedcovers had been turned invitingly back, and by the flickering firelight she saw a new Durham quilt of pink and cream, and her mother's finest linen. She reached out a hand to touch the deep, fine crocheted lace edging on the crisp, white pillowslips. 'Aren't they lovely? My mother's mother made them. I've only ever seen them used once before, and that was when Emma and Jimmy came back here after they were married.'

'Very pretty. All it needs to make it perfect is a beautiful young woman, naked and eager for her husband.' He turned her round and sat her down on the mattress, then knelt down to unbutton her natty little white high-heeled boots.

'It'll take you hours to get them off,' she said.

'Help me then.'

'Go and fetch the lamp. We'll do better with a bit more light. Better lock the door, as well. I'd hate anybody to walk in and catch us.'

He disappeared, and she hung up her hat and her jacket and wrap, then removed the fireguard and picked up the tongs to put a few more coals on the fire. So this is what her mother had been doing, all that time during the dancing when she was nowhere to be seen.

Freddie was back with the lamp and set it on the dressing table, where it cast a pool of light on a bowl of forced tulips, duplicated in the mirror. 'My God, but she's been busy. She's even polished the fender, and the coal-scuttle,' Lizzie remarked.

'It all looks wonderful,' Freddie agreed, throwing off his coat and unbuttoning his tunic, his eyes on Lizzie all the while. 'And if you're not undressed before I get these off, I give you fair warning...'

'You're a lot too fast for me, Freddie. I like to take my time.'

'What a frightful little prick tease you are, Lizzie. You'll drive me wild before you've done, if I allow it.'

'Or Wilde,' she said, removing her skirts. 'But I'm not a Wilde now, am I? I'm Lizzie Bowman. It does sound strange.' She stood in her cami-knickers, decorated with his regimental crest, and began unbuttoning her blouse.

'It sounds perfect to me,' he said, stepping out of his trousers. 'We're one flesh now, Lizzie, or we will be, jolly soon. *One* flesh.' He kissed her, and with his lips still on hers he pushed her backwards until she stood against the bedroom wall, then nudging her knee aside with his he inserted his fingers inside that flimsy garment and began a tender, rhythmic stroking. His grey eyes searched hers with a desire in their depths so intense it made her afraid. 'Tell me you want this as much as I do. Tell me.'

Pinned to the wall so close that she could scarcely move, she nodded her assent.

'No, that won't do. I know you want it. I can feel it. I can feel it, Lizzie – concentrated essence of joy. It's simply oozing from you – but I must hear you say it. Say, "I want you inside me, Freddie, I want you to make love to me".'

She felt a blush rise to her cheeks, and her heart began to pound as in a whisper she repeated words she could never in a million years have imagined herself saying.

'That's right, you do. And there'll be no running off to the bathroom this time, Mrs Bowman,' he said, holding her so she had no escape. 'None of that, tonight.'

'Oh,' she gave a gasp of mingled fear and pleasure as she felt him press himself into her. She felt the wall hard against her back as he moved towards her. She had told the truth when she said she wanted him. With her eyes half closed she put her arm round his powerful shoulders and sought his mouth, opened herself to the invasion of his tongue in a long, sensuous kiss and thrilled to the

251

sensations he created in her, the masculine scent of him, his mastery of her, and his delight in her. She closed her eyes the better to feel the swell of him inside her. Too soon, too soon, her climax was upon her and all strength drained away until she could hardly support her leg and would have sunk to the floor but for his hold on her.

She opened her eyes and looked into his face, a little flushed, his forehead moist. Intent now on his own pleasure he kissed her briefly and without pause in the rhythm of his movements. A final couple of thrusts, strong and deep, and he was still. She buried her face in his neck, tasting his salt moist skin on her lips until at length he released her. With her legs trembling she looked down, and saw that she still had on her boots.

He continued his undressing, kissing and caressing her from time to time as she unbuttoned blouse and boots, but when she slipped down the strap of her cami he stayed her hand and motioned her towards the bed.

'No,' she shook her head. 'I want to get washed. I'll mark the sheets, like this.'

He took her by the hips and applied her damp behind firmly to the bed. 'Your mother will think there's something wrong with us if we don't mark them,' he said, barring her exit from the bedroom whilst stripping off the rest of his clothes. 'She's had six children, after all. If we lived in Italy, she'd be expected to hang a bloody sheet out of the window tomorrow morning.'

'Lucky for us we live in England, then.'

'Lucky for me too,' he grinned. 'I wouldn't

contemplate marrying a woman I hadn't had the pleasure of.'

'You're a strange one, Freddie. Most men want a virgin to walk up the aisle with.'

'I suppose they imagine that that guarantees she'll be faithful afterwards, but it doesn't, not always.'

'You'd rather I'd been a virgin when you met me though, wouldn't you?'

He moved her along the bed and climbed in beside her, then propping himself on his elbow he looked down into her face with eyes full of amusement. 'Well, I've no grounds for complaint, have I? "And you won't even be getting my virginity!"' he mimicked. 'As if a man would expect virginity in a girl he'd hired for a night. It stunned me rather, Lizzie – and you said it with such a *defiant* stare.'

'I did, didn't I? But you told me a big lie.'

'I know,' he grinned. 'But after your declaration I simply couldn't help myself. Do you forgive me?'

She forgot her preoccupation with pregnancy and laughed. 'You are an idiot, Freddie.'

She lay on her left side in a light sleep, facing the window as the first light of a grey dawn fell on her face. She heard the hooting of an owl far away and became drowsily aware of the pressure of him against her.

'Freddie!' She tried to turn towards him.

'Shush, shush, Mrs Bowman, and keep still,' he murmured, 'We're one flesh again, you see. No separation between us, just as it should be between man and wife. Keep still.' He raised her right thigh a little then pulled her tight against him and kept her still. 'Did you hear the tawny owl?' he murmured, perfectly motionless.

She nodded, 'Yes,' her mind less on the bird than on that delicious sensation of distension within her. She tried to turn and kiss him, but he prevented her. 'Keep still, and listen.'

She had little option but to lie there, inhaling the lavender scent of her mother's pillow, with her eye taking in the pattern of its pristine white lace edging and the pretty cream and pink of the quilt.

'Hear that?' she felt his breath on her ear.

'What?' she asked, and then heard it, a liquid chirrup chirrup chirruping, paused and then repeated.

'It's a robin,' he murmured.

'What time is it?'

'About quarter to four, I think. Listen, listen. Now a mistle thrush. Hear that, like a little flute?'

'Kiss me, Freddie.'

'Soon. Keep still for now, my darling. There's a blackbird ... and now a woodpigeon. One can't mistake them. They'll all be nesting, Lizzie, and doing just what we're doing now, and the hens will soon be laying their eggs.'

They lay for a while in silence, listening to the noisy dawn chorus, and it suddenly struck her how much she'd missed those sounds in London. The air felt cool on her cheek, but not icy. Frozen winter was nearly over and springtime would soon blow in on the cold March winds, and Selfridges would be full of new fashions, and...

'Kew gardens will be full of spring flowers soon, won't it?'

'Yes, it will. This is awfully s'nice, isn't it? Do you like this sort of treatment, Lizzie?'

'Yes. It *is* awfully, awfully s'nice, Freddie,' she agreed, and feeling pleasurable waves of contraction deep within her, she had an almost irresistible desire to turn towards him, to feel his mouth on hers. Instead, he pushed her onto her belly, and separating her knees with his he pulled her hips upward until she was kneeling with her head and shoulders on the lavender-scented pillow, and he between her legs. 'Oh, Freddie, kiss me.'

'Soon, my dearest, sweetest darling, soon,' he soothed.

Again he restrained her, but once recovered from her lethargy she wouldn't submit, not this time. She couldn't. 'You'll have to let me go, Freddie,' she said, 'you'll just have to. I want the lavatory. I shall wet myself if you don't let me go.'

'Very well, but I'm coming with you. I don't want you doing anything to yourself.'

'What do you mean?' she demanded, eyebrows raised and eyes wide open.

He calmly met her gaze. 'You know exactly what I mean. You're my wife now, and I won't have you getting up to any prostitute's tricks.'

Shocked, she protested, 'God, Freddie!'

But he accompanied her, and as if she were a child he stood beside her whilst she answered nature's call. She was Mrs Bowman now all right, and she knew she had a master. She was Freddie's property, and no mistake.

He was blindfolded and with an envelope pinned to his chest to show where his heart was, and he was so drunk they had to carry him to the place of execution and tie him to a post. Twelve trained infantrymen were aiming their rifles at him, waiting to shoot him for being too much in love. She watched and held her breath as they waited. Waited for the order to 'Fire!'

Then the little ghost whooshed past her, brushing against her face. She uttered a long, soundless scream and awoke with her heart thundering in her ears to see the curtains pulled back and the pale winter sun a little higher in the sky and Freddie standing by the bed in his pyjamas, stroking her cheek.

'You were dreaming. It's almost noon, and I've brought you some tea.'

She shuddered and shook herself, and sat up to rearrange her pillows. 'Have you? Is my mother back, then?' She leaned back against the pillows and took the cup from him.

'Not yet.'

'Why, who made the tea?'

'I did.' She must have looked as surprised as she felt, for he added, 'I'm a man of many talents.'

'So you must have lit the fire for the water.'

'It wasn't very difficult.'

'Goodness,' she said, taking a sip of very good tea, 'goodness, where did you learn to do all that, Freddie?'

'At school.'

'I'd have thought they'd have servants to do

that, at a public school.'

'They did, but I rarely went home in the holidays, you see, and I used to get very bored and fed up, and ended by spending most of my time hanging round the cook, or the gardener, getting in their way and generally making a nuisance of myself until they let me do things. The gardener was my favourite. I liked the cook, but she was very intolerant of mess in her kitchen. I used to get round her by offering to make her cups of tea.'

'Crafty little Freddie. And now you're getting round me.'

He laughed, and tousled her hair. 'Yes, I suppose I am. I annoyed you rather, didn't I?'

'Yes, you did. But if you want to get round me I'll tell you a better way.'

'What's that?' he asked, getting into bed beside her.

'Get Philip out of the army, and back where he belongs with our Ginny. It'll kill her if anything happens to him, and Martin as well.'

'We'll go and see her today. There might be something we can do, between us.'

'One sixteen-year old's enough for them to murder. If anything like that happened to Philip...' She felt a prickling in her eyes and held the tea to her lips, to feel the comforting steam from it moistening her face.

'It isn't very likely, Lizzie. The relevant sections of the Army Act are read out directly the new recruits arrive in France, and regularly on parade. There's no excuse for not knowing them, and very few... Lizzie? Don't cry! He hasn't got a sweetheart, has he? No girl who's likely to let him down?'

'No,' she said, her voice thick with tears. 'Have you got a handkerchief?'

He found her one, and took the cup from her whilst she blew her nose. 'Well, then,' he said, 'well, then, he's got no reason to go absent without leave, so it's not likely to happen, is it?'

'It already has! It's happened to that poor ... poor...'

'Poor Lizzie.' She felt his arms around her, and he was rocking her like a baby.

'Have you ever been court-martialled for anything, Freddie?' she asked, as they walked hand in hand towards the Cock along roads cleared by the thaw, a few dirty clumps on the verges the only remaining evidence of snow.

'Certainly not! I generally obey orders.'

'Except when you write letters that might spread gloom and despondency. Have you ever sat on a court martial?'

'No. I had to give evidence once, and I didn't enjoy it very much. That's rather an understatement. I hated it, in fact.'

'What had the man done?'

'He was charged with drunkenness. It's very common. He's a very good chap, but drink, you know, with some men, it's an awful weakness, especially if they're under strain. It was perfectly frightful, having to stand before a court of highly decorated senior officers and give evidence against the poor chap, and him within arm's reach of me – especially knowing that what I said would condemn him, probably finish his career in the Army for good. It was all the more unpleasant because apart from anything else, we'd become friends, you see. Quite one of the worst things I've ever had to do in my life.'

'Imagine what it must be like to have the death sentence pronounced on you, then, and only sixteen.'

'I won't, if you don't mind, Lizzie. I can't take on *all* the misery of war. I'm only one insignificant captain, with no power other than to carry out my orders and do my bit, and so I do my best to mask the horror and the pity and the tragedy from myself, and just get on with it. I've seen a lot of things, some so frightful I couldn't speak about them, and if I were to dwell on it all I should be useless. Perfectly useless. And I don't want to be useless, because bad as things are, if we lose the war they'll be even worse.'

'But they shouldn't have ordered him to be shot.'

'They had no choice, Lizzie, given the evidence against him. There was no possibility of bringing in a not guilty verdict, and the penalties are laid down; they have no discretion except to recommend mercy, which they did. They had to act in accordance with military law.'

She glanced up at him, with his rigid jaw and his blank grey eyes, and almost hated him. He was cruel and callous. She withdrew her hand and after a sullen silence said, 'It's funny though, isn't it? Military law doesn't seem to mind turning a blind eye when it comes to enlisting boys before they're old enough to fight. They should have sent him back home to his mother where he belonged, instead of killing him.'

'You took your time. Had you forgotten it's Shrove Tuesday? We thought you would be here long before this, didn't we, lads? Stand back, now.' Ginny was at her kitchen range surrounded by Emma's lads, with the frying pan held in both hands. She tossed a pancake into the air, and caught it again.

'Me and Tommy had to go to confession this afternoon. Did you go to confession, Uncle Freddie?' asked Jem.

'No, I'm afraid I didn't.'

'Why not?' asked Tommy. 'Have you not done anything wrong, like?'

Jem's expression was doleful. 'Everybody's done something wrong,' he said, 'and it doesn't matter whether you have or not anyway. You still have to make your Easter duties. And tomorrow you have to go and get the ashes on your forehead, and the priest says "Remember, man, that thou art dust, and unto dust thou shalt return."'

'It sounds frightfully serious,' said Freddie.

'Freddie's not a Catholic, Jem,' said Lizzie's mother. 'He's Church of England.'

'Aye, well, forget about that now, Jem, we're having some pancakes,' Ginny said, and addressing herself to Freddie, added: 'Maybe it's just as well you didn't come earlier. The first few were a disaster.'

Lizzie gave her mother a hug. 'Thanks for all you did, Mam. You made it look lovely.'

Her mother whispered, 'I'll just get on home

260

now, and clean up a bit, but you'll have the place to yourselves at night until you go back down to London. I've decided I'm sleeping at Ginny's.'

'Thanks,' Lizzie squeezed her hand, and looked towards Freddie. He seemed too entranced with Emma's urchins to hear what her mother had said.

'What did you do with them, the disasters?' he was asking them.

'We ate 'em!' they chorused, laughing and rubbing their stomachs, their eyes glowing, all apparently as pleased with Freddie as he was with them.

'All right, lads! Who shall we give this one to, Freddie or Lizzie?' Ginny asked.

'Freddie!' cried Jem.

'No, Lizzie,' Joe and Bob contradicted.

'Why do you think Lizzie should have it, you two?'

'Because she's the bonniest,' Joe piped up. 'She's like a princess.'

'And why do you think Freddie should have it, Jem?'

'Because he's the bravest.'

'Why, who shall we give it to, Tommy, the bonniest or the bravest?'

'Why, the bravest, man, definitely,' said Tommy, 'but maybe's when he gets it he'll give her a bit.'

'How old are you, Tommy?' Freddie laughed.

'Eight. Our Jem's nine, our Joe's seven, and Bob's five. We've got a bairn an' all. He's not one yet. Me Aunt Elsie's looking after him. We come here from school when me Mam's at work.'

'Here, Jem, squeeze some lemon juice on this,

and you sprinkle some sugar on it, Tommy. Then you can roll it up and give it to your uncle Freddie,' said Ginny, sliding the pancake onto a plate. The boys crowded round the kitchen table, pushing and jostling to have a hand in the task, all intent on their squeezing and sprinkling.

'Their fingers are none too clean, Ginny man,' Lizzie observed, when Jem gave Freddie the plate.

'Never bother. You'll take no hurt,' Ginny said, handing Freddie a fork.

'I'm sure I shan't. Well, boys, it's always ladies first. Here you are, Auntie Lizzie.'

'*Auntie!*' Tommy mimicked, and the lads burst into noisy laughter.

'We just call her Aunt Lizzie, like,' Jem informed him.

'Aunt Lizzie?'

More laughter, and protests, 'No – *Ant* Lizzie.'

Freddie brought the laden fork towards her. 'Well, Ant Lizzie?' he smiled, and with the lads' eyes all on her she opened her mouth and allowed him to insert an inch of rolled pancake.

'He's feeding her, just like me Mam feeds the bairn!' Bob said, his eyes wide in wonderment.

'See?' Freddie laughed, 'I'm feeding you just like their Mam feeds the bairn.' He put plate and fork on the kitchen table and sat down and then dragged her onto his knee, and tried to feed her with another piece. 'Is this how she does it?' he asked the boys.

'Aye, it is.'

'Why, aye!'

'Aye.'

'Come on, open your mouth and eat your lovely pancake!' Freddie insisted, and Lizzie was surrounded by the four boys, all staring pop eyed, three of them shouting encouragement to Freddie, and Bob watching her and opening his mouth wide, as if to encourage her. She struggled vainly to free herself, then couldn't help opening her mouth to laugh. It was quickly filled with pancake, to shouts of triumph from the boys.

'You'll stop for your tea, will you not?' Ginny asked them, when the laugh was over. 'It's nothing elaborate, like. Just meat and potato pie and veg, and baked apples stuffed with raisins and syrup for after, but there's ample. Emma and Jimmy are coming, and our Elsie and John with their two, as well as me Mam, and you two, I hope. Oh, aye, and our Arthur's Kath, but she's leaving her bairns with her mother. We'll have to have two sittings – us first and the bairns after.'

Chapter Sixteen

'Me dad's not a soldier,' Tommy announced when six o'clock struck and the adults sat round Ginny's big draw-leaf dining table in her spacious living room upstairs at the Cock. 'They wouldn't let him join up because he's got a wooden leg.'

'Aye, all right, son,' said Jimmy, a little testily. 'Everybody knows I'm not a soldier. They know I've got a wooden leg an' all, or they do now if they didn't before. Go and read your *Boys' Own*, or play at marbles with Jem.'

'You'll not be the only one with a wooden leg before this war's over, man, Jimmy,' said John. 'There'll be plenty keeping you company.'

'All our soldiers are called Tommy. Did you know that?' Freddie asked the child. 'Perhaps you'll be a soldier one day.'

'Aye, I might. Our Phil's joined up. He'll be in France soon.'

'I don't think he will, Tommy,' Freddie said. 'He's too young, isn't he?'

'Aye, but he had a bad attack of enlistment fever,' said Jimmy. 'I wish you'd been at home, John. He might have listened to you.'

'He wouldn't, Dad,' said Jem. 'He said, "I'm going, and nobody'th going to thtop me!"'

'Your uncle Freddie's going to stop him. Aren't you, Freddie?' Lizzie demanded, sounding more aggressive than she intended.

'He'll have a job,' said Ginny. 'I was down at that recruiting office as soon as Phil told me, and all the sergeant would say was, "Well it's too late, like. He's in the Army now."'

'How old is he, exactly?' Freddie asked.

'Sixteen years and two months,' said Ginny.

'Well, there you are, boys, he *is* too young. He can't go to France for another three years. Where is he now, Ginny?'

'North Moor Camp, Cramlington. It's near Newcastle.'

Freddie caught Ginny's eye. 'I'll speak to his commanding officer. Perhaps something can be done.'

'He won't thank you for it,' said John.

'I know,' said Freddie.

'Why, what does that matter?' Lizzie shrugged, gladdening at the relief she saw on Ginny's face, and the knowledge that it was there at her behest. It gave her a pleasant feeling of control to have turned the tables on capable Ginny, and to be dispensing favours instead of begging them.

'He'll be best off out of it,' said Kath, her eyes intent on Lizzie's face. 'That's what our Arthur says. And trust you to get a man that can do it, Lizzie. Arthur tipped you would get a good catch.'

'I'm afraid you give me more credit than I deserve, Kath,' said Freddie. 'Like Ginny, I can only ask. I've no power to make anybody comply. But if I don't succeed, you could write to your MP, Ginny, or see a solicitor, as a last resort.'

'Aye, I'll do that, Freddie.'

'And I hope you get him out, between the two of you,' said John, 'but this lad's back down on the train tomorrow, leave over. It seems to have flown past, man.'

'It does. You seem no sooner home than it's time to go back,' Elsie sighed.

'And I only have another three days,' said Freddie. 'I wish I'd had a motor car. I should have liked to see something of the countryside.'

'You can borrow the bicycles if you like,' said Ginny.

'Thanks awfully,' said Freddie, looking pleased at the prospect. 'I suppose you can ride, Lizzie?'

She nodded.

'Well then, perhaps we will. We could ride out to some pretty place and stay overnight. What do you say, Lizzie?'

His eyes were smiling, expecting a truce.

She pulled a face. 'I don't really fancy it, Freddie. It's cold, and it'll be too windy.'

'It's a sin you married that lad,' Ginny said, as they stood in the kitchen washing and wiping pots. 'That's what you ought to be confessing to. You don't love him, and it's a sin you married him.'

'What? Because I won't go bicycle riding with him? I don't want to go bloody bicycle riding in the freezing cold, getting my hair blown about all over the place.'

'You would have at one time.'

'Aye, well, maybe I would, when I was young and daft.'

'And in love.'

'What makes you think I'm not in love with Freddie?'

'I know you're not, because you never touch him and you hardly ever look at him. When I married Martin, I couldn't keep my eyes off him, or my hands. I never used to leave him alone. Even our Emma, she was forever gazing at Jimmy, and she still does at times, and the same with our John and Elsie. And when you were courting Tom you couldn't keep your paws off him. I've seen you just about chew his bloody face off.'

'Well I've grown up a lot since then, and I've learned to be more polite. We're not all like you, you know. Some people have got a bit of self-control. They don't like to make a show of themselves.'

'Self control my arse.' Ginny's eyes expressed

something bordering on contempt.

Lizzie gave a defensive little shrug. 'Well, if I don't love him he'll never know, and what he doesn't know won't hurt him. I'll make sure I keep my half of the bargain. He'll get plenty of what he wants.'

'And what's that?'

Lizzie coloured a little, and with another little shrug said, 'Same thing they all want.' Ginny thought she knew it all, but she could have no idea what Freddie was really like, and she wasn't going to explain it to her.

'A man that marries you wants a lot more than that, Lizzie man, and he deserves a lot more an' all, especially these days. Men want real love, just like women do. And that's what you promise in the marriage service.'

'It's not like you to be so bloody sanctimonious, Ginny. I thought you were all for you-know-what.'

'I am, and I'm all for plenty of love to go with it an' all.'

Lizzie gave a little cluck of annoyance. And this was all the thanks she got, and after all her efforts persuading Freddie to get Phil out of the army. She wondered why she'd bothered. Ginny was trying to make out she'd cheated Freddie but she hadn't, not really. She did love him – in a way.

She gave a sudden, secret little half-smile at the thought of that way. Some of the things he did – they were shocking, disgusting. Like this morning. People would be horrified if they knew, and she was half horrified at herself, for liking it so much. She couldn't imagine her mother ever having allowed anything like it, or Emma, or even Ginny – and in broad daylight! There must be something warped about her, she thought, but there was no getting away from it; she loved him in bed, or at least she loved the things he did to her there. And if she didn't love him out of bed, so much the better for her. Real love's too terrifying. When you give people *that* sort of love you give them the power to destroy you, and she would never do that again.

'Goodbyeee, goodbyeee, wipe the tear,
Baby dear, from your eyeeee...

The platform at Durham station was full of soldiers like John, all piling onto the train for the journey down to Southampton, thence to France. Lizzie saw Elsie's eyes fill with tears as John gave her a final, lingering kiss, and, feeling a lump rising to her own throat, she handed Elsie her lace-edged hankie. All the train doors but the nearest were slammed shut, and the stationmaster was poised with his flag raised and his whistle to his lips before John reluctantly let go of his wife and jumped aboard.

'Oh, John...' Elsie's voice broke.

'Why, never mind, bonny lass,' he said, hanging out of the window as the train drew out of the station, 'we've had some good times, haven't we? With Freddie and Lizzie, and the rest of 'em? And there'll be plenty more good times to come, Elsie hinny, plenty more... You'll be all right. They'll look after you, you'll be all right.'

When the train was quite out of sight Elsie

dabbed her eyes and blew her reddening nose. 'I wonder how long it'll be before I see him again?'

Freddie said nothing, but with Elsie's unspoken 'Will I *ever* see him again?' sinking deep into her heart, Lizzie put her arms round her brother's wife, and pulled her close.

'What a perfect little gem of a town.' Freddie stopped her outside the railway station to stand and admire Durham cathedral outlined against a pale blue sky, mellow and magnificent.

'City, Freddie, it's a city,' Lizzie told him

'Of course. I know that. I should, standing here staring at the cathedral. But the place is so compact that it hardly seems more than a town. And it's a dream for anyone with an interest in architecture. It's a far cry from the devastation that used to be Ypres, though I suppose that was as pretty a place, before the war. I don't think I shall ever tire of Durham, Lizzie. Now stand still, ladies, I want to take a photograph of you. Move over there, the light's a bit better, I think. That's it.' He pressed the shutter. 'Would you mind taking one of us, Elsie?' he asked, handing her the camera, and Lizzie felt a rather proprietorial arm around her waist as they stood for the photograph.

That done, they walked towards Elvet Bridge, to find somewhere to have a cup of tea with Elsie.

'Have you got much shopping to do?' Lizzie asked her.

'Not much, but I just like looking round the shops.'

'So do I. And it'll cheer you up a bit.'

'We'll leave you to do that, Elsie,' said Freddie.

'There are several fascinating buildings I should like to see, and explain their finer points to Lizzie. We could spend the whole morning here, and then get a spot of lunch before going on to Cramlington.'

It was on the tip of Lizzie's tongue to tell him he could go on his own and she'd go shopping with Elsie, but the thought of the criticism she'd get from Ginny prevented her. So she resigned herself to traipsing round for hours in the wind and the freezing cold, looking at boring buildings she'd seen hundreds of times before and couldn't care less about, just to show she did love him.

She stretched her lips in her most pleasing smile. 'I'd love to keep you company, Freddie. I must have seen them all hundreds of times without ever really taking any notice of them, but now I've got you to explain all their finer architectural points to me it'll be really interesting.'

He took her hand and squeezed it, his eyes fired with such enthusiasm and smiling so delightedly into hers that she couldn't help returning a genuine smile. Oh, well, she thought – roll on lunchtime, and another nice warm hotel. They were the only buildings she cared anything about – and nice, warm department stores of course, the bigger and more luxurious the better.

'Jimmy's boys are engaging little chaps, aren't they?' he commented as they journeyed on to Cramlington in a comfortable carriage with a handful of officers. 'Intelligent, funny little characters. If ours are half such fine little fellows, I shan't complain.'

'We haven't got any yet, and when we do, they might be girls.'

'I suppose they might. I suppose girls bring out the protective instincts in a chap.'

'But you'd rather have boys.'

'I'd be happy with either. Or both.'

Liar. 'You'd rather have boys,' she said, and knew she was right from the expression on his face.

But he wasn't going to admit it. 'Which would you prefer?' he asked.

I'd prefer none. I'd prefer to get another leading part, or try my luck with Fred Karno and live as free as a bird, with no responsibility, and not have any kids for years and years, but she kept that sentiment to herself. Aloud she said, 'I don't mind.'

He leaned towards her and whispered in her ear, 'I hope you're pregnant, Lizzie.'

She pulled a face. 'Well it won't be your fault if I'm not, will it?'

'You wouldn't mind very much, would you?'

'It would be all the same if I did,' she said, 'but I think it would have been better to wait until the war's over and you're back home for good.'

'Let's just let nature take its course. I've a very strong feeling I shall come through. People seem to know when their time has come out there, you know. It's uncanny, but I've seen it time and time again.'

She hadn't much option but to let nature take its course with Freddie guarding her the way he did after you-know-what. Still, he'd be back in France before the week was out, and she'd have to be really unlucky to be in the same condition she'd been last time she'd ridden the rails to Newcastle. And anyway, she was respectably married now, so even if the worst came to the worst it could never be as bad as it was then.

She stared out of the window, lulled into lethargy by the rhythm of the wheels and the gentle rocking of the carriage; idly watching flights of birds, coal black against the pale sky. They looked like blackbirds – no, too big for blackbirds.

'What are they, Freddie, rooks or ravens?'

Rooks. They were rooks. She watched them wheeling overhead, over ploughed fields, and fields of sheep with their newborn lambs.

'I like your family awfully much, Lizzie,' he said. 'I didn't expect to, but I do.'

'You haven't met our Arthur yet,' she said.

Elsie was at her mother's cottage when they got back, setting the table for tea.

'What did they say about Phil?' she asked.

'Not much,' said Freddie, drawing out a chair and sitting down. 'I told the CO he was his parents' only child, his father was already in France, and his mother needed him to help with the family business, although running a public house is hardly a starred occupation. He told me Philip will probably still be his parents' only child when he's eighteen, but he promised to "look into it", no more than that. I have a feeling they'll let him go, though. Hello, Pip old fellow,' he greeted the child who had come to stand at his elbow.

'Ginny'll be glad,' her mother said, looking up from the dish of potatoes with onions and cheese she was cooking at the range. 'Put the kettle on, Lizzie. Elsie and the children are staying for tea.'

'Pip was named for Philip, you know,' Elsie told Freddie, 'but we thought it would be a bit confusing to have two Philips, so you're Pip, aren't you, pet?'

Lizzie moved to the sink to fill the kettle and after setting it on the range reached up to the cluttered mantelpiece for the tea caddy. 'Isn't it time you threw some of this rubbish out, mother?' she asked, picking up a little book of pressed flowers, rather rubbed round the edges.

'It's not rubbish. You gave me that when you were seven years old. I'll never throw it out.'

'Why not? It's seen better days, and it wasn't any good in the first place. And God only knows why you're keeping this old thing,' she said, holding up a piece of shale.

'Your dad gave me that, not long after we were married. I wouldn't part with that, either.'

'Mother! It's only an old fossil he found in the pit. Nobody else bothers to keep them. They're not worth anything.'

'It's an imprint of a fern, made millions of years ago, and he brought it home when we were newly married. They're love tokens, Lizzie. They're worth everything to me, especially now you're all away from home, one way or another.'

'I once gave my mother...' murmured Freddie, and stopped. Her mother and Elsie looked expectantly towards him, wondering what he was going to say next. With all their eyes upon him he began to fumble in his pockets for his cigarette case.

'Give us a one, then, Freddie,' Lizzie said.

He reluctantly offered her one, then struck a match and gave her a light. 'I don't really approve of your smoking.'

'I don't, either, Freddie,' said her mother, 'but she only does it to copy you. I hope you won't mind me saying this, but you smoke far too much, and if you didn't do it, neither would she.'

'Wouldn't she?' Freddie sucked furiously on his cigarette. 'I'm not entirely convinced about that, but I don't mind your saying it at all. And you're quite right about my smoking too much. I really should try to cut down, and I will – *après la guerre*.'

'It was a little necklace of green stones I found on the pavement on my way home from school. I ran all the way home to give it to her, frightened all the while that the rightful owner would pounce on me and take it back. I suppose it was quite a tawdry little thing really and the catch was broken, but it seemed something magical to me. I wonder if she still has it?'

'I'd bet my life on it.' Her mother had long ago returned to the Cock Inn and left them to themselves, and despite his determinedly keeping her in bed after their lovemaking she lay in Freddie's arms that night feeling well disposed towards him. His dominance gave her a curious feeling, a mix of childish resentment and pleasure, and a thrill such as she imagined a high stake on the roulette wheel might give – 'Will I be pregnant or will I escape? How terrible if I lose, and lose everything!'

It hadn't hurt her to give him the answer he wanted. He must have loved his mother to run away from school and find his way back to her. And when he had, she'd betrayed him. 'Did you ever stop hating her for sending you back?' she asked.

'Yes, when I began to understand how powerful my father really is, and how the world works, especially against women like her. She could never have withstood him. He'd have beaten her in the end, and she had to consider what would happen to my brother, too.'

'Was it always horrible at school?'

'I've very few happy memories of it. The very best time was when I had mumps and I was isolated in the sick room. Matron went to the library to get me a few books to pass the time, and one she brought back turned out to be a book of Norse myths, full of wonderful illustrations. I was very taken with it, especially Odin's spear maidens, the Valkyries, you know, the choosers of the slain. I liked the idea of these indomitable warrior women searching the battlefields and taking the bravest back with them to feast in Valhalla. That's where we get the word "valour" from; did you know that? It captured my imagination rather.'

'Like when you were a patient after you were wounded, and they gave you morphia. You dreamed about them then, the Valkyries.'

'Yes, I did. Those stories must be buried deep in my brain, mustn't they? But I wouldn't have swapped you for dozens of Valkyries.'

'What are the other happy memories – of

school, I mean?' she asked, and thought: I'm getting like him, looking on the bright side, masking off the bad.

'Being in the kitchen with the cook, or in the garden with the gardener, or playing chess with some of the nicer masters. I hadn't any real friends among the boys, you see. Some of them might have befriended me, but most people want to run with the herd no matter what direction it's going, and fear of being targeted themselves made them give me a wide berth. "What does it say? I can never make out what the beast is saying!"' Freddie drawled, in perfect clipped-vowel public school English. 'Nobody wanted to be tainted by association, you see. So I was left out of all the fun, with little to do but concentrate on schoolwork, except, as time went on, I began to distinguish myself at sports: boxing, rugby, cricket, and that sort of thing. That gained me quite a few hero worshippers and I suppose it might have won me some friends, but by then it was too late. I'd adopted the school patois, but I'd also learned to rely on myself, and I'd become rather stand-offish and contemptuous of my schoolfellows. I thought them either bullying and stupid or weak and petty, and I knew I was more talented than they, and they knew it too, and hated me for it. It sounds terribly conceited I know, but it's true.'

'Yes, you've certainly got a talent for blowing your own trumpet, anyhow,' she said.

'Believe it or not, I don't. Or I never have, to anybody except you. And none of it did me much harm in the end. I was a misfit, so I learned to

276

stand on my own two feet. There was nothing for me to do but work and the more you learn about things the more interesting they become, so I developed a perfect fascination with mathematics, and then with architecture. The result was that when I went up to Cambridge I did rather well.'

'It was the best thing that could have happened to you in the long run, your father putting you in public school.'

'Except I seem to have lost myself, somehow. John was telling me that he nearly emigrated, but he's glad now he didn't, because he belongs here. I don't feel I belong anywhere, certainly not in my father's house, nor among any of the fellows from school.'

'At your mother's?'

'Would I? I'm not sure. I'm not the same little chap she lost; public school made sure of that. We've lost a lifetime of knowing each other. I often wonder what we'll think of each other if I ever do find her. I belong to you now, and you to me, and after the war we'll have a proper home, and that's where I'll truly belong.'

She snuggled into him, and kissed his cheek.

He turned towards her and nuzzled her ear. 'How I hate the idea of going back to France, now. I love you, and I don't want to die.'

'There's a raven,' Freddie said, pointing upwards to a large nest like a fantastic crown of crystal studded frost, atop which sat a bird like a thick, black dart, still and silent, surveying the territory.

'That's a cruel looking beak it's got,' she said.

'But it's not always cruel. Ravens are the

earliest birds to pair, and I once saw a couple locking and unlocking beaks exactly as if they were kissing.'

Lizzie looked again, and could imagine no use for that powerful beak other than tearing flesh. 'They're sinister looking things,' she said, 'They remind me of funerals. And they make a horrible squawk.'

He laughed. 'Yes, they do, but again, not always. They have a variety of cries, and one that sounds rather like "corpse, corpse," which isn't at all endearing, I admit. But they also have a call very like laughter, and when you listen to a breeding pair chattering to each other they sound as tender as any other lovers.'

A shaft of sunlight pierced the frost-rimed trees and danced on the gurgling waters and stones of the beck, and Lizzie squeezed his arm and huddled into him for warmth.

'It's cold, isn't it,' he smiled. 'But I so love a frosty morning, don't you?'

'As long as I'm well wrapped up.'

He pulled her red woollen Tammie down over her ears, took hold of a length of her thick scarf and gave it an extra turn around her neck. 'Me too. And beautiful though it is, this weather's hard on the wild life. Only the strongest will survive. And your nose is beginning to look like a little red cherry, Lizzie,' he said, dropping a kiss on it. 'Perhaps it's time we went back. Have you ever tried mulled wine? I should like to get you a little tipsy.'

'No, I haven't, but it's a bit early to start filling me up with gin just to make me sin. It isn't noon yet.'

'Imagine your suspecting me of doing that. Still, I suppose you've got grounds. I'm a frightful beast, aren't I? My mind seems to run on one track when I'm near you, and that's how to get nearer still. But there's so little time before I go back.'

'You'll be on leave again in a few months.'

'If I'm lucky,' he said, turning her in the direction of the Cock Inn, and walking a little faster. 'But what if I'm not? It'll be months and years before I see you again. I shan't need a shell to blow me up. I shall explode of my own accord.'

The woods were still, except for the rustle and crackle of leaves and twigs beneath their feet, the coo coo of woodpigeons, and the song of smaller birds. They walked on for a while in silence, and then he sighed. 'The woods do look beautiful though, don't they, Lizzie; the way the sun catches the frost and makes it glitter. It's a place of enchantment, a land for elves and fairies.'

No. It was a land of pain and sorrow, for the gurgling beck and every boulder in it, every ice rimed tree and ivy leaf, every frosty tussock and gorse bush, every fallen branch and reed and blade of grass reminded her of Tom.

Freddie stopped and turned towards her, put his knuckle under her chin to tilt her face towards his. 'You look so mournful, little wife. Cheer up; the war can't go on forever.' She met his eyes, full of unexpected gentleness. 'Come on,' he said, 'we've got a fair walk back. Lively now, we must make the most of these last days. Yo ho ho, to the Cock, for steaming coffee – laced with a bottle of rum.'

Chapter Seventeen

'Quite a bit of post, Lizzie,' he said, when she unlocked her pigeonhole on their return to the flat in Bloomsbury Square. 'Who writes you so many letters?'

It had been a tiring journey, and she was cross and out of sorts. 'I don't know, Freddie. I haven't opened them yet.' She scooped the letters up and led the way up to the flat, leaving him to follow with the luggage.

'God, it's absolutely freezing in here, and dark, as well,' she said, putting the letters down by Georgie's lamp, and crossing to the fireplace. Lucky she'd thought to buy a bundle of sticks and fill the coalscuttle. Still in her coat, she began to rake the cold ashes from the grate. 'Will you light the lamp, and draw the curtains?'

'Yes, all right.' He put the luggage down and found a match, but made no move to close the curtains once the lamp was lit. His attention was fixed on her letters, which he picked up and began to examine. 'You have half a dozen from France, and one from Holland, as well as a few posted in London. Who are they from?'

'God, Freddie, how do I know? I haven't had a chance to look at them yet. I'll open them and read them all to you as soon as I get the fire going; before I've even taken my coat off, if you like.'

'No need for sarcasm, Mrs Bowman,' he said abruptly, taking off his greatcoat and hat and hanging them up, 'but I should certainly like to hear them. Who do you know in Amsterdam, for example?'

'God, Freddie!' she protested. 'Put a match to the fire. I'm going for some milk.'

'It's Sunday. Had you forgotten?'

'There's a very Christian lady lives downstairs. I'll beg some from her.'

When she returned Freddie was holding a newspaper over the fire to pull a draught under it.

'I thought you'd be reading the letters,' she said. 'You're used to censoring them, aren't you?'

He folded up the newspaper and turned to face her. 'No,' he said, quietly. 'I wouldn't read your letters, Lizzie; but you shouldn't mind telling me who writes to you and what about. I *am* your husband after all.'

Fuming, she said, 'Very well. Which one do you want to know about? The one from Amsterdam? I can tell you who it's from before I open it.' She took up the letter and tore it open. 'Just as I thought. It's from Irma.'

'Irmgarde Meyers?'

'Yes.'

'Give it to me.'

With cheeks blazing she did as he asked. Without another word he threw it onto the fire and took hold of her shoulders to prevent her from snatching it out again.

'You're not to have any more to do with her, Lizzie. She's not a fit woman for you to know.'

Enraged, she demanded, 'Why not? Because she's half German?'

'No, not because she's half German.'

'Why, then?'

'I've already told you. Because she's not the sort of woman that any self-respecting man would allow his wife to know. Now, who else is writing to you? Open the next letter, Lizzie.'

'Because she's had a few lovers, that's why, and you'd have been one of them if you hadn't decided on me instead. When it comes to it, you condemn her for the self-same things you do yourself. Men are such *hypocrites*.' She found the caddy, and threw a couple of teaspoons of tea into the pot and splashed a drop of milk into each pretty china cup.

After a long silence he said, 'And is that what you think of me?'

'And what is it *you* think of *me?* That's more to the point.' He was accusing Irma of being a whore, and she hardly knew how she managed to prevent herself from asking him how he judged his own mother if that was the case. But that would have been too low a blow so she swallowed the words and said no more, and turned to the gas ring to make the tea.

Taking the cup she offered he said, 'You're my wife, and I love you. That's what I think of you.' He sat in the armchair and indicated the foot-stool. 'I don't want to quarrel with you, Lizzie. Come and sit by me, like you did the night before we went to Annsdale.'

'While I was still a free woman, entitled to my own letters, do you mean?'

'Lizzie, when you were a free woman you wanted to be married. And now you are married you must play the game. I know women must make bigger changes in their lives to accommodate a husband than a man makes for a wife, but you *must* make that change. Surely you realized that becoming a wife would entail some loss of freedom?'

'Rather a lot of *musts* there, aren't there? But I'm sure you shouldn't have done that, Freddie. I'm sure it's illegal to burn other people's letters.'

'Whether it is or not, I don't regret it. What do you suppose John would say if he knew Elsie was carrying on a correspondence with a woman like Irma? Would he encourage it, do you think?'

She shrugged, and sank onto the footstool, knowing full well that John would not.

'Very well, if you won't answer me, we'll pass on to the next letter,' he said, handing it to her. 'Who's it from?'

'Georgie.'

'Georgie. The sodomite, do you mean?'

'What a horrible thing to call anyone. Georgie's my friend. Half the stuff in this flat was given to me by him. The tea you're drinking was boiled on Georgie's gas ring. I'm looking at this letter by the light of his lamp. The curtains are his. Lots of things.'

'I'll buy you a gas ring of your own, and a lamp, and everything else you need. I don't want you using anything of his. And I don't want him writing to you. I can't stand fellows like him, and I don't want them near my wife. You're to give him his things back, Lizzie.'

'I can't, there's nowhere to take them. He's in France, and he's given his flat up. That's why I've got his stuff.'

'As soon as I get my next leave, you're giving this flat up, and we're going to have a place of our own, with nothing in it except what we get together.'

'Am I allowed to have any say in these decisions, Freddie? Am I a wife, or am I a slave? I mean, are you my husband, or my gaoler?'

He said nothing, but groped for his cigarettes, found them, and lit one.

'What about me?' she demanded.

'Well, I don't want you to smoke, either,' he said, handing her the lit cigarette with a wry smile, 'but I'll give you one to avoid being called a gaoler or a slave master.'

'Good.' She returned him a half-smile.

'Now don't call me that again,' he said, lighting one for himself.

'Don't act like it then.'

He inhaled deeply and blew a perfect smoke ring, then said: 'I'm acting like a responsible husband.'

'You're acting like a tyrant.'

'Oh, no, I'm not,' he smiled, and began stroking her hair.

'Oh, yes, you are. I suppose you want the next letter now.'

'No, I don't. I want you to take your clothes off and get into bed. I want to give you lots and lots of treatment.'

Another gamble in the dangerous game of pregnancy roulette, Lizzie thought, and the thought stirred her. She raised her cigarette, to her mouth, and inhaling slowly began, with mounting excitement to unbutton her blouse with her free hand. She gave his face a sly, sidelong glance and was surprised to see not the sensuality she'd expected but a thoughtful expression, with a trace of anxiety around the mouth and eyes. She'd put that look there, that uncertainty; by sticking to friends he feared might lead her astray. If only Tom had been as jealous of her. She almost laughed at a sudden sense of her power over Freddie, but she didn't want that now. In bed, she wanted her master and she thrilled to be his slave.

He put down his cigarette and took hers from her, then got up to turn back the covers of the bed before helping her undress

'I so love you,' he murmured, nuzzling into her neck. 'I love you, Lizzie. I love you, I love you.'

'I like your family awfully much, Lizzie.'

'Yes, I know. You've said so before. And they like you.'

'I wish you'd stayed with them. You'd have been so much safer away from London and among your own people.'

She'd expected another inquisition about her unopened letters that morning, but Freddie had studiously ignored them and urged her to get dressed, asking her where she wanted to go on this, the last day of his leave. And so with a blustery March wind chilling their cheeks they were leaning against the rail of a ferry bearing them up the Thames.

'But, Freddie, how could I stay in Annsdale

285

when you're either here or in France? Besides, there's nothing for me to do in Annsdale.'

'There are five little nephews who need somebody to help look after them whilst their mother's at work, there's a lonely mother who'd love to have you back with her, and two sisters you could help. There's plenty to do there, Lizzie. You haven't a job, and there's absolutely no reason for you to work at all now we're married.'

'But I want to, Freddie. I want to do my bit. We can't rely on your father for anything really, and with a bit of luck I might be able to earn some decent money. I want to do my bit for the war, too. I think the soldiers need entertaining every bit as much as they need nursing. Nurturing for the spirit, as well as for the body. I'm sure it raises their morale.'

'I'm sure it raises yours,' he said. 'All the applause, and getting yourself written about in the papers. That letter you wrote me about the pantomime was the liveliest I've ever had from you.'

The words sounded ironic, but not unkind. She laughed, and fingered his lapel. 'I admit it. I enjoy performing. But there is another reason for my wanting to be in London, you know, Freddie. I want to be here for when my husband comes home on leave, bruised from the war and in need of some treatment and a little wife to be s'nice to him.'

'Don't say any more about that just now, or you'll make me wish I'd kept you in bed, and not brought you out at all.'

She gave a chuckle of satisfaction. Freddie was

proving surprisingly easy to manage after all. She'd managed to override his wish that she bury herself in the cottage in Annsdale, making herself useful to her family. Not bloody likely. Emma shouldn't have had the five little nephews if she didn't want to look after them.

She felt elated, but just as she was certain she had the upper hand he turned away from her to stare into the dark, swirling waters of the Thames and said, 'I hope that's all it is though, Lizzie. I hope you were sincere in the promises you made to me last week. Adultery can sometimes be forgiven in a man you know, but never in a woman.'

They went straight to the dining room for lunch. 'The food should be very good,' Freddie told her. 'Karno – Wescott, I think his real name is – employs a fellow by the name of Luigi, he's said to be one of the world's greatest maitres d'hotel.'

She nodded, and sat obediently in the chair he drew out for her. The room was certainly beautiful, with a décor of grey and purple the like of which she had never seen before, but she could take no pleasure in it. They studied the menus, and she found she had very little appetite for anything. Freddie ordered for her. He'd made attempts at conversation ever since they got off the ferry, but his insinuations about her had struck her dumb, and then made her feel so vexed that she wanted to cry. Except that she didn't want to show herself up by crying, but she couldn't carry on as if there were nothing amiss, either. With her feelings in such turmoil the whole day at the Karsino was going to be ruined unless she had it out with him.

'Was that a slur on me, or on performers in general, Freddie, what you said?' she asked.

He knew exactly what she was talking about, because he answered straightaway. 'Neither. It's a statement of fact.'

'But you make it because I want to carry on performing. You think all actresses are loose women.'

'No, I don't think that, Lizzie, but it's not unknown in some of them.'

'If you think that of me, why did you marry me?'

'I love you. I love you, Lizzie, and I don't want you to do anything that will make our life together impossible.'

'And you think I might.'

He shrugged. 'I don't know why, but I can't feel entirely sure of you. Not as sure as a man should be of his wife, anyhow.'

The waiter returned and placed two steaming bowls of some sort of soup before them. It smelled very good, and Lizzie picked up her spoon and dipped it in the soup. Before she could bring it to her lips a large tear ran down her cheek and splashed into the bowl. Without a word, Freddie handed her a handkerchief.

'You've made me cry,' she said.

He said nothing, and it made her more vexed than ever.

'Aren't you ashamed of yourself, Freddie? Aren't you sorry for saying such a horrible thing to me?'

'Not if it prevents you from doing something that will make us both cry,' he said.

They strolled around the landscaped gardens after lunch, and then danced in the ballroom. Lizzie felt the eyes of other men on her, but, very subdued, she neither looked at them nor smiled, and she felt Freddie relax.

He took her to watch the show in the palm court concert pavilion in the evening. A few people recognized her from the pantomime and came to congratulate her on her performance, and she couldn't help it, she came to life again and, with Freddie looking on, she told them how much she'd enjoyed it, and how desperately she wanted to perform at the Karsino, to work for Mr Karno.

This was the reason she'd come back to London, she thought, when she'd stopped enthusing and the people had drifted away. It was nearly a month since the pantomime had closed, and if she'd stayed away much longer no one would have known her from Adam. This wasn't the time to let her face slip from the public consciousness; she had to build on her triumph while people still remembered her. She loved the stage, she loved the life of a performer, and Freddie would just have to let that be, or marriage was going to suffocate her.

They said very little to each other on the way home. He'd soon be gone back to France, thank God, and then she could do as she liked, so she decided she'd humour him, behave like the demure, adoring little wife and soothe him with flattery, but he saw straight through her act and told her so. Very well, she thought, and as soon as they were inside the flat she dropped all pretence, and threw his *Adultery can sometimes be forgiven in a man, but never in a woman* in his face. 'It's rankled all day, Freddie. In the first place, I'm accused before I've even thought of doing anything wrong. In the second place, it's not fair. What's sauce for the goose is sauce for the gander.'

'Not in this case. It's a far worse thing in a woman.'

'How?'

'Because I'm sure it's a more agonizing thing for a man than for a woman. A woman at least knows her own children. It's impossible to impose any others on her under the pretext that they're hers. But a man has to trust his wife, and she must be worthy of his trust.'

Still fuming, but unable to think of a suitable answer she snatched up the kettle and stormed down to the bathroom to fill it. As she stood there with the cold tap full on, impatient for it to discharge its sluggish stream into the kettle, there came into her mind an image of that other victim of love and war, not the sixteen-year-old, but the grown man who was found with one foot bare and the top of his head blown off.

Her unopened letters were still under the lamp when she got back to put the kettle on the gas ring. She pushed Freddie into the armchair, sat on his knee and picked up the first letter. Still in a pet, she said, 'It's from Georgie. Poor Georgie, he'd die a thousand deaths if he knew I was reading this to you.

"Dear Eliza,

"It's not too bad over here so far. I'm in a transit camp, and when we're not doing fatigues or yet more training, some of us are getting up a bit of a show to entertain the boys. We call ourselves the Whizzbangs, after those wicked little German shells. I've never been a female impersonator, but of course, I let them persuade me to be the leading lady. You should see me when I'm done up, I'm just as beautiful as you, and I've got better legs, *so there*. I'm getting a few of the boys interested in becoming Thespians, and we have great fun together in rehearsals. I'll tell you all about it when I see you. Much too much to write in a letter, and much too entertaining for the censor.

"Someone gave me this photo of a dog wearing a gas mask. The French use them to run over no man's land with messages, apparently because they're much faster and more agile than men, and harder for the snipers to hit. But a dog wearing a gas mask, Lizzie – I ask you, isn't it just about the weirdest sight you ever saw in your life? Absolutely *killing*, my dear. Keep the photo for me. I shall have it framed..."

Freddie put his hand over the letter and stopped her from reading. She removed his hand and read on, one letter after the other, until the kettle boiled and she got up to make the tea.

He stood up. 'You must be frozen. Shall I make a fire?'

'Is it worth it? It's bedtime.'

'I think so. It won't be so cold then when I get up tomorrow morning.'

291

Her anger quite gone, she put the kettle down and threw her arms around him.

'Poor boy,' she said.

'Yes, isn't it childish?' he said, squeezing her and kissing her hair, 'but that's exactly how I feel. It's been a wonderful leave, Lizzie, and I'm sorry I spoiled the last day, but how's a chap to control his wife without telling her these things?'

'A chap should leave his wife to control herself.' She caught the look on his face, and added, 'You needn't have any concerns about me being like Irma, Freddie. I'm not. It's just that I love the stage.'

'I know. But I simply can't stand the thought of any rival. Still, there's one comfort, I suppose; the stage can't sire any children.'

'You'll have to do that yourself. But not for a long time, I hope.'

He gave her a kiss, lingering and sweet. 'Within the next hour, *I* hope. If I haven't already.'

'We are Fred Karno's army,
Fred Karno's Infantry
We cannot fight, we cannot shoot,
What earthly use are we?
And when we get to Berlin we'll hear the Kaiser
     say
Hoch hoch, mein Gott, what a bloody fine lot
Fred Karno's sent today.'

Another vast, crowded railway station with the air reverberating with the rattle of men's boots, under which could be heard the hum of conversation between people soon to be parted. A group

292

of soldiers were leaning against the wall singing and joking with each other as Lizzie went in on Freddie's arm; waiting for friends, she supposed.

Freddie gave a wry smile. 'You'll be joining that yourself, as soon as I'm out of sight, I daresay.'

'What?'

'Fred Karno's army.'

'Perhaps. He's very particular who he takes, you know. Only the best stand an earthly. He might not want me.'

'I hope not, but I rather suspect he will. I hope you can't get work anywhere, and you have to go home to Annsdale and let your family take care of you. I've no doubt you think I'm a perfect beast for saying that, but I mean it. I should feel so much easier about leaving you if I knew that would happen.'

'Freddie, I'm a grown woman. I'm used to fending for myself, and I don't need anybody else to take care of me.' Seeing the look on his face, she added, 'Except you, of course.'

They walked towards his train. One last kiss and he boarded one of the carriages reserved for officers and hung out of the window. 'It's such a wrench, parting with you, Lizzie. I can't wait for this bloody war to be over. I don't mind telling you I'm absolutely fed up with it.'

'Let's hope it really will be over before next Christmas,' she said, above the noise of slamming carriage doors and the whistle of the station-master.

'Yes. Another winter in the trenches is something we could all do without. I say Lizzie, do you know...'

The train began to pull out of the station and she walked alongside it. 'What? What?'

He hesitated, then said, 'I don't want to leave you. Write to me every day, won't you? And don't forget you have a husband in France who loves you.'

'No, I won't. Bye, Freddie, bye, bye!' She raised her hand to wave and froze, taken by a sudden fancy that his mother must have been the last person to have seen that strained, boys-don't-cry expression on his face, on the day his father took him away – or the day she'd had to give him up, perhaps. Tears started to her eyes, and she put her fingers to her lips to blow him a kiss but it was too late, he was gone. Poor boy, poor boy.

No, no, no. She checked herself, and the flame of real sympathy that that glimpse of his suffering had kindled in her heart guttered and died. That was enough of that. She'd gone down that path once before and she'd seen where it led. From now on, she'd lay her life down for no man, husband or no bloody husband.

She stepped out of the station into sunlight bright on her face and rejoiced to be free. Better than free – she had all the advantages of marriage, a guarantee that her flat was safe and all her bills would be paid come what may, and an indemnity against conscription into a munitions factory – without a man like a dead weight round her ankles, keeping her back, preventing her from doing all the things she wanted to do, demanding to decide who she knew and who she didn't know, and who she corresponded with. Freddie was a lot too dominant, which might be glorious in bed but she wasn't in bed all the time, and she was damned sure she wasn't going to be dominated out of it. Not while he was in France, at any rate – and not when he came home either, if she could help it. She was going to write to who ever the hell she liked, and do what she bloody well pleased. The life of London was buzzing all around her and she revelled in it. She felt liberated, elated, and she almost danced down the street towards the motor-bus.

Home, now. She'd get home and put the kettle on and read through all her letters, absolutely scour them, especially the one from the governor offering to act as her agent.

She shuddered as she got on the bus, at the thought she might be pregnant. Hope to God she wasn't, that's all.

Handing her money over to the lady conductor she decided on a change of plan. She had the whole day before her, so she'd go to see the governor at home first and take him up on his offer, and then she'd have somebody she could absolutely trust to do his best for her. It would be good to see him again, and tell him all her news, and if anybody could get her a booking with Fred Karno, it would be him, knowing him personally as he did. Then she'd go home and read through her letters, and answer as many as she could, and maybe write to Irma and explain what had happened to her last letter.

Chapter Eighteen

'You got my letter, then?' he said, leading her into a spacious drawing room. 'Margery's gone off to some committee meeting or other; can't remember what it's for, something to do with the war – aren't they all? Not my cup of tea, but since the kids ... well, she buries grief in good works. The house is like a morgue these days, but lucky we've still got it, eh? Lucky it was in her name, and those bloody liquidators couldn't get their greedy hands on it.'

Her eye took in the Persian carpets, the grand piano, the mirrors and pictures and plush furnishings, the large, walled town garden beyond the French windows. 'Well, you did say they were going to take everything *you* owned, didn't you? So it was lucky you didn't own all this. Or was it a bit of good management?'

He laughed, and tapped the side of his nose, then lifted her hand to examine the wedding ring. 'Well, and you've gone and got yourself married! Where's the husband?'

'He's in France,' she said, 'but I'm still keeping my own name; and I'm not going to broadcast the fact that I'm married. I'm taking the ring off as soon as I get home. I want to earn some money, governor, the more the better. I really want to get on with Fred Karno. Being seen at the Karsino doesn't hurt anybody, does it? Can you make it happen?'

'Yes, I think so. I think you'll do for Fred. In fact, I can almost guarantee it. He's always on the look-out for new talent.'

'Tell him if he's got Lizzie Wilde, he's got everybody. I can do Vesta Tilly, Marie Lloyd, Florrie Ford, and even Harry Lauder, if he wants. Tell him I'll do anybody or anything he wants me to do – I'll even do myself. I can use all Ginny's old songs, if he wants. I'll even do slapstick.'

'What about other bookings?'

'I'll take any you can get, as long as they don't stop me taking work at the Karsino, and they're not too far from Bloomsbury.'

'The Karsino's bloody miles from Bloomsbury, Lizzie.'

'I know. But I want to work there. Everybody who counts for anything goes there, and I want to be seen. I think he'll pay me enough to cover the fare, don't you?'

'I wouldn't guarantee it. He's a bit of a stingy bugger, Fred. But he *is* a genius. You'll learn a lot from him.'

'Oh, well, I'll go and see what he does pay me.'

'There's another thing you ought to know about him. If he gives a girl an audition, he usually expects her to be *very nice* to him, and the nicer she is, the more likely she is to get a booking.'

'Hm,' said Lizzie. 'So I've heard. Just tell him I can't do my act in the horizontal position, will you – but I'm so good he ought to employ me anyway.'

Another change of plan took her into Selfridges to look at the spring fashions.

'The women in Paris aren't depriving themselves of pretty things to wear,' one of the young assistants assured her, 'just because there are lots of casualties at Verdun. You soon realize that, if you read the fashion columns in the papers. Frenchwomen think it's even more important to keep up a good appearance during the war than it was before. But Parisians have more style than anybody, haven't they? They put us to shame when it comes to style, don't you think?' She glanced at Lizzie's left hand, and saw the wedding ring. 'I suppose your husband's in France, is he, Madam?'

'Yes. He's a Captain in the Middlesex,' Lizzie told her, and was gratified by the impression it made.

'Well, Mrs?'

'Mrs Bowman.'

'Well, Mrs Bowman, I'm sure the Captain must be very proud to show his wife off, you're so elegant. Shall I show you what we have for the new season? With a figure like yours, you could wear anything. What about this ensemble, in light blue? Or the lilac? Or perhaps a stronger shade would suit your colouring. Will you try them on?'

With her purse full of Freddie's money, Lizzie was very willing to be persuaded, and the assistant whisked her away to a dressing room, talking all the while. 'In fact,' she pronounced, 'all the men need to see beautiful women, and all the women who can afford it should dress themselves nicely, it's the least they can do. And obviously that gives work to poorer women who need it, so they feel the benefit too, in wages.'

With a fleeting pang of guilt Lizzie wondered if Freddie's mother might be one of the poor women to benefit by the money she was about to lavish on new clothes. Was she still making copies of Paris fashions, or might she be in some ghastly sweatshop making uniforms for soldiers? Lizzie had a flash of inspiration. His mother must have had to register under the Act, like everyone else so it must be possible to trace her through the registry offices, unless she'd married. That would please Freddie, at any rate, if she found his long lost mother, and it would be something to fill in the time whilst she was waiting for work. And wouldn't he think she was clever, if she succeeded?

But there might be snags. Would it be a good idea from her point of view? She was probably a lot better off without a mother-in-law – she'd never heard any woman say she had a good one. And if they found her they'd find the brother, and what might he be like? Whoever heard of anybody going looking for two *poor* relations, it might be like looking for a couple of millstones to tie round their necks. She'd give that idea a bit more thought. Let it be for now.

And that was a good day's work she thought, on arriving home with her parcels late that afternoon. 'Mrs Bowman,' the sales assistant had called her. Mrs Bowman, who was married to Captain Ashton. Lizzie wondered what she would have made of that had she known, but she'd rather destroyed the girl's illusions about the officer's wife anyway, by insisting on carrying her own parcels home.

The fire was still in, so she carefully revived it and pulled her armchair nearer. There was still enough light to read by, so she'd sit in her coat and read her letters until the kettle boiled and the fire burned up a bit. She'd start with Georgie's. They were her favourite; she always enjoyed his letters. What a shame she hadn't got Irma's, it would be fascinating to know how she was getting on with her 'worthy burgher'. She'd probably replaced him by now. Lizzie picked up her pile of letters and sank into the armchair.

A couple of hours later she roused herself and gathered her towel and sponge bag, and her nightdress. What relief, on undressing in the bathroom, to find she had no need to worry about any babies. Considering he was so good at mathematics she'd better leave it for a couple of weeks before telling Freddie there was no 'endearing little chap' in the making.

After her bath she made herself a cup of cocoa and sat in bed to drink it, looking at their photograph on the mantelpiece, of Freddie behind her with his hands on her waist, holding her. She finished her cocoa and went to put her wedding ring beside the photograph, then snuffed the lamp and climbed back into bed.

How empty it seemed. As still and quiet as the grave.

BEF France

Dearest Wife,

Thanks awfully for the parcel you sent me.

300

Magazines are always welcome and can be passed on when read, which makes a chap quite popular. Cigarettes are something else we can't seem to get enough of, so you're quite a hit with the company just now.

We're being sent up the line in a day or two. What's the worst thing about being at the Front, you asked me. Is it the cold, the foul food, the trenches, going over the top? The rats, the mud? The jolly old poison gas, or shellfire, or machine guns, or the sniper's bullet? Well, it's been all of those things at various times, but now none of it's half as bad as being separated from you. I had such a marvellous honeymoon in Annsdale with my little wife that I've hardly thought of anything else since I left you. I'm sorry I upset you, but you soon forgave me, didn't you? What an absolute little darling you are. I think of what John said, about 'more good times to come,' and it keeps me going. I'm storing up heaps of kisses, and everything else for you. Simply bursting with them. I'd better sign off now I've got into this vein, or Heaven knows what I'll say next.

Your *very loving* husband,
Freddie

He'd written almost every day since he went back, and Lizzie replied nearly every other day, because most of the time there wasn't much news, anyway. Not that there was ever much that was really new at his end. His letters were full of the same sort of thing: thank you for the parcel, everybody enjoyed what you sent; who's going on leave and isn't he a lucky dog; how much I'm longing for my next leave; what filthy trenches the last lot had left when we went up the line to relieve them; wiring parties, trench raids, who's been killed or wounded; what a narrow squeak I had when ... and I'm sure it's my lucky horseshoe kept me safe; so and so's lost his nerve – but no good getting depressed about things, is it? – or alternatively, you've got to stay optimistic out here, or you'd jolly soon go under, and always, always, ending with how much he was looking forward to getting back to her, for some *s'niceness* and *treatment*.

At the end of March she thought of telling him he wasn't going to be a Daddy, and then thought again. She'd tell him if he asked. She gave him a full account of her first triumph at the Karsino though; she was so full of it she couldn't help herself. And to celebrate, or to assuage her guilt, she sent him a small hamper from Fortnum and Mason's, even though she knew his father was sending them as well.

It all fell so easily into her lap. She got bookings everywhere. The ones at the Karsino were the ones she loved the best, but there were never enough of them. A balanced programme was what Mr Karno needed, and plenty of variety, so that the show never got stale, and to that end, the bill changed regularly. The life of a music hall artiste was harder than she'd thought, what with the constant shuttling in cabs to different theatres, it was exhausting. The money wasn't as good as she'd imagined either, though it was better than theatre. And conscription was biting, so there were too few male artistes. The talk was that the Actors' Association was blacklisting men who were shirking their duty by working abroad, and the Variety Artists Federation had sent a cablegram warning American Artists not to accept engagements in England.

'No foreign artistes are going to come here and pinch our jobs while we're fighting. We won't stand for it,' an aging tenor told her one night.

A consumptive-looking juggler cried him down. 'You think they'd take any notice of a cablegram? It wouldn't put *me* off. No, it's the U boats keep them at home.'

And so there were more jobs in the theatre than men to fill them, but sadly for Lizzie, with women, the boot was on the other foot. If only Georgie had been in London they could have perfected their tango and done exhibition dances and that would have been another string to her bow and might have got her more bookings with Fred Karno. But she could only write to him and bemoan the missed opportunity for them to be in that glorious place together, among good artistes, performing for all the officers and their families on that wonderful stage. He wrote back and told her what marvellous times he was having playing 'female parts' in France. He'd even had French officers flirting with him, and bringing him flowers. The war was a bore, but France was wonderful, in many ways.

She was sitting with a couple of other artistes after the show, and the middle-aged major with the thick, slightly greying moustache 'simply had to come across and congratulate her,' he said. 'Your impressions are most convincing, Miss Wilde. One might almost imagine one were seeing the original artiste. More them than they are themselves, so to speak. Which do you enjoy portraying the most?'

He'd spoken to her before, when he'd been at the Karsino at one of the matinees a couple of weeks ago, with his wife and daughter. He'd been very complimentary then. She would have introduced him to her companions, but he'd made so little impression on her she couldn't remember his name. To cover her awkwardness she flashed him a smile. 'Oh, Florrie Ford, without a doubt.'

'Ah, yes, what an artiste she is. Such a wonderful repertoire. "The Lady with the Glad Eye", "Hold Your Hand Out, You Naughty Boy", "Hello, Hello, Who's Your Lady Friend". Yes, marvellous. Your pastiche is the best I've ever heard – and I flatter myself I *am* an authority.'

Lizzie wasn't averse to his flattering her, at any rate, so she allowed him to buy her a drink, and conversed with him for a few moments, telling him all about her career. What about her husband, he wanted to know, and when she told him he was in France, 'He must be awfully proud of you,' he said.

They discovered they were near neighbours. He and his wife had a house in Bloomsbury, and: 'I would offer you a lift home,' he said, 'but I suppose you've already arranged your transport.'

'No,' Lizzie told him, 'I get digs in Hampton when I'm playing the Karsino.'

'Another coincidence! My wife's in Hampton

with our daughter; visiting her mother. I have to pick them up before going on to Bloomsbury. Perhaps I can offer you a lift there.'

Well, Lizzie thought, if they were going to Bloomsbury anyway, why stop at Hampton? She might as well go with them, save her the trouble of getting home tomorrow – Easter Sunday.

The distance to Hampton was very short and the major's wife would surely expect to sit in the front of the car, so Lizzie was more than happy to be ushered into the back. She sank into the soft leather upholstery and left him to crank the engine into life. It fired, he jumped in and they were off. The car was warm, and hummed smoothly and pleasantly along the empty roads. It was awfully rude, but the Major's conversation bored her, and what with the car humming along, and him droning on, she felt her eyes beginning to close. She smiled, remembering something Freddie had said about being so tired he needed matchsticks to prop his eyelids open sometimes in the trenches. He'd been joking, but she knew what he meant. If she were on sentry duty now, she'd be facing a court martial.

Her head lolled forward, and she gave a sudden start. They were on a stretch of very dark and lonely road and it seemed hours since they'd left the Karsino.

She stifled a yawn. 'We must have left Hampton ages ago. Where are your wife and daughter?'

He stopped the car, and turned to her and something in his expression made her flesh creep.

'Actually, that was just a tiny fib,' he smiled,

and in the blink of an eye he was out of the driving seat and blocking her way out of the rear door, pushing his way in to join her on the back seat. She backed away from him and pulled at the other door, but it was useless, the door was locked and he'd made doubly sure of blocking her escape by parking next to a stone wall. 'They're already in London, you see. What say we rest here for a while, my lady with the glad eye, and get to know each other better?' He stroked her cheek. 'You look a very willing little showgirl. You're not going to make any difficulties about this, are you?'

She arrived home shaking. Hard to believe she'd been taken in like that, but it would be the last time. And there was nobody she could tell. Nobody. Laughing, almost hysterical, she went to the bathroom to get out of her filthy clothes and clean herself up. Never, never again, she thought. Never, never again.

'Trust them to kick us when we're down. I shouldn't be surprised if they're up to their necks in intrigue with the Germans!' Freddie's late April letters were full of indignation about the rebellion in Ireland, as well as the usual preoccupations. In May he had some good news. 'I've got four days' leave. I'll be home for Whitsuntide, so if you've got any bookings, cancel them at once! And better wear your *oldest clothes* – for the first twenty-four hours, at least – I'm liable to explode like a Jack Johnson – one of the biggest Bosche shells! Remember our wedding night? What a beast I was, but you know how impossible it is for me to restrain myself when I'm near you, don't you? So beware...'

She felt a pleasant flutter of anticipation and laughed, glad to cancel her bookings because Mother Nature's urges had begun to trouble her now and then – though nowhere near as much as they seemed to trouble Freddie.

'I say, this daylight saving idea of the Government's is wonderful, isn't it? Ten o'clock at night, and still light,' Freddie said, as they surveyed the panorama from the Thames Embankment.

'Wonderful for us, I suppose,' Lizzie said, linking his arm as they resumed their stroll. 'But I'm not sure the people who're having to work longer hours will think so. What did you think to the revue?'

'All right. At least it wasn't some wildflower of an actor, who's kept himself well away from any fighting, talking a lot of patriotic gibberish about dying for King and Empire and giving hell to the cowardly Hun, and telling us how very worthwhile all our sacrifice is. I can't stand shows like that, they make most people want to be sick. Yes, it was a pleasant enough bit of froth. I suppose you're sorry you had to sit in the audience with me.'

'No. Not at all. I rather liked it.'

He squeezed her hand. 'You surprise me.' He leaned towards her and murmured, 'And what did you think to your undies? I spent hours poring through Madam Venn's catalogue, and I think I made a good choice, don't you? That pale blue silk will look simply splendid on you, with your black hair. I think I like it even more than the cream.'

She gave him a sharp glance and a little smile, but made no comment.

After a while he said, 'I put a man's name forward for the VC the other day, you know, and he deserves to get it. We had a wounded man left in no man's land as dawn broke after a raid, and nobody would go out for him, with German shells and bullets whistling about. I couldn't have because I was the only officer present. So this tender-hearted corporal tied a handkerchief to a stick and hopped over the bags. That took some pluck, you know, with bullets whistling round his ears. He got to the fellow without being fired on, and gave him a water bottle and a couple of morphine pellets, and told him we'd bring him in after dark, And to give them credit, when the Germans saw what he was about, they let him get back unscathed. If there *is* anything glorious or inspiring about war, it's courage like that, and what men will do for their chums, and the decency of the enemy, sometimes.' He paused, and smiled. 'Now that's enough of my news. By Jove, I've hardly shut up. Talk about stung with a gramophone needle. It's time you had a turn. Tell me how you've been doing at the Karsino.'

'Stopped going there.'

'Any particular reason?'

'I just got fed up with it, Freddie. I wanted to do it, and when I had, it didn't attract me anymore. In fact I'm fed up with music hall altogether. I'll be back into real theatre the minute somebody offers me a decent part.'

'I see.' They strolled on for a while, looking out over the river, and then he said: 'Bad job about poor old Kitchener, wasn't it? An army man all his life, and then to end by being sunk by a mine in the North Sea.'

'Yes, it was.'

'At least Admiral Jellicoe's chased the German ships back into their ports.'

'Yes.'

'I think there's going to be a big push soon, Lizzie. The French are being bled to death at Verdun, and we're expected to do something to take the pressure off. If we can just make the breakthrough we'll drag the Hun out of his trenches and get back to open fighting. With any luck, we might soon see an end to the war.'

'That'll be a relief for everybody, especially our Ginny. She wrote and told me they'd sent Phil home from Cramlington, and a week later he ran off down to Yorkshire to enlist there.'

'I thought something like that might happen.'

They walked on in silence, until he said: 'Lizzie, there's something wrong, and I think you'd better tell me what it is.'

Later, white-faced, sitting on the footstool and hugging his knee, she ended her sorry story. 'And I realize now how stupid it was, but he was an officer, Freddie, and I'd seen him there before with his wife and daughter, he'd even introduced me to them. So when he said he was picking them up for the journey back to London, I believed him. But it was a lie, and he stopped miles out of

309

town and got into the back of the car with me, and he tried to, you know, but he never did because I was so terrified my stomach heaved, and I was sick – all over him, all over myself, and all over his lovely car. You should have seen the look on his face. And I felt as if I was choking in it so I tried to stand up and get past him, and I threw up over the driver's seat, as well.'

She snorted with laughter at the memory of the Major's face, and looked at Freddie, half expecting him to be laughing too, but he sat in stern silence, his jaw clenched. 'I couldn't help it,' she said, 'I just kept spewing, and spewing, and it stank his car out, the way vomit does. It certainly cooled him off though. He kept saying "You dirty, filthy..." I won't repeat it, but he left me alone and wiped the driver's seat with a bit of rag, then got back into it and drove. He couldn't wait to get home to get himself changed, I suppose, and he threw me out of the car in Bloomsbury. I often wonder what excuse he made to account for the mess in his motor car.'

She waited anxiously for his reaction, thinking that the least he would say would be 'I told you so,' and wondering whether he was going to lose his temper with her, but although his expression was grim, all he said was, 'And are you certain you can't remember his name?'

'Yes.'

'In view of the fact that he has a family, perhaps it's as well you can't – because I have a terrible premonition that if you could, he wouldn't survive the war.'

'I wasn't going to tell you. I thought you'd

blame me.'

'You've been very silly, and you've had a very lucky escape, but I don't *blame* you, Mrs Bowman. Drink your tea, and promise me you'll never do anything so foolish again.'

'I promise. Men are so lucky, Freddie. They can go everywhere and do anything they like, knowing that whatever happens at least they can't be raped.'

After a long and thoughtful silence, he said, 'Yes, I suppose you're right. *Men* are very lucky. And you've never worked at the Karsino since, you say? I'm very glad about that, Lizzie.'

When she parted from him at the station, after his too fleeting four days' leave was over, he looked deep into her eyes. 'Well, you've learned your lesson, I hope, and you'll be a sensible girl from now on. You know, I trust you completely, Lizzie. I must, and I will.'

'And I'll trust you, to be a good boy among all those naughty French girls,' she quipped.

'Kiss me then, to seal the bargain. I'll behave myself, and so must you.'

After a last tender kiss she left the station thinking how curious it was that he'd been so good about that horrible incident in the major's car, and how easy it had been to tell him – the last thing she'd expected.

A week later she started at the sound of rattling glass in London, caused by the guns on the Somme.

On a blustery autumn evening Lizzie spotted

311

Ethel in Harrods, the first time she'd seen her since they'd been together at de Lacey's. She approached her unseen, and, leaning towards her, whispered, 'Are you still doing your bit for the soldiery?'

Ethel started, and turned to her. 'Oh, Lizzie, it's you.'

'Come and I'll treat you to tea at Lyons Corner House. I'm a bit flush, and I'm going there now.'

Lizzie ordered tea and cakes, and after an awkward silence Ethel said: 'I've never been as bad as you thought, you know, Lizzie. I'd just been let down by my young man, and then there was that raid that burned my poor little niece to death, and I really didn't care what happened to me after that, I got so low.'

Lizzie could sympathize with that, and felt herself blush for shame. 'I'm sorry, Ethel.'

The girl gave her a genuine, generous smile. 'Well,' she shrugged, 'I will admit I felt sorry for the soldiers, and I thought if I had a few, and one of them let me down, there'd always be another to step into his shoes, so it wouldn't matter. But then I fell in love again, and he loves me, and I've been faithful ever since I met him. We're going to be married on his next leave.'

'It's love! *That's* why you're looking so well!' Lizzie laughed.

Ethel was good company and after they'd shared a lot of reminiscences of everybody at de Lacey's, Lizzie didn't want to part with her to go back to her empty rooms. She suggested they round off the afternoon by going to the pictures to see the new film of the Battle of the Somme.

By the light of the usherette's little electric lamp and the flickering film they found their way to a couple of seats in the stalls. The orchestra was playing, and above that was the noise of the woman next to Lizzie, crackling sweet papers and sucking and crunching sweets.

'God, some people!' Ethel exclaimed.

Lizzie leaned towards the woman and in her best officer's wife manner said: 'I say, do you mind?'

The crunching stopped. Lizzie offered Ethel a cigarette and lit it for her, then lit one for herself, and settled back to watch the film. The screen was full of men tending other men on stretchers, some of them wearing white armbands with a cross. Then the camera moved on to a scene of men in tin hats filing through muddy trenches. She leaned forward, doubting what was before her eyes. Was that a dead boy slumped in the trench? She watched in horror, and the slow, surreptitious sucking and crunching began again. Lizzie gave an audible tut of irritation, hissed: 'Bloody woman!' to Ethel, who said nothing, riveted by the film.

Men were lined up at the bottom of a trench, waiting. When they all began to scramble over the top, the orchestra stopped playing and the cinema was filled with an awful silence. One poor man slid back down the trench as the others went over, and seemed to cling to the wall of earth for his very life. Lizzie could almost feel his fear, and knew the poor devil would probably be shot for it. She shuddered. Killed by the Germans or murdered later by some vengeful military bigwig who kept himself safe far behind the lines, there was no escape for the poor bloody infantryman. The crackling to her right had stopped, and out of the corner of her eye she saw that the 'bloody woman' was perfectly motionless, holding a sweet about six inches from her open mouth with her eyes glued to the screen.

Now men were lifting their comrades on to stretchers, but were they dead, or wounded? Stretcher after stretcher, they struggled through trenches. Were they going to dressing stations, or graves? It was hard to tell.

'My God, they're dead, they're dead!' Ethel exclaimed, and burst into tears. Lizzie took her by her elbow, urged her to her feet and towards the aisle. A man in front of them got up in the same instant. His right sleeve was empty, and as he turned his face towards her to squeeze past the row of cinema-goers, Lizzie saw that he was crying.

This was what Freddie had been telling her about. This was what she had never understood, what lay beneath words like 'we were in a stunt', or 'a minnie hit our trench, six killed and ten wounded', or 'my nerves were rather shot after the last show, but I'm all right now', and the recurring – 'no good getting depressed, is it?' This mud and filth and murder was his daily life, but apart from one story about a sixteen-year-old deserter none of it had touched her before; none of it had held any reality.

She put Ethel in a cab and sent her home, then walked back in the eddying wind to Bloomsbury

Square. Freddie had been carried through trenches on one of those stretchers, and lived. Who said the days of human sacrifice were over? Every nation in Europe seemed intent on sacrificing its best and bravest to the God of War, eager to hurl them into the furnace. The thought chilled her.

What had seemed a distant abstraction was suddenly a hideous, immediate reality. Freddie really might die. She might actually become the officer's widow of her calculations, might bask in public sympathy and enjoy the eminence and the pension that went with the part.

Horrible, horrible thought. She turned into the Square and saw that the leaves were thickly falling.

Chapter Nineteen

My Own Darling Lizzie,
1st November 1916

What a shocker you are, to think of getting the registrars to find my mother for me, and using the pretext that you need seamstresses for war work, of all things. I never suspected you of being quite so devious – it's rather alarming.

Since I came out here, I've been searching for my brother, too, looking for his name on every roll of soldiers I see, and into every man's face – for a masculine version of my mother's, I suppose.

He was very like her as a child of three or four. There's absolutely no hope that he's an officer, so whenever I think of the men in some of the ghastly billets they sometimes have to put up with – barns full of filth, for example – I wonder whether he's in the same sort of place. I can't stand a filthy place at any price, either for myself or my men if I can help it, and I'm getting quite a reputation for turning the men into housemaids and supervising their spring-cleaning operations.

I don't know whether I'm glad or sorry you saw the film, but don't get anxious about it *at all*. In the first place we aren't always in the front line. We rotate, perhaps four days opposite the Germans, then the same in support, and in reserve lines, and in rest billets. Rest is the wrong word, because there are always fatigue parties to be got together for one thing or another, picking up salvage after battles, rebuilding trenches after shelling, doing work directed by the engineers, and sometimes more gruesome tasks. But we do manage a game of footer or cricket sometimes. There are even people teaching country dancing, and to watch men holding hands and daintily tripping along in their boots two by two is quite amusing. There's even a thriving amateur drama group at the YMCA. The men enjoy that enormously, although I suppose you'd think it very poor stuff.

When the 'hate' is in full flood though, things can be simply hair-raising. If I were alone, I think I should shoot off down the trench never to be seen or heard of again, but when all the men's eyes are on you, relying on you to lead them, it's oddly calming. And months and years of all the horrors out here seem to have made some of us quite callous, and we take things now that we'd have found absolutely horrifying before the war as a matter of course. So, you see, the film wouldn't affect me as it did you. I've seen so much death and had so many narrow squeaks that I'm quite battle hardened, and I'll tell you something very strange. I took part in a stunt the other day, with machine guns rattling, and shells exploding around and about, and I *knew* I wouldn't be killed. *Simply knew it.* I couldn't tell you how, but I sensed it very deeply, something like a revelation. A really peculiar, inexplicable sort of feeling. So don't worry a bit about me, Lizzie. I'll worry about you instead, with all those filthy Hun Zep raids on London.

Nobody seems to be getting leave. I don't know when I'll see you again. I'm absolutely fed up with the war and especially this Big Push on the Somme, this glorious breakthrough that anybody with half a brain knew within a week was never going to materialize. Any Tommy could have told High Command that bombardment wasn't going to cut the wire – it just heaved it up and tossed it down again, in a worse tangle than before. A great pity the brass hats and politicians sitting in their clouds above the Olympian Heights amusing themselves with our lives aren't so quick to catch on, but they're far too exalted to heed any advice from the ranks. As we sing here below: 'I don't want to be in la belle France no more', but we've little choice.

Love and kisses by the tankful (you must have

heard of them? They're a wonderful new invention for getting us over enemy trenches without getting shelled or machine gunned, which sounds marvellous in theory; but in practice the damned things are always breaking down.)

Eternally yours,
Freddie

Lizzie walked down the Mile End Road, and turned off into Spitalfields and then went deeper and deeper into the slums until she found the alley she sought and made her way along the bottom of a chasm almost too narrow for the sun to penetrate, between two walls of blackened, crumbling brick interspersed with filthy windows. She picked her way over rubbish and around swarms of half-dressed, dirty children sitting or playing on the slimy pavement, passing the few women standing outside their doors. She felt their eyes upon her, some curious and some hostile, and began to wish herself less well dressed and far less conspicuous. At last she reached the address given to her by the registrar, and with as much courage as she could muster she knocked on the door, her eye taking in the peeling paint, the crumbling brickwork, the dirty windows with their tattered curtains.

'Oo yer lookin' fer, laidy?' one of the women demanded.

'I'm looking for a lady called Mary Elizabeth Bowman.'

'Bess? What d'yer want with 'er?'

'I've got some work for her, if she wants it.'

'I 'opes it won't take long, then. She ain't much

longer fer this world. She coughs something terrible, I 'ear 'er when I'm working, and all night – cough, cough, cough. Second floor up, and better pay 'er in advance.'

Up a narrow, foul stairway, striding past a group of young urchins, and she reached the vile, airless little hole where Freddie's mother lived, worked when she could, ate, slept, and was about to die. What billet in France, she wondered, could possibly be worse than this?

'My God, Freddie!' She stood with her hand on the handle of the open door, too surprised to say any more.

'Yes, Freddie!' He swept her into his arms, strode into the flat and kicked the door shut behind him before depositing her on the bed. 'You must give me a key, you know. I came earlier, but you weren't in. However, I made good use of the time. I went to my father's and touched him for some extra money. I told him I needed it so that I could see my high-priced dollymop, which is near enough to the truth. He was falling over himself to get me the spondulicks; seemed quite proud of his lecherous boy. Can you imagine how cheated he'd feel if he knew it was all legal and above board? Come on, get yours off too,' he urged her, tearing his clothes off, his grey eyes dancing with laughter. 'It's twelve o'clock, the witching hour. And I want to witch my little witch – in bed!'

'You're too sudden for me, Freddie,' she protested, half laughing herself. 'It's disgusting! You haven't even asked me how I am, or told me why you didn't let me know you were coming. It's like somebody gorging a meal without setting the table, or even putting the food on a plate.'

'It is, isn't it?' he gave a joyful chuckle, and dropping his trousers to display the bulge in his underpants he stood by the bed to help her out of her clothes. 'I won't bother to ask how you are, because I can see you're all right. And you can see how I am. I'm like a horny toad who can't wait to get a firm grip on his female. Come on; hurry up and get into bed.'

'What a sight you are,' she said, but couldn't help laughing, 'and you've still got your hat on.'

'Never mind about that. There are no ladies present, I hope – except Lady Toad.'

'I'm not a toad.'

'No, you're a trout.' He threw off his hat, tossed her clothes onto the floor then pushed her along the bed and began to tickle her ribs.

She squealed with laughter. 'Get off, Freddie!'

But he wouldn't. 'You're Mrs Trout, who requires a little tickling to make her compliant,' he told her, and his lips descended on hers in a surprisingly tender kiss.

Afterwards, he lit a cigarette. '"The Great Fuck-Up?" That's how they refer to the Battle of the Somme in the ranks. And with twenty thousand dead and twice as many wounded on the first day, it's difficult to argue the point. There's been a sad neglect of intelligence and some monumental miscalculation – with the result that the enemy who were supposed to have been knocked out by the bombardment came streaming up from their deep concrete dugouts as soon as it stopped and manned machine guns and mortars they had strung out all along the Front. Every inch of it was covered. As soon as we went over the top you could hear the swish, swish of the bullets, mowing our men down like a scythe. Those of us who managed to get to that German wire – that was supposed to have been severed by the shelling – found it so dense you could hardly see daylight through it, and it's thicker than ours, you know, and more barbed, and what a bloody tangle it was in. They must have been reinforcing it for months, and hundreds of our men were dead on it, just like fish caught in a net. And still they kept sending men up, line after line, into all that – sheer murdering madness. The carnage in our sector was as bad as anything at Verdun, if not worse. The whole place was littered with the dead, stray limbs, mangled bodies, severed heads – you could hardly move without treading on bodies, or parts of bodies. Absolutely in-describable. We couldn't get the wounded away so they stayed moaning and screaming where they were until they died and rotted among the rest. I never saw a body buried that first fort-night, and the stench, with the heat of summer, you know. And flies, great black clouds of them, I'll never forget them as long as I live, and then they come and crawl on you, and crawl on the food you have to eat.' He sucked at his cigarette, and exhaled, before going on.

'The French did better. A short bombardment, not too much warning for the Hun, then up and over and all their objectives achieved with only a few thousand losses. We blast the place to Hell for a week to give the Hun plenty of notice that we're coming, and then we have to lead men over the ground we've churned up – without any cover. And brave men have stuck it and stuck it and stuck it out there until they've been either maimed, or killed, or gone raving mad; and to ask men to go back to it, again, and again, and again, when you know you've had every last ounce out of them and you're driving them beyond the point of endurance, well – and then you think of others, shirking at home ... well, I'll tell you what I think. I think all war-mongers and all war profiteers should be hanged, but men who won't do their bit to help us now we're in the thick of it, they're beneath contempt.'

He blew a perfect smoke ring. 'So, that's what it was like to spend the summer and autumn with the B.E.F. in the vicinity of that little French river called the Somme, and after all that slaughter the breakthrough failed. But are we downhearted? Will we admit defeat? No, because we did as much damage to the enemy as he did to us, and we've learned a good many lessons from it all.'

'My God, Freddie, that's terrible. Is that all you can say about the thousands of men who've been killed and maimed? That we've done as much damage to the Germans, and we've learned some lessons?'

'Can't afford to think about it in any other terms; we still have a war to win. Thousands of good men are dead, and it's a thousand pities, but there we are. Those of us who're left alive have simply got to get on with it. It's pointless to sit bemoaning our fate and feeling sorry for ourselves. We must learn from it, learn everything we need to learn to get on and *win*. It's a mighty struggle, but that's what those men sacrificed their lives for, after all. Lucky for me I'm not the sensitive literary sort, but there's a poem that sums up what they'd want us to do now:

'Take up our quarrel with the foe,
To you from failing hands we throw
The torch.'

'But you write poetry, Freddie.'

'Not lately. I gave it up after the first month of the Somme. It doesn't do to think too deeply about some things. Poor old Yates, you know, had to be invalided out. He's in some hospital or other, twitching and shaking all over the place.'

'I'm sorry about that.'

'So am I. But mathematics is to be my medicine, and it'll do me good. I'm to spend the next three months at Aldershot, teaching trigonometry and sound ranging, along with other arts and sciences of war so that we can find enemy guns and put them out of action before sending men over the top. Other things as well. We're learning new methods, reorganizing platoons, making better use of scout planes. And our artillery's poor, and a third of our shells were duds – all that's got to change. We need accurate, up-to-the-minute maps, better shells, better guns, and better gunners. The science of mechanized warfare, Lizzie. That's what we've got to get to grips with. We shall soon be much more efficient killers than the Prussians. Now that's something to rejoice over, isn't it? And so we must, now they've started bombing our civilians from airplanes as well as Zeppelins.'

'A Zep was shot down a mile off Hartlepool the other week. Twenty seventh of November, I think it was.'

'You're right. By a pilot from Seaton Carew aerodrome. Good man, I hope they give him the V.C. I'd like to see them all shot down in flames, make London a lot safer for my little Mrs Trout. And me as well, as it happens. I shall be able to come up to see you every Saturday night, and stay all day Sunday. Isn't it marvellous?'

He was wide-awake, obviously winning the war in his head, but Lizzie was exhausted. She wouldn't tell him about his mother yet; that would be something else to keep him awake. By far the best thing to do would be the thing that might help them both to get to sleep. She kissed his cheek, toyed with the hair on his chest, ran her hands down well muscled flanks, fondled that pleasing part which now lay flaccid on his thigh, and felt it come to life. 'Freddie?'

He smiled down at her, said: 'Hello, Lady Toad,' and crushed his cigarette into the ashtray.

She handed him his cup of tea the following morning. 'We'll have to drink it without milk and sugar. There's none to be had anywhere, not even from the saint on the ground floor. Oh, yes, and I've just remembered that I forgot to say: "I told you so," when you told me about your course yesterday,' she said, getting back into bed beside him. 'If I'd let you persuade me to stay in Annsdale, you wouldn't have been able to come and see me, would you?'

'I would, but it would be pretty exhausting, I admit.'

'There's another thing I didn't tell you yesterday, Freddie. The governor's got me a part in pantomime. It's *Aladdin* – not half as good as I had last year, but not bad. I get a few of the funny lines, and I make them funnier. But the leading lady's awfully sniffy about her rank – not a bit like Irma; but Irma didn't need to be like that, she was so good she wasn't frightened of competition and I flatter myself that I'm not, either. Don't say it,' she held up a warning finger, 'I know you don't like Irma, but she was always good to me. I'm just hoping Aladdin gets an attack of something, and then I'll pounce on her part, and I'll do it so much better. But,' she grimaced and drew in her breath with a tiny hiss of apprehension, 'we're playing on Sundays, as well.'

'Oh, Lizzie, that's ... that's damnable. Can't you give it up?'

'If I get a reputation for being unreliable, I might never get work again.'

'That shouldn't matter now.'

'But it does, Freddie. What else am I going to do while you're away? And I like it so much better that music hall, being with the same set of people all the time. And I'm sure it's safer, being among people I know and who know me, and not having to travel round so much. And it's near home.'

'But what am I going to do while you're there? I was going to take you dancing. You'd like that, wouldn't you?'

Poor Freddie. He looked so disappointed, but how would he take her next news? 'Yes,' she said, 'I would, and we could easily go dancing after the show. But while I'm in the theatre you could go and see your mother. That's the other thing I didn't tell you. I've found her. But she's ill, Freddie. Desperately, desperately ill.'

Before they were two hours older she was leading him along streets the cabby refused to go down, the same streets she'd traversed alone a week previously. Now, even without Freddie beside her she would have felt entirely safe. The neighbours had seen her coming and going, knew what her errand was, and approved. She took him in at the rotting front door, up the sordid staircase, and into the one-room hovel his mother called home.

She was sitting by the window and turned to greet them, her chest contracted and shoulders bent from hours of toil. Lizzie felt a pang of pity for the older woman, whose son, far from displaying any pleasure at their reunion was staring at her, looking aghast at the sight of her grizzled hair, her whey face with its hollow cheeks and bloodless lips. The feverish black eyes under their dark arches were the only sign of life.

'That's not my mother,' he breathed. 'It's an old woman, not my mother. It's not my mother.'

'Look at her hands.'

Around her right hand was entwined a little necklace of green glass. He took off his hat and crossed the tiny room in three hesitant strides. Squatting beside her chair, he held onto the arm

326

and searched her face for something recognizable.

With infinite tenderness she touched his thick, brown hair and sighed, 'Freddie.'

'Oh, Mamma.' He rested his forehead on her knee and wept.

Consumption. The mere word made her shudder. Such a degrading, disgusting disease, even the sound of it was full of the stench of poverty, the stink of slums and squalor. When she'd seen his mother cough blood, Lizzie had jumped, actually leaped back for fear, and she knew the older woman had seen the terror in her eyes. But the thought of catching that shameful, deadly disease, it was terrifying. This time Lizzie went no further than the doorway. 'I'll wait for you downstairs,' she said, and unsure whether he'd heard her or not, she left, glad to get out of that room.

'If you think that was bad, you should have seen the place when I first went,' she told him when he joined her outside. 'She was half-starved and sleeping on a mattress on the floor, not a stick of furniture in the place, and the rent hadn't been paid for weeks. She'd have been in the workhouse in another day or two. It might have been the best place for her because they'd have had to put her in the infirmary. They couldn't have made her work. She's not fit. But of course, she wouldn't go. It's the shame of it that people can't stand, isn't it?'

He was quiet, the marks of crying round his

eyes and nose.

She went on. 'Consumption, that's what it is. She's been coughing blood. I wanted to shift her out of there, get her somewhere better, but I'm sure she thought it was a trick to get her into the workhouse. She said the neighbours were good to her, and a couple of your Aunt Clara's daughters live in the municipal dwellings over there. I went to find them and at least their places are fit to live in, but they're healthy, with husbands earning so they can afford the rent. Even then, though, they can barely make ends meet, that's why your mother's in the state she's in. One or the other of them goes to see her every day. I said, "Hasn't she got a son? What's he doing about it?" "Well," they said, "he's in France, and the army sends the allotment money, but it doesn't go far enough, because she's got nothing else coming in." So I got her a couple of chairs and a rug and a decent bed and bedding; I even had to get her some clothes; she'd hardly got a rag. And I've had the doctor to her. He says she's got to have milk and meat every day, so I left money with her cousins, and they've been bringing it in for her. And they take the washing as well, and I've given them the money for that. She's supposed to have fresh air, but there's not much chance of that here, is there? You can't even open the window in that room, and I know because it was the first thing I tried to do.'

'Thank God for Aunt Clara and her girls. And thank God for you, Lizzie. That building over there, did you say? Give me the address and I'll go and see them this evening, while you're at the theatre. My poor mother. I've thought of it for years, this meeting, and I never imagined her living on a dung-heap like this. But she's going to have everything she needs now, absolutely everything. Perhaps we'll get one last Christmas together; as good as we can make it. That's something, isn't it?'

She took his hand and squeezed it. 'Yes. And I suppose she showed you the pile of letters from your brother. You'll be able to find him now.'

'Thanks to you. And Lizzie, I didn't leave enough money for all you've done. I'll pay you back, every penny.'

Did he really think she was so grasping that she wanted to be paid back to the last penny for helping his dying mother? She let go of his hand.

She was sitting gossiping among a group of chorus girls before the matinée performance, snatching a quick smoke and putting on her greasepaint when the callboy announced: 'America's declared war on Germany! It'll soon be over, girls. And there's a lady at the stage door in a nurse's uniform waiting to see you, Lizzie. Says it's important.'

Lizzie looked round in alarm. 'Send her in, then,' she cried, but gave a little grunt of disgust when her eyes met those of Alice Peters.

'Tom's been wounded, at Arras,' Alice announced. 'He's in the officers' hospital in Highgate. He'd like to see you.'

How well Lizzie remembered that authoritative tone. The high-ranking lady was talking to the lower orders in the well-remembered manner, and eyeing Lizzie's short red satin costume and the half-dressed girls surrounding her with obvious distaste. Lizzie raised her eyebrows and copied Alice's voice and hauteur.

'Must I? I'm awfully sorry, but it's quite impossible.'

A couple of the girls looked round and giggled as Alice recoiled at the mimicry. She never had liked to be made fun of. Lizzie smiled, and put her cigarette to her scarlet lips.

'Do you know what it's like, at Arras? Four thousand British casualties a day! That's what our losses have been. My brother has risked his life in defence of his country, and you have the...' Alice stopped, took a deep breath and began again. 'He fights so that people like you can continue to earn your excessive incomes and live your comfortable lives unmolested. The least you can do is come and see him.'

'Oh, I doubt your brother's made any sacrifice for people like me.' Lizzie exhaled reflectively, breathing her smoke in the direction of the lady in the VAD uniform, watching as just a very little colour rose to her superior cheeks and her imperious green eyes averted their gaze. 'What on earth does he want to see me for, anyway? And I shouldn't think somebody with your high principles would be encouraging a man to renew any acquaintances with women he knew before he was married. Especially not *theatricals*.'

'We were friends once, and it's Tom's wish to see you, that's all.'

'Hm. I see you're doing your bit for King and country, anyhow. How very noble of you. Just what we'd all have expected.' Lizzie slowly ground

330

the stub of her cigarette, mastering an impulse to snatch up the heavy glass ashtray and hurl it at her visitor's head. An overpowering anger was making her hands tremble, but she rose to her feet and looked Alice steadily in the face. 'All right. Tell him I might come tomorrow. If I'm not too busy.'

Alice left without another word. Lizzie watched her go, then followed, firmly closing the door on the sordid little dressing room. Consumed by fury, and most of it against herself, she walked towards the stage.

She wanted to go, and she didn't want to go. She'd unpicked the past in her fantasies, pictured herself back with Tom for so long that she shrank from the reality of seeing him again. Had he realized, in the trauma of battle or illness, that she was the love of his life; that he should never have broken with her? Why would he want to see her again otherwise? Perhaps he wanted to tell her that he would never have been parted from her but for his sister's lies and meddling; that his marriage had been a ghastly mistake, that he loved her and wanted to spend the rest of his life with her, righting the terrible wrong he'd done.

She wanted it, and she dreaded it. She resisted going to see him for two full days, and then could resist no longer. Poor Freddie. Back in France, winning the war to keep her safe, to do this to him, and after the blow of his mother's death. She grieved for his grief at her betrayal, and wished she could shield him from the harm she would do him.

331

Chapter Twenty

She found him sitting in bed propped up by pillows, and he gave her as easy a smile as if nothing had ever been amiss between them.

'Well, Lizzie. It's nice to see you, and after so long. And you're living in London. Extraordinary.'

She stood transfixed, waiting for her heart to begin its fluttering, for that sweet thrill of love that had always flooded her senses at the sight or even the thought of him, for tears of joy on seeing him again, or grief at their ever having parted.

She felt nothing. She looked into the familiar blue eyes, the same, and not quite the same. There was a weariness in them, and the smile had lost some of its old merriment. Hardly surprising after a sojourn in France and a Blighty wound, she thought, although most men were overjoyed to get a Blighty.

'Yes,' she said. 'Extraordinary, isn't it.'

'Extraordinary. Pull your chair nearer, and tell me what you've been doing since I last saw you.'

She hesitated and sat down, but before she could open her mouth he filled the silence with talk about himself. Incessant talk. She sat with her gloved hands folded in her lap and listened to the torrent of self-congratulation he poured forth about the brilliant career he'd had with the firm, until he'd made the supreme sacrifice and joined up, just before conscription. And what a sacrifice it had been because he was a full partner now, able to charge astronomical fees, and Uncle William was having a terrible struggle managing without him. He dropped the names of local worthies by the score, boasted about cases he'd won, never mentioned losing any, and told her of the gratitude, the gifts of appreciation he'd received from so many important people.

'How interesting,' she said. His flirtation with socialism hadn't long outlasted his flirtation with her, then. Her eyes flickered over a face now sporting the obligatory officer's moustache. How old must he be? About twenty-nine? How was it she'd never noticed how mousy his hair was, how effeminate his jaw, how plump and smooth and hairless his hands and wrists, how stubby the fingers, how the nails were cut – not straight across, like Freddie's; he'd manicured them into an *oval*. And they were longer than hers! They were hardly like a man's hands at all. How was it possible that a man who four years ago had been the height of human perfection could have shrunk into this complacent nonentity? What malevolent deity had wrought such a change in him?

It began to seep into her mind that there was no change in him; that the change was entirely in her. The scales of love had fallen from her eyes to reveal him as he was, this paltry man for whom she would once have sold her soul. She caught his eye, and watched him start to transform himself into the flirty young fellow with the banjo she'd fallen in love with, seeming to take it for granted that she was still in a state of blind adoration for him, that she was as in love with him as he was with himself. She heard someone come through the door, and turned. 'It's Alice,' she said.

It was Alice, and his face lit up at the sight of her. 'Oh, yes,' he said, 'she comes to see me every day, and stays for at least an hour, although she's frightfully busy with her nursing, aren't you, Alice?'

Alice took a seat at the other side of the bed. His face became even more animated and it was evident he was still a god in his sister's sight. The flow of words continued under her approving gaze, about his wonderful house, his treasure of a gardener, his beautiful motor car, his wife's inheritance, his wonderful sister and her wonderful cause, and her wonderful nursing, and how highly the doctors thought of her.

His wife's inheritance. There was no competing with that; Lizzie would never have one of those to offer. But was that the only thing about his wife worth talking about? His conversation was grating on her nerves, and if he didn't see it, Alice did.

'Is John at the Front?' she asked. 'I suppose he's an officer and a gentleman by now.'

'Even if only a temporary one? That's what they call men promoted from the ranks, isn't it – TGs? Not as far as I know, Alice. He was a company sergeant when I last saw him.'

'Has he any children?'

'They've got two.'

'And Emma, how many has she got?'

'Five, at the last count.'

There was a pregnant pause, with both brother

and sister silent, looking at her, waiting for something. Her face a blank, Lizzie looked into his eyes and said: 'And you, Tom, have you got any children?'

'Not... That is, no.'

Another silence, then Lizzie said: 'I wonder why you wanted to see me, Tom? After all, we only knew each other for a few weeks, for a few short cycle rides.'

'Surely more than that. We knew each other for six months at least, and you invited me to your house, and your sister's. And you came to lunch at Uncle William's.'

Oh, yes, she thought, and more besides, but he wasn't going to admit to that now, and neither would she. She gave an indifferent shrug and rose to leave. 'Oh, well, six months then. Give my regards to your wife, although I never met her. I hope you'll be better soon, Tom, after this honourable sacrifice you've made for your country.'

He seemed surprised that she could think of leaving, and rather awkwardly said, 'Thank you.'

Alice followed her. Not caring who heard her she stopped and said: 'Excuse me, Alice, but it doesn't look to me as if there's anything much the matter with him. Is he a case of what they call neurasthenia?'

'No, he was wounded, but he's making a good recovery.'

'Where? There's nothing to see.'

Alice lowered her voice. 'In a place that isn't immediately obvious.'

'Whatever do you mean?'

Alice didn't answer that, but lowered her voice

still further and said: 'Did you have his child?'

Astounded, Lizzie replied, 'It's a bit late in the day to ask me a question like that! It's four years since he jilted me, after all.'

Alice glanced towards the few interested faces looking in their direction, flushed, and said nothing.

With her cheeks burning and her eyes flashing fire, Lizzie went on, 'Oh, no, Alice, I did not have his child. Most certainly not. An honourable man like your brother would never have abandoned a girl in that condition – would he? No. If there'd ever been the remotest possibility of that, an honourable man like your brother would have done the honourable thing, and made an honest woman of her – wouldn't he?'

And so that was what the entire pantomime had been about, all that 'has this one got children?' and 'has that one?' and finally, 'did you have his child?' Well, tears and sighs, regrets and offers to make amends had all evidently been too much to hope for, and it was plain she was never going to get them. He'd damaged her in ways he could never atone for in a million years, even if he wanted to. Now he was suddenly curious about the child he knew he'd left her with – *knew* he'd left her with. It must be his wife's fault, she thought. She must be barren. Or might it ... could it possibly be on account of his having sustained 'the wound that every soldier dreads'?

No, that would be too ridiculous. His wife was barren, and the thought of dying had prompted him to find out if he had any children at all.

336

Either way, she thanked her lucky stars she had no child; that she would never know the sort of anguish Freddie's mother must have faced. For her, it was finished. Now, far from envying Tom's wife, she pitied her from the bottom of her soul.

Outside the hospital she breathed deeply and then walked along the street with a spring in her step. The thought pursued her – that perhaps the war had avenged her, freed her, and made her quits with Tom Peters. She began to whistle that jaunty, disreputable song of some of the London Regiments:

'I don't want to join the army,
I don't want to go to war,
I want to hang around Piccadilly Underground
Living on the earnings of a highborn lady.
I don't want a bayonet in my belly,
I don't want my bollocks shot away,
I want to stay in England,
Merry, merry England,
And fornicate my bleedin' life away!'

Anger, pain, relief, amusement, and malicious joy; she'd felt a maelstrom of emotions, but half an hour's brisk walking calmed her and made her contemplative.

She debated with herself: whose are the worst wounds? Who suffers more, a soldier emasculated by the war, or a girl made pregnant and then abandoned by her false lover? Or is it the child who is worst injured – cast out of its despairing mother's womb, dead before it lives, denied its claim to love and the sweetness of life?

She took down her hair that night staring at her black eyes in the mirror over the fireplace, thinking how like Freddie's mother's they were. Poor mother, to have missed so many years of knowing her son. Poor son, how she'd pitied him when his mother died, but she'd so dreaded her disease that except for the ordeal of Christmas Day she'd hardly ever gone with him to see her. She put the hairpins by the photograph of her and Freddie, then picked it up and looked at him, so full of courage, so determinedly hopeful.

She wouldn't have swapped him for a thousand like Tom Peters.

BEF
20th April 1917

Dear Lizzie,

I see the enemy's submarine campaign is having just the sort of effect they want, what with half a million tons of our cargo sunk. I hope the harvest is good this year, or I can see England starving. We're all jolly pleased that the Americans have declared war, but it'll be months before we see any American troops ready for action here.

You've probably read in the papers that the Bosche have fallen back, and dug themselves in deep farther off, along the Hindenburg line. They've made themselves as safe as possible with concrete boxes to fire at us from, with barbed wire strung between them, a hundred feet thick. They seem to have even less stomach for another Somme than we've got.

The devastation they left when they fell back from Peronne and Noyon absolutely beggars description: villages demolished – hardly one stone standing on top of another; roads destroyed; land flooded; wells poisoned; every fruit tree cut down; and all this deliberate destruction wreaked on people whose homes they've lived in for months, whose children they've played with. When they evacuated Noyon, they forced fifty girls to go with them, to act as 'orderlies'. The Huns excel at dirty tricks, don't they? One French private here told us he came home on leave for the first time since the war started to find his wife nursing a boy of about twelve months old with flaxen hair and blue eyes. Both he and his wife are dark, needless to say, so wasn't that a joyful homecoming for him? How I should feel in his shoes, I simply can't imagine.

You've no idea how lucky we are that England hasn't been invaded for hundreds of years. The air raids are bad enough, but if you knew some of the things that have happened in France – they don't bear repeating. Some of the women who lived round here looked very cowed. I think a good many of them were starved into sub-mission.

Still, as far as dirty tricks go, there are people nearer home who take the biscuit, aren't there? When my mother told me he'd promised her marriage and then married another woman two years after I was born, it absolutely felled me. I loved her, but I always blamed her, in a way; I thought he was already married when she met him. We have too much time for thinking sometimes here, and I can't get it out of my mind. I've decided I'm going to have it out with him when I get back to England. I wish I hadn't let you talk me out of it while I was there. Married officers below the rank of major can claim an extra £104 a year now, and I don't want anything more from him. I'll work my way up from the bottom whatever I do. I've seen nothing of my brother yet. I suppose it's too much to hope for.

People are saying that only the most severely wounded are going to be sent to England from now on, so no good hoping a Blighty will bring me back to you, is it? No, count the days off to the next leave, when I can see you again. We'll make it a happy one. And Lizzie, small blame to you for insisting on marriage. I'm glad you did. That's another thing I've been thinking.

Have you any news for me? I keep hoping so; we've been married for over a year now, after all. But we haven't seen enough of each other, that's the trouble.

Yours till death,
Freddie

'No, governor, you don't understand. It's not the principle – it's the money! What use are principles? They didn't pay the doctor's bills, or keep his mother comfortable for the last months of her life. Principles don't keep people out of the workhouse, and if you'll excuse me saying so, they don't keep people out of bankruptcy courts, either.'

The governor looked more than a little affronted. 'Steady on, Lizzie!'

It sobered her, but couldn't stop her. 'I'm sorry,

340

but before that business with his mother, Freddie would have been the first to agree. He seems to have gone off his head because of it – he's lost all sense of proportion. You don't give offence to people like his father and expect anything good in return. All he has to do to keep a good allowance and everything else he'll get is to keep his mouth shut and say nothing, and it shouldn't be hard, because he hardly ever sees him. The thought of losing all the money he might get is making me *ill*.'

Lizzie was standing with her bottom propped against the windowsill in the governor's living room and her hands curled round a cup of tea. She took a sip, then replaced her teacup in the saucer, and flung herself back onto the sofa, thoroughly disgruntled.

She got more sympathy from Margery. 'She doesn't mean it. She's upset. But can you do anything to stop him, Lizzie? Try to think calmly about it.'

'He said he'd have it out with him on his next leave. I just hope to God he won't put it in a letter before then. That's what's really worrying me. If only I could see Freddie face to face, I know I should be able to talk him out of it.'

'When is it, his next leave?'

Lizzie shrugged. 'God knows. You never really know.'

'Mr Dorrien's in France. Not the first time, either,' said the governor. 'He's with a troupe touring base camps. They work themselves to death, what with all the travelling, and the number of performances they give and the conditions are sometimes terrible, performing in packed YMCA huts, and worse. He goes for weeks at a time, and comes back worn to a shadow. You've got to admit, he's a game old bird.'

'What brought that on? Nobody was talking about Mr Dorrien,' Margery said.

'But Lizzie was talking about wanting to see somebody in France. It just passed through my mind, that's all.'

Lizzie was curious. 'How much do they pay him?' she asked.

'I think they're expected to do it for nothing, just about. But now I think about it properly, it wouldn't do. They wouldn't let someone who was married to a serviceman out there.'

But at the words 'expected to do it for nothing' Lizzie had lost interest. After all, there'd be little hope of running across Freddie – she might as well look for a needle in a haystack.

Mr Dorrien in France though, who would have thought it? 'I wonder if he does his "Drake's Drum",' she said, leaping to her feet to strike a pose that was a perfect caricature. With hand on heart and the other arm outstretched she declaimed:

'Drake he was a Devon man and ruled the
   Devon seas,
"Capten art tha sleepin' there below?"
Rovin' thro his death fells he went with heart at
   ease
And dreaming arl the time of Plymouth Hoe
"Take my drum to England, hand et by the
   shore

Strike et when your powder's runin low,
If the Huns sight Devon, I'll quit the port of
    Heaven
And drum them up the channel as we
    drummed them long ago"...'

'If he tries that on, he'll get a pretty poor reception. Freddie says the front-line soldiers can't stomach all that patriotic drivel.'

The governor and his wife were laughing in spite of themselves, but seemed to feel obliged to protest on Mr Dorrien's behalf. 'Oh, I don't know,' Margery defended him. 'He told me it goes down rather well.'

Lizzie held up a finger, a gleam of triumph in her eyes. 'He does do it, then!'

They laughed again at that, and it was time for Lizzie to go. She enjoyed her Sunday afternoon visits to their house. It was a safe place to let off steam.

No, she wouldn't be risking her neck to go to France and wear herself out for nothing. She'd stay a supporting actress in comfortable revue, among people she'd got to know and hope a gentle letter to Freddie would persuade him not to do anything hasty.

BEF
30th May 1917

Dear Eliza,

I'm getting myself into a very nervous state about Ollie. He's in one of the regular divisions that had it pretty rough a couple of weeks back, and I haven't heard from him since. I've made some enquiries but I can't get any news so I'm hoping he's been taken prisoner and he's in Germany working on a farm or somewhere, safe until the end of the war. I refuse to believe that anything horrible has happened to him because I simply couldn't bear it. I wonder if it would be too tactless of me to write to his wife and ask if she's heard from him?

Write to me by return, Lizzie, and tell me something frightfully funny. I badly need cheering up. Life is so desperately grim out here.

Love, from
Georgie

BEF
10th June 1917

Dear Lizzie,

Did you hear the explosions on the 5th, when we blew the top off Messines Ridge? The papers said it woke Lloyd George up in his office in Downing Street. The tunnelling company went right under the German Lines and laid twenty-two mines – it took over a year. Well, bonny lass, we blew the lot. It went off champion. You could feel the earth shake under your feet and the whole bloody hill went up in a column of fire. I thought my eardrums would have bust. I haven't a lot of sympathy for the Germans, but I felt sorry for them then. We took hundreds of prisoners. Let's hope it'll not be long before the war's over. Be a good lass and send us a few razor blades in a nice parcel. Put plenty of fags in it. Fags and mags, and plenty of razor blades, and decent grub.

Arthur

How like her younger brother. She folded the letter, thinking she would send him a parcel just to give him a shock, and was startled to hear explosions much, much nearer to home. Her heart started pattering, and her hands and feet went cold as she flew to the window. They seemed to be coming from the East End, bang, bang, bang, one after the other. German bombs again, and dropped in broad daylight this time. From huge aeroplanes.

She bought a paper on the way to the theatre. Seventy-two bombs dropped from Gotha G. IVs, and two had gone through the arched roof of Liverpool Station. Over 160 people dead so far, more than twice as many wounded, and there had been no defence. The Government had been useless.

As she expected, Freddie's next letters were fulminating against the Germans. One man in his company had learned that his daughter had been one of seventeen kids killed in a school cellar on the first of the daylight raids. The Hun, as usual, was full of filthy tricks and not playing the game, and the Government had better wake up. She gave a wry smile and thanked the Hun for taking Freddie's mind off his father for a while.

The following month the City was hit in another daylight raid. Lizzie had seen the Gothas dropping bombs further east from where she stood in the Strand, and after the raid she walked on towards Billingsgate, to see more of the same – the front walls of houses blown off, wharves destroyed, carts overturned, horses and people dead in the devastated streets and the pubs doing a roaring trade, full of women reviving themselves and their children with drink.

Freddie's letters came until the end of August, and then nothing but field post-cards until he sent another letter, very terse: 'Something has happened here that is terrible beyond words, something so awful I can't bring myself to write about it. I might be getting some leave.'

The air raids went on until people's nerves were wrecked. Half of London took refuge in Brighton until the end of the harvest moon, and the other half took shelter deep in tube stations and tunnels under the Thames. At times it would have been cheaper to close the theatres than try to keep them going.

There was one bright spot in all the gloom, though. The wheat harvest of 1917 was the best in history, so to hell with the U boats, Lizzie thought. Maybe it's *Gott mitt* the Englander, after all.

Chapter Twenty-One

'I'm not a soldier, Lizzie. I was never meant to be a soldier. I'd never seen anyone die before, except on stage.'

He was facing her, but his eyes were flitting from left to right as if watching the war unrolling before them. 'No,' he said. 'On stage, the coup de grace is dealt cleanly, perhaps from an assassin's bullet, or with a rapier to the manly bosom. Our hero's always clean, and whole and handsome, with courage and defiance in the tilt of his chin, and stern resolve aglint in his eyes. And he's always so terribly *well-dressed*. His noble sacrifice brings tears to the eyes, it inspires, and the curtain goes down. And then the hero springs to life, and takes his bows, and people rise to their feet and clap furiously and shout Bravo! Bravo!

'No. Stage heroes aren't gassed; they don't lie gurgling and gasping with bulging, bloodshot eyes, struggling for every suffocating breath. They don't take hours to die in filth, with the tops of their heads blown off, they don't stiffen in no man's land with lice running off their corpses, and their bodies aren't stacked into trench walls to provide cover from the enemy, or shelled to smithereens.

'No, Lizzie. Stage soldiers are nothing like us. We lie out in no man's land rotting in the shitten mud, with our faces turning all colours and our bodies blowing up with gas and stinking to high heaven – obscene objects. We're fodder for lice and guns while we live, and when we're dead the rats gorge on us. You should see them, rolling with fat, almost too obese to move, slithering along in mud and slime. When I look at their evil little faces I see the people in power – the politicians, the financiers and industrialists, all gorging themselves and fattening on us. They could have stopped it all. We heard the Germans had made overtures to Asquith suing for peace, but what did our Government do? They backed Lloyd George and the war, and Asquith resigned. They don't want this war to end. If anybody cared a damn, there'd be a bloody outcry. We hate them. We hate them all.'

Not knowing what to say, or what else to do, she poured a generous measure of Freddie's whisky into a cut-glass tumbler and handed it to him.

'Aah, Lizzie, my angel. Never mind. However bad it gets, there's a profit for the distillers, and the worse things get, the more they profit. It belongs to your latest admirer, I suppose. Or have you begun a love affair with the bottle yourself? Plenty do, these days.'

'Can you keep a secret, Georgie? It belongs to my husband. I still call myself Wilde, but I'm Mrs Bowman now. We're keeping it dark, though, or at least, I have been; we might lose money if his father gets to know.'

He studied the golden liquid, and took a gulp. 'Ever the crafty little cat. Imagine not telling me, your best friend. How long ago?'

'About eighteen months. His father's rolling in it, and I'm not what he'd have chosen for a daughter-in-law.'

'I see.' He sat for a while in silence, taking in his surroundings. 'It's like being at home here. So comforting, with all my old things, my lovely lamp, and my net curtains, and my pictures. Do you mind if I stay the night? You know you're in absolutely no danger.'

'Look, I'll have to go, or I'll be late for the performance. But I would rather you went home,

Georgie. What about your mother? She'll want to see you.'

'Do you know, Lizzie, you're the only person in the world who tried to keep me out of all that insanity in France. I'll never forget you for that. My mother didn't. She was overjoyed to see me marching off in my uniform, even if only as a private. I'd done something respectable at last, and she could hold her head up among her friends. There's little likelihood I'll win a medal, but I suppose getting myself killed would give her even more prestige – *mort pour la patrie*, as our allies say. I have a horrible suspicion she'd prefer it to having me scandalously alive. Put up with me, just for tonight, will you, Eliza? I want to stay with the one true friend I have left, among things that remind me of happier times.'

He was still sitting in the armchair when she got back, gazing into the dark, with the curtains still open and the fire nearly out.

'Do you love him, or was it a marriage of convenience?' he asked, watching her light the lamp. Even by its gentle light his face looked drawn, and much older.

'Yes. I mean I do love him now, I suppose.' She was surprised to hear those words on her own lips.

'I'm glad. It would be a crime not to. Don't look at me like that, Lizzie. I'm not joking; I'm serious. We must love our lovers while we can. Really love them.'

She crossed to the windows to draw the curtains, and with her back to him said: 'It's Ollie,

349

isn't it?' When she turned and saw his face she knew she couldn't throw him out.

'Lizzie, in your foulest, filthiest nightmare, you couldn't imagine it, what I've seen. Unless you've been there and lived in it, you can never understand.'

She was gasping, desperate for a hot cup of tea and crossed to the gas ring to lift the kettle. It was still full, and the cups clean. He'd had nothing, either to eat or to drink. She turned on the gas and replaced the kettle, and then hung up her coat and knelt down to revive the fire. Georgie sat in silence while she swept the hearth. It was on his mind anyway, so she said: 'Make me understand then. How did he die?'

'A bullet, I hope. He'd been missing nearly three weeks, and he was intact, you see. He must have been buried by the earth thrown up by the shelling. I have nightmares of him being buried alive, but buried he must have been, because the weather and rats and maggots and everything else would have eaten him to the bone otherwise.'

'Oh,' Lizzie shuddered. 'Oh!'

'Oh, yes, "Oh, oh." We bury our dead when we can, and sometimes the next bombardment uncovers them, or we do, when we're building and repairing saps and trenches.'

He was quiet, his eyes were still, fixed on something far off. She didn't prompt him, and eventually he went on. 'We were being strafed pretty badly and I threw myself over the lip of a shell crater just as a flare went up, full length, right on top of him, and ugh, the air came out of his putrid lungs, right into my face. God, God, it was horrible. He always used to say: "Got a kiss for me, Georgie? To show me you love me?" And I saw the thick blonde hair, you know, and that moustache, and those lips I'd kissed so many times. I couldn't mistake him. His beautiful body that used to feel so warm and alive next to mine, it was cold, and putrid. Putrid. And his eyes were sunken and shrivelled, but his mouth was smiling, as if he were saying it – "Got a kiss for me, Georgie? Go on. Go on, show me you love me *now*.""

He'd come straight from France and all his stuff was filthy, so she gave him a towel and a pair of Freddie's pyjamas and his dressing gown and sent him to the bathroom, hoping there would be enough hot water for a decent bath. By the time he came back the fire was hot enough to make toast, so she sat by the hearth on the footstool with a thick slice of bread on a toasting fork, holding it to the flame. Georgie sat in the armchair and watched her.

'Thanks, Lizzie.'

She looked up and smiled, her cheeks pink from the heat. 'What for?'

Pulling at the dressing gown as if to show her he said: 'For lifting a lead weight off my chest. I haven't been able to tell anybody, you see. I couldn't have spoken about him to anybody else. I could never have admitted I loved him, that we'd been lovers, I mean.'

'Oh, Georgie.' She looked into the fire to hide eyes brimming with tears, then heard a noise and glanced up.

Freddie stood there, filling the doorway. He looked into her eyes, then looked at Georgie – and was gone.

He had stripped it off for her, that armour of self-sufficiency and coarse carelessness he'd plated himself with since childhood. He'd thought she loved him, and trusting her he dropped that shield around his softer self. Now he reeled with the shock of the wound she'd dealt him.

'Freddie, Freddie, come back!' He could hear her crying, screaming after him and looked back to see her running along the pavement without her shoes, but he couldn't, wouldn't turn round again to let her see the pain she'd caused.

He moved swiftly down Southampton Place, keeping near to the houses, in safe shadow. Was that a body over there, or just a bundle of rags? There were bodies everywhere, but as he drew nearer he saw nothing. Nothing at all but paving stones, not even a rag. And that fellow had been drinking his whisky and wearing his dressing gown, and his pyjamas, too. He turned the corner and pressed himself against a wall, gasping for breath, feeling as if his heart would burst.

'Freddie, Freddie.' Her voice was weaker now. He stood straight, walked swiftly on, turned into Kingsway with the sight of her flushed face filling his mind, with her eyes full of tenderness for that filthy actor. Such tenderness as he'd never seen, that had never been there for him, never. But Elsie had looked like that when John left her for France – because she loved him.

She must have hurt her feet, but she'd never

catch him now. Down, down Kingsway and onto the Strand, and over Waterloo Bridge to the station. And he'd been so desperate to get back to her to lose himself in her embraces, her scent, her warmth, her love.

March, march, march and wait for a train back to Southampton, back to France. Back to apocalyptic ruin, and his company of men; men who would always play the game. Men among whom he'd found comradeship, for the first time in his life. Men he could trust. He reached Waterloo Station, cold and comfortless, and sat down at last.

'Oh, Lizzie, oh, Lizzie, Lizzie, Lizzie.' He raised his arm and drew his sleeve across his eyes.

What, weeping? What was the matter with him these days?

The train ground its way out of the station. Exhausted, he closed his eyes and sank not into the oblivion he wanted but into Flanders, that nightmarish country where constant shelling and the worst autumn rain in living memory had turned the earth into a morass in which men were exhausted after half a dozen strides. Where liquid mud and slime made green from poison gas sucked down gun carriages and horses, mules and men, and drowned them in its treacly filth. In that tormented wasteland of waterlogged shell holes his men had picked their way to the Front with the sweet smells of poison gas and rotting flesh in their nostrils, on slimy, slippery roads and tracks swept by artillery fire, not daring to move either right or left to escape it for fear of falling into the swamp, and every man dreading the injury or the lost footing that would send him into the engulfing mud. Men had broken their backs and lost their lives in that place trying to free comrades from the deathly embrace of the mire.

After they were relieved he'd sent his men back behind the lines, scraping mud from their eyes, carrying rifles so thick with mud they looked like trees, men without boots, men bloodied and lame, all exhausted and trudging wearily on, too tired to care much about catching a bullet. Stunned with tiredness himself he was following some distance behind when he heard feeble cries for help. Following the sound he came upon a horse and gun carriage up to the limbers in mud and a young corporal chest deep beside it, his dark eyes old and mad with suffering after a shrapnel wound to his leg and two fearful, struggling, sinking days. With neither a horse nor a mule in sight and men too done and too far away to help there was no hope of freeing either of them, and if there had been, the lad was certain to die of tetanus or gangrene from that filth. Freddie gave him three pellets of morphine and calmed him, reminded him of his mother, and promised him he would get back to her. Keeping his voice full of optimism he promised a rescue he knew was impossible, and when he saw the poor chap's pupils shrink to pin-pricks he held his service revolver to his head and freed him, and shot the poor dumb beast as well.

He had borne his burden alone for weeks, aching to go home to his wife, to feel her arms around him, and to see love and understanding and mercy and forgiveness in her face when he told her how it was he came to kill his brother.

Horror upon horror, those eyes still haunted him. Waking or sleeping, he saw them in his dreams.

He leaned against the rail when they weighed anchor from Southampton under circling observation planes in grey winter skies. In his mind's eye he saw her crying and shouting after him, running, following him with her poor little feet bare, and the November night so cold. But she couldn't catch him, and she must have known he would never go back, for he heard it wrenched from her, that last sobbing scream: 'Freddie. Oh, Freddie.'

He crossed his arms over his lifejacket, hugged himself. 'Lizzie. Oh, Lizzie! You shouldn't have done it! You shouldn't, you shouldn't have done it.'

A soldier further along gave him a queer look, then felt in his pocket and retrieved a packet of Woodbines. He held them out to Freddie. 'Coffin nail, Captain?'

He took one and briefly smiled his thanks, found and struck a match and shielding the flame from the breeze he managed to light the other fellow's cigarette and then his own.

'Woman trouble?' the soldier asked.

Freddie gave a non-committal shrug, inhaled on his cigarette, held it up in mock salute, said: 'Thanks,' and turned away, to stare at the receding coastline. The soldier took the hint and wandered off to join the hundreds of other servicemen swarming over the decks. Freddie turned and with his back against the rail he watched him go.

Woman trouble? He hadn't thought so on his last leave, when she'd found his mother for him, and looked after her. She'd surprised him then by refusing the money he'd tried to repay, astonishing in one so keen to earn and hoard, so determined to keep a grip on his father's money.

And now, to find her with that dirty gigolo. When he'd voiced his suspicions before they were married her protests and her laughter had seemed genuine, and he'd believed her. Now he remembered their tango in that den of a dance hall. The way they'd danced, he should have known. She loved that filthy blighter, no doubt about it; he'd seen it in her eyes. He was the sort that batted for both sides, and she was the sort who would sell her charms for a stake in an old man's fortune.

How many times had he told her he loved her? A thousand, or more? How many times had he written it? Probably in every letter he'd ever sent her, and although he'd hoped for it, he'd never yet heard those words on her lips. Never, never. Nor had she ever written them, and he'd scoured through every letter he'd ever had from her.

They'd soon be in Le Havre, and he'd be back where every man was – who was a man at all – with his regiment. He'd take his chances with them. He'd go back to France and forget her. Forget she ever existed. He couldn't mask life's horrors from himself any longer, and he'd go back to France to spend his last hours among decent men, and hurl himself into the abyss. And he would write to his father and tell him to go to hell.

Freddie's pyjamas were neatly folded on the armchair when she got back to the flat, and Georgie was dressed and ready to go. She saw the wretchedness on his face and tried to reassure him.

'It's all right. He's gone off like this before. He'll come back.'

'I hope so. I'm going, in case he does. I'll get the tube to Pimlico.' He put a hand on her arm. 'I wouldn't have done this to you for anything on earth, Eliza, old thing.'

'He'll come back,' she repeated.

With a doubtful downward twitch of his mouth Georgie kissed her forehead, and after one last, regretful glance round the room he lifted his kitbag and left. Lizzie picked up the pyjamas and sank into the armchair to hold them, and wait.

Freddie found his regiment near Neuve Eglise, in 'rest areas'. Little rest to be had, with men needed for salvage duty, or working parties for Engineers and Pioneers, and constant work on defences. And then there was training and assimilation of new drafts. Work was unceasing.

Yates was back. Too many bloody officers in Craiglockheart, he joked, few of whom he had liked. The only man on earth he would have confided in, Yates sat listening like a Dutch uncle while Freddie poured his heart out about finding his brother up to his neck in mud, wounded and out of his mind with pain and fear at Poelcapelle. 'I still see his eyes, staring at me, and I can hardly believe it really happened – but it was so nightmarish, it must have.'

'The quacks tell you to talk about these things. It stops them creeping up on you in the middle of the night. What else could you have done, Freddie?'

'Rescued him.'

'How? What with?'

'I don't know.'

'Neither do I. You saved him from slow drowning in that mud, knowing every moment what was happening to him.'

'Maybe.'

'Which would you have chosen, a bullet or slow suffocation in filth?'

'His eyes, though, Yates, old chap. I see them in my dreams.'

That night, though, the laughter of children echoed through his dreams, and he awoke feeling lighter. Yates had done him good, and as soon as he was free he went in search of him. He found him playing patience and stood looking over his shoulder for a moment or two, then placed a couple of the upturned cards and drew up a chair.

'Ah, Freddie. You've come to spoil my game.'

'No, but two heads are better than one. I want to talk to you about Lizzie.'

Yates scanned his columns of cards. 'What about her?'

Freddie poured it all out, and ended with: 'You didn't like her, did you?'

'I think it was more that she didn't like me. You have to remember, I didn't meet her under very favourable circumstances. You're a rather primitive sort of chap at times, Freddie, and it has to be admitted – my errand wasn't terribly honourable, was it?'

Freddie placed a column of cards. 'I suppose not. Still, I did the decent thing and married her, and look how she's repaid me. I've told you what happened, and there's no room for doubt. Is there?'

'You married her because she refused to live with you, Freddie. I wouldn't say there's no room for doubt, either,' Yates shrugged. 'It looks bad, but you didn't exactly catch them in the act, did you?'

'Not quite, but he was in my – *my* bloody pyjamas.'

'And dressing gown. I know.' Yates thought for a while, then said: 'Look, old man, if you had her before a court martial, you'd let her tell her side, wouldn't you?'

'Of course.'

'Well, then.'

A week after that awful night Lizzie saw his writing on an envelope, and tore it open.

20th November 1917

Dear Lizzie,
I think you owe me an explanation.
Freddie.

One terse sentence. But she'd already written to him, had written to him every single day. Their letters must have crossed in the post, or perhaps hers had gone astray.

Georgie had insisted she could say anything she liked about him if it would get her husband back for her, so Lizzie wrote again and told him everything. But it was two weeks before she had an answer, a mundane, colourless little missive which contained no reference to his finding her with Georgie, no reaction to her explanation, no fulminating against the Hun, no endearments, no longing for his next leave, no threatened explosions.

She wrote again, with more forceful explanations and stronger denials, and a threat that she'd make Georgie write himself. His answer to that came by return of post – he wouldn't have it. She must do no such thing. After that his letters were infrequent, and so polite they almost broke her heart.

By the end of the year Freddie was billeted in the Convent in Poperinghe, known to the troops as 'Pop', with the luxury of clean white sheets, a room that smelt of polish, the kindness of the nuns, and the tranquility of their unvarying routine. It must be easy to believe in God in such a place, he thought. A few days before Christmas he was surprised and very bucked to get a hamper from Fortnum and Mason's – game pie, smoked salmon, pheasant, tins of ham, and salmon, Christmas Cake, Scotch Bun, whisky, brandy, cigarettes, the inevitable and always welcome pairs of socks – no end of stuff. Everything he liked, and all of it from Lizzie. She'd spent a fortune. What a wrench it must have been to her miserly little soul to part with all that money, but he was glad she had, it was the only parcel he would get, after the breach with his father. How would she take that news, he wondered?

He scanned her letter. 'I don't know what else to say to you... I feel as if I'm writing to a stranger... Do you want me to stop writing? Don't you love me anymore?'

What was the use of her saying anything? Her every denial deepened his conviction of her guilt, and the stronger her denials the stronger was his disbelief of them. But did he want her to stop? He scarcely knew. She was headstrong and dishonest, and what hope had he of controlling her, separated from her by so many miles? And how could he have any confidence in her after seeing her with *him*, the sort of fellow whom she *knew* he loathed? He'd had enough of that sort of filthy blighter at school. Impossible to tell a woman *why* that was, but he'd been so deeply angry he'd wished that he no longer loved her.

Strange though, to stop loving wasn't as simple as he'd imagined, not like snuffing out a candle, or turning off a tap. And he was touched by her gift in spite of himself and it was Christmas, the season of goodwill, and she was his wife, after all. He put on his greatcoat and hat and spent a freezing cold morning wandering round Pop looking in the shops, but Lizzie had such exacting tastes, and he saw only tawdry lace, unworthy souvenirs and untrustworthy watches, none of which she would like. So he sent her a gift of money and wrote to her explaining why, suggesting she get 'something nice' in London.

He had a fancy to hear a Mass. His mother had been a Catholic, though not practising, and he had an urge to experience something of her religion, to feel it, and feel closer to her. So, he went to Poperinghe's fine ninth – or was it eighth – century church at midnight on Christmas Eve and stood, and sat and knelt along with the rest of the congregation, smelling incense and listening to a Mass sung in Latin. It struck him as mysterious and meaningless, until the voice of a soprano soared to heaven, pure and crystal clear in a hymn he'd never heard before. 'Lord, have mercy, have mercy on me,' was her refrain. It pierced him to the quick and stayed with him long after he'd left the church, the sound of that sublime voice repeating and repeating again those words of supplication.

He fell into a reverie during his walk back to the convent that freezing winter's night under a brilliant moon and stars. And were they the same moon and stars that had shone on him aeons ago when, wrapped in blankets with his mother and brother, he'd journeyed on carts through the poorest parts of London? No stable could have been more lowly than some of the places they'd lived in, but what laughter they'd shared, and what joy he'd often felt in those mean streets of his childhood. And now it was all lost to him forever, and his wife was faithless. Except for his gallant company of Diehards he was alone. And what, he wondered, would he do at the war's end, when they were gone too, those men he'd learned to love? He tried to hum the catch that ran through his brain, but the lump in his throat choked it off.

Lord, have mercy, have mercy on me.

The battalion was in reserve positions in January, with, to his amazement, a party of American officers attached for instruction. The enemy were quiet, too quiet, during the worst two months of that most bitterly cold of winters, like the calm before the storm. Then in early March, when they were in the front line Fritz started shelling them with gas as well as explosives, the gas shells unmistakable with their slopping, hooting sound and the velvety plop of their bursting. The masks went on, but too late for some. Mustard gas this time, almost odourless, with its sly, insidious fumes that took men unawares – until the damage was done. Then they clutched their throats and gasped, with their eyes writhing in the sockets, struggling for every breath, their blue faces masks of fear as they lost the sight in their oozing, blistered eyes. Cursing the hellhound who invented the stuff, Freddie sent men whose lives had become so enmeshed with his that he thought of them as brothers on to the dressing stations. His own eyes began to discharge. The MO gave him an eyewash, then he was back to the trenches, wondering what would come next.

Day in, day out, their ranks were being thinned, in preparation for – what? He had a deep sense of foreboding, but when, in the middle of March, he was offered a few days' leave he took them. He wanted to get away from death and trenches, and visit that other world, the world of pampered, sleek civilians. He wanted to see Paris, its architecture, and its women.

The skies were full of grey clouds and the trees on the boulevards still bare, but in spite of the cold there was an unmistakable feeling of spring in the air. Apart from the air raids, and the fact that several people were wearing black, there was little sign of the war. On the whole, Paris was a place of ease and plenty. Sacrifice, it seemed, had been firmly delegated to the men at the front.

He wanted to be among women, beautiful women, and if they were whores, and if they were mercenary and shallow, what of it? So were most women, and it didn't stop men needing them. He wanted, more than anything, to be in that place where he had never yet failed to find solace, the arms of a woman.

It was mid-afternoon when he heard laughter and turned into a hotel, empty except for a handful of customers and three young *filles de joie* who were seated at a table, their dresses shorn well short of the ankle and their sprawling postures displaying a good deal of deliciously rounded calf. They were smoking and chattering together in French, and either assuming he couldn't understand the language or not caring whether he could or not one of their number began describing her experience with a feeble fellow who started lovemaking and quickly failed. 'He went pump, flop flop!' she exclaimed, illustrating the scene by gesture.

This was a hotel with women on the menu. Amid gales of laughter Ashton made his way to a table and beckoned a waiter. When the laughter had subsided and the place was almost quiet a pretty brown-haired girl in red, the most lively of the trio, suddenly thrust her shapely arm into the air several times and burst out: 'Well, he pumped like a little jack-rabbit with me!'

They all shrieked again at this and Ashton, laughing too, ordered champagne and sent a bottle over to them. When they turned to thank him he pointedly raised his glass to the brunette in red and winked. A sensuous, uncomplicated, fun-loving French girl, she was just what was needed to raise a man's spirits and drive dismal thoughts away. He would have her, if she'd let him.

He threw off his tunic and gazed into a pair of roguish brown eyes that widened under their thick, shapely brows when he began swiftly and expertly to strip her. Her skin was smooth and honey coloured, her breasts firm and full, more than his hand could hold, the nipples large and brown. Her belly was soft and rounded. She was typically, brazenly, beautifully French. She laughed and began coyly to unbutton his trousers, but he had no patience with her slowness, and tore off his clothes himself.

'Une petite femme mignonne et brune,' he murmured, pressing his lips against hers and thrusting his tongue easily into her willing mouth. He pushed her back onto the bed and lay at her side, kissing her face, her neck, and her breasts.

Finally, putting his hand between thighs that fell too readily apart he found her liquefying.

She might have been a pleasing little dumpling, this hireling, but somehow the scent of her, and the taste of her skin and her kisses were all wrong. She lacked the touch and even the accent to keep him aroused and his enthusiasm for the assault plummeted. After a little fondling he lay back against the pillow and stared despondently at the ceiling. She leaned over him and making a little moue of disappointment, began to stroke his hair.

'*Tu es triste.*'

'*Oui, ma petite, tu as raison. Je suis tres triste.*'

'*C'est la guerre.*'

'*Non, ce n'est pas la guerre; c'est une femme. Une femme Anglaise, et tres mechante.*'

She cast her eyes upwards in a look of disapprobation. '*Ah, les Anglaises!*'

He took her hand and kissed it, then got out of bed to stand before a mahogany framed cheval glass. His eyes met their melancholy reflection in its surface, travelled downwards to the lifeless part and fixed there. What a disgrace, and what fun those little French minxes were going to have at the expense of *le capitaine Anglais* with his flop, flop, flop. With his eyes still on the offending part he heaved a theatrical, comic-mournful sigh and asked in pleading tones: 'Oh, why won't you stand up?'

His petite femme must have understood him, for she rolled about the bed howling with laughter. Ashton turned and gave her a rueful smile, feeling he'd let down his little partner, himself, his regiment, and the entire British Expeditionary Force, and at heart, caring very little about it. He dressed, put a week's pay on the table and left. That girl wasn't doing too badly from the war.

Wondering whether Lizzie imagined he did this sort of thing all the time, he walked back to his hotel, wishing he'd gone home after all. He might as well have. He'd spent his whole morning wandering round the Marais looking at architecture that had failed to interest him because he was too busy searching the faces of women for a face that looked like hers. If he was going to chase whores, he might as well chase that frightful, mercenary little whore he was mad for – his wife.

That was what he would do next time. He'd go home and oust that filthy little shirt-lifter, put the fear of God in him; and if he survived this bloody war he'd never spend another night away from her. He'd keep her well under control, and he knew exactly how to do it. He'd keep her well fucked; give her a few babies to make sure she'd no time for any stage nonsense, and keep her well away from all those bloody stage people with their damnably lax morals. He'd make certain she never needed another man, nor had any time for one. Then he'd be able to feel sure of her.

He changed direction and walked towards the boulevard Haussmann to see if he could find a nice little present for her – something expensive in the jewellery line that she'd be sure to like. And when he got back he'd go and see his CO and claim the married man's allowance.

Yates screamed and fell beside him, sinking to the ground as they were overwhelmed by hundreds of Bosche. Freddie stooped beside him and tried to haul him to his feet.

'My back! I can't move my legs,' Yates gasped. 'I've had it, old man. Leave me, and get on. I've had it, Freddie. Get on.'

Get on? A swift glance round assured Freddie that there could be no 'getting on.' There was nothing to be done but surrender. They were taken completely by surprise and outnumbered hundreds to one, and resistance was futile. He knelt beside Yates, and raised his shoulders. The colour drained from his face.

'God, I'm cold,' he shivered.

Freddie quickly stripped off his greatcoat, and tucked it round him, as if he were tucking in a child, then fumbled for morphine. Yates gave a feeble smile and grasped his hand. 'I never told you how much I love you, did I, old man?'

Startled, Freddie stared into Yates's pain-filled eyes. 'I know, old chap, and I love you – like my own brother.'

'No,' Yates winced. 'Not like that, Freddie. More than I could ever love any woman. Do you understand?'

Freddie froze, then felt a German bayonet prodding his back and had little choice but to raise his hands. 'Good luck, old lad,' he said, as, very much against his will, he got to his feet. 'They'll come for you soon, don't worry!' he called, as he was herded away.

Poor old Yates, he must have been mad to say a thing like that – 'I love you.' Or he'd known it was the end of him. Poor fellow, he'd probably be doctored by a bayonet in his belly, or simply be left to die. Freddie stumbled on, blind with tears.

Neither was he safe himself. Herd the prisoners into a hut or a dugout, chuck a couple of Mills bombs in after them, and no more trouble with the prisoners. No guarding them, no risk from them, no having to sacrifice rations to feed them. Both sides did it. If he ever saw England and his wife again, he'd be a very lucky man.

Chapter Twenty-Two

Christmas again, the worst bloody time of the year, and this year people were beginning to think the country was running out of food. Lizzie had done her share of panic buying along with the rest, and had her very own hoard of sugar and flour and tinned food under her bed, but nothing as luxurious as the stuff she'd sent to Freddie. And for him to send money in return, that was even worse than those fortnightly letters containing nothing but polite enquiries about her family, and her health, and her career, and giving nothing away about himself. It was as bad as the time he'd wanted to pay her for looking after his mother. The smallest gift he'd chosen himself, anything would have been better than money and had she not been too sick at heart she would have been furious with him. But his letter was friendlier, and she wondered if he'd been drunk when he wrote it. The thought gave her some encouragement, because that's when the truth comes out, when people have had one too many.

She had a couple of field postcards around the end of March, telling her he was all right, and then she heard no more from him. A horror of what she might find prevented her from making any enquiries of the Army or poring through the casualty lists, although it was obvious they were growing longer. She would trust that no news was good news, and then it would turn out so. But she became more and more unsettled, and in mid-April, wandering by sheer force of habit through a department store full of the new season's clothes she stopped to look at a beautiful evening gown. She might get something like that before his next leave, but better keep tight hold of her cash for now. On leaving the store she bumped into Ethel, dressed from head to toe in black, as most people seemed to be these days. Oh, evil omen.

'Who is it, Ethel?' she asked, although she knew. Ethel's pale blue eyes looked into hers and brimmed with tears. It was her fiancé, died of wounds in some French hospital at the end of March, and buried in France.

And who else would it have been, after all? Lizzie sympathized, and could have done more. She was going to have some tea, and could easily have invited her. That would have been the Christian, charitable thing to do, but seized by a superstitious fear that bereavement might be contagious she hastened away, to keep Freddie safe.

She followed her familiar track and slipped thankfully into Lyons Corner House, where who should she see but Mr Dorrien, just giving his order to the waitress. Poor old thing, he looked worn out. If he only knew how ridiculous his hair looked. He'd much better let it go grey, and stop trying to be young altogether.

Unterseeboot. That was the name, or so she'd heard, and when they cast off a little frisson of fear ran down her spine at the thought that any of those deadly U boats might have slipped through the channel's defences and be lurking in the depths below them even now, intent on consigning her to a watery grave. She looked up and saw airmen soaring aloft, circling like hawks in the blue April heaven. Down below destroyers were patrolling the sea. How stupid to be fearful. The British Navy was on the alert and guarding her sea-lanes pretty well. She breathed a little more freely. She had attached herself to a troupe of entertainers led by Mr Dorrien, and he bolstered her confidence. 'Do you know, Miss Wilde, not one life has been lost so far on this crossing,' he said.

She shivered. 'Is there a nice warm bar, somewhere the officers might congregate?'

He looked doubtful. 'I'm not a very spirituous person myself, Miss Wilde, and when we get to France we mostly perform in YMCA huts and such places, you know, and they rather frown upon...'

'And well they may, Mr Dorrien, but,' she lowered her voice, 'when I let you persuade me to

371

come to France you did promise to help me find my husband, didn't you? I'm sure that awful misunderstanding about Georgie Bartlett is the reason he's stopped writing, and I want to make things right with him.'

'Shush, Miss Wilde,' he said. 'I warned you, you mustn't let on you're married to one of the officers. If it gets out, the Army will send you packing. They won't allow wives or sweethearts anywhere near the soldiers.'

'It won't get out. It hasn't yet, except to one or two of my close friends. But you do sympathize, don't you? If I'm to have any chance of finding him I must look in the right places, and Freddie told me it's phenomenal the amount of whisky the British Army drinks. He should know, he drinks a fair bit of it himself, so it seems obvious that wherever they serve the hard stuff is the place to start making a few discreet enquiries.'

'It's not very likely they'll allow it, Miss Wilde. They're very touchy about their rank. I'm sure they won't let us in.'

'Perhaps if I get into my Tommy uniform, and we offer to give an impromptu concert, for all of them, men and officers alike?' she said. 'Everybody likes a concert, that's why we're here. And that would give me the chance of talking to lots of people afterwards. It always does, and we might get invitations, after that.'

A rough and ready show, given by those members of the troupe who weren't too seasick, in a room packed to suffocation with men and their kit, it was, in spite of all, fairly successful. At least

372

it broke the ice and led to lots of chat afterwards, mostly about the acts. She saw some of Freddie's regiment, and made her way across to them.

'Can yer shoot as good as yer look, Miss?' asked a cheeky little bandsman, who looked about twelve.

'Give me a rifle, an' I'll show yer!' she challenged, with the self-same accent and attitude.

'Yer'd look a lot better in a dress, though!'

'Nearly as good as some of the female impersonators in the army shows, do you think?' she asked.

'A lot better, I'd say!'

After an exchange of Cockney banter and demands to see her pay-book, she said: 'I know somebody who was there when we took Peronne and Noyon. And now the Germans have broken through and taken them back again. I feel sorry for the French.'

'Yes, Miss. We'll be fighting over ground we've fought over three times already,' said one corporal, sounding very dispirited.

Thousands of men from all regiments had been killed, and as many taken prisoner was all she could learn, but before she left them she couldn't help it, couldn't forbear asking in as light-hearted a manner as she could affect if any of them knew of a Captain Ashton, who was an acquaintance of a friend of hers. Then the tenor of the conversation changed, and she sensed she must be very careful not to arouse suspicion, or turn them off her.

'As bad as old Antonio, is 'e, Miss? Left 'er on 'er onio, 'as 'e?' one of them quipped, after an awkward silence. Lizzie laughed and said: 'That's right. 'E's as bad as old Antonio and Kelly from the Emerald Isle put together, that one.' They laughed at that, but if they were to be believed, none of them knew anything about Freddie. She excused herself and left them, thinking he must have been taken prisoner. The possibility that he was dead was something she refused to contemplate.

Although she'd seen a few sly smiles from the men during Mr Dorrien's dramatic monologues, on the whole they'd gone down better than she would have thought. At least he'd had the sense not to sing any patriotic songs, or talk about worthwhile sacrifices. It was her act she had doubts about. Enthusiasm for women impersonating soldiers had definitely waned, and Hun bashing and flag waving seemed to have fallen out of favour along with 'Rule Britannia' and 'Hearts of Oak'. A good many Tommies resented talk from civilians about cowardly Germans, and said so. It was clear that what went down well with London audiences wouldn't do in France. Her repertoire needed some adjustment.

'They're amazingly cheerful, aren't they, considering what they've been through, and what's still facing them over there,' she commented, when she found Mr Dorrien.

He lowered his voice. 'A surface cheeriness, I think. Their lives are so precarious, you know, they live for the day, and who can blame them? That's why these concerts are so very important, Miss Wilde. Some of these men will be dead before the week's out.'

'What a morbid thought, Mr Dorrien,' she protested.

'I know, and I do try to be uplifting in the stuff I give them. But you should hear some of the songs sung by the soldier entertainers, if you think I'm being morbid. Things about poor blind boys, and children depressed at losing their fathers, and an even worse one about somebody being shelled to bits:

'His right hand dropped in Paris,
His eyeball's in Tralee
They haven't left an atom
Of my pal's anatomy.

'Not quite "Tipperary", is it? Terribly, terribly depressing stuff, but some of them absolutely love it.'

'Mm,' said Lizzie. 'It's what they live with at times, I suppose. It sounds terrible, but do you think they might be poking fun, Mr Dorrien? Making light of things by being a bit ironical, I mean?'

If they were, it was lost on Mr Dorrien. 'Oh, no, not at all,' he said. 'They look perfectly mournful.'

Motor ambulances were driving up one after the other in an endless stream when they arrived in Boulogne and men with bloodstained bandages covering missing limbs and head wounds were being carried on stretchers up the gangways and onto the hospital ships. One man looked straight into her eyes, and inwardly she shivered, imagining how gladly he'd probably marched away to fight for England. Now he was crippled and mutilated, how much would England do for him? What and who was 'England' when you came to think of it? That look he'd given her seemed to say it was her; and she shivered again at the thought.

She hardly knew what she'd expected France to be like, but Boulogne seemed hardly French at all. The air was full of the sound of English voices, even of English spoken in French accents. British uniforms were everywhere, and the streets reverberated with the tramp of British feet. It was near noon when their little troupe made its way through a harbour thronging with soldiers, horses, guns and all the paraphernalia of war, and streamed out with the rest towards the British Front. Allied aircraft wheeled like birds of prey in the cloudy skies.

In three weeks, the little concert party travelled behind the lines from Ypres to Amiens by way of Arras, and back again, sometimes giving three shows a day along the way in any improvized theatre they could find. YMCA huts were most frequently used – light, airy barns which were invariably clean, sometimes enlivened by pretty curtains and vases of flowers and always cheered by the stalwart daughters of the British middle-classes serving behind the counter. Packed to capacity, they could hold almost two thousand men.

Mr Dorrien was deeply impressed by them, and

enthusiastic in his praise. 'Such pleasant places, you know, Miss Wilde, and very well spoken of by the soldiers. They're guaranteed a cheery welcome and a good, cheap meal – so rare in France.'

No doubt everything he said was true, but unworthy though it was, she agreed with her brother Arthur's description, 'all tinkling pianos and *parsons*, and soprano helpers warbling "Bonny Charlie's Noo Awa'." The Tommies might have enjoyed a risqué joke or a suggestive song, but who would dare attempt one, knowing that they were expected to fold their hands in prayer at the end of the show? Not Lizzie. It was like performing before the Lord Chancellor, and she was disgusted at having to ditch some of her livelier impersonations.

Much more to her taste were the few more full-blooded shows they did in conjunction with the soldier entertainers in barns and aircraft hangars, and theatres purpose built in concrete. There, free from the watchful eyes of the over-virtuous she could give a more ebullient performance, and enjoy herself. Those joint shows also gave her the chance of mingling with the army's performers, many of whom knew Georgie, but none of whom, unfortunately, knew anything about Freddie.

Poor old Dorrien, he was so worn out he looked like a ghost by the time they embarked for England, but he'd been game to the last, and so protective of her. 'There appear to be no holds barred to the soldier entertainers, Miss Wilde,' he apologized when they were on the boat. 'Very indelicate to a lady's ears. It's as well you're used

377

to music hall.'

'Hmm,' she said.

He paused for a moment, then said: 'After that last show, some of them actually told me they'd toned it down, just for our benefit. Well, all I can say to that, Miss Wilde, is I shudder to think what it was like before!'

'Yes,' she said, but she was miles away. The tour had been a revelation. It had also been a washout, because for all her discreet enquiries she was no further forward. Freddie seemed to have vanished off the face of the earth, and all she could do now was to hope that she'd arrive home to find he'd written to her. Drained, she made her way to her cabin, too exhausted to worry about submarines, or torpedoes, or anything else the Hun might throw at them.

She dumped her suitcase, and went straight down to see the tenant in the ground floor flat. The door was opened almost before she had time to tap. She gave her brightest smile and asked: 'Any letters for me, Mrs Hawkins?'

'Come in.' The invitation was softly spoken, but there was no answering smile as Mrs Hawkins led her inside and made her sit down in a clean little sitting room crowded with cushions and crochet work, and innumerable little nick-nacks. 'My sister's had a stroke you see, and I had to go and stay with her, so I've been away from home nearly as long as you, and I'm still going to see her every day. I haven't been here to take in any letters, but there was nothing in your pigeonhole when I got back.'

'I'm sorry to hear that, Mrs Hawkins – about your sister, I mean,' said Lizzie, though more concerned with her own disappointment. Mrs Hawkins went through the kitchen and into the yard, and came back with a blackened parcel. 'I was here when this came, though. I kept it in the coalbunker outside. It smells so awful.' She went to the mantelpiece and found a letter. 'I'm so sorry, my dear. I'm afraid it's bad news.'

He'd been posted missing at the beginning of April, during the massive German breakthrough. He must have given her name as his next of kin, and she read the letter from his commanding officer half a dozen times, then unwrapped the parcel and sat in her armchair staring at the greatcoat, stiff with mud and blood, stinking of putrefaction, and with its bullet hole so unmistakably Freddie's. She could have repaired that for him. Could have done, should have done. Too late now. She searched the pockets and pulled out a handkerchief, a few verses scribbled on a sheet of writing paper, a battered little book of Norse myth stamped with the crest of his public school, and a letter. It was dated the first of December, and beneath the embossed address was scrawled one short sentence: 'As you wish,' and then his father's signature.

But where was Freddie's hat, his whistle, his revolver, periscope, watch, all the rest of it? Where were his field glasses and his wallet?

An overpowering smell of the graveyard pervaded the room, seeping into every crevice. No wonder the saint downstairs had left the parcel in

379

her coalbunker. Lizzie went to the window and lifted the sash, hung Freddie's coat outside and brought the window down on it, trapping the collar between the frame and the sill. The night was fine, and it would air like that, get some of the stink out of it, and tomorrow it could go to the cleaners.

She lit the gas ring and put the kettle on, then picked up the verses and read:

And the soldiers, ah, the soldiers,
We that go like lambs to slaughter
We that crouch in trench and crater
Wounded moan.
The fiery shell-shards near us
Their red-hot shrapnel sears us
And the dead eyes of the slain
Seem to mock such sacrifice, so little gain.
Seem to mock our shell-torn flesh
And splintered bone.

Who seeks glory in so rolling
On the human heart a stone?
They are neither man nor woman,
They are neither brute nor human
They are Ghouls.

It was so unlike the Freddie she'd known, to compare himself to a sacrificial lamb like that.

Chapter Twenty-Three

'Well, they liked you at the Karsino, Lizzie. Fred says you can do a spot there, any time you like. I can't understand why you stopped going,' the governor told her.

'Freddie didn't like it, that's why,' she said, 'but he's not here now, is he? So I might as well go back. Music hall pays better than the theatre by a long chalk, and now I'm on my own again, I'd better go for something that pays decent money. I'll do a bit of charity stuff, but not too much, and none for shows organized by titled ladies, if you don't mind. I'm sick to the back teeth of being treated like dirt by high-handed ladyships who take all the credit for our efforts. The last show I did, the titled madam who organized it all told *us* – a bunch of half-starved penniless per-formers who'd just done an afternoon's work gratis – to take a collection among ourselves, because the takings had "fallen considerably short of expectations", if you please!'

Margery gave her a look of sympathy. 'You're not struggling for money, are you? Have you heard anything about your widow's pension?'

'No, and I don't want to. They'll only make me pay it back if it turns out he's alive. Your garden's looking well just now, Margery.'

'Yes, there are still a few bulbs flowering, but it'll soon get very overgrown. There's no help to be had these days, and I've rather lost interest in it, I'm afraid. There are things that matter so much more.'

'You're on some committee, aren't you?'

'A few of them. The Prisoners of War Comfort Fund, The Variety Artistes' Concerts at the Front Fund, the British Women's Hospital, and one or two others. It keeps me busy, now that the children are gone.'

How could she bear to mention that? Lizzie thought of their grief at the funeral, and wondered that the governor and his wife had survived it. Perhaps it was better that Freddie would be buried in France if his body were ever recovered, because her feelings now were nothing like theirs had been when their children had died. She had none. It was as if it were happening to somebody else a million miles away and nothing to do with her at all. Curious, because she'd thought she loved him. But she might have been turned to stone, for all she felt.

Ah, well, lucky for me, she thought. It just goes to show I never really loved him after all.

'Bloody hell, Eth. *The Mumming Birds?* That sketch has got whiskers on it. It's the one that Chaplin used to do before he went to America, isn't it? Fancy Mr Karno sending for us to take part in that.'

Lizzie had been engaged at short notice for the week to do a male impersonation and sing a couple of comic songs, and had arrived early so that she could enjoy a stroll round the Karsino's gardens before getting ready for her act. She regretted it now, however, for the beauty of the gardens brought back memories of her time there with Freddie. It was a relief to see Ethel coming towards her, looking a picture of blonde English purity in a pale blue dress with a Peter Pan collar, trimmed with white.

'Well, it was always a great hit with the public. "That side-splitting, rip-roaring show of the nineties," the governor calls it. And a lot of younger people haven't seen it,' Ethel said, 'so I suppose it won't hurt to do it again, now people need cheering up so badly. We'll be doing it in the open air if the weather holds. The governor says I'm to play the little singer that the drunk takes a fancy to. I'm a rotten singer, but that's all the better for the comedy, isn't it?'

'I hope the drunk takes a fancy to me too. You get things thrown at you if he doesn't, don't you?'

'Yes, so they tell me. No doubt we'll get directions.'

'No doubt. It probably *will* be muddle and mayhem, with none of us rehearsed. Karno must trust us. But it's only half past four, Eth, and the first show doesn't start until six. Shall we take a boat out for half an hour?'

'Can you row?'

'Anybody can row, Eth.'

'Don't go far. We don't want to get swept out to sea.'

'Not much chance of that, from Tagg's Island.'

They walked towards the small boats bobbing on the Thames, thoughtfully provided by Mr Karno for the pleasure of his guests, and the attendant helped them in. Lizzie pulled the boat away from the side with a few easy sweeps of the oars.

Ethel lazily trailed her hand in ripples of shining water. 'I should have my parasol. I'd look like a Victorian Lady in a picture then.'

'Your skirt's too short.'

Ethel removed her hand, and shook the wet off. 'I suppose it is. And the water's too cold, as well.'

Lizzie rowed on, and caught sight of the window of the bedroom she'd stayed in with Freddie, with the sun glinting on its panes. Thank God she hadn't left him to sleep in that chair all night; she'd be hating herself now if she had. If only she'd known how it would end she'd have followed Eth's example and given him everything he wanted.

'Have you ever been to a séance?' she asked.

'No.'

'Would you?'

'I don't know anybody who does séances.'

'I do. A Mrs Hawkins, who has the ground floor flat in the house I live in. She's having one on Sunday evening – a "home circle", she calls it. Do you want to come? You'll be quite safe. You can sleep with me afterwards if you like, and go home on Monday.'

Ethel looked doubtful. 'I'm not sure I believe in that sort of thing?

'Only one way to find out though, isn't there? Come and judge for yourself. She's a nice old thing. We'll probably get a bun and a cup of tea at least. I always thought she was an ordinary churchgoer, somebody like my mother. You could have knocked me down with a feather when she told me it was the spiritualist church she went to. The spirits want to help us, she says.'

'But why should you need help from the spirits, Lizzie?'

She hadn't told Ethel that Freddie was missing, and she couldn't bear to talk about it just now. 'I don't. I just want to see what a séance is like,' she said. She'd tell Ethel later, if she felt up to it.

They were booked for two shows, the first at six and the second at ten past eight. The place was packed, and the audience of officers and their families as appreciative as any artiste could wish. Lizzie stepped onto that beautiful stage in a man's evening clothes to sing her songs and be waved away before she got to the end of them by a disdainful drunk. Hundreds of torsos shook with laughter, mouths roared and shrieked, faces were creased with mirth, and eyes watered – the moustachioed ones most of all. The place rang with merriment.

At the start of their spring offensive the Germans had plunged forty miles into the British rear, had regained Peronne, Noyon, and Soissons and dealt the hated Englander an appalling 300,000 casualties. Most of these men in the audience were convalescents, some probably wounded around the same time that Freddie went missing, within the first week of that devastating enemy attack. Many had probably survived horrendous fighting and unimaginable horrors, and would have to go back to face more of the same in a last-ditch attempt to turn the Germans back from Paris. They deserved all her sympathy, everything she could give them, but when she looked out at them, row upon row, all she could do was wonder at the sheer unfairness of it, why it had to be them here, living and loving and laughing – and not Freddie.

They walked through the doorway of Mrs Hawkins' small but comfortable flat, and into the sitting room on the right hand side of the passage. It was quiet, well insulated from the ceaseless noise of the city. All the ornaments had been removed, to keep them safe from mishap, Lizzie supposed.

'One or two of these ladies and gentlemen are regular sitters,' Mrs Hawkins said, 'the others come occasionally. We usually have about twelve, more or less. I like my sitters to get to know each other as much as possible before we start. It helps the conditions. And we alternate men and women round the table as far as we can for the same reason, although I don't think we'll quite manage that tonight. There's a seat for you here, Ethel, and one over there for Lizzie. I'll leave you to chat for a few minutes to break the ice, and don't be frightened to laugh. The spirits like laughter.'

Ten chairs were arranged at a round table that filled most of the room. They seated themselves, and drew the chairs in. Lizzie was facing the man seated next to Ethel, whose snow-white hair was an odd contrast with his pink complexion and youngish face. She couldn't remember his name, but Mrs Hawkins had said he had a responsible position in some leading London business or other. 'I always thought it was only women who were given to strange fancies,' she challenged him.

'You're very critical, I see. Well, nobody's expected to leave reason outside the door when entering a séance room. I never have.'

'No. A keenly active mind doesn't upset conditions,' the lady sitting next to Lizzie concurred.

'But hostility, and anger, they vibrate the ether in a way that obscures the spirit world – rather like interference on a radio receiver – they make the message very difficult to decipher. The vibrations of people who are hostile are very different to those at peace. You must have noticed as much in ordinary life,' the white-haired man explained, with a touch of reproach in his voice.

'I think my vibrations are all right,' she said.

He gave her a patient smile. 'Very peaceful, I hope. That encourages them. Another thing to remember is that the spirits who come through might be people who died years and years ago. Your grandparents, perhaps. So if you hear a name you don't recognize immediately, it might still be a message for you, from an old neighbour, or somebody like that. The unlikeliest people watch over us, and time means little in the spirit world.'

'I suppose not,' she said, and thought, if there is such a thing.

When Mrs Hawkins returned, she squeezed past them to take a seat furthest from the door, with the thick, drawn curtains at her back.

'A note of caution,' the white-haired man murmured. 'A séance can be dangerous for the medium. Mrs Hawkins takes a considerable risk when she holds these circles for us.'

'How?'

'Oh, a medium is susceptible to shock, especially if anybody knocks or jars her. Some have died of it.'

'But we hold hands, don't we?'

'Yes, that's much the best course.'

Mrs Hawkins seated herself, looked brightly at them all, and said: 'We'll begin with a prayer to God and the spirits, as usual, and then a nice hymn. Music helps harmony, and that gives us the best vibrations.'

The white-haired man led the prayers for all the people on the earth plane and in the spirit world, and then he started the singing. Someone put the lights out and they sat with hands on the table and fingers touching, in the dark and the warmth and the silence. Lizzie heard somebody playing a harmonium, slow and soothing, faint and far away. She had been sleeping badly, and was so exhausted she began to doze. Coming to with a start, she opened her eyes and saw a green light flitting about the room. She squeezed her eyes together, and then opened them again.

'Ah. The Grey Lady's taken possession of her,' she heard the white-haired man whisper to Ethel.

Mrs Hawkins' eyes were still and apparently fixed on something far distant, and her face was bathed in a greenish light. She sat quite impassive, in spite of a violent rapping on the table and a voice intoning: 'Come, spirits, come.'

'I hear a C ... Clive coming through. Clive, Clive, is that you?' Mrs Hawkins said.

The white-haired man claimed Clive, and then Ethel ventured to say that Clive was her fiancé's name.

'Folkestone. Folkestone's connected with Clive.'

Ethel's Clive embarked for France from Folkestone after his last leave. The white-haired man's Clive had lived in Folkestone.

'A star,' Mrs Hawkins pressed on. 'I see a star.'

Ethel gasped, 'My fiancé had one star. He'd just been made a second Lieutenant when he was wounded.'

'Yes ... yes, it's coming through,' Mrs Hawkins said: 'The message is for Ethel. Lieutenant Clive wants her to be comforted.'

'Oh, oh,' Ethel was overcome. 'Is he speaking to you?'

'He wishes Ethel to know he is happy in the spirit world.'

'Oh,' said Ethel, 'can you see him?'

'I see a shape – a young man – yes, an army officer. Now I see his face – a handsome face – in the sunlight. He's smiling.'

'Smiling? Is his wound healed, then?'

They waited in silence, with no answer other than the scratch of a pen on paper. Ethel began to sniff, and broke the circle to find her handkerchief.

Had it not been for Ethel's distress, Lizzie thought she would have burst out laughing.

After almost two hours in the circle they returned to Lizzie's room and made tea. Ethel held the steaming cup to her lips, replaced it, and said:

'Half his jaw was blown off. I never told you that, did I, so how could she have known? He died of wounds in a hospital in France, and his captain wrote and told me it was a mercy. I didn't know why that should be, until one of the boys he enlisted with told me he'd hardly have been able to eat or talk, because his poor face was destroyed. I'd have had him back anyhow though, Lizzie. I loved him so much; I'd have looked after him. But he'd been so handsome, and a bit proud of it, you know the way they are, and I know he couldn't have borne going about looking like a gargoyle, like some of the men you see these days. You hardly dare look at them.'

Ethel's eyes dropped to her scrap of Mrs Hawkins' automatic writing, her message from the spirit world. 'You can't imagine what a relief it is to know his wound's healed, and he's all right. I couldn't bear to think of him suffering like that. And he's happy, and waiting for me. When I felt him put his hands on my shoulders, well, I can't explain what I felt like. It was as if his spirit was all around me.'

Lizzie caught Ethel's glistening blue eyes. Couldn't she see it had all been a swindle? Nothing but stage magic and fishing for information, and trickery? Lizzie knew, just *knew* that the white-haired man had been Mrs Hawkins' accomplice, and that it was solid, flesh and blood hands that had been placed on Ethel's shoulders. The poor girl's need to believe had done the rest. People could find meaning in anything if you encouraged them to look hard enough, especially desperate people trying to reach across an aching void of grief. Lizzie was convinced there was a lot of chicanery on the earth plane during Mrs Hawkins' circles and the only spirit world was in the sitters' imaginations. The best you could say was that it had helped Ethel to believe that her fiancé was happy, and Mrs Hawkins had taken no money. But, Lizzie wondered, if she could see she'd drawn you in, if you grew to depend on comfort from the spirits, would Mrs Hawkins take your money then?

Not from Ethel, she wouldn't. Ethel had gone through enough, and she wasn't going to have her made a fool of if she could help it. 'The minute they ask you for money, Eth, go home, and don't come back again,' she said.

'I'm sorry your husband didn't come through,' Ethel said, then, 'no, that's wrong, Lizzie. It probably means he's still alive, doesn't it?'

They went to bed and put out the light. Lizzie lay in the dark thinking of Freddie. She had no sense that there was any sort of afterlife or that he was in it. Her mind drifted to the night he'd promised marriage, when she'd refused to let him make love to her. How bitterly she regretted that now. How she longed for him, and how she wished he were beside her, lusting and laughing at it. One thing was certain. Alive or dead, he was in France or Flanders, and not in any ether.

He couldn't be dead. She wouldn't believe it.

She'd collected his greatcoat a week after taking it to the cleaners, and when she got it home and hung it up the dark stains hit her in the eye. How was he supposed to wear it, looking like that? He wouldn't have it near him. She bundled it up and marched straight back to the shop with it and laid it out under the assistant's nose, pointing to the marks. 'I'm not satisfied with it,' she exclaimed. 'You'll have to do it again.'

The woman pushed Freddie's coat firmly back across the counter. 'It would be pointless, Madam. Unless it's dealt with immediately blood makes a stain that nobody can get out, and it's had time to set. I'm sorry, but there's nothing more to be done with it.'

It was something about her attitude that did it. Lizzie felt such a passion boil up inside her she could have committed murder. Didn't this stupid woman understand that they'd killed her husband, that he was dead somewhere and she'd never see him again, the stupid bitch? And all these other idiotic people standing gaping, hadn't they any idea? She leaned over the counter and with cheeks pale and eyes like gimlets she ground the words out. 'You should have made that clear when I brought it in. You told me then you could clean it, and you've made a mess of it.'

The woman frowned and opened her mouth, but before she could say anything: 'If you can't do anything with it, I want my money back!' Lizzie's voice was full of menace. 'I want my bloody money back!'

Seeing her face, the woman hastened to count the money out. She handed it over without a word.

Clutching the greatcoat and the money Lizzie left the shop slamming the door behind her and strode along the pavement with her cheeks flushed, seething. It wasn't enough. The money wasn't enough, not half enough. No amount of money could give her the satisfaction she wanted. She wanted his greatcoat made as good as new, and she wanted him inside it, and if she couldn't have that, she wanted blood. She wanted vengeance.

It should have been Tom. It was the wrong one who'd been killed. Where was God? Where was divine justice, anyway? God should have taken Tom – he was the one who deserved it, the spoiled, smug, lying, treacherous ... if it hadn't been for him, she'd have loved Freddie from the start; she wouldn't have been terrified to love him. But that was God all over, to play a trick like that. She wanted nothing more to do with Him. She walked on and on, oblivious of the passage of time and of everything around her, until she stood outside the governor's house.

He answered the door, took one look at her face and said: 'You'd better come in.'

She followed him into the drawing room, threw the coat on the sofa, put her fists to her lacerated heart, and howled.

That night she dreamed she was walking along the duck-boards at the bottom of the deepest trenches in Spitalfields, looking through the slats at the stinking slimy water with the filthy bricks of the houses towering above her. She saw the station ahead and knew it couldn't be many minutes before the train left, so she sped along to the ticket office and asked: 'Which platform for Passchendaele?'

'Why do you want to go there?'

'To find somebody I know.'

She flew down miles of dark stairs, passing jostling people coming out into the light. Deep in the bowels of the earth she reached a place with mile upon mile of track, but no train. She asked again.

'Up those stairs, and when you get to the top...'

A whistle blew as she got there, and she spurted on towards a massive, antiquated old train to wrench open a carriage door.

'Is this the train that will take me to Captain Ashton?'

A half-rotted corpse wearing a captain's stars and gold wound stripes on his sleeve leaned towards her. 'Who is he?'

'Somebody I know.'

'This is the train to Hell. Is Captain Ashton there?'

She hesitated. The train began to move. She walked alongside it with a terrible dread in her heart, but soon it was going too fast for her to get on, and, coward that she was, she watched it go.

She awoke with a feeling of desolation, and fearful of the dark opened her curtains to let in the moonlight. With trembling hands she lit the lamp, illuminating that stained and silent witness to the horror of war hanging on her bedroom door, Freddie's greatcoat. The bed was cold and empty and she lay tense and shivering, remembering the nights when she'd laughed at him for his eagerness for her and after his lovemaking had lain against his warm body, drowsy and fulfilled. If only she could recapture that feeling of bliss she'd had from him, that feeling of ease and fulfilment that went through to her marrow.

She got out of bed again and went to the mantel to pick up their photo. Two solemn people stared out into the future, seeing nothing. How sad the girl's eyes were. Funny she'd never noticed it before. Instead of replacing it, she kissed his face, and took the picture back to bed with her, to hold it next to her heart.

Chapter Twenty-Four

There must have been a mix up. There was no body to prove he was dead, after all, and none of his belongings either, except the greatcoat. He'd been taken prisoner. That was it; he'd been taken prisoner, and maybe he'd escaped, and his letters had gone astray because of Mrs Hawkins not being at home to keep them safe. Or he hadn't written because he was still brooding about Georgie. She'd go to see if his father was at the flat. He might have heard something.

At the flat in Knightsbridge she handed his father's three-word missive over to an old man-servant. 'Show that to your master, and tell him there's somebody waiting to see him.'

He showed her into the spacious, oak panelled hallway and she was confronted with Freddie's grey eyes, looking solemnly down on her from his full-length portrait. She stared at him for many moments, aching with pity for herself and for him, then finding she'd forgotten her hand-kerchief, she dashed away her tears with the back of her glove. Just as she regained some comp-osure Freddie's father appeared and there it was again, that flash of recognition that ignited in his eyes and just as swiftly died. Without preamble she strode towards him and began: 'They told me Freddie was dead, but I don't believe it. Have you heard from him?'

'Not since I got the letter that prompted this,' he replied, holding up the letter she'd brought.

Deflated, she turned to go, and had just put her hand on the heavy brass doorknob when he asked, 'What did he tell you about me?'

Still facing the door, she answered, 'Nothing, except you dragged him away from his mother when he was seven and stuck him in a boarding school. And you're a diamond merchant.'

'Yes, I suppose you took good heed of that, and much good it will do you. I did everything I could for him. I recognized him, and I put him into school. What chance would he have had with her? A lifetime spent in some low, drudging, menial work far beneath his talents. I didn't consider that a fate worthy of my son, so I spent a small fortune on his education and fitted him for the life of a gentleman. I'd have done more for him as well, but what thanks did I get? He wouldn't have it.'

'You didn't marry his mother – you could have done that for him. Did he tell you she's dead?'

'Yes.'

'Why didn't you marry her?'

'She wasn't the sort of woman a gentleman marries. She was the sort he has a liaison with until he marries someone from his own background.'

She turned to face him. 'Like me, then.'

'Yes, like you,' he grimaced. 'She was a little seamstress; you, I hear, are a little entertainer. An expensive little entertainer. Same type. You're like her in looks, and in temperament too, I imagine. Did he tell you that?'

'No,' Lizzie shrugged, 'but it hardly matters now, does it?'

She was halfway out of the door when he called after her, 'I've often wished I had married her, though. Before she had that other boy. Too late now.'

Closing the door after her, she gave a short laugh, murmuring, 'Much too late.'

Here she was again, wandering around Selfridges. The once-coveted evening gown was still there, and gazing at it she wondered: what am I doing here? I've no interest in any of this stuff. It's all useless. Useless clothes, useless arrangements of flowers, silly, self-important assistants, puffing their useless goods. What does any of it matter?

She left the store to find a telephone, and clutching at a straw of hope began discouraging days spent telephoning every hospital in London and everywhere else she could think of. None had a Captain Frederick Ashton nor even a Captain Bowman, and she was fast sliding into a slough of despond. Plenty of hard work, that was what she needed. That's what Margery said the doctor had told her, after the children had died. Keep busy; find plenty to do. It stops you going out of your mind.

She agonized over whether she ought to go to France again, or whether she should give Freddie up as a lost cause. John's letter made her even more depressed. The army, he said, was losing heart after so much ground lost instead of gained, and at the cost of so many good men killed and maimed. 'Fed up with the war' was the phrase on everybody's lips, and men were asking themselves why they were in France at all.

The following day was Pentecost. Just as she was setting out to meet the governor and Margery she heard the familiar, threatening sound of German planes overhead, and the shrieking of shells. More love gifts from the Kaiser to burn and blast defenceless civilians. She ran for the safety of the tube station wondering whether that was what the Bible meant when it talked about tongues of fire. Before she descended into the earth she heard the anti-aircraft guns open up, and saw English planes in the sky. It looked as if Jerry was going to get a bit of opposition this time.

After the raid she went to help people searching through the rubble for survivors. The Germans had had too much of their own way for too bloody long. Before the Americans came in, people had started talking as if England were going to lose the war, and she'd been surprised how angry it had made her, so angry that she'd begun to sound like Bert, the old flyman at de Lacey's. She was sick of feeling terrified, running like a rabbit in her own country. It was time to turn and fight instead of sitting in London waiting for German bombs to drop on her head.

What was it Freddie had said? Take up our quarrel with the foe? Well, a little music hall artiste couldn't do much – but she could do something. Whether Freddie was alive or dead, whether she found him or not, whether he wanted her or not, she was going to France again. She was going to put a bit of heart into the troops, or at least give them something to laugh at. Or die in the attempt.

Lizzie looked about her, trying to imagine what the place must have been like when it was full of swells in evening dress and gorgeous women in colourful gowns, all pursuing their intrigues and amours and gaily throwing hundreds of pounds away on the turn of a card or a roulette wheel. The people in charge of the place were playing for different prizes now – the lives and limbs of wounded servicemen, and the hearts and livelihoods of their families at home. The game was harder, and the stakes higher. 'So this used to be the Boulogne Casino!' she said. 'Nothing like a casino now, is it? Everything's white. It must have had a bit more colour before the war.'

'It stinks of hospital,' said Ethel. 'I hate that smell.'

'At least it's a clean smell, and the place is spotless,' Mr Dorrien approved, as the RAMC officer led them to their audience.

'This is our biggest ward,' he informed them. 'I'm told it was the Baccarat room in the old days.'

Weedy little Archie Higginbottom, a Northern comedian of five foot two that Lizzie had managed to tempt onto the tour with the promise of mere subsistence asked: 'Baccarat? What's that? Back-a-rat into a corner and shoot it?'

'Yes. Very funny,' said the officer, without a trace of humour.

Lizzie smiled. Some of Archie's witticisms might be a bit feeble, but he did a beautiful drunk. She was jealous of him. When she'd asked Mr Karno if he'd let her take *The Mumming Birds* on tour in France she'd wanted desperately to play the drunk herself, but certain it would fall flat with a woman in the role, albeit a woman dressed as a man, Fred Karno wouldn't have it. He agreed to her doing the sketch only on condition she gave him full credit for it, and employed a man for the drunk's part. They wouldn't be doing it here, though. There wasn't room, for one thing; the ward was packed. There were men lying in cots, swathed in bandages from head to foot, men hobbling on crutches, and men sitting in chairs, all cramped together. The skin of many a face was drawn tight over the bones, and some of the eyes had that exhausted, leaden look that Georgie's had held the night he told her about finding his lover, a look she called 'trench eyes'. In spite of everything, every face that could was turned cheerfully towards them. Perhaps Freddie had lain in just such a place, perhaps this very one, Ethel's fiancé, too. She glanced at Ethel, expecting to see distress on her face, but she was serene. The spirits had certainly wrought a transformation there.

Lizzie walked between the men to the little platform to do a turn. Some of them looked as if a good belly laugh might kill them, especially the ones with abdominal wounds, so no *Mumming Birds*. The programme would be made up of two or three of Lizzie's impressions, a couple of ragtime songs, a few sentimental ones accompanied on the piano, and a smattering of Archie's patter. It would be a straight little concert, the best they could give.

It had hurt her to cut herself off the photograph she and Freddie had had taken together, but she'd done it, because she'd been warned that the military authorities wouldn't tolerate any serving soldier's wife anywhere near the troops. She'd given it to Mr Dorrien, for him to show around on her behalf, and now, as they were snatching a quick cup of tea with an RAMC Captain and some of the staff, he produced it. 'Have you seen him lately? I'm a friend of his family.'

The orderly next to him peered at it. 'Sorry, no.' He passed it on, but the response from all of them was the same.

It was what she'd expected, though far from what she'd hoped for. 'The men look wonderfully well cared for,' she commented, once the photograph was safely back in Mr Dorrien's pocket.

'We do our best,' one of the nurses said. 'But there's only a few of us, and no end of them. It's heavy going most times.'

'I'll tell you something, though,' said the Captain. 'You've done them good, as much good as we could do them in a week.'

'Oh, nonsense, nonsense,' Mr Dorrien said.

'But you did,' one of the orderlies insisted, with a wary look at the Captain. 'I've never heard anything like it from them, all that laughing and clapping and cheering. I've never seen them look so alive, better than any amount of medicine.'

'Oh, no, no,' they protested, with self-deprecating smiles on their faces, then caught each other's eyes and smiled again. Of course they'd done the men good. Why else had they come to France?

That night, at a convalescent camp on top of the cliffs a mile or so outside Boulogne in a YMCA hut as big as a barn, they gave another show to over a thousand cheering, clapping, singing roaring men – most of them a lot further along the road back to health than the men at the Casino. They could certainly stand Karno's sketch, Lizzie thought. When she winked at Archie he took her meaning at once, and, very inebriated, he staggered over to sit among the convalescents. They tried to suppress him at first with disapproving looks, then by shouting him down, and finally by threats of a beating with the nearest crutch, until enough of them realized what was going on. Roars of laughter followed that, and at the end of the show the applause was deafening. The piece was a resounding success.

But again, nobody seemed to know anything about Freddie.

They spent the night in the same modest hotels used by the staff of the YMCA, and the next day joined the melee in Boulogne. The hot June sun shone down on all the industry and equipage of war, and the gentle breeze caressed motor lorries, ammunition wagons, supply trucks, horses dragging heavy guns and trees in full leaf. The army driver soon had the little troupe rattling along at a lick in the general direction of Ypres, on a surprisingly good road.

'Isn't it green?' Ethel raised her voice above the noise of the motor. 'From what everybody told me, I expected everything to be mud, and the trees shelled to stumps!'

'There's been no shelling here – yet – but the German guns have shelled Paris,' the driver told them.

'Hell of a lot of traffic, though,' said Archie. 'It's worse than the middle of London.'

'Haven't you heard? There's a war on!'

A couple of generals with red bands round their hats passed them, lolling in the back of a limousine, smoking and talking.

'Have you told them that?' asked Archie.

'Ha, ha.'

There was a shrill blast from behind. The driver pulled into the side of the road and stayed there while a motorcycle went tearing past.

Ethel gave a tut of disapproval.

'What did you give way for?' Archie demanded. 'Feller's got no manners.'

'Despatch rider. Everybody gives way to them. It's the rule.'

'Even the generals?'

'Even the King.'

At first, all the traffic was going their way, but before long a stream of traffic flowed towards them and Boulogne. Some of the trucks were empty, but others were laden with all sorts of salvage, everything from broken rifles to old shoes.

'What's all that lot?' Archie asked.

'Salvage. Men pick up everything that's left after a battle – rifles that have been dropped or thrown away, bayonets, knives, coshes, boots, shoes, bits of uniform, anything and everything that can be mended and used again. Nothing's wasted. Saves the taxpayer such a lot of money, you see.' A motor ambulance was approaching, a vivid red cross emblazoned on its side. 'Going to the hospital in Boulogne, or maybe on to Blighty, lucky so and sos,' the driver commented.

'I should think one would want to know what's wrong with them, before pronouncing on their good fortune,' said Mr Dorrien.

'Well, did you ever?' said Archie, as they approached the middle of a village. 'Just look at this. A policeman directing traffic. You'd think we were in the middle of Leeds.'

'It's so sunny, and everything's so green – not how I imagined France at all,' Ethel repeated.

'How old must they be?' said Lizzie, nodding towards a stooped old couple working in the fields.

'About ninety, I should think. It must be hard on them with all the young men gone, especially when it gets to harvest time. Incessant labour, and at their age.' Mr Dorrien spoke with feeling.

'Just the same in England.'

'Hell's teeth!' Archie exclaimed at the sound of an explosion. 'Hear that? I don't know about not letting us get near the Front. I think the Germans will bring the bloody Front to us if they get much further.'

Subsisting on the shoestring budget provided by Margery and her committee ladies, the little troupe travelled all over France and Flanders, playing wherever they were allowed to play, in camps, villages, tents, barns, aircraft hangars and YMCA huts, anywhere and everywhere a show could be staged. Initially, owing to recent German successes they found the mood of their soldier audiences fairly flat, but now calling themselves 'The Mumming Birds' they gave the piece everything they had, varying the acts it contained to stave off boredom in themselves and their audiences. Anyone who could do a turn was dragged in – soldier entertainers, YMCA helpers and even chaplains. The shy and nervous among these conscripts found an ally in the drunk, the more robust and rambunctious were dispatched without ceremony, to roars of delight from the audience.

Their days were filled with travelling and performing in so many camps, villages, hospitals and towns they could hardly distinguish one from another and sometimes lost track of where they were, or even what day it was. They sometimes saw men going into houses which displayed lamps outside, sometimes blue, sometimes red. A French soldier put her wise – they were the

405

places where the 'bad women' waited – in the blue lamps for officers, in the red for other ranks. She wondered whether Freddie had ever seen the inside of one of them, and sadly acknowledged to herself that he probably had.

After her turn, Lizzie would watch the rest of the show and the audience's reaction to it and, infected by the laughter, would laugh with the rest. At night, though, lying in an unfamiliar bed, she was sometimes too keyed up to sleep. One of the Tommies' favourite songs often ran through her mind, 'Keep the home fires burning, while your hearts are yearning...' That was the name of the pain inside her – a yearning, a long, long, longing for Freddie and for his kisses, and the times she used to lie in his arms, completely relaxed. How fervently she wished she could get it back, that wonderful feeling that followed lovemaking and preceded blessed sleep. Then she would read a story from his book of Norse myth and picture him being borne to Valhalla by some dauntless spear maiden, or take his photograph from under her pillow and stare into his bright, optimistic eyes, and grieve at having failed to see the good in him while he was still hers.

She could find nothing out about him until they were in Poperinghe, when Archie showed his photo to the rotund, bespectacled, untidy looking chaplain at the club for servicemen there. He pushed his black-framed glasses farther up his nose and examined it. 'Yes, I remember him well, nice chap. I spoke to him quite a few times. He was billeted at the convent over Christmas. Haven't seen him for months, though. No idea what happened to him.'

A sigh escaped her. Not much comfort in that.

Before they left Ypres, they found Ethel's fiancé among the thousands of sleepers in Flanders fields; his grave marked by one of the in- numerable little wooden crosses. They watched in silence as she placed a simple bunch of corn- flowers tied with blue ribbon on his blanket of earth. 'I wish I'd had his baby,' she said, and looked at Mr Dorrien. 'Does that shock you?'

He put a sympathetic arm round her shoulders and gave her a squeeze.

I wish I'd had his baby, Lizzie echoed in her heart.

In August casualties among the allies soared, but oddly enough, so did morale. 'Do you know how many stunts I've been through lately, Miss? Six! And I've had some narrow squeaks, I can tell you. But you should have seen how many pris- oners we took near Abbeville,' one wounded and exhausted Tommy boasted at the month's end. 'Enough to fill a dozen football fields! Thousands of Jerries with their hands up, shouting *"Kamarad, Kamarad!"* Nothing but kids, some of them, and couldn't surrender fast enough. Just about throwing themselves into our arms, they were.'

The story was the same everywhere. At last there was something to be seen for the sacrifice. Optimism crackled in the air. It was Fritz's turn now, and he was losing heart as he lost ground. Paris was saved, and The Mumming Birds voted to award themselves a few days off to see the French capital.

'Well, I reckon I'll go and see what's left of the naughty nineties,' Archie said. 'See the Folies Bergere, if they're still on the go. Let somebody else do the entertaining for a change.'

Mr Dorrien seemed extraordinarily pleased. 'Oh, Paris! That will be wonderful.'

Lizzie's eyebrows shot up. Hard to believe that the upright Mr Dorrien was a devotee of saucy shows.

He caught her look, turned pink, and hastened to explain. 'You might not have noticed, but I touch up my hair from time to time, and I've run out of the ... you know, the *dye*. The French do a rather nice henna based one, so much more natural looking, and I'm sure to be able to find it in Paris.'

'Mr Dorrien, I'd no idea!' Lizzie just managed to keep her face straight.

There was plenty left of the naughty nineties, and Archie took full advantage. Lizzie was surprised to see a couple of English shows in the theatres, *Tipperary* and *Roses of Picardy*. They spent a few days seeing the sights, and then went in search of the British soldiers' pied-à-terre in Paris, to meet the Chaplain, and Georgie Bartlett.

'Well, the idea is to distract our innocent boys from the more traditional pleasures of the capital,' Georgie told her, 'save them from going on the sick list with any wounds from Cupid's arsenal. What a hope! Still, we do our best, and we've put on some passable shows, but novelty and variety's always wanted. Fred Karno's piece will go down very well.'

Lizzie looked round the vast hall of the society's headquarters in the Rue Jouffroy. 'Ten thousand meals a *week*, did you say? It's impossible to imagine.'

'It happens though. The Tommies get their meals, and a game of billiards if they want it, and books, records, help writing letters, they can even get their money banked, if they've got any. Oh, yes, and city tours thrown in. The chaplain's kids take some of them.'

'Must be a different sort of parson to the one where I live. Well, the place is certainly big enough,' she said. 'Seems a strange setting for you, though, Georgie – *chaplains?* The Continental and Colonial *Church* Society?'

'It does, very *queer*. I'm frightfully careful to mind my ps and qs; the chaplain's such a straight-laced old thing, but his heart's in the right place. Funny they gave me this nice safe job after I'd ceased to care whether I lived or died, isn't it? Perhaps it's a case of the wicked being given time to repent.'

They played there for a week, and Lizzie was overjoyed to meet people who'd seen Freddie in Paris before the German breakthrough in spring. She was so glad to hear anything of him that it took her a minute or two to realize it didn't help her. She already knew he'd been alive in March, from his letters.

After Paris, their lives again became a series of

409

one or two night hops, playing at camps and towns from Rheims to the North Sea, in tents, barns, schools, theatres, or any sizeable building left standing. Near the old Front they saw something of the ravaged countryside, the ruined farms and houses, craters full of slime and filthy water and shell blasted trees standing like charred and broken ships' masts in a sea of mud. Ethel said: 'This is what I imagined France to be like, ever since my fiancé told me about it.'

'This is what they meant when they said "devastation", and told us they couldn't tell us what it was like. It has to be seen to be believed. Poor people. Their country's destroyed. You can't imagine how anybody will ever live in it again.'

'They will, though. Nature will take charge, and heal it,' said Mr Dorrien. 'The summer after our Somme offensive there was a profusion of wild-flowers on that churned up ground. Dog daisies, poppies, all sorts of wildflowers, brilliant against the pink and white clay, and clouds of butterflies. So beautiful.'

It was a comforting thought, now that rumours of peace abounded. 'Have you heard the news, Miss? The Kaiser's abdicated, and Crown Prince Willi's renounced his claim to the Throne! I wonder if there really will be an armistice?' Cynicism seemed to be receding from the faces of the soldiers they met, and in its place the glimmerings of new hope.

That night, they took part in an Allied revue. One of the acts was a tableaux of Germans seizing a young village girl and putting her in chains to lead her away, to the hissing and booing

410

of the audience. At the end of the piece she was rescued by a French soldier, with a Tommy rushing on to help him release her from her chains, to cheers and clapping and the playing of the Marseillaise. The Mumming Birds got nearly as enthusiastic a reception, and when the applause and the laughter had died away a young soldier entertainer stepped forward to thank all the artistes and to end the show.

'Give us a song, Bert!' some in the audience were shouting, and wouldn't be quiet until Bert had nodded to the musicians. They struck up with a verse of 'When This Bloody War is Over', and played it once. A hush fell.

When this bloody war is over,
Oh, how happy I shall be!
When this bloody war is over,
No more soldiering for me.
No more rising at reveille,
No more going on parade
No more visits to the trenches,
No more bringing in the dead.

Bert stopped, and his last words reverberated round the place, deep and wistful. There was absolute silence for a minute, then: 'God,' Archie murmured, 'I'm covered in bleedin' goose flesh!'

'Me too,' said Lizzie.

The following morning they heard from the officers that the rumours had been confirmed; an armistice was to be signed that day and the war would be over before bedtime. All the towns-

411

people were out and a couple of French soldiers were carrying a little boy shoulder high through the streets, to tumultuous cheering and applause. Lizzie asked a French soldier why.

'As ze Bosche march, 'ee kill one wiz a rifle, and zey can't catch 'eem, 'ee 'ide in zee trees,' he said, nodding towards a copse. 'We make 'eem ze Legion d'Honneur!'

People who had toiled for years under their German conquerors had had their honour restored by a child who could hardly be ten years old, and they were jubilant. The sight of their glad faces brought a lump to her throat, and unable to bear it she fled the place and didn't stop until she came to that deserted wood that had hidden the boy hero. And where was her hero hiding, where was he? Surely not dismembered and rotting in that vast, stinking latrine, that mass grave that filled half of Northern France and Flanders? Surely not. Not Freddie. If only she could don her gleaming breastplate and mount her white charger and ride out with the Valkyries to rake those dark, polluted wastelands until she found him, her warrior.

A Valkyrie in the form of a raven, Lizzie flew low over miles of corpse littered battlefields, over filthy trenches and slime-filled shell craters and slippery duck-boards which zig-zagged over the mud – on and on in an endless search for him and finding only other eyeless, long-dead soldiers who lifted their decaying arms, beckoning to her – choose me, choose me.

She awoke with a shudder and lit the lamp.

Hadn't somebody told her once that ravens visit battlefields to peck out dead men's eyes? She crossed her arms over her chest and grasped her shoulders to hold herself, to stop her shuddering.

Chapter Twenty-Five

It was odd to be sitting on the deck of the ship carrying them to Folkestone with only the gulls gliding in the sky, and no U boats in the depths below to threaten them. Strange to feel no flutterings of fear inside. She was getting cold, but lingered for a while beside Mr Dorrien, gazing out to sea.

'We've done well,' she told him, and transferring her gaze to the veined hands resting on his knees, she thought how frail they looked, how blue the fingernails.

'Yes.' It sounded like one long sigh. His head slumped forward onto his chest and his hat fell off, revealing the white hair just beginning to show at the roots of the deep brown. She leaned forward to look into his face, and saw that his eyes were wide open and still. His face had turned a light purple colour, and his lips were blue.

'He died in harness. It's what he would have wanted,' the governor said, after they'd watched Mr Dorrien being lowered into his grave on that cold December morning. Margery nodded her agreement.

'I suppose you could say he died for his country. He was such an absurd, ridiculous, old-fashioned old stick. Patriotism never lost its gloss for him, did it?' Lizzie said, looking round the black-clad gathering. 'It's amazing how many people are here for the old ham, though, just about everybody in theatre and music hall. He'd never have lacked for friends if he'd lived to be a hundred.'

'You sound a bit cross with him, Lizzie,' Margery said.

'I am. He's gone and abandoned his post, the old deserter,' Lizzie sniffed, swallowing her tears.

'I think you loved him in the end,' Ethel said.

'I'm not ashamed to admit it. You look awful, Eth.'

'I feel it. I won't come back your house if you don't mind, governor. I'm going home, and then I'm going straight to bed.'

Watching Eth go, Lizzie had an impulse to follow her, to see she got home all right. But the governor and Margery had organized a meal for a crowd of them, and it seemed unreasonable for another guest to cry off at the last minute, and so she stayed. 'She's been looking forward to going to more of Mrs Hawkins' séances,' she told them, still watching Ethel's retreating figure. 'Her face fell a mile when we found out she'd given her flat up and gone to live in the house her sister left her. So no more spirits. I wasn't very happy, either, because nobody seems to have a forwarding address so if she's taken any letters in for me I'll be lucky if I ever see them.'

'I hope you got my note.'

'Yes.' Lizzie held the door open, and indicated the armchair. 'Shall I take your coat? Would you like some tea?' she asked, wondering what on earth had prompted the visit. Georgie could hardly have been exposed to enemy fire in the Rue Jouffroy, and anyway, the war was over, but the look in the brown eyes that held hers for a moment augured nothing good.

'Thank you.' There was a tiny smile of gratitude and an awkward pause as Georgie's mother took off a very good cashmere coat – black, as most people's things were these days – and handed it to her. No wonder Georgie was such a looker, Lizzie thought, surveying the tall, still-slim, brown-eyed blonde who sank gracefully into the armchair.

'I believe you knew George very well. He talked about you a lot.'

Lizzie placed the coat carefully across the bed, and turned to light the gas ring. 'He was awfully kind to me when I first came to London. We became very good friends.'

'I used to hope when he talked about you that he'd found someone to settle down with, at last.'

Lizzie could barely suppress a smile at that, until she saw her visitor hide her face and start fumbling for a handkerchief. Then the impulse to laugh was gone.

'I did so hope for grandchildren you know, but it's not to be.'

'Oh,' Lizzie said. It was the worst news, then.

His mother was silent for a long time. When at last she was able to speak she said: 'He died in

415

France – of influenza. I know you were keeping some of his things for him. I'll take them away if you like, but if there's anything you want to keep, you may.'

Really, another one! It was too ridiculous of them. Oh, Georgie, she thought, you silly, silly man, to come through all that, everything you endured at the Front, and then to die of a sneeze in gay Paree – a place that was made for you, if ever there was one. As you'd have said yourself – my dear, it's too, too, funny! She collapsed into the armchair and laughed until she was weak. Thank God they buried the silly idiot in France. Mr Dorrien's was bad enough, but Georgie's was a funeral she really couldn't have borne to attend.

How wrong he'd been about his mother, though. Luckily she'd had enough tea left in the caddy to scrape a weak cup for her, but now there was none left, and no Mrs Hawkins to borrow from. Damn. Her throat felt as if it had been scrubbed with a file and she was desperate for a cup of tea, so despite feeling like death she had no option but to drag herself out to buy it. She came back to her empty room and, shivering, made her tea. If only she had Freddie to share it with, if only she could reach out to him, touch his hand, feel his skin on hers.

The saddest words in the English language, those, 'if only'. Unless they were 'too late'. 'If only' or 'too late'? It was a toss-up, really. She was weary, sick to death of this craving, craving, craving inside her, for Ashton and the love he could have given her. It gnawed at her constantly, like rats feeding on the fallen, wearing her away and making her thin and shrunken, while it got fatter. She threw the last coal she had on the dying embers and extinguished them, and then all her energy drained away, leaving her limp. Oh, well, she'd have an early night rather than re-light it, though it was only half-past four. How dreadful she felt. She drained her cup, took off her coat and skirt and blouse and had just enough strength left to pick up her photograph and crawl into bed in her underwear. Her head ached. Her bones ached, and she was racked by a dry, irritating cough. Thank God she was 'resting'. Thank God there was no theatre manager relying on her turning up for work tomorrow.

Her eyelids fell, and laughing audiences, boys being shot, ten-year–olds with rifles, gun carriages, limbers buried up to their axles in mud, French wives with German babies, wildflowers and butterflies, decaying men and horses, fields full of wooden crosses, rats and ravens and her last sight of Freddie's face all swirled together in the slough of grey despond that swallowed her.

They stared at her with eyes devoid of pity and the one in the middle of the three spoke for them all. 'You're here on a very serious charge. Very serious indeed. Has the prisoner anything to say in her defence?'

Lizzie stood in her khaki uniform before a bench of generals in their red banded hats and red tabs and their tons of medals and miles of gold braid, wondering what bloody business they thought they had, dragging her here with her hands tied behind her back. Her defending officer quickly rifled through his copy of the Army Act, casting apologetic glances at them all. The court grew restive. He became even more nervous, and gave up with a shrug. The generals conferred among themselves, and the one in the middle held a pen, poised to sign her death warrant.

Her defence was suddenly inspired. 'There are mitigating circumstances. She's a woman.'

The prosecuting officer sprang up to protest. 'That deepens the crime, her being a woman; we were all agreed on that!'

The defence shrank back, and the general applied the nib of his pen very deliberately to the paper. Lizzie's heartbeat dinned so loudly they must all be deafened by it, and an awful fear stopped her breath, until she caught sight of the charge on the warrant, there in black and white: 'cowardice in the face of the enemy'.

It was a travesty of justice. Bewildered, she asked, 'Who is the enemy?'

The generals rose as one, leaned towards her and boomed: 'Love is the enemy!'

She felt the hands of the guards on her, blind-folding her, pinning an envelope to her tunic and then pushing and heaving her out of the court towards the firing squad. She resisted, a fearful rage at their stupidity boiling within her. 'Fools,' she shrieked, 'fools, you're all fools! Love's not the enemy. Fear is the enemy! Bitterness is the enemy – not love!'

She awoke, repeating it. 'Fear is the enemy, bitterness is the enemy, not love.'

418

'Ethel's dead,' Margery said. 'She fell on her way home from Mr Dorrien's funeral and died on the pavement. Isn't it terrible? Spanish Flu, they said, like Mr Dorrien. Her family are burying her on Monday.'

Weak and ill as she was, it took Lizzie a minute or two to take it in, then: 'Lucky Ethel,' she croaked. 'What day is it today?'

'Friday.'

'I don't think I can go, Margery. I can hardly get out of bed, and my head's splitting. I've hardly slept for three nights for coughing. I'm lathered in sweat one minute, and shivering the next. If it hadn't been for one of the other tenants filling a water-jug and bringing me tea now and then, I'd be done for.'

'You've got it as well, Lizzie. Come and stay with us. You're not fit to be by yourself.'

'No. I couldn't move if I tried, and I don't want you to catch it.'

Despite all entreaties Lizzie wouldn't change her mind, so in the end Margery went out for a small bag of coal, aspirins and other provisions, lit a fire, brought water, made tea, and left.

Her throat felt a bit better; it must be the aspirin. Glad to be left in peace with that lovely fire now burning cheerily in the grate she curled up in bed and let her swollen lids fall over her reddened eyes. Poor Eth, she was past needing séances now. Lizzie suddenly saw her, lovely in her blue dress with the Peter Pan collar, jumping the bags and, with her blonde hair streaming behind her running over that dread no man's

419

land that divides the living from the dead, to find her beloved in that longed-for spirit world of hers.

Bravo, Eth.

'You can't waste your life waiting for somebody who's never going to come back, Lizzie. I'm being cruel to be kind. You're young enough to start again.'

Lizzie turned to stare out of the cab window. No danger now from air raids, and London was beginning to look festive with brightly lit displays in the shops, and cheerful crowds anticipating the first Christmas of peace. 'Start again? Get a new husband, you mean? Now, you're not going to say: "There are plenty of men out there," are you, Margery? Because there aren't. Not now.' And even if there were, she thought, whoever would *want* to start again, after enduring all this?

Another week of illness and isolation in her room had made Lizzie feel as if the walls were coming in, and so in the end she'd let herself be persuaded to stay with Margery and the governor for a few days.

Suddenly she sat up straight, her nose pressed against the window. 'He's there. He's there!'

'Where? Where?' Margery leaned over her shoulder, craning to see.

Lizzie pointed, fingering her little black cat with the sapphire eyes as the cab drew nearer, but he'd vanished. Deflated, she sank back into her seat.

'It still happens to me, and it's three-and-a-half years ago,' Margery commiserated. 'I see my son's face on a boy in the park, or my daughter's on a little girl coming out of a shop. I see a gesture, just like theirs, or hear a child's chuckle, and my heart turns over. But it never *is* them, and it never can be, because they're *gone*.'

Gone, Lizzie thought. What a dismal word is 'gone'.

'I'll have no clients left soon,' the governor said. 'Ethel and Mr Dorrien dead, and half a dozen others besides. How am I going to make a living? And now you.'

'Don't worry about me,' said Lizzie. 'Only the good die young.'

'But you're not going to be working, are you? You're mad, Lizzie, giving your room up and clearing off to the back of beyond. People are soon forgotten in this business, and there are half a dozen jobs I could get you for Christmas.'

Lizzie shrugged. 'Oh, well.'

The governor threw up his hands in despair. 'Oh, well? Is that all you can say? When are you coming back?'

'I don't know.' She felt too ill to work, and not only that, she'd lost every scrap of enthusiasm for it. She was tired, tired, tired, and low on funds, and she'd seen enough with Freddie's mother to know that she didn't want to be poor in London. She would have to overcome that superstitious horror she had of applying for her widow's pension, she supposed, but not just yet. Barring the governor and Margery, everybody she cared about seemed to be gone, one way or another, and she wanted to be at home for Christmas, among her own people. She'd planned no further than that.

Except she decided she was giving up her room. Why fork money out on rent, when she might never come back? She'd go to the Post Office and get them to redirect her letters, and send Georgie's things back to his mother as well. They reminded her too much of that awful night she'd lost Freddie.

Her mother's house was in darkness when she got to Annsdale, with nobody in to answer her knocking. She'd only herself to blame. Why, oh why hadn't she written to warn her mother she was coming?

It was the final straw, and she sat down on her luggage and dropped her head into her hands. But inside her was a well of grief so bottomless that once she loosed the spring she would drown in tears, and now was not the time. After a moment or two she stood up and lifted her suitcase. There was nothing for it now but to tramp all the way to the Cock.

'Where's me Mam?'

She found Ginny in the taproom, talking to half a dozen customers clustered round the bar. 'Ee good heavens, it's our Lizzie!' Ginny's eyebrows almost met her hairline, and then her face relaxed into a strange expression of amusement, overlaid by mock reproach. 'She's at our John's. You might have let us know you were coming, Lizzie man.'

Lizzie shrugged. 'How's our Em?'

'A lot better than last time you saw her. She packed the munitions factory up, and went to help old Walter on the farm. I told you in my letter.'

'I never got it. I went touring in France twice, and the woman who was supposed to be looking after my post did a flit without bothering to leave her new address. What about everybody else, then, our Sal, and John and Arthur, and Martin, and Phil?'

'Our Sal's nursing, in Newcastle. John's already home. He got sent back straight away, they want all the miners back at work. Martin's still in France; he can't get demobilized. He reckons he might get sent to Germany. Phil never even got to France. He's still at the Training Camp.'

'Lucky for John and Elsie, then. Not so good for you.'

'I'm not complaining,' Ginny said. 'My lads are alive, and they've not been maimed. Our Arthur's still in France, but he's all right. We're a thankful family, Lizzie.'

Lizzie rolled her eyes, and gave a little grimace, but said nothing.

'And now we've got you back, an' all. By, we'll have a grand Christmas this year, Lizzie.'

The customers at the bar were watching them intently. 'Are you not going to tell her, Ginny man?' one of them asked.

'Tell her what?' Ginny asked, looking him straight in the eye. 'I've told her all there is to tell. You'll want the key then, Lizzie?'

She'd never have believed it of her sister, to be so bloody callous. 'Well, I've just come all the way from London, Ginny. I wouldn't have minded a cup of tea and a bite to eat before I walk home again. And I'm sorry to put a damper on things, but I won't have a smashing Christmas. I hate Christmas, and I'll hate this one more than any other.'

But Ginny was still surveying her, smiling, with a sort of mockery in her face. One or two of the lads began to laugh, and Ginny's grin broadened. 'Why away upstairs and put the kettle on then, hinny. Cut yourself a couple of slices of bread and have a bit cheese with it. Then go to bed for an hour. Sleep all night, if you like.'

Lizzie let herself through the bar to the stairs leading to Ginny's living quarters. Everybody was safe but Freddie, and Ginny'd never even asked about him, never even mentioned his name, just stood grinning like the bloody Cheshire cat. And here she was, with her misery magnified by all these happy people; expected to have a 'grand Christmas' with her poor husband dead in France, without even a little wooden cross to mark his place.

Who seeks glory in so rolling on the human heart a stone? Well, whoever it was had rolled one on hers, and no mistake.

She pushed open the door of Ginny's sitting room and felt all the blood drain from her face at the sight of Freddie's ghost, just as he'd been the first time she ever saw him at de Lacey's theatre – the same well-cut suit of grey flannel, same clean-shaven face, same thatch of wavy brown hair parted at the side and swept back, same lustrous grey eyes that crinkled at the corners as they smiled into hers.

She squeezed her eyelids together and shook her head slightly before opening them again. No, it wasn't a ghost. No ghost ever stood warming his backside at the fire with a cigarette dangling from his lips, nor ever came rushing forward to catch a person before she fell, with the cigarette still dangling, mumbling: 'I say, little wife, you've gone as white as a sheet. Am I such an awful sight? I thought I'd come through without a blemish!'

He swept her up in his arms and deposited her on the sofa.

'Freddie, you're skin and bone!' She kneaded his arm and his shoulder, wondering at their solidity, that they still existed at all.

'Prison camp diet; we've lived on watery black bean soup since April with an occasional bit of herring and chunk of black bread. I used to see that hamper you sent me in my dreams, old thing. And our men got the worst fatigues on the camp, to pay them back for being "Englanders". The French got off more lightly. Odd, isn't it? And after the armistice they simply left us to get home as best we could. I only crossed to England a few days ago.'

'They told me you were dead.'

'So I heard. I bumped into the old girl you used to borrow stuff from when I went looking for you at your old address. "Two minds with but a single thought," she said, when we both found ourselves shivering outside your door – and you gone. Neither of us had a clue where to. She told me she'd been round half a dozen times after she'd moved, trying to find you in. So we concluded that you must have moved as well, and I thought it would be quicker to get the train up here and find out for myself what was going on. And I've nowhere to stay in London now, apart from my club.'

'I know you've been written out of the will.'

'Pretty comprehensively I think, that's if I was ever in it. Do you mind?'

She gave an ironical little chuckle. 'It would be all the same if I did, wouldn't it? But I don't, as a matter of fact. Do you?'

'No. But I'm glad you've taken it so well.' She basked in an approving smile for a full minute before he came to himself and said: 'The old girl gave me a stack of letters she'd been keeping for you, mostly from me. Said she thought she'd lost them, until they turned up at the bottom of a tea chest.' He nodded towards a pile of letters and a tiny cardboard box on the sideboard.

'Oh, I don't think I'll bother reading them, Freddie,' she said, unable to keep the sarcasm out of her voice. 'They'll only say things like: "The weather here is frightful. We got a rather inferior lunch of dog biscuits and horsemeat today. How are all your family? Must close now, as I have a frightfully important appointment with my lice."'

'No they won't. They're the ones I wrote to you after I'd been on leave in Paris. I did miss you, Lizzie, and I wished more than anything I'd come home to you.'

'Did you?'

'Yes.' He threw his cigarette onto the fire and reached into his pocket for his cigarette case. 'Here,' he said, opening it and offering her one, 'just to prove what a tame husband you have these days.'

'No thanks, Freddie. I don't want a tame husband, or a cigarette. I haven't fancied them since I had influenza.'

'Poor little wife. You do look rather pale and skinny. You're getting better now, though, aren't you?'

She nodded.

'Well, if you're not having a cigarette, I won't either.' He snapped the case shut and went to the sideboard, returning with the cardboard box. She opened it, and finding a little necklace inside, looked up at him and smiled.

'Green glass.'

'No. Emeralds. Not many of them, I admit, and very small, and probably not the first quality, but I spent every penny I had on it. Stand up and take your coat off.'

She did as he asked, and he fastened the necklace round her neck. 'I love you, Lizzie.'

She looked in the mirror over the mantelpiece, admiring it. 'And I love you, Freddie.'

He put his hands on her waist and kissed the top of her head. 'That's the first time you've ever said that to me.'

'Is it?' She caught sight of their reflection, a thinner pair than the couple in the photograph, and he was looking down, and her eyes were full of hope.

'Yes,' he said, 'and it's awfully, awfully s'nice,

but one day it will be even s'nicer.'

'When?'

'When you say it before I do.'

She thought about that for a while, then turned towards him and felt for the string round his neck to hook out the little golden horseshoe. After fingering it for a moment she put her arms round him. 'Ginny said I should go and lie down after I'd had a cup of tea. If you were to come with me, we could bolt the door and give each other some treatment.'

'Do you really want the tea?'

'I do.'

He gave her a squeeze. 'Don't be long with it, or I shall explode.'

She smiled. 'I do love you, Freddie.'

Sprawled and sleeping, she felt his lips on her face, then her breasts. 'Merry Christmas, darling girl.' His hand travelled down her flanks to rest between her thighs. Smiling slightly but too drowsy to open her eyes, she parted her legs a little more and felt his breath, warm against her ear.

'There. There, my little wife, lie still. You like that, don't you?'

'Mmm.'

'Yes, you do. My pretty kitten ... you're beginning to purr. You'll soon be ready for some more love, but not yet, you're not quite... But you're like a little trout ... a plump little trout who likes the tickling so much ... that in the end ... she won't mind getting caught. It's so s'nice, isn't it, darling?'

'Hmm. Mmmm.'

'Yes, it is ... so very ... very ... s'nice. I know it is... No, I won't kiss you yet, just a little more ... my love. A little more gentle tickling, now ... a little more ... for my pretty Mrs Trout.'

'Mmm.'

'Yes. Yes ... and now your breathing's deeper ... and you're such a sweet, darling little wife ... and so yielding ... and so very, very... I think my little wife wants her husband now. Does she?'

'Hmmm. Hmmm.'

'Yes... Yes, I thought so... There, darling... Oh ... th ... e ... e ... re.'

'Hh! ... mmmmmmmmmmmm ... mmm ... m.'

The publishers hope that this book has given you enjoyable reading. Large Print Books are especially designed to be as easy to see and hold as possible. If you wish a complete list of our books please ask at your local library or write directly to:

Magna Large Print Books
Magna House, Long Preston,
Skipton, North Yorkshire.
BD23 4ND

This Large Print Book for the partially sighted, who cannot read normal print, is published under the auspices of

THE ULVERSCROFT FOUNDATION